MIMI AND HER MIRROR

UYEN NICOLE DUONG

MIMI AND HER MIRROR

PUBLISHED BY

The characters and events portrayed in this book are fictitious. Any similarity to real persons, living or dead, is coincidental and not intended by the author.

Published by AmazonEncore
P.O. Box 400818
Las Vegas, NV 89140

ISBN-13: 9781935597308
ISBN-10: 1935597302

ACKNOWLEDGMENT

My thanks go to Terry Goodman, David Downing, Emily Avent, Wendy Jo Dymond, Sarah Tomashek, and all the staff at Amazon who have helped me bring this novel to the public, giving it the best of their skills, dedication, and professionalism.

This is the story of Mimi,
the younger sister of Simone, the protagonist in

DAUGHTERS of the RIVER HUONG

by the same author.

Note: On April 30, 1975, Saigon fell, and the Vietnam War ended. The U.S. evacuated approximately 150,000 Vietnamese refugees and resettled them in America. These were the lucky ones—the first wave of Vietnamese Americans. Those who stayed behind—South Vietnamese associated with the fallen regime—were sent to hard-labor camps by the Communist government.

In the seventies and eighties, millions of Vietnamese escaped Vietnam by boat. Many died at sea. Many were stranded for years in Southeast Asian refugee camps awaiting resettlement. These were called "boat people," as distinguished from the airlifted evacuees.

Mimi's family was among those 150,000 lucky airlifted evacuees.

CONTENTS

THE FAMILY TREE

Huyen Phi (1880–1930)   +   Prince Buu Linh (1870–1945)
(The Mystique Concubine)   (His Royal Highness Thuan-
                                          Thanh, King of Annam)
                                          /reign: 1884-1910/

/MARRIAGE/

AMONG THE DESCENDANTS OF
HUYEN PHI AND THE KING OF ANNAM

Princess Que Huong
(Madame Cinnamon, or Grandma Que)

DESCENDANTS OF MADAME CINNAMON

Mi Suong   +   Tran Giang Son
(Dew)   (Hope)
Born 1934   Born 1934

/MARRIAGE/

CHILDREN OF MI SUONG AND TRAN GIANG SON

"Simone" (Mi Uyen) (born 1955)
"Mimi" (Mi Chau) (born 1959)
"Pierre" (Phi Long or "Pi") (born 1965)

ONE
JOURNEY WITHOUT SHOES

Saigon, South Vietnam
Tan Son Nhat Airport
April 27, 1975

I stepped onto the icy floor of the C-130 cargo plane. The back of the plane—that cold, gray metal door—opened like the mouth of a big, ugly shark. It swallowed me.

I stepped inside. The chill shot from my heels all the way to my head.

In the rush of things, I had lost my shoes. I was going on bare feet.

A journey without shoes.

My heels froze, but my body seemed on fire. The hot and humid air of the night stuck to my skin. I curled my toes, arching the soles of my feet away from the floor's terrible cold. My bare feet felt as though they were shackled.

The back of the cargo plane—its entry and exit—was still open. I had to turn back to look behind me, one more time. The yellowish lights emanating from the plane competed with a sky full of silver stars. There was something deadly and menacing in the silence of the night and the sickly yellow light.

I turned to look at my parents for assurance, but panic had struck their faces. Wrinkles deepened at the corners of their reddened eyes. Their mouths drooped.

And then the silence broke.

My father, of all people, my father—the stern and aloof philosophy professor of the University of Saigon—had broken down and was openly weeping. His bookworm glasses dangling to the side of his jaw, my poor father held his head with his hands and sobbed. The wailing sound he made could have cracked open my throbbing skull.

I looked to my mother, just in time to catch her. She had collapsed. My father held her up, and her head fell onto his shoulder.

In a split second I realized the role reversal: my parents were no longer my protectors. I had taken on that role. My mother was unconscious and my father was weeping; I was conscious and I was not crying, and my little brother Pi was holding on to me. The Pan Am bag I carried on my shoulder suddenly felt heavy, as heavy as that big rock pushed by the Greek tragic hero. What was his name? Sisyphus. Some French philosopher had written about the arduous climb of Sisyphus. In this instant, I had become a young, female Sisyphus, and the weight was well beyond me.

I reached for Pi's tiny hands. My ten-year-old brother held on to me.

We were at the airport getting on the plane. My big sister, Simone, and my maternal grandmother, Grandma Que, were still in central Saigon.

—

The crowd squatted on the floor, filling up the belly of that immense metal shark. I could smell their sour, salty sweat, even their hot, salty tears. My father had squatted down, dragging my mother to the floor with him. So I squatted, too, pulling Pi down to the floor.

The icy floor of the plane became my refuge, but what a cold refuge it was.

The airplane engine roared, thick and throaty like an angry tiger. The threatening sound of the engine vibrated through the stuffy air. No bullets flew. No rockets. For an evacuation at the end of a war, the night was too peaceful to forewarn of any approaching apocalypse.

Where was the apocalypse?

I shut my eyes, but the wailing of the people allowed no escape from this reality. I had to open my eyes again and look. It wasn't just my father, but everyone in the whole airplane. The sobs became a mourning refrain.

Terror struck me and the realization sank in. To the mob of panic-stricken Vietnamese squatting on the floor, the moment, the night, marked something so historically dreadful, so tragic, it had to be the signal of death.

The face of the U.S. marine standing motionlessly at the back of the plane came into focus. A young, rosy, chiseled Caucasian face with glassy blue eyes, a long nose, a thin mouth, and a shiny forehead. An emotionless, immobile figure towering over a squatting, crying crowd. The door—the back of the plane—was being closed behind him, and I caught the last glimpse of Saigon's skyline edged against the blackened sky dotted with stars like rhinestones on a velvet coat, sparkling in competition with the white streaks of bulbs lighting up the rooftop of Tan Son Nhat airport's passenger lounge. The lights lasted but one second more, and then the back of the airplane was completely closed, like an enormous metal shield shutting off a dreamy world. The tall American marine stood between me and that world, his arms folded before his giant chest, a statue in a soldier's uniform separating me from everything I was leaving behind.

For a few minutes I silently planned for days ahead and made my resolution. Wherever I ended up, I would pretend the life before this night—in the world shut behind the marine—was just a still frame of a blackened sky lit up with stars. The plane had swallowed me, and the following day, wherever the plane landed, I would crawl out and that would be my rebirth. I would be born a sixteen-year-old girl with no memory of the time before this departure.

In the days to come, I would teach myself the illusion that this night never existed at all.

Pi kept poking his soft, tickling fingers at my back and waist. I put a hand on the fuzzy head of the frightened boy. I held his head and smoothed his fluttering eyelids. His lashes were matted, wet.

Soon he would sleep, and so would I.

——

I was awakened by the dull, steady sound of the plane engine. The plane, already in the air, bumped up and down in harmony with the pulse in my temples. I glanced around. No more weeping. Most people had fallen asleep. Mouths opened and nostrils flared, frowns and furrows deepened on faces that still registered anguish, even in sleep. My parents, too, had fallen asleep, nestled against each other like a pair of traumatized birds.

I reached for my Pan Am bag, the only piece of luggage I had carried with me on this journey. I found a pen, but there was no paper.

I crawled across the floor, making my way through the sleeping crowd. I awakened a few, who stirred and mumbled their protests. It took me a while before I got to the back of the airplane.

I pulled on the boots and pants of the tall U.S. marine. He did not look down at me.

"Where is destination?" I wrote across my palm with the pen. I kept pulling on his pants legs until he had to look down at my pleading face. Then, I held my hand up as though I were worshiping him. I showed him my open palm.

The marine stared down at my palm with those glassy, emotionless blue eyes of his. He took my pen and grabbed my wrist. He wrote something across my wrist and handed the pen back to me. He folded his arms again, his face remaining emotionless. Our eyes did not meet.

I read what he had written on my wrist: *Clark A.B.*

Where was Clark A.B.? I thought I was going to America. Clark A.B. did not sound like one of the fifty states.

For months during the spring of 1975, the rumors had been going around Saigon that the evacuees airlifted by the United States could all be dumped onto some deserted land to work as laborers for the new world. Could Clark A.B. be one of those labor camps? But anything was better than a communist hell, the elite and middle classes of Saigon believed. Even a schoolgirl like me got all the hard facts.

I crawled back to the small space next to Pi and my sleeping parents. For one fleeting moment I was terrified they were all dead, and I was left alone to carry on the exodus by myself. I curled up and embraced myself once more, bringing my knees to my lap. In the dark, I imagined tiny circles of lights that jelled into a bright spot, in which there was a road sign: Clark A.B.

Sleep came again before I could think through all possibilities. Sleep came, deep and exhausting, a coma in which no dream was possible.

And that was how I left Vietnam to enter the dreamland of America.

TWO
HER NINE WORDS

Diamondale, Illinois, 1976

In 1976, the Vietnamese Student Association at SISU—Southern Illinois State University, located in the college town of Diamondale—had about twenty members. Most were engineering and accounting students who'd come to America on scholarships. It took a year after the fall of Saigon for them to straighten out their immigration status, acquire alternative financial plans, get through the shock, and move on with their lives.

Everyone in the Association knew of "the Crazy Man" and his life story.

The guru first appeared at the beginning of the fall semester, on the steps of Krost Hall, the building that housed the political science department, located between the Student Center and the Woody Administration Building. He set up his shop on the first floor of Krost. He sat on his blanket or sometimes stood, gesturing and talking to himself. Around him were self-published pamphlets and flyers, all about democracy in the Third World.

I was beginning my second year at SISU. The first time I saw him, I recognized the Vietnamese features of his face, although I knew nothing about him then. The high and flat cheekbones, square jaw, dark skin, and full mouth all spoke of the Vietnam I had left behind.

Not at all a crazy face.

I felt a sense of déjà vu about the face. I must have seen it before. I liked his face immediately, but somehow I also felt pain. I did not want to understand or acknowledge where the pain came from. So I shook my head and attempted to wipe away the familiarity of the man's face.

For the first few weeks, students formed a circle around him out of curiosity and listened to him talk. Some even shouted objections and expressed their views about Vietnam. Then he was left alone. Soon, most students trashed his pamphlets right before his eyes. Before long, his presence became a normal sight at the entrance of Krost Hall. Nobody cared anymore.

I was part of the crowd circling him, but he did not notice me that first day. I was wearing an old scarf that covered up half of my face. In early fall, the weather had not gotten cold, but I was too skinny and shivered all the time as I walked on campus. I picked up a flyer from him and glanced at the word *Vietnam* in bold face. I winced and walked away, not wanting to read on. Around the corner from the hallway of Krost, I tore the flyer into pieces. Into the trash can went those words about Vietnam.

After that first day, every time I passed by Krost Hall, I would slow down to observe the Crazy Man from a distance. Even when he was preaching to himself, he exuded an air of genuine ardor that suggested passion, not insanity. Day after day he still did not notice me. I stood five feet two and weighed ninety-five pounds, an unobtrusive, fragile, and forgettable little figure like my mother, lacking completely the lofty, striking, asparagus-root slenderness of my big sister Simone. I did not have her height, nor her distinguished good looks and elegant, dainty stature. I was Simone's duckling sister who had neither grace nor curves.

—

The first time we spoke to each other on the steps of Krost Hall, the Crazy Man had just given me a pamphlet. The title said, "Did the War Belong to America or the Middle Class of South Vietnam?"

"Who's the middle class of South Vietnam?" I asked.

He looked at me, apparently recognizing the genetic features of my face. "You and me," he said. That was no answer, I thought. He and I alone did not make up the middle class of South Vietnam. I could not imagine who would belong to such a middle class.

After that, every time I walked by Krost Hall, we exchanged glances. One day, as I dropped a one-dollar bill into his box, he looked at me intensely, and I had a chance to observe him in close proximity. At about five feet eleven, he stood taller than most Vietnamese men of his generation. He was also darker and more muscular than most of them. His eyes sparkled, his brown skin gleamed, and his hands were large, bony, and strong, with long fingers, square at the tips. His hair was cut very short, a crew cut like a soldier's.

And that familiar face.

My mind came up with an explanation for the familiarity. The square jaw, full, tight lips, pointed nose, and starry eyes reminded me of the black American actor Sidney Poitier. At the SISU Communications Center, I had seen a movie about a black guest who came to dinner at the home of his girlfriend's white family. I must have retained the image of that handsome face, full of dignity and determination. The Crazy Man could be the Vietnamese version of Sidney Poitier. He could also pass for a revolutionary leader, I thought. Intense, rigorous, and righteous.

The sense of familiarity still disturbed me after I'd come up with the Sidney Poitier rationalization. Could I have seen such a face even before *Guess Who's Coming to Dinner*? The discomfort lingered in the core of me. I was facing my pain again.

On an impulse, I ran away from Krost Hall, confused and breathless.

When I stopped, I realized I had given the Crazy Man my meal money for the day. I promised myself not to do that again. I was a student worker in the Woody Administration Building, making minimum wage. Every day, I ate a McDonald's Big Mac. In 1976, it cost almost a dollar. That was my only big meal each day. An apple, a few crackers, a banana, or a piece of cheese from vending machines sufficed for the rest of the day. My ninety-five-pound body did not need much food.

———

I could not resist the urge to help him. The following day, I was back at Krost Hall, dropping my one-dollar bill in his box.

"I know who you are." He flashed his Sidney Poitier smile at me, showing two even rows of teeth, which appeared much whiter against his dark brown skin. "You are the pretty, bright girl that the newspaper talked about."

The *Southern Illinoisan* had run a human interest story about a young freshman at SISU who scored the highest on a statewide English grammar test required of all English and communication majors. No professors had expected the highest scorer to be a Vietnamese refugee who'd been in Illinois less than a year. The Crazy Man must have heard of this.

"You should eat more," he said, staring at me. "You are too skinny. You barely look fifteen years old!"

I said nothing and walked away.

In the Woody Administration Building, I emptied my purse for some coins to buy a bag of potato chips from the machine—a substitute for my Big Mac. I vowed to myself that I would never again give my one dollar to the Crazy Man.

Yet, I did it again and again. One time, he gave me a new pamphlet. Its title was "Vietnamese refugees—the newest flowers in the United Garden of America. Why are their children paying out-of-state tuition to SISU? Are they paying 'out-of-state' taxes?"

I was on scholarships for academic excellence—a university scholarship for having made straight As during my freshman year, and the prestigious Hearst Scholarship for outstanding journalism students—so his flyer about Vietnamese refugees having to pay out-of-state tuition did not concern me. Yet I did not take my one dollar back. It remained in his box.

"I know all about you." He stared at me.

All about me? How could he know all about me?

"What do you eat that makes you so smart?" he asked.

McDonald's Big Mac, I wanted to tell him. Only one a day. Although I was not too crazy about American food, I had no choice. Despite the snacks, my stomach was perpetually empty, making grouchy noises. But I rarely had any appetite. I studied hard. My goal was to graduate from SISU in three years. I was the kind of girl trained by my maternal grandmother, whom I called Grandma Que, to have big plans for herself.

"Wasn't that a difficult test, the one that the newspaper said made you a star?" he asked, his eyes alight.

"Just a multiple-choice test." I shrugged. "Besides, English grammar is relatively easy," I told him. "You don't conjugate verbs too many times, and you don't put objects before verbs. I LOVE YOU, not I YOU LOVE."

I took this example from my knowledge of French. I used to put my head down on my palms to sleep in my French elementary school in Hue, Vietnam. My big sister got all the attention, all the adoration. All the French Catholic nuns at Jeanne D'Arc Institute had high hopes for beautiful Simone, and all ignored the messy younger sister. I was left to sleep in class whenever I wanted to.

"Interesting comparison between English and French," he said. "You are very smart," he added. "I will make you my vice president."

"Vice president?"

"Of the new Republic of Vietnam."

"Oh!" I was speechless.

"Or you can join my cabinet. The only requirement is that you can't be corrupt. Are you corrupt?"

"I don't think so!" I answered, but not too convincingly. I knew I was not a saint. As a baby, I was a mess. Unlike Simone, I frequently vexed my parents with my bizarre habits—putting rice in my shirt pocket, saving half-sucked candies by sticking them on the wall above my headboard. As a teenager, I continually challenged my parents' authority. Was I corrupt? Perhaps.

All of a sudden, I became very sad.

Those days at SISU, I had bouts of unexplained sadness and disabling hopelessness. Quite often images of the April 1975 airlift of Vietnamese refugees flashed through my head. Somewhere airplanes roared their angry sounds and swallowed me into their metal bellies. I heard in those angry sounds my own cries for my childhood in Vietnam—what I had left behind. Those wailing sounds of ghosts and spirits who all wanted to tell their sad stories.

"What should I call you?" he asked.

"I am just ME. ME."

"Let's talk phonetics now. In Vietnamese and Mandarin, 'me' means beautiful. It also means America. America the Beautiful. With a different accent mark, 'me' is also the generic term for a princess, daughter of a Hung King, in the Kingdom of Van Lang, the ancient predecessor of Vietnam."

I nodded. I knew all the various meanings of a phonetic "me."

"Or you can be Michelle. *Michelle, ma belle. Ce sont des mots qui vont très bien ensemble. Très bien ensemble,*" he continued.

So the Crazy Man was a Beatles fan. Like the rest of the world. The thought of Beatles music must have animated him. He smiled broadly, repeating that I deserved to be his choice for the vice presidency of the new republic.

I walked away from him, feeling unhappy. There would never be a new republic that consisted of him and me. The country I once called home had been replaced by the Socialist Republic of Vietnam, and we were a bunch of refugees running away from it. No Vietnamese there in the new Vietnam would vote for the Crazy Man, even if a general election took place. Particularly when all he did was pass out pamphlets in Southern Illinois.

—

My one-dollar bills kept going into the Crazy Man's box.

One day, he threw a surprise at me. "Do you want to be a first lady?"

"What?" I was more than startled. I thought of dreams born under a *longan* tree, its branches tilting down, laden with heavy clusters of fat *longan* fruits wrapped in nets. Lovebirds were singing everywhere, mingled with the clear soprano voice of my sister. Simone was the singing lovebird of the family, and the sun

13

danced around her. I, too, was running around her, somersaulting, a spectator of Simone's fabulous performance.

Born in a Third World Confucian society like Vietnam, of course I had no hope of being a female president. So I had long settled for first lady instead. I had never mentioned a word of this to anyone, except to my collaborator, Grandma Que. I had grown up with this idea in my head, and everything I did in my life in Vietnam had been to prepare for this goal. My teachers called me a child prodigy, so I deserved to be the future first lady of the republic, according to Grandma Que.

The dream, as outrageous as it was, had died with the fall of Saigon in 1975. Any remembrance just brought back the painful thought of Grandma Que, who had stayed behind and could not make it to America.

—

"I want to marry you!" the Crazy Man insisted.

"You are indeed crazy," I said, blushing.

"That's what they say about all great men who refuse to be mediocre. I mean it. I want to marry you."

"Why?"

"You are first lady material. One of a kind. Like me."

"I am too young to be married."

"One can never be too young to love. Or be loved."

The mention of love made me even sadder. I had become so withdrawn after the fall of Saigon, and my parents would never approve of a jobless boyfriend, a bum, especially when we were refugees needing to build a new life in the U.S. I walked away, miserably self-conscious, eyes locked upon my socked toes underneath the straps of my sandals (a gift from the women of the Diamondale Lutheran Church).

From that day on, each time I passed by Krost Hall, he winked at me and called out, "Hello, my first lady!"

—

I had a strange dream one night. I saw a Vietnamese Sidney Poitier face grinning at me. I had seen the face before, between crashes of thunder and among streaks of a brutal, blinding light. The man was wearing an air force flight suit stained with blood and with some slimy white substance stuck to its collar. Like John Wayne he walked around, bowlegged, with two guns in his hands. He fired three gunshots, and gunpowder came out of his eyes and mouth. I rushed toward a roaring cargo airplane and heard someone say, "Farewell, Saigon"; the word *farewell* was written on a handkerchief smeared with blood. I woke up and found my pillow soaked with tears. For a heart-stopping moment, I thought my tears were blood. I bit my teeth into the pillow and wished once and for all I could forget.

"No, no, no," I cried out to myself. Those images. I had determined to forget.

Hours passed. I could not forget, nor could I go back to sleep. So I got up, sat on the bed, and began writing. It was all factual, nothing too emotional, too tragic. After all, it was just about the beginning of our American life. Our story was just one of the many.

—

In June 1975, at the Fort Chaffee refugee camp in Arkansas, we reunited with my big sister Simone, who had boarded the last helicopter atop the U.S. Embassy in Saigon. Simone had traced us to the refugee camp in the middle of the United States. She reported to us that she had been unable to persuade Grandma Que to leave.

Gone was Saigon. Gone was our Grandma Que.

In July 1975, my parents and their three children—two girls and a boy—arrived in Diamondale, Illinois, hoping that SISU would give my father a teaching job. SISU had once invited my father to its campus to teach Vietnamese culture to a class of about five students. My father had been hopeful that such a past tie would secure him employment with the university. But the fall of Saigon had changed academic needs, and SISU was no longer interested in hiring Vietnamese scholars to teach Vietnamese culture.

Except for the university, Diamondale had little else to offer a bunch of shell-shocked immigrants craving good jobs. The sponsoring Lutheran Church gave us old furniture and temporary accommodations in a modest two-bedroom house fifteen minutes from the SISU campus. The house was too old; it looked and felt like one of these beat-up haunted houses in the movies. The only nice thing about the house was the fact that it was on Pecan Street, bordered with beautiful, tall trees. I had always loved tall trees.

We made it day by day through the summer of 1975 with the help of the church. Members of the congregation gave us old clothes, bedsheets, groceries, and homemade pecan pies. My first American experience was devouring pecan pies topped with whipped cream—a contribution from the Lutheran congregation. Those days, nothing could taste better than such an American pie.

Eventually, my father got a university fellowship. He also worked part-time in the library shelving books. My mother found an assembly job at a shoe factory—the town's only industry. My oval-faced, porcelain-skinned, French-speaking, twenty-year-old big sister Simone waited tables at the town's only Chinese restaurant, the Ming Dynasty. Things seemed to be working for a short while. I was prepared to enroll in SISU as a freshman.

Within a few months, the structure of our new life crumbled. The owner of the Ming Dynasty made a pass at Simone and placed his oily hand on her breasts. She went home crying that night, recounting the humiliating experience, and opted to be unemployed.

In the old house, she and I shared a bedroom. Little Pi slept on the couch. The remaining bedroom was for Mom and Dad. I woke up one early morning to find Simone sitting in a corner, crying and talking to herself. Her hair was wet—she must have washed it in the middle of the night—and she went on and on about how she hated the Ming Dynasty. It wasn't just the man's oily hand, she sobbed. Simone also hated the smell of deep-fried egg rolls that clung to her luscious, velvety black hair. She was sickened by the smell of cooking oil, stale egg roll skin, and soy sauce, and the ceaseless, lustful stare of her boss lifted goose bumps onto her porcelain skin. He tried to pinch her bottom at every occasion he could find. Once he had locked the door to the kitchen and attempted to take off her blouse. "I feel dirty everywhere, everywhere, so dirty, so unclean!" She became hysterical. "Forgive me, forgive me," she kept saying. And then she threw an envelope at me, told me she was heading to the bus stop for New York City, and stormed out of the bedroom.

I was still in bed, not yet wide awake. I had heard every word she had said, but because I was badly nearsighted, I could not see head from tail and just could not grasp what was happening. In my half-blind state, I noticed, however, that she had the Pan

Am bag with her, the same bag that had served as our luggage from Vietnam during that hasty departure in April 1975. The first sunlight of the day was just entering our tiny bedroom through the window when I heard the front door open and close. I felt numb, unable to move or cope. I couldn't concentrate. But I knew Simone was gone.

When sunlight eventually filled the room, I pulled myself together and brought the envelope she had thrown at me closer to my eyes. It was sealed and addressed to my parents. I ran to their room, banged on the door, woke them up, and showed them the envelope. My mother read the handwritten note inside, passed it on to my father, and cried. My father read the note, put on his coat, and took a walk. I wanted to read Simone's note, but my mother said no. She went to the kitchen and burned it. She told me that Simone had to go to her American husband in New York City, and possibly my big sister would not be coming back, although she promised to send us an address and money as soon as she was established in New York City.

"Her American husband?" I asked, confused. Simone had no husband, let alone an American husband.

My mother broke out crying again. "Just pray for Simone," she said, and then explained that in April of 1975, Simone had secretly married some old American man in Saigon to get us space on a flight out of Vietnam. So Simone had sacrificed herself to secure our freedom, like Lady Kieu in Vietnamese ancient literature, who sold herself to secure the release of her father. But my mother told me I should not think of beautiful Simone as Lady Kieu, who eventually became a courtesan. Rather, my mother wanted me to remember Simone's porcelain, oval face in the image of the beautiful, sacred female Buddha Quan Yin, a savior, a goddess representing the pure, compassionate heart. I was to be grateful to Simone and not to think badly of my big sister because she had left so abruptly.

At dinner that night, Pi kept asking about Simone, and my mother gave the same explanation, reiterating the Quan Yin savior image but omitting the reference to Lady Kieu. From that day on, at dinnertime, my mother often looked worried, staring pensively at the empty seat once reserved for Simone.

Now that I knew how and why our family had been able to board the plane away from Saigon, I could be grateful to Simone, but I had problems thinking of her as the savior Quan Yin. To me, the image of Quan Yin meant holiness and magic. For thousands of years, victims of shipwrecks in the South China Sea had claimed the beautiful female Buddha would appear on the turbulent sea, saving drowning victims. She walked on waves and floated on a beautiful lotus bloom, holding a holy jar containing a magic potion that could cure sufferings and assure safety and salvation for all mankind. At times she would even hold a child, a symbol of motherhood. Simone had saved our family from staying behind in Saigon after the Communist takeover. She had given me a chance for a better future, but to me, Simone could not be my Quan Yin.

I knew she had not saved me. I had my own pain to bear. More than just pain—my nightmare. Here, in America, I often got up in the middle of the night, shivering, seeing again in my mind the streak of lights from the row of poles along the runway. In the dream that awakened me, I was all alone. No Mom and Dad. No Grandma. No Simone. Not even my little brother Pi. Just me. I heard myself crying on the way to the airplane. The pitiful crying of some poor little house pet about to be sacrificed. There were beasts behind me, in a jungle no one knew about. No one could ever know about.

No, no, no, Simone had not saved me!

—

We had little time to absorb or wonder about what might happen to Simone, because bad luck did not stop there. My mother, with her fragile, ninety-pound frame and tiny hands, could not make the quota for shoe production at the factory. The bald-headed foreman asked to speak to someone in the family who could communicate in English. So I went to work with my mother and stared at the man's big red nose while he complained about my mother's incompetent shoe packing. He told me he actually liked us Vietnamese, but business was business, and the weekly quota had to be, at a minimum, some 570 pairs of shoes per assembly line worker. My mother, a former teacher of Vietnamese literature, could barely process 250. I listened to the foreman's speech about how bad a worker my mother was, and learned to fear the combination of shiny bald heads and big red noses ever after.

When my parents made a decision to leave Diamondale for Houston, Texas, for a better future, they took Pi with them and decided I should stay on in Diamondale to finish college. I said nothing, just quietly packed the few pieces of secondhand clothing—all courtesy of the Diamondale Lutheran Church—and moved into Smith Hall, the cheapest dormitory on campus.

Some twenty-five thousand out of Diamondale's thirty thousand inhabitants were students who disappeared during Thanksgiving, Christmas, and spring breaks. During that first year at SISU, I stayed in the empty dorm in sleepy Diamondale throughout all three breaks. The shivering silence of the deserted college town buried under winter snow became my image of small-town America. I had no money to travel to Houston to visit the family, nor did they have any to send me. I was on my own and survived on scholarships and my minimum-wage earnings as a part-time student worker. From Houston, Texas, my father wrote me a postcard for my first Christmas in America and told me the best thing Diamondale could offer us as a welcome gift to America was my going to college. I accepted his words and understood my own blessings. I was a teenage refugee who could immediately go to college and did not have to work in a factory like my mother, or in a restaurant like beautiful Simone who had run away on a bus to consummate a loveless marriage to some American man. Who knew what had happened to her since. She had not written me that first year.

In that state of mind, I had no desire to socialize during my freshman year. I stayed away from American classmates and had no friends. I didn't even care to join the Vietnamese Student Association, called the VSA by its members. In fact, I deliberately stayed away from the VSA and its crowd on campus. I wanted badly to forget the fall of Saigon. I considered myself born seventeen, without a past. The denial was part of my vow of rebirth.

The Crazy Man changed all that. It was because of him that I decided to join the VSA in the fall of 1976. I could have attributed this decision to Dr. Joseph Morgan's journalism class. Dr. Morgan had assigned me to a beat: foreign students on campus. He had seen the Crazy Man and encouraged me to write about the guru. I could have said no. I could have picked a different topic and justified my choice to the liberal-minded, easygoing professor. I could pretend I had forgotten the fall of Saigon, but I could not be dishonest to myself and deny one obvious fact—the Crazy Man had more than invoked my curiosity. His face had become the focus of my life.

By the third week of the fall semester of 1976, I broke out of my shell and contacted the president of the VSA, an engineering student named Vu. I wanted to pay the Association dues with my scholarship money. A week later, I found myself attending the VSA's monthly meeting at Denny's, where Vu worked as a late-night waiter. Vu had invited me to the meeting to welcome me as a new, dues-paying VSA member. Vu called the meeting the "decompression hour," where the Vietnamese students of SISU congregated and chitchatted about campus life. I sat among Vietnamese engineering and accounting majors, my arms crossed tightly in front of my chest. I sipped at a glass of iced water and asked careful questions, which provoked all kinds of rumors about the Crazy Man. All the details of the man's life and family background were tossed around among the handful of VSA members at Denny's that night.

When the evening was over, I knew all there was to know about the Crazy Man. I had my story for Dr. Morgan's journalism writing lab.

Deep down inside, I knew I had a personal interest in his story, all beyond the journalism class. During that semester, there was never a day when I did not think about the Crazy Man.

—

The night seemed to last forever in my dormitory room in Smith Hall. I went on with my dry, purely factual writing. I had no typewriter with me, so I wrote on a yellow pad while playing contortionist on my bed. Words poured out relentlessly on my yellow pad. They were no longer about me. All about the Crazy Man. Nothing emotional there, either.

To help me write, I created a film screen in my head, on which appeared the images I wanted to describe. Appearing on the screen was a twenty-seven-year-old Asian version of Sydney Poitier, an eloquent, charismatic PhD candidate in the political science department, who, like the rest of the Vietnamese students at SISU, was cut off from financial support when Saigon fell. In April 1975, the world knew the North Vietnamese had defeated a great power, the United States of America. South Vietnam disappeared on the world's map, since only one unified Vietnam existed from then on. Many people saluted the people of Vietnam for their victory. Others turned away in shame. The SISU Vietnamese students all cried over news stories showing a panic-stricken Saigon with its flow of refugees climbing onto the last helicopter atop the U.S. embassy. There were Vietnamese students who went into shock and skipped classes. Professors excused their absences and sympathetically avoided the topic of Vietnam when the Vietnamese students resumed classes. The Vietnamese students shared one thing in common: they were all too pained by their own problems to remember the then president of their Association.

Until he became the Crazy Man.

I contorted myself on my narrow bed in Smith Hall to project all angles of what happened onto the film screen in my head. At Denny's earlier that night, the VSA members had filled me in on the Crazy Man's North Vietnamese revolutionary family. His father, a national hero in the resistance movement against French colonists, led Vietminh troops that hauled cannons up the hills of Dien Bien Phu.

Hell in a small place, I wrote, and on the film screen of my mind appeared the dust-filled valleys of Dien Bien Phu, which, in 1954, became French soldiers' hell. Little, malnourished

Vietnamese men and women hauling cannons up a hill, those heavy war machines supplied by Russia and China, well hidden under tree branches and green leaves. They moved swiftly yet silently, like arduous little ants, their bony bodies packed into Vietminh mustard green uniforms and brown peasant pajamas all covered with dust. Perhaps little drops of sweat fell underneath their army hats. Perhaps I could even hear the footsteps of their rubber shoes, accompanied by the haunting chants of spirits—those who had died along the way.

What happened, then, to those Dien Bien Phu fighters who survived? I scribbled on a different page: *The nameless tragic heroes of the Indochina War. Tham thuong thay nhung anh hung khong ten tuoi.* I could still hear those Vietnamese words spoken by the VSA members, lost in the sounds of late diners' conversations at Denny's. The students told me how the Crazy Man's father had died in North Vietnam. The Vietminh's victory at Dien Bien Phu in 1954 made the Crazy Man's father into a national hero, but victory had yet to be celebrated when the hero turned tragic. During the Land Reform movement implemented in North Vietnam, the national hero of Dien Bien Phu heard the news that his parents, denounced as antirevolutionary landlords, had been persecuted to death by his Vietminh comrades.

The Land Reform movement and the persecution of Vietnamese landlords. I began another page with those words. *Cai cach ruong dat.* I saw an old Vietnamese couple, shackled together and displayed at the village's meeting hall, the *dinh,* with its curved roof over its dirt floor in the classic style of ancient Vietnamese architecture. The peasants of North Vietnam squatted in their black or brown pajamas and cone hats, their bare feet appearing glued to the earth. A few of them had been instigated by the political commissar, who had trained them to persecute and denounce the landlords. These vocal ones led the crowd. The rest just perked their ears to listen to the recitation of the old couple's crimes committed against the people of Vietnam—from buying and selling children to whipping poor farmers and renting out rice paddies at exuberant prices. One peasant even swore that she had seen the old couple cut up pregnant peasant women and eat fetuses in a soup as a delicacy. The peasants' flat faces bore the expression of dazed schoolchildren thrown together after an arduous, confusing class, forced to absorb a lesson well over their heads. Yet, one by one, they got up and uttered strings of hateful words. Vietminh cadres sat in the audience, commingling with the peasants, occasionally yelling out their slogans, "*Da dao dia chu!* Rise against the landlords!" Day after day the persecution continued until all villagers had contributed to the trial. Eventually, they ran out of crimes to recite. When the public trial ended and the cadres were gone, a few peasants stayed behind, cried their tears, and whispered to the old couple, "I am truly sorry; I didn't mean to. I just had to do it." And then the old couple was left by the dirt road. Their house and rice fields had been confiscated. They dragged themselves from door to door asking for food from villagers who used to work for them, but no one dared to feed them anything. The old couple died from starvation in each other's arms, in the rice paddies that once had belonged to them.

Really, the VSA members had no intention of gossiping at Denny's, especially about the politics of a Vietnam in turmoil in 1954. Some of them were not even born then. Nor did they want to dramatize anything. But one thing led to another, and the way I innocently raised questions about the Crazy Man kept the conversation rolling. All the VSA members did was tell me about the 1954 Communist Vietnamese Land Reform Movement, modeled after Mao Tze Tung's Land Revolution in China. It was believed to be part of the Crazy Man's family history.

What happened to the tragic hero? I started a new page. While the old couple were being persecuted, their son, the celebrated warrior of Dien Bien Phu, was held up by the Party in Hanoi and could not do a thing to help his parents, except to receive the news of their death, followed by the news of his own demotion. The Party expected him to acknowledge his parents' crimes. He never did. Instead, he locked himself up in his office for days and never came out. When the neighborhood police knocked the door down, they found him blue and purple in a pond of blackened blood. His head had blown up, and his brain was stuck to the walls. He had shot himself. Sorrow killed his widow shortly thereafter, leaving two surviving sons, a little boy and his big brother.

"You haven't heard anything yet until you know about the big brother," Vu said, lowering his voice with a touch of mystery when he brought us more french fries. (Denny's french fries were incredibly greasy. I picked up a small piece and dipped it in the ready-made tomato sauce that came out of a glass bottle, which they called *ketchup*. I saw nothing French about the greasy potato sticks, just as I didn't understand why the fat-filled pink sausage was called *hot dog*. But those days I accepted the wonders and surprises of America without question and was simply grateful for everything, especially homemade pecan pies.)

The legendary big brother, Vu said, was a high school dropout who had to take care of his baby brother while planning an escape from the Communist North. No one knew how the big brother had done it, but he walked from Ha Dong, east of Hanoi, to the port town of Hai Phong, and then onto the Seventh Fleet waiting for refugees at sea. The whole time, the little boy, six years old, was in a pack bag behind his big brother. The ten-year gap between the two brothers was a result of their father's long absences during his guerrilla fighting career and participation in Ho Chi Minh's revolution.

How could one hopeful PhD candidate become the Crazy Man? I wrote. It all started with an orphan raised by his older brother. I tried to sketch a boy on the next sheet. I made him crawling on the floor because no one cared for him. His parents had died their tragic deaths. Other than that, he was a normal, beaming six-year-old little boy, too young to realize the tragedy that had befallen his parents and grandparents or the parental burden his sixteen-year-old big brother had undertaken. Of course, he would come to understand, much later, after his big brother told him how they had become orphaned. I closed my eyes and imagined how it must have felt to know the past only as it was revealed in words. What it was like to be indebted to a big brother who had stepped into the role of parent. Gosh, they must have loved each other very much.

So, after the Geneva Conference in 1954, which ended up with an international accord dividing Vietnam into two zones, North and South, the brothers joined the flow of refugees and reached the Saigon harbor safely via the Seventh Fleet. At that time, President Eisenhower had decided to rescue Vietnamese refugees from the North and bring them safely to the South, as America stepped into the vacuum left by the French in Indochina. In Saigon, the older brother did odd jobs for a while and then joined the American-backed South Vietnamese army. His lifetime passion was to fight the Vietcong, the successors of the Vietminh he held responsible for the deaths of his parents and grandparents. The undying passion and deep-seated hatred helped him climb the military career ladder, and he eventually became the presidential security chief of the Saigonese government.

Studying abroad. The dream of any excelling Vietnamese student. I wrote down the beginning of a dream. One day in 1967, the presidential security chief put his baby brother on a plane so that the high school graduate could become a mature young man in America, with all the wonderful education America had to offer. The next thing the young man knew was SISU, where there was once a Center for Vietnamese Studies. The young man spent the next eight years of his life working toward a PhD in political science. He was elected president of the VSA. He announced to all VSA members that his goal was to build Vietnam into an independent nation free of both colonialism and communism. VSA members all knew how their president had become orphaned, because the young man kept it no secret. They all knew his ambition was to return home to run for public office. He had never been shy about sharing his dream.

Yet by fall of 1975, like all Vietnamese students at SISU, the PhD candidate found himself having to adjust his visa status, and then to take on a job at Steak & Ale, located on the feeder road of the highway connecting the tiny airport in Marian, Illinois, to the SISU campus. Worst of all, he heard the bad news. After the liberation of Saigon, the incoming North Vietnamese Communists immediately sent his brother to a "reeducation camp," a euphemism for the Vietnamese gulag, and the man died shortly after that—sharing the fate of his "antirevolutionary landlord" grandparents and his Dien Bien Phu "tragic hero" father after two decades of war. The rumors alleged that, in the haste of evacuating U.S. personnel from the American Embassy, U.S. officials had forgotten to burn intelligence files. A roadmap to the identity of U.S. sympathizers, employees, collaborators, and agents was left at the fingertips of the winners of the war.

Krost Hall, I wrote. The next chapter of a life broken in two. What happened when someone with a big dream had to pick up the broken pieces to create a new version of the dream? I contorted myself into new positions on the tiny bed. I dotted the *i*'s and crossed the *t*'s in my sentences, my fingers gone numb and clumsy so I had trouble holding on to my pen. In fall 1976, the PhD candidate abandoned both his dissertation and his job at Steak & Ale to become the Crazy Man. Krost Hall became his permanent residence, furnished with a blanket, flyers, pamphlets, and a money box. He solicited contributions for the reclamation and reconstruction of a new Vietnam, announcing to the student crowd that the struggle between North and South was not over.

Not in his mind.

———

I was finishing my story when the phone rang at ten o'clock that night. I reached for the telephone and heard Vu's voice. Pimple-faced Vu. Studious Vu. Nerdy Vu. Future brilliant engineer Vu. Lucky Vu, whose family had boarded a fishing boat, reaching international waters hours before the fall of Saigon and then arriving safely in California months later. At Denny's earlier that night, Vu had talked of how the Association should organize Tet, the Lunar New Year's celebration, for the newly arriving refugees in Southern Illinois. He had asked me whether I would mind performing a solo dance, and I had said I would think about it. So when I said hello on the phone, Vu sounded real happy at the other end. He wanted my commitment for the dance, and I gave it to him, as long as the Association could throw together the traditional costume for a North Vietnamese country girl: a big, flat hat made of bamboo leaves; a puffy, earth-brown skirt falling to the ankle; and a split-open overcoat-tunic the color of ripened, yellow rice paddies.

"The Crazy Man," I changed the subject. "Did he just snap after Saigon fell?"

I thought I heard Vu's faint sigh. Or I must have imagined such a sigh.

"All his life the man has wanted to occupy the highest public office in a tumultuous, underdeveloped Southeast Asian country," Vu said. "It was crazy, because even now he still thinks he is meant to be the president of Vietnam. The saddest thing is that I don't think he wants this because of self-interested ambitions or his own greed. I think that to someone like him, it was a matter of ideals. Being born into a family like that, at a time like that."

I said good-bye to Vu abruptly and went to bed. I lay down and closed my eyes. I saw the Crazy Man's face appearing on a stamp like a national treasure, the face of the young and handsome president of the Republic of Vietnam. But that would require a country over which he could preside.

I had once envisioned my own face on such a stamp sold all over Vietnam, when there was still a country that could distribute stamps. A country I could call my own.

—

Quite often during my first year at SISU, I had dreamed of a cargo plane that circled a calm green sea. My luggage—all those dresses my mother had made for me in preparation of my graduation from high school—floated on the emerald surface. I was hanging onto the tail of the plane with one hand and with my other hand attempting to catch the floating clothes that seemed to dance upon the bubbling waves. The fear of falling and the desire to catch the clothes made every root of my hair stand up as the wind brushed against my face. And then in my despair, my beautiful sister Simone appeared on the calm green sea like the female Buddha Quan Yin, in a white blouse and black silk pantaloons that fluttered above her rosy heels. She glided on the water's surface like a roller-skating champion, picking up all my floating clothes so gracefully, and then jumping onto the plane, she landed so lightly, as if from a parachute, pulling me inside and telling me everything would be all right, and we would be going home to pick up Grandma Que. The dream always ended there, and I never could see Grandma Que's face. When I woke up, I could still hear the roaring noise of the plane, my eyes blinded by all that green sea.

I did not want to sleep after I had written the Crazy Man's story, fearing the same recurring dream would haunt me and I would wake up in the morning with my heart pounding and the roots of my hair pulsating upon my scalp. So I lay in bed awake, staring at the ceiling for the remainder of the night.

In that state of exhaustion and concentration, I recalled, for the first time since the fall of Saigon, Grandma Que's face as I remembered it from my childhood in the city of Hue.

—

Once Grandma Que had taken me before the family altar and showed me a piece of radiant green jade carved into the shape of a phoenix spreading its wings, imprinted against a matted plate of reddish gold molded into the shape of a flying dragon. A dragon signified a king, and a phoenix symbolized a queen, she explained. The jade phoenix was a royal seal designed for a queen, and it belonged to a powerful spirit. The spirit, she said, was that of my great-grandmother, a royal concubine, wife of an exiled king and the uncrowned queen of Annam. Grandma Que was Madame Cinnamon, the princess of the South Sea Pearl, proud daughter of the Mystique Concubine and His Royal Highness Thuan Thanh, king of Annam. According to Grandma Que, the Mystique Concubine had died young in her sleep in the middle of the Indochina War, and her ashes were spread over the River Huong, which flowed through the heart of our ancient capital where I was raised. So the Mystique Concubine became the Spirit of the River Huong to protect the ancient capital city. The romantic imperial city of Hue.

The spirit thus carried the substance of a queen, and she would pass that substance on to the next special girl in a long bloodline. I could be destined to become the next in line, and this would be my sacred bond to Hue. If I accepted the spirit, the River Huong (called the Perfume River by the French, and made popular as such by tourist agencies) would symbolically flow in my bloodstream and bring the spirit to me. The spirit would guide me as to what it took to be a queen. Being a queen meant responsibility for the populace—to discharge duties and make her subjects happy and prosperous. A queen also represented the state. She was to portray a role model of courage and dignity. Being a queen was the predestined job for only one unique and very smart young girl, out of millions, a young girl chosen for a special future and a special mission—the sovereign representative for the nation-state. And since the monarchy had been replaced with a republic, I would not be a crowned queen, but rather, a first lady. The first lady of a modern Vietnam.

"Why would the queenly spirit want me?" I asked Grandma Que that day before the altar.

"It is a matter of choice," Grandma Que said. Simone did not want to become a queen. She only wanted to sing, and a diva on stage was not a queen in life. Nor was my mother enthusiastic about this queenly ambition. When my mother turned sixteen, she had been sent to the Couvent des Oiseaux boarding school in the highlands for the best education the French could offer their colony. The Couvent cultivated the minds of future queens in Southeast Asia, and it cost Grandma Que a fortune to send her only child there. My mother went along for the excitement, but when she got to the highlands, the cold climate and isolation depressed her. She cried for days and did not want to stay. She told Grandma Que she did not want the best Couvent education. My complacent mother did not wish to have the fire in her heart, nor the queenly spirit in her veins, as those notions did nothing but make her miserable. My mother preferred and accepted normalcy.

Not me. Those days I was called Mi Chau, the younger daughter of Ong Ba Giao, Mr. and Mrs. Schoolteacher.

Do you want to have this spirit in your veins? I remembered the question Grandma Que asked of me in her tonal Hue accent. The dialect, when coming from her curvy lips, sounded light and soothing like ethereal music. I looked up at the altar, mesmerized by the radiant green of the jade phoenix, and I said yes, yes, with all the ferment and fire in my young heart.

But it would be indeed a long time before I could become a queenly adult. Those days I stood barely one meter and weighed twenty kilograms, a diminutive waif who could not handle food. I ate like a slob and acted like a nervous fool. Give me a small bowl of rice and it would take me an hour to finish, and when the bowl was empty, Grandma Que would find rice grains and brown fish sauce stains in my shirt pocket. I stunk like fish sauce and old rice, and she had to bathe me each time. At some point I gave up on food, losing my baby fat so quickly that Grandma Que had to force-feed me three times a day. She would tell me stories from the history of Vietnam—all about those kings and queens and generals and female warriors who fought against the Hans, the Mongolians, and the Manchus. The stories mesmerized me. So caught up in the tales, I would automatically open my mouth and take in those spoons of food she placed at the tip of my tongue. Telling me stories was her only way of getting me to open my babyish mouth and swallow my rice.

Grandma Que told me I was a sullen baby who spoke too little. While my big sister Simone sang all day like a bird, I just stood in a corner and stared into space, with my fingers in my mouth. I was always dirty. Even when Grandma Que employed a nanny to take care of me, I would slip from the nanny's arms and go about doing my own things, usually in a corner somewhere, messing up my linen clothes and smearing food on my bald head. I grew up into an antisocial little girl who preferred reading stories by myself and who was too shy to play a sport.

Everybody in the family remembered me as a nearly hairless baby. At three, I was still bald like an old man. Grandma Que worried herself sick that I would not grow any hair, so when I turned three, she began to give me the *boket* nut treatment. She boiled those hard-shelled black nuts, which would never go soft no matter how long they stayed in the pot. All the heat did was to excrete a clear reddish brown broth from the nuts that smelled like pungent herbal medicine. Grandma Que had worked the magic potion on my big sister Simone, and it had worked. Simone's hair had grown so fast, thick, and long. When Grandma Que tried pouring boiled *boket* juice over my fuzzy head, I broke out laughing, wiggling my body, splashing water everywhere, and causing a mess. I was ticklish on my scalp and Grandma Que had to hold me down. The ordeal proved worthwhile, though, because within a year my hair grew longer and longer—never as thick and shiny as Simone's, yet abundant enough to burden my midget and toothpick body.

With or without hair, I was never grand enough to appear queenly. Grandma Que said I still had plenty of time to grow so long as I worked on my posture. "Hold your chest out proudly. Tug your stomach in gracefully. Do not bend the small of your back, and keep it upright and forward. Walk like a queen always. Good posture is everything—what makes a classy lady forever classy," she said. She never thought I was hopeless. Further, she claimed the queenly material was indeed in my eyes. Our eyes, the reflection of our soul, would not change with time. My eyes resembled hers, she said. Like black *longan* nuts. They stay shiny black and lively forever, she told me.

Grandma Que once called the *longan* tree the signature of the old French villa built by her mother on the slope of Nam Giao in Hue. Simone paid no attention to the *longan* tree in the back of the villa. She loved only the magnolia tree in the front yard. Grandma Que said Simone could have the magnolia tree, but the strong and tall *longan* tree would belong to me symbolically. Every child needed a shady tree under which to recite poetry, Grandma Que said. Wherever we went when we grew up, Grandma Que said, Simone and I should always find ways to grow a big, tall tree in our own yards. One day the war would stop, and all the women of Hue who had been stranded elsewhere would return to live peacefully in their City. Not just any city, but the City. My great-grandmother's spirit would wait for us, the women of Hue, in the famous River Huong flowing through the heart of Hue, the river we all carried in our heart. It would only be a matter of time before we, the stranded women of Hue, all came home. That necessarily included, according to Grandma Que, the return of

Simone and myself, should we ever leave Hue to study abroad. One of these days when I turned old and gray, I would return to the villa in Nam Giao to live and to reminisce on my extraordinary life.

Grandma Que had everything figured out. She talked to the spirit in front of the altar every day. She always knew best.

How could one be so sure of the future, I asked, and she told me of my own history. All of the signs were there, she claimed. Of course, I had heard my own story a thousand times. Back then, in the early sixties, Dad had gone back to France on a graduate scholarship at Sorbonne, and Mom had decided to go back to school to study horticulture, having entrusted both Simone and myself to Grandma Que's care. One day Grandma Que came home from the wet market and found me crawling on the floor, reading a book and reciting Vietnamese classic poetry. She had hired a high school student from Lycee Dong Khanh to babysit me. The sixteen-year-old teenager had taught me the alphabet. Left alone with her day after day, I learned to read a storybook on my own. What's more, I had listened to the babysitter's practiced recitation for a Vietnamese literature class, and I repeated all those classical poems by heart.

So naturally!

According to Grandma Que, I learned all the anecdotes of Vietnam and became a storyteller at barely five years of age. My favorite stories had always been about those queens and princesses of Vietnam.

I did not recall learning how to read on my own or from the babysitter, but the first grade bored me terribly, as though I were just born one day and instantly knew how to read, and the first grade was nothing but a needless repetition of the obvious. If Grandma Que said so, it had to be true that I had learned to read on my own. Grandma Que confirmed that I showed signs of an extraordinary mind—the real substance of a first lady. What was more, I had virtues, she said. I was always a sweet, humble, and kind little girl. These extraordinary genes and traits ran in the family, she said.

I knew what she was referring to, because, again, she had explained at least a thousand times. The good gene had started with my great-grandmother, that uncrowned queen of Annam who had turned into the Spirit of the River Huong. My protector.

With the spirit serving as my guardian angel, according to Grandma Que, all I needed to do was to wait, and wait patiently, for the realization of dreams.

Of course, I would wait, and wait patiently. I had to grow up first.

—

In childhood, I equated Grandma Que's concept of waiting with the soothing shade of my favorite *longan* tree and the pleasant devouring of its saccharine fruits, all taking place in the backyard of the French villa in Hue.

But in Diamondale, memories of Hue came only in occasional dreams, in scattered images rushing through my mind, when, after a long day of school and work, I could no longer hold my eyelids open. Sleep simply meant I passed out from physical and cerebral exhaustion. Then I became the young girl eating *longan* fruits in a garden full of shady trees.

She looks up to a blue sky, and the sparkling sunshine is making its way down in between leaf shadows that weave themselves into a dark, green net separating the girl from the sun. The net divides the sunshine into long gleams like thin diamond necklaces hanging down from the sky.

The door of Grandma Que's French villa opens, and her silhouette slips out, carrying a basket full of longan fruits—round nuts enveloped in the texture of saccharine longan meat, grapelike, well contained inside a brown, grainy peel. Peel it off, and the transparent meat lies invitingly, puffed with sugary juice. Bite into it, and the juice drips down all the way to your chest. The soft, plump texture of a longan fruit either sticks between my teeth or melts at the top of my tongue, its syrup permeating down and coating my throat. I laugh and devour it, and the syrup runs from the corner of my mouth down my neck, cooling my chest as the summer breeze slides over the pores of my skin, leaving on it the stickiness of dried syrup.

"More, more," I say loud and clear, and the silhouette of the woman turns around and catches me in her arms. I curl up into the silhouette. I am inside the womb again and am whole, and before I disappear, I see her face under a cone hat. It is Grandma Que's face, and her loving black eyes shine upon me together with the diamond necklaces of the gleaming sun. Her pupils are indeed two longan nuts, the deep, shiny, lacquer black color drawing me in. I never want to go anywhere except inside the blackness of her eyes; there I am bathed in the sweetness of longan syrup, where I am to rest and be safe.

And that was how, in the early days of my life in America, I relived the senses and feel of my childhood—in my late-night, exhausted sleep, filled with the sight and taste of longan fruits and other things that had once characterized Grandma Que's kitchen and altar. When a baby girl crawled out of her cradle to be nuzzled by an adult, she remembered what the senses registered—the smell and feel. In Smith Hall, during those early morning hours, my senses lingered among corked-lid bottles of coconut oil, herbs boiled in clay pots over burned straws, boiled mung bean cupcakes, dried chrysanthemums, and lotus seeds, all wrapped in soft, fragrant lotus leaves or the crispy, translucent wrapping papers that tore, turned brittle, and wrinkled so easily under the child's greedy fingers. Once there had been an ancestral altar in a dark room, filled with incense smoke. Grandma Que moved quietly, placing these food offerings on the altar and lighting the candles that cast their flickering, yellowish color upon the array of objects. She burned an incense stick and said her prayers to the Spirit of the River Huong, who could make my dreams come true—the creation of a queen, the first lady of a new republic.

All it took was the patience to wait. Under the shade of a *longan* tree.

—

But it was 1976, and I was suffering from insomnia in my tiny room in Smith Hall of SISU, Diamondale, so Hue was just the flashing of a dream unfulfilled, and the memory of Grandma Que made my stomach hurt.

The following morning, I got out of bed and tore up all the yellow pages I had written the previous night about the Crazy Man. I tossed them into the air. Pieces and pieces of papers cascaded down on me. I thought of golden autumn leaves swirling in the air, and shivered at the image.

I knew what I needed to do. I would go to Dr. Morgan in the morning and ask to change the beat for the journalism class. I could not write this story about a man who wanted to be the president of Vietnam. There would not be a Crazy Man story, ever, from me. That was sacred ground. My American classmates would say, *Too close to home, too close for comfort!*

—

I walked by Krost Hall one late afternoon and the Crazy Man sneaked out behind me, holding out a news clipping. It was the *Southern Illinoisan* article, and I recognized my picture in it, a skinny, studious Asian girl wearing a cheap pair of thick, nerdy glasses.

"I know everything about you," he said, waving the clipping in his hand. "Your real name is Mi Chau, the name of an ancient Vietnam's princess. You are a prodigy, aren't you? It says here you also won the Hearst Scholarship for outstanding journalism students. That's not the kind of honor they casually bestow upon a refugee fresh off the boat and nonnative English speaker, you know."

My face felt hot, and I looked down at my toes to avoid his eyes. The English grammar test and controversial journalism scholarship application of months ago all at once became fresh events, and I felt like crying. When I looked up, his eyes grabbed mine, and they, too, seemed a little red.

"What's wrong?" he asked. "You should be proud of yourself. Come and talk to me." He pulled on my elbow.

We walked side by side toward the steps of Krost Hall and sat down on his blanket together. There was nobody around at six o'clock in the evening that day, and the round sun was hanging over a building roof. The sun had just turned brownish yellow, and its beams were changing into the reddish color of sunset. Our shadows formed a blob on the concrete steps of Krost Hall, and I turned to look at him. We had never been this close before. He needed to shave, and I could see the roots of his facial hair around his mouth and chin.

"You are…hairy," I said.

He threw his head back and laughed, his white teeth gleaming underneath those full, light brown lips that reminded me of the color of milked mocha or boiled chestnut shells. He took my hand and placed it upon his chin and cheeks and made me feel them. The contact with his skin made me uncomfortable, but his palm felt warm and soft. My fingers touched the rough facial skin, full of hair roots. There was something very intimate in the way we sat and looked at each other. I felt natural and comfortable in his friendly gaze.

I withdrew my hand and said, "You felt…rough and…normal."

He laughed again. "Of course I am normal."

"You are…not crazy."

"Of course not. You think I am?"

I remained silent and watched the sun die on his crew-cut hair. His was a big head that looked strong, and perhaps that meant he had brains enough to occupy the presidency of a war-torn Third World country. The somber-colored sunset was bestowing upon us darkened his skin almost into a shade of ebony. He had placed that big head of his onto his two palms. When he looked up, I found sadness in his eyes.

"It sucks, doesn't it?"

"What does?"

"The fall of Saigon. It rips flesh from my bones at night."

The raw image made me quiver. I thought of pain that exceeded the limits of verbal description. He was speaking into his palms, and I cocked my head, straining to catch his words.

"I once wrote a six-hundred-page dissertation, day and night, for years. It was the sketch of a dream, and my heart and all of me went into it. I don't care about anything anymore. But I still care about the dream."

He looked up at me from his palms, and his eyes sparkled again. Day would be turning into night soon, and it was about time for me to walk back to Smith Hall.

"I knew it the first time I saw your face," he murmured. "We are unusual people with dreams larger than life. But where is the place for us now? In America? As what?"

I nodded without knowing what I was agreeing to. I did not know I had shed a tear until he put a thumb to my face and smeared it over the hot skin of my cheek.

"Tell me, Princess Mi Chau. What is it? What's bothering you?"

He held my hand and kissed the tips of my fingers. Small, repeated kisses. I thought I would die because of a sharp stabbing pain above my stomach, just beneath the heart compartment. My limbs felt weak. The stab repeated with every touch of his lips, along with a sensation that rolled through my body in small waves.

In that palpitating state, I decided to tell him my story.

———

My story began with my conference with Dr. Joseph Morgan in his office next to the writing lab in the spring of 1976, my second semester at SISU. This journalism professor and supervisor of the lab had the reputation of being the sweet white father of the black students in the department, an I-know-your-pain defender of all minorities, always recommending nonwhite kids for scholarships. The man sat among piles of papers, his wire-rimmed glasses falling over the bridge of his high nose (and this reminded me of my bespectacled college professor father).

Sitting on the other side of Dr. Morgan's small desk, I could see the perspiring pores of the professor's white facial skin. One of the buttons on his navy blue cotton shirt, around the stomach area, had become undone, showing a patch of skin white like tuna fish. I could see the black and gray hair that seemed to grow out of his navel. He was talking on the phone, signaling for me to sit down in the chair in front of his untidy desk, and I automatically followed the motion of his index finger. I sat down, and he was standing behind his desk, his stomach pressing against the edge of the desk, and the exposed navel was just a little below my eye level. I wished he would fix the button of his shirt so the black and gray curly hair would not jump out at me. I felt nauseated, perhaps because of the stuffiness of his office, perhaps because of its overwhelming untidiness, or perhaps because I was not accustomed to seeing navel hair on the big, protruding belly of a middle-aged white man. At least the black and gray coloring matched his mass of hair, like a bird's nest situated at the top of the professor's head. Thank God he did not have a shiny, bald head and a big red nose like the mean man who fired my mother; otherwise, I would never have trusted Dr. Morgan.

The professor was a university teacher like my father. Watching him talking into the telephone, I could not help contrasting Dr. Morgan's fat frame with my father's skeletal shoulders and sunken chest, or the loose skin of my father's soft belly that hung over his skinny, hairless legs, the smallness of which caused his knee bones to protrude and appear larger. The very image of a skinny, bookish Vietnamese father. I could not help noting to myself that Dr. Morgan was nothing like my father. The two of them looked so far apart physically that they served as a perfect illustration of how East was East and West was West and the two would never meet.

Dr. Morgan remained on the phone for what seemed a century while I wiggled slightly and nervously in the big chair, wondering why he wanted to see me after class. It was another century before Dr. Morgan hung up the phone and looked into my face. I noticed his short, bushy brows—something I had missed about his face when I saw him from afar during his class lectures. The bushy brows matched his bird's nest hair.

"Hi, *My Chow*," he said, giving me a warm, friendly smile. Like everyone I had met in Southern Illinois, he mispronounced my birth-given name, Mi Chau, and that was OK. I had no need to be addressed by the correct pronunciation of a name that no longer spoke of the reality I was facing every day. I could be Mi Chau to my parents in Houston, Texas, and My Chow to the rest of the world, and it would not bother me a bit.

"Amazing, amazing." The professor stood up, pacing back and forth behind his desk. "Your English test score was so high. The verbal skills portion of the test would qualify you to pass the GRE and enter graduate school at an Ivy League school. You know what that means, My Chow?"

"No."

"It means you are supersmart. It also means that bilingual minds work in wonderful ways. Tell me, you've been here, say…"

"Nine months," I finished his sentence for him.

"And where did you learn English?"

"In a high school in Saigon called Trung Vuong, named after a Vietnamese queen and female warrior."

"Did you speak English at home?"

"Speaking English at home? No." I raised my brows. The whole idea of speaking a foreign language at home was alien to me. Grandma Que would have frowned upon it as snobbish and totally unpatriotic.

"Amazing," he said again. "In my ten years of teaching I have not seen anything like this. A foreign freshman scoring high enough to enter an Ivy League graduate school. Let's see, you ended up here because…"

"The Lutheran Church. And my father used to teach here. Vietnamese culture and language in a class of five students. He couldn't find a job and left here already. My father has a philosophy degree from Sorbonne, Paris." I gave Dr. Morgan the facts as I knew them, emotionlessly.

"So, you come from a middle-class, well-educated Vietnamese family." He brought his big white hands together with satisfaction and sat down. "You are not one of those villagers whose hut got blown up, like in My Lai."

I nodded. I had never consciously thought of myself as middle class or well educated or compared myself to the slain villagers of My Lai. I was Mi Chau, the middle daughter among three children of a slender Vietnamese schoolteacher, a man who loved to read, and his fragile wife, who loved to plant flowers.

Dr. Morgan leaned against his chair and pulled a document out of his desk drawer. I recognized it as my first feature story submitted for his writing lab. It had my name at the top left corner. I had carefully reversed the order of the first, middle, and family names to conform to the American style. I even hyphenated my compounded first name. *Mi-Chau Thanh Tran.*

"This story," he pointed at my paper, "was incredible." He paused for my reaction. I had none. I had written about factions of Iranian students on campus fighting for recognition from the student body and the university administration. I was simply doing my job. No big deal. The political conflicts among these student groups forewarned the day of an Iranian Revolution. But I had my own pain to bear about the revolution in Vietnam, so I wrote the Iranian story without emotion. It was the best way to write journalism. No wonder Professor Morgan liked my story.

"You write better than ninety percent of the kids around here," he went on. "You made typos, and you will have to learn how to pay attention and edit your own work. But overall, you have a natural way of analyzing and summarizing facts for clarity. The Iranian mess was a mess, but you explained it with an intuitive sense of organization and a fluency and ease with language that I would not expect out of a student who speaks English as a second language and who has been in this country, say, how long? Nine months. How did you do that? My Spanish is so pathetic despite my years of learning it."

"*Analyse grammaticale*," I blurted out unintentionally, and he said, "Excuse me?"

"Nothing," I said, not wanting to explain. Professor Morgan must not have heard of the French phrase. In Vietnam, I had learned French grammar by a method called *analyse grammaticale,* the same method that had produced thousands of bureaucrats and technocrats who drafted correspondence for French colonists in Vietnam for almost a century. The method trained students of French to perform a conscious analysis of every element of a sentence, its grammatical structure, and syntactical properties. I simply took the French *analyse grammaticale* and applied the method to English. After all, there were sufficient similar words between the two languages.

The professor threw my paper into a pile and laced his fingers together. Those white fingers reminded me of Vietnamese white yam sticks. He placed his yam-stick fingers on the desk and tapped them slightly on the wood surface. He was giving himself a speech.

"My God, that senseless war. At Kent State I marched against it. I personally feel the Vietnam War is among the biggest mistakes this country has ever made. The only good that came out of it is that it brought bright kids like you into this country. I am glad you are here, My Chow, and I am going to help you."

I widened my eyes and looked at him without a smile, uncertain whether it was safe to share in his enthusiasm.

"My God, don't look at me with those scrupulous and defensive eyes. All of these are compliments, My Chow." He threw his hands over his head. He leaned back against his chair one more time and squinted his eyes slightly.

"You are also a good-looking young woman. Maybe you ought to try radio and TV. A new Connie Chung, perhaps."

I lowered my eyelids—a nervous habit whenever I did not know how to act. Good-looking? He had not seen my sister Simone.

No one, except this old, kind professor, had said such nice things to me in America. He even said I should be on TV like Connie Chung, the beautiful morning anchor I watched in the Student Center. I had not so dreamed. Since the fall of Saigon, I had developed a nasty habit. Occasionally, I stuttered. Always at the wrong moment. Connie Chung never stuttered. Me, as the next Connie Chung? I became breathless.

By then Professor Morgan had realized his shirt was unbuttoned over his stomach and quickly buttoned it, so the mass of his navel hair no longer flashed itself at me. And then he asked me to describe how I lived. I told him, in short sentences, that I lived in the cheap, rundown dorm, got a university scholarship that waived tuition because I had made all As my first semester, received some government grant to pay for the dorm and fees, ate one McDonald's Big Mac a day, and worked as a student worker filing student transcripts to earn my pocket money.

The professor blinked and asked me if there was anything I needed. I told him timidly yes, I would like to buy a pair of contact lenses. Simone had perfect 20/20 vision, and I was badly nearsighted. In the Arkansas refugee camp, the restrooms and shower facilities were organized into Men and Women. I could not see well and frequently got into the wrong side and embarrassed myself. Either Simone or my mother had to go with me to prevent disasters from happening. When I applied for free prescription glasses at the camp's Red Cross headquarters, I got an ugly pair. I was very self-conscious about my glasses. They made me look nerdy and stupid, and they gave me headaches. In fact, one lens had already cracked because I had accidentally sat on my glasses. Yet I still had to wear them. I desperately wanted to get rid of my glasses.

"OK, My Chow. Tell you what," the kind professor said. "I have nominated you for a Hearst Scholarship, and that should give you sufficient money each year to buy your contact lenses and support you all along. You will automatically receive funds each year for the rest of your time here, provided that you continue making all As on your course work all the way to your senior year. And I know you will."

My mouth and eyes had opened widely, and I was trying to close them when I heard the professor add the undesirable word "But…" He paused a little before saying, "There is a problem." He was unconsciously scratching his stomach. I twisted in my chair, afraid the middle button of his shirt would burst again.

"I have a problem with the department chair, Dr. Henry Stone," Professor Morgan said. "Dr. Stone does not believe your test score. He does not think multiple-choice tests are reliable. That's why I wanted to see you today. I want you to go the second floor of the Communication and Fine Arts Building and speak to Dr. Stone. Maybe after he sees you and your writing, he will believe you deserve the scholarship. Go now. He is expecting you."

Dr. Morgan leaned his heavyset body even farther and farther back, his head cocked, his chin lifted toward the ceiling. For a moment I was genuinely concerned the chair could not take his weight, and he would somersault backward over the chair and land on the floor. He was oblivious to the risk and was talking to himself.

"Henry Stone is a properly mannered East Coast man with a PhD from Princeton, and that's the problem. His knowledge of people kind of stops there. At Princeton. So I have done something extra. I contacted the *Southern Illinoisan* and gave the reporter a lead. They probably would do a story on you about your incredible test score. Once that's in print, Henry won't be able to say a thing or vote you down."

So, at Dr. Morgan's instruction, I headed toward Dr. Henry Stone's office. I did not feel nervous or challenged. I was going through the motions to fulfill Dr. Morgan's plan. I was kind of floating through a sleepwalker's dream. That was how I had operated whenever I was put in a difficult situation, since the fall of Saigon.

—

Dr. Henry Stone's lanky limbs contradicted both Dr. Morgan's stockiness and my father's refined, Asian slightness. Everything about Dr. Morgan spelled thickness, width, and abundance, while my father represented the Hollywood vision of a frail, small, ivory-skinned Tonkinese. Everything that made up Henry Stone, however, was excessively long and lean. Dr. Stone had Abraham Lincoln's body and a bad version of Henry Fonda's thin, thoughtful, and angular face. Even his ears and chin were longer than most ears and chins, giving his countenance a distinctively vertical look. His long arms hung on both sides of him like a chimpanzee's. The elongated look was enhanced by his long pillar legs, which ended with two long, shiny black shoes showing themselves underneath his wool pants, upon which his long torso rested expertly, as though the excessive height had never been an obstacle to his movements or his vision when he had to bend or look down at his shiny shoes. Dr. Henry Stone's height alone would make me forever look up to him.

Like Dr. Morgan, Dr. Stone had a habit of leaning against his chair and stretching his body backward when he talked to me. What's more, he swallowed each and every time he finished a sentence, and I nervously watched his Adam's apple shuttle up and down the length of his neck, stretching the wrinkled skin of his throat. He talked slowly and kindly to me, his speech formal, elegant, and precise, so unlike the racing words and warm tone of the overweight and messy Dr. Morgan. I listened to Dr. Stone describe the Hearst Scholarship, absorbing his lecture on how the honor should be reserved only for that special student who demonstrated extraordinary potential for a reporting career in print journalism. Then, he wanted me to explain how I'd come by my English grammatical skills. I knew I would have to explain the *analyse grammaticale* method, but as I made ready to start, my vocal cords played a trick on me. I began to stutter. I had just begun to talk of how I learned French and English at Saigon's Trung Vuong High School. The phrase *grammatical analysis* had already appeared in dark, bold-faced print on the screen of my mind, when a huge lump blocked my vocal cord and I could not go on.

"Aa…a…a," I began, unable to carry myself onto the next sound. My tongue refused to obey my mind. Dr. Stone's long ears seemed to perk up, and he leaned his lanky body forward. He was all into listening.

"Aa…a…a…" I said again, intending to say "analytical," but could not connect the vowel *a* to the consonant *n*.

"A…a…" I forced air through my mouth, yet could not breathe. The word still stuck at my throat. I was exhausted, and my eyes could have popped out of their sockets with the mental effort to fight my stuttering. Dr. Stone was frowning, watching my lips.

"Aa…na…l." I finally got the *n* and the *l* out.

"Annal?" he asked, puzzled.

I shook my head.

He was eager to help me get the right word. "Annual?"

"No, no, no," I said in despair, "not that. Anal…y…t."

I had to stop there. The T sound got out only halfway. "Tut…tut…tut…tut…" I heard myself sounding sick and stupid.

Finally, I stopped trying. I turned completely silent, my hands clutching the arms of the chair.

"That's OK. I understand," he said, comfortingly. "You are trying too hard to pronounce words properly. English is a difficult language."

No, it isn't my English. My vocal cords, my breathing, my head, all have betrayed me. I am simply too anxious. If I could just get back into my sleepwalker modus operandi, then I would be fine. These subtitles appeared on the film screen of my mind, yet I could not say a word. I would only stutter again. Words forever stalled in my pained throat and became my worst enemies. All I could do was to look at Dr. Stone and force a smile. It must have looked quite idiotic. Dr. Stone graciously thanked me for having stopped by to see him, promising he would let me know very soon about the Hearst Scholarship.

I got up with the intention of heading toward the door, feeling like crying. Yet I did not cry. My eyes felt tired and my facial

muscles tingled. Dr. Stone was bending down over his desk, looking up and down a page in the pink campus directory. He was
no longer looking at me. I turned, opened the door, and walked
through it, eager to leave his office as soon as possible so I could
cry to my heart's content.

Something was terribly wrong.

In an instant, I had been met with total darkness. There was
no way out, just the dark. I turned around, and the realization hit
me and froze my feet.

I had walked into Dr. Stone's coat closet.

—

Something held my feet in place. I could not move. A bright
shade of light appeared in my mind, took on a life of its own, and
began to work. It quickly reviewed the embarrassing situation of
how I had got here.

When I'd walked toward the door, Dr. Stone had not been
looking at me. If I walked out now, he would see me coming out
of the coat closet. I would look like a fool. I would be remembered
forever in Dr. Henry Stone's mind as the young Vietnamese girl
who could not get words out of her mouth and who walked into
his coat closet. Yet that same clumsy girl had the nerve to ask for
a nomination to the prestigious Hearst Scholarship. Things could
not get any worse.

The bright shade of light in my mind began to direct me.
Having quickly assessed the situation, it told me I was better off
staying in the closet. It was almost five o'clock in the afternoon.
Soon Dr. Stone would have to go home. Then I would sneak out.
The plan would work. Lucky me. It was springtime, and Dr. Stone
did not need to carry a coat. There was no coat in the dark closet.

Otherwise, at five o'clock, he would have opened the door, got his coat, and found me nestling inside. And then my clever plan would not have worked.

I stood in the total darkness for a time, afraid to breathe, and then I carefully opened the door a little, just enough to receive a crack of light through which I could see the lanky Dr. Stone at his desk, dialing his telephone.

"Hi, Joe," he said and paused.

Joe had to be Dr. Joseph Morgan.

"The young Vietnamese woman, Chow Chow," Dr. Stone continued, "she was just here, and she…"

He had, as many others, misspoken my name, changing Mi Chau into Chow Chow, making my name sound like a Chinese restaurant or a dog. He had stopped mid-sentence. Apparently, at the other end, Dr. Morgan was speaking.

"Listen, Joe, she seems intelligent and is probably the kind of student who will apply herself. But she can't speak English."

My temple pulsed and I felt the headache spreading. The expert assessment was made. I could not speak English.

"Look, Joe. She sat before me and said some gibberish. She couldn't pronounce a word…"

Another long pause. The kindhearted Professor Morgan must have been defending my English competency. It was all hopeless.

"Of course she was self-conscious. That did not change the fact that she couldn't say what she wanted to say. I think she had a problem with diction."

Another pause, and then Dr. Stone was trying harder to speak. Yet he kept having to stop, could only speak a few words here and there, never a complete sentence, as Dr. Morgan must have continued to interrupt him.

"The test? How could I know why she did so well? Joe, it's a multiple-choice test. Her writing samples? Foreign students are often better at writing than speaking. But I tell you, Joe, I just can't in all my conscience give the Hearst award to someone who can't speak English and can't pronounce words…

"What do you mean, she speaks beautiful English? With kind of a Welsh accent! Joe, come on. She couldn't say the word she wanted to say. How could I know what the word was if she couldn't say it to me?"

I leaned against the back wall of the dark closet, feeling sick in my stomach.

"What? Well, certainly. Fine. Come on over. We'll discuss it then." Dr. Stone hung up the phone.

He sat down at his desk and began to write profusely. I glided down into a squatting position. The crack in the door shed barely enough light for me to observe my surroundings. I was definitely in a closet. I was a small girl and could manage inside a small, claustrophobic space.

My hands felt and my eyes saw a pair of gigantic boots. They smelled like sewage. I was disturbed by the unpleasant thought that Dr. Stone's feet could be this long, this big, and this ill-smelling. My hands felt, too, stacks of old papers and newspapers. An old tie. A wool hat. And then my fingers felt the sleekness of a magazine cover.

I squeezed myself into a corner, taking the utmost care not to make a sound. Through the crack at the door, I could see Dr. Stone writing at his desk. Then, he stopped to reach for the telephone. He was about to make another phone call. I was determined not to listen. Out of self-respect, I reasoned to myself. To avoid listening, I needed something to occupy myself.

I picked up the magazine, bringing it closer to the crack at the door. I could see the cover. It was titled *Penthouse*, featuring on the cover a naked blonde woman sticking her behind to the camera. She wore nothing but a man's tie around her neck. It hung down in front of her, together with the pendulous momentum of the side view of her huge breasts and long nipples. She looked backward at the camera, her fierce blue eyes firing a wicked gaze, her hands resting on her knees, her crimson lips pouting.

I dared not turn the pages.

And then I heard footsteps.

Through the crack of light at the closet door opening, I could see the fat Dr. Morgan making his way into Dr. Stone's office. The two professors shook hands, and Dr. Morgan settled into the same chair where I had been sitting before. He was raising his voice.

"Henry," he said, "if I hadn't known you for a long time, I would say you were full of shit. Pardon my French. You are denying the Hearst money to the most amazing kid I have run across in a long time."

I took a deep breath. They were talking about me again. Should I rush out of the closet, apologize to the two distinguished journalism professors, and then run to Smith Hall and cry alone for hours because I had messed things up?

"Read this." Dr. Morgan threw a document on the desk. "She wrote this story and finished it within two hours in my writing lab. I saw her do this with my own eyes. She has been in this country for nine months. Nine months, Henry. Nine months. Could you have done the same, Henry, writing this well in a foreign language, had you found yourself in Russia, the Arctic, or the moon?"

On the other side of the desk, Dr. Stone said nothing. His chin and ears appeared longer.

"She misspelled words," Dr. Stone said without much assurance, holding my story in midair.

"OK, so she misspelled a few words. But how could you say someone who wrote this couldn't speak English? I am afraid she speaks it better than I." Dr. Morgan was loud, and his face was red. "She might not speak it exactly the same way we do, but it is English."

I shifted my body. The *Penthouse* magazine fell from my hand, making a noise, but Dr. Morgan was so ardent and loud in his speech the two men apparently did not hear the noise from the closet.

"Henry, I brought you something else. I called the admissions office. She showed up here last year, daughter of a former Vietnamese visiting scholar with a philosophy degree from Sorbonne. She had no authenticating papers with her, and her father wrote an affidavit attesting that she was seventeen years old and was ready for college. They made her take the TOEFL, that English proficiency test for foreign students, as well as the GED, the SAT, and she scored high on each and every one. And guess what, listen to this…"

Dr. Morgan paused. Dr. Stone was listening behind his desk. I was listening behind the closet door.

"Listen to this," Dr. Morgan said slowly. "She seemed a little distracted and withdrawn, full of nervous energy at times and melancholy at times, so they sent her to a psychologist. They did give her some sort of a psychological test, which was inconclusive probably due to cultural issues. They also gave her an IQ test. Guess what, Henry? She scored 164. We have here in our department a genius, an eighteen-year-old genius who came out of that war. Henry, let me repeat. It's the IQ score of 164, that of a genius…"

—

An hour must have passed by the time I concluded my story. The Crazy Man had been laughing intermittently, his eyes brightened, his white teeth shining under those chestnut lips.

"So, Princess, you sat in the closet and eavesdropped," he summed up with great amusement.

"Stop laughing at me," I said, unable to conceal my displeasure.

"How did you get out?" He raised one index finger and touched the tip of my snub nose. I winced.

"I sneaked out after Dr. Stone had left his office for the day and had locked his door. Fortunately, the door could be opened from the inside, and only the janitor saw me in the hallway. Still, I felt very bad, so the following day, I went to Dr. Morgan and confessed. He laughed so much, just like you now, but he promised to keep my secret. Everybody laughed at me…"

"I am not laughing at you," he said, the chestnut lips closing with the last word. His eyes shone, and he squeezed my hand.

We both sat in silence for a long time. I rested my chin on my knees until he gently patted my back, "So they finally believe you are a genius. I already know you are a genius. Go home, genius. Go home, my first lady," he said.

He left me and walked toward the open space outside the hallway of Krost Hall, as though he were walking into the sunset. For a while he stood immobile, a lonely figure, edged against what was left of the reddish sun. Then he began moving his limbs, precisely and deliberately, slowly at times, swiftly at times, as though each movement had become a graceful samurai sword cutting through the air.

Against that dying sun, he became a warrior, a knight, a kung fu fighter displaying his art in preparation for embarking upon a new mission.

His warrior dance came to a stop with his right arm held in midair, as he froze himself into a statue. A moment passed in utmost solitude, and then the statue turned toward me, the fisted arms held tightly close to his sides. He bowed solemnly as though I were a throned spectator judging his art. Then he went back inside the hallway of Krost Hall, picked up his blanket, spread it in a dark corner, and lay down. He closed his eyes, his two hands folded behind his head. He was going to sleep.

I got up from the steps of Krost Hall and walked toward the dormitory complex. The sky had darkened, and the sun was completely gone.

——

The weather got colder as the fall semester of 1976 went on. Cool autumn was approaching, manifesting itself on branches that gradually became barren and upon leaves that changed their colors and flew in the damp air. The Crazy Man did not stand anymore. He sat on the concrete floor, his dirty blanket wrapped around him. No one looked at him but me.

He told me again one day, "I want to marry you. You are my pretty woman."

"Why are you doing this to yourself?" I was about to cry.

"Doing what?"

"This." I pointed at his pamphlets. "It's meaningless."

"Don't you ever tell me that."

"Sorry, I am not even twenty years old. I don't know much."

I looked at his face again. Fiery eyes, tight corners of lips reflecting the stubbornness of a righteous man accepting his fate, his roots, with absolute pride. I knew I had seen a similar face before, not in the image of Sydney Poitier of America, but in my past in Vietnam. I shook my head to clear away the image of the man.

I changed the topic. "Why should I marry you?"

"Because I know you have a beautiful belly and a sensuous belly button."

My cheeks grew hot. I should have been shocked and offended. I should have said something in protest. But I could not move my lips.

"Soft skin, smooth with a line of tiny, fuzzy, colorless baby hair running from your navel down to the tops of your thighs. His eyes were closed. He was in his own world and could care less about my reaction.

"You are crazy," I sighed.

"What is there to live for in life, except pursuing a cause and putting your head on the belly of the woman you love, kissing her belly button?"

Words finally blurted from my mouth. "You don't love me. You are self-centered!" I ran away from him, stopping momentarily around the corner outside the Krost Hall vestibule, yelling at the top of my lungs. "You are obscene and irresponsible. And you are playing a game with me!"

I was angry at him, intimidated by his sensual remarks. But a ticklish feeling lingered for a long time in my lower abdomen as I recalled what he said. This bothered me. I was determined never to let him talk to me that way again.

———

I had the same dream again. The Vietnamese man with a Sidney Poitier face sneered at me. Three gunshots. And then he bent over and kissed my mouth. The ticklish feeling in my abdomen became a knife cutting me in half. I became two fish swimming toward an ocean. And then my fish tail turned into legs. There were two of me, two pairs of legs, running with the man. Like John Wayne he jumped on a horse, and I went with him. The anxiety of having to traverse the night made me choke. I woke up, coughing, and found the pillow damp with tears again.

I sat in my bed, wishing I could have a glass of water and that someone would pat my back. There was no one, and the kitchen in the dormitory was on a different floor. So I lay down again and stared at the ceiling. I wanted to tell the Crazy Man about my nightmare and my pain. I trusted him, and he knew about pain. It would be a relief to be able to tell someone. My insomnia persisted through the night, and I wished I could write down the story I would be telling him—what happened to me when a regime collapsed and a country changed boss.

The night passed. I knew I was alone.

——

Just before midterm, I brought the Crazy Man an apple. He took it immediately, was about to raise it to his mouth, and stopped midway.

"Fate makes you my love," he said. "We met."

"What is fate?" I asked.

"I'll show you what fate is. Fate is this apple." He pointed to the little stem at the top of the apple. "I will say from *A* through *Z*. When the stem breaks, the letter that corresponds will be the name of my future First Lady. That's fate."

He began twisting the little stem, and I took a deep breath, nervously watching his square-tipped fingers at work. When I raised my eyes, his black pupils took mine in. *"A, B, C, D, E,"* he said, beginning the alphabet.

He said, *M*, so slowly, his lips closing on the consonant. I looked down at the apple. The stem had broken.

"It's you, my dear ME. Princess Mi Chau. *Michelle, ma belle,"* he almost whispered.

I shook my head and interrupted him. "You broke the stem deliberately on the M. You planned this. You are playing with me again."

I walked away, leaving him with his apple. Soon he would eat it. His white teeth would dig into the crusty, juicy texture, and he would make noise with his smacking lips.

I turned back and shouted, "You are phony!"

"Don't say that. Come back here, ME, ME," he shouted after me. "I am never phony. A country should never have a phony man in the highest office of the land. *Nguyen thu quoc gia*'s got to be an honest man who keeps his promises."

I wanted to escape his words. *Nguyen thu quoc gia.* Head of state. An honest man.

"Come back here, *ma belle*. Apologize to me. Otherwise, you may never have a second chance."

I kept on walking.

That night, I examined my face in the mirror. I might not be as pretty as Simone, I decided, but I have an honest face.

———

Autumn arrived in its breathtaking beauty, with golden leaves flying in the cold air, occasionally hitting my cheekbones and landing sadly on the ground. When I walked on campus, I wrapped my long hair around my neck. I was known among my classmates as "the quiet, skinny Oriental girl with hair wrapped around her neck."

I had not been by Krost Hall for weeks. And I was busy studying. One day I had to cross the forest between Krost Hall and the Morris Library to reach the Communications and Fine Arts Building. I had to attend a drama practice at the University Theater on the other side of the forest. In apprehension I had signed up for a drama course. Each drama practice was a test of my strength. I was never sure I could even open my mouth to deliver the lines. I began to stutter a lot.

That day I walked by Krost Hall with Shakespeare caught between my lips. On the steps of Krost Hall, there was no Crazy Man. He was gone.

No more blanket. No more silly talks. No more pamphlets or flyers.

No one missed him. No one noticed he was gone. At one time, I had thought they would install him permanently on the pavement of Krost Hall, so he would become an institution. Like Krost Hall itself.

I stood where he used to stand. Shakespeare was gone forever from my mouth, and I did not know what to do to overcome the unexpected feeling of loss.

I walked through the double glass door into Krost Hall. Inside, I picked up a copy of the campus newspaper.

"Vietnamese Guru Severely Beaten by Unknown Suspects," the headline said. Below the headline appeared a picture of the Crazy Man passing out pamphlets. I felt dizzy and had to lean against the wall.

The news story reported that the Crazy Man was a robust man. His wounds should have been fatal; a weaker man would have died instantly. I could see him performing his warrior dance, brave like a soldier, kicking, striking out with his fists, breaking all his ribs, damaging his kidneys, and cracking his skull. He must have fought so bravely, the story concluded, but the result of his heroism was the intensive care unit.

The news story raised all possibilities. Robbers? Unlikely, because he had nothing on him, and his moneybox, full of coins and one-dollar bills, remained intact. Hate crime? The bitterness of some Vietnam vets? Those Americans who lost their sons and daughters in the war and resented the Vietnamese refugees? Any Klan members, white supremacists, oblivious and unidentified in the rural areas of Southern Illinois? Even any of newly arrived refugees, broken, angered, maladjusted, needing a scapegoat? Or was it personal vendetta?

In any event, the reporter pointed out, it happened on a peaceful, liberal campus, outside the building that housed the history and political science departments. The social sciences and the humanities. Nothing like this had ever happened in sleepy Southern Illinois and SISU. His assailants had meant to kill.

The reporter had interviewed the Crazy Man's dissertation advisor, who gave a summary of the young man's abandoned dissertation on Vietnam. The Crazy Man had constructed a model for rebuilding the countryside. Oil exploration along the coast. Exportation of rice. Toward a complete stoppage of American, Russian, or Chinese intervention. A stronger middle class, with freedom of speech so ingrained in people's minds it became a habit, an attitude, a norm of life. All of those ambitious, wonderful things I no longer wanted to think about.

The dissertation was the work of an idealistic man, the news article concluded.

—

Somehow I knew in my heart I would never see my Crazy Man again. I had never had a chance to tell him about my pain. Gone was the opportunity to share. I was to bear my pain alone, from now on.

I left Krost Hall and headed for the Communications Building to attend my drama practice. First, I had to cross the forest.

Autumn appeared before me on the mattress of gold, reddish, and mustard green leaves covering the earth. A single morning breeze awakened them. Tiny, evasive sounds emanated as the passing wind touched the leaves. Those tiny whispers turned into the crispy sound of breakage as my shoes pressed onto the damp ground, crushing the awakened leaves. Then came silence. Like a stagnant painting, the forest after its morning breeze froze into serenity, and the rows of trees stood silently, countless leaves waiting breathlessly in that dense silence. They throbbed as I raised my heels and stepped, as though they had souls.

Leaves are crying! I thought to myself.

They are indeed crying, I repeated. I could hear their cries. Distinctly. Those small cries together filled up my ears in a requiem for imminent death.

I began to see, among broken leaves, the dark, fiery eyes of a disillusioned Vietnamese graduate student who had decided to throw away his long years of education, and who had called me his first lady.

I stood in the heart of the woods, burying my feet in the corpses of broken leaves. My eyes blurred and my temples pulsed. For a moment, I forgot where I was. Images of roaring cargo airplanes and people walking through barricades of MPs wearing black bands on their arms and shiny pistols around their hips rushed through my mind, and I had to sit down on the ground to gather myself. I sat among crying leaves and could recall no Shakespeare lines from class. Instead I composed my own monologue.

I am going to my drama class in America for Shakespeare. All of this excitement of a new life, and yet here I am, carrying my broken heart, alone among autumn trees and leaves and all this beauty. What do I want now? I want to turn the clock back so I can redo a departure. I want to pack properly. I want good luck and bon voyage and welcome gifts. Where I am going, I will see the changing seasons like rows of silent evergreens and all that pure, sparkling snow whitening the earth, and I will jump up and down and roll myself around on that pure snow to celebrate the season and know the great joy of being alive. But I am not rolling. Instead, I have made timid footsteps on broken leaves.

On the Boeing airplane that crossed the Pacific from Guam to the U.S, I came across a Newsweek *cover showing people standing behind banners: "Only Ford wants them." "Why this banner? Are we not wanted?" I had asked that day, and my father yanked the magazine from me. Too late. I had already seen the angry rejection of the host country. In confusion I slept through the flight, and when I woke up, I had already crossed the ocean. When the ocean no longer spread its green underneath the gray wings of that impersonal plane, I thought I was still walking in a dream, forever a dream, that sleepwalker's dream, a girl with no past born to be sixteen, a young refugee with no luggage but her nightmare and solitude. Yet I am supposed to celebrate freedom and a new life. But separation is the fate of the exiled, and for a traveler in exile, every departure is but an old déjà vu beginning. So through this life I will repeat my departures, meeting forests of leaves that change colors, telling me of the season and the transient nature of life. I am whispering to the dying leaves about my end—when life and death become one, and I, too, will return to the earth, joining those leaves and disappearing into the ground. Perhaps then I will turn into the cool autumn air, and there will be no breakage, no separation, no past, no present, no running, no search for a new place, no repeated departures, because I have become the air, inseparable from its sky, and no one, nothing can cut the air in half and break life in two to create a new beginning that multiplies. The air I have become will permeate everywhere. But as young as I am, why am I thinking about a time when I will change into the autumn air? It must be because of what happened to me during the exodus—the pain of secrets that I alone have to bear, and there is no one to tell it to—the wretched exchange for the freedom I am supposed to cherish. So instinctively I know that only in the transformation of flesh and bone into air will I attain complete safe harbor. Change me into the air, and I will attain absolute freedom and the ultimate sanctuary of peace. But once a refugee, always a refugee. I'll be running forever, until I reach the farthest edge of the planet, until there is no more earth on which to run, when I will turn into the ultimate vacuum called the air. Until that final moment comes, I am to cross the forest, toward a stage.*

"Are you sure you can handle Shakespeare?" a classmate named Steve once asked. I didn't know what to say, but I could see the doubt in his eyes.

———

On that day in autumn of 1976, I delivered my monologue in the woods, while listening to the cries of dying leaves. At times, I heard the leaves throbbing, pulsing, in harmony with the sobbing timbre of my heart. A strong wind blew by, and all of the leaves awakened for the last time before their death. Their cries became a symphonic crescendo, filling the low sky. I held on to my shoulders, shaken by nature's requiem for those dying leaves.

Standing up from the bed of leaves, I started to cry.

And that was how I reached the stage of the drama department. There, I would be delivering the role of a lawyer, in front of a crowd who might be doubting my ability to handle the job.

"*The quality of mercy is not strained. It droppeth as the gentle rain from heaven upon the place beneath. It is twice blest. It blessed him that gives and him that takes. 'Tis mightiest in the mightiest it becomes the throned monarch better than his crown.*"

I was speaking Shakespeare! I curved my tongue and then darted it underneath the upper row of my front teeth. I gave the soft *th* and pushed my breath through the blockage between the tongue and teeth to pronounce the breathy *th*. This sound did not exist in Vietnamese. It sounded English, and I became Shakespeare's English. I found a spot in front of me, a spot with no face, no name, and I spoke my words to it. I gave the words all the volume I could draw from the ninety-five pounds and five feet two inches of me. Words poured out of my soul, and when they escaped my mouth, they sounded so alien. They leaped toward the spot I had chosen. There, in that spot, I reigned. Yet I felt so rotten inside.

For the performance, I had signed my full Vietnamese name. The drama coach could not comfortably pronounce it. It was a problem. My Vietnamese name was problem. Nobody cared how I was once so proud of the long, winding name that said something about my roots dating back to the Spirit of the River Huong who watched over me. Here, I was better off without that name on this stage. They had given me a new name. *Portia.* Easily slip on and off. So long as I could articulate the beautiful words, I would become *Portia*.

I was on stage as a woman disguised as someone else to speak the clever words and help someone she loved. *Mercy. Justice. A pound of flesh.* A woman more powerful and shrewder than men. An advocate. No one cared who I was. No one recognized me. No one was supposed to. I became Portia. The spot to which I spoke was no longer Hue, DaLat, Saigon of the Vietnam I knew. It became Venice with all those gondolas and plenty of olives. "*That in the course of justice none of us should see salvation. We do pray for mercy.*" I was speaking outward still, yet a smaller voice spoke inside me. *Salvation,* the tiny voice told me. To reach salvation, one must forebear. Forgive. Forgo. And forget.

I put the sharpness of my pain into the words.

"*Take then thy bond, take thou they pound of flesh. But in cutting it if thou dost shed one drop of Christian blood, thy lands and goods are by the law of Venice confiscate unto the State of Venice…*" I thought of the next step after SISU. Did this mean no more first lady? Just a stage?

"*Therefore prepare thee to cut off the flesh. Shed thou no blood nor cut thou less nor more but just a pound of flesh.*" In the spot to which I spoke, I found the Vietnamese Sidney Poitier's grin. Those shining white teeth. *I am speaking to you. Can you hear these clever words? I am supreme and powerful and I can make things happen. I won't succumb. Forebear. Forgive. Forego. And forget.* I was speaking forever, though it felt so bad inside. I enunciated the *t*'s and the *s*'s. I was careful and perfect with all letters, vowels, and ending sounds. When the lump rose in my throat, and my tongue refused to obey, I stopped and removed my eyes from the spot. In the rows of seats in front of me and below me, they all waited, their eyes fixated, thinking I was highlighting something. My eyes back to the spot. To him and me. Mercy. Salvation. A pound of flesh.

And then it was all silence.

Until I heard a few hands clapping. And then a few more. My eyes left the spot where he was, and everyone in the theater was clapping, and the roaring sound reminded me again of that fated cargo airplane that had swallowed me that day in April 1975.

I rushed off the stage. I thought I would collapse.

But I did not collapse. Instead I stood still, somewhat dazed, and someone was approaching me. I recognized him. The curly hair. Big brown eyes. Big teeth. He smoked and called himself an actor. "Hey," he said. The SISU students all said that. *Hey, hey, hey, oh yeah? Cool! You guys, the dude, the gal, my pal, what do you know good? Hey hey hey…come on, it hurts so good….oh swell.* His name was Steve Something. Steve Whatever. I couldn't remember. Steve Something or Steve Whatever from the drama class.

"Hey, it was really good. I was just…surprised. I couldn't believe you could do it as well as…" He faded off. His brown eyes also spoke the language of sincerity.

"So when did you first learn all this? At the beginning of the semester or last night? Quite impressive." Steve was still speaking. He did not know when to stop. He was genuinely surprised to discover I could almost outdo him. Just almost.

They had given me a blonde wig to get into the part, and I had tucked my long black hair under it. It looked utterly ridiculous, and I was taking it off, but actually, no, I would not take it off! I had decided to become Portia. All I needed was a wig, plus one Big Mac a day.

"When I was a baby girl, I learned about *The Merchant of Venice* in Hue, Vietnam," I explained to Steve. I meant for my eyes to speak the language of sincerity. I was telling the truth. I was sharing my past with him. I traveled back to the time when my father was teaching English and American civilization to twenty-two-year-old college women at Hue University. Those young women had taken turns translating pages from *The Merchant of Venice* and *A Farewell to Arms* into Vietnamese. They handwrote the translation in a hardbound coffee-table book, pages beautifully bordered in flowery motifs and art emblems of the Faculty of Letters, sharp black ink on the best of grainy ivory paper. Some of the women were artists-to-be, and they drew illustrations with ink and watercolors, and these artworks were inserted in between pages of translation. The beautiful book had been given to my father as a gift at the end of the semester. I had seen these pages, words written in beautiful penmanship, those black and blue ink strokes reminding me of dancing swans. It was the most exquisite thing I had seen—this wonderful handwritten book that commemorated my father's teaching career.

"What? You learned Shakespeare in Vietnam? You must be kidding me." Steve was lighting a cigarette, and people were leaving the theater. "I don't believe it," he said. "I know about Vietnam. My brother was there in the army. People wore black pajamas and village huts were blowing up. Couldn't have Shakespeare taught to a little girl in a place like that."

I looked back to the spot to which I had been staring while on stage. The Crazy Man was hovering like an angel, waving at me.

"Hello, my first lady."

"How difficult is it to become a first lady in America?" I asked Steve, and then my face felt hot. I swallowed with difficulty, my mouth all dried up, and I felt sorry I had even asked the question. The echo of the Crazy Man's voice became louder and numbed my ears.

"Hello, my first lady."

Steve had not extinguished his cigarette, his eyes darting around the theater. Naturally, he did not see the hovering Crazy Man.

"You mean like Jackie Kennedy?" he asked. "I don't think you can play her. She's five feet seven. Besides, you're Oriental."

I looked away to avoid the smoke coming from his cigarette and the reality it painted. I was Oriental, as in Oriental rugs. I was no Jackie Kennedy. I could eat ten Big Macs a day and I would never be five feet seven. I looked to the spot above again, but the Crazy Man was no longer there. He had flown away.

"Hey, are you crying?" Steve was still smoking, and everyone else had left the theater. "Don't feel bad, kid. So what if you can't play Jackie? This is America. Everyone is a first lady. Everyone is the president. It's a democracy. It's the American dream."

———

My instinct was correct. I never saw the Crazy Man again, since only a day later, the campus newspaper reported that he had died in intensive care.

He had no family in the United States, so the Vietnamese refugees in Southern Illinois pooled their resources to hold a funeral. The campus administration, several student antiviolence groups, and churches in the area also contributed. His burial invoked as much gossip as the rumors about his life. Fearful of his killers and the prospect of hate crimes, many refugee families were too afraid to attend his funeral. Some started lying about where they were from. Others hopped on a bus and immediately left for California after the funeral. After all, California is the Promised Land for Asians.

I did not attend the funeral, for a different reason.

On that day I skipped classes and tried to sleep while snow fell outside. For Vietnamese, white was the color of mourning. His funeral coincided with the first snowfall of the season. I stayed in bed the whole day, and between short lapses of sleep, I heard again the sounds of gunshots and airplane engines. Déjà vu. Images of falling leaves and falling snow dancing on an all-white path dashed through my head. Even the leaves had turned white.

I heard again the cargo airplane engine, emanating rhythmic pounding noises, and I wondered what it felt like to stop breathing and die, lying underneath the hammering of nails onto a coffin lid. I wished I could lie in silence, under beds of roses and tulips. Yet I tossed and turned in my bed, hearing pounding noises above my head as my temples pulsed. I knew the Crazy Man was gone, and I lived on.

———

To the Vietnamese students at SISU, the Crazy Man became a myth.

Vietnamese believe in the luck of the number nine. I believe that all important things in life should be summed up in nine words.

For the years to come in my life in America, I kept wishing I had delivered my nine words to him. Either to the man I knew, or the symbol he had become in my head. Whenever I thought of him, I still felt the ticklish sensations in my abdomen, together with the urge to cry. I thought, too, of all the ideals and dreams that had died when I crossed the ocean in 1975, revived shortly when I had exchanged words with him and during my first appearance as Portia on the SISU stage.

I let myself daydream one day and thought of all the what-ifs, and I wrote down in my diary combinations of my nine words. On the page appeared the following:

Dear Mr. President of the new Republic,

> *I think I have fallen in love with you.*
> 1 2 3 4 5 6 7 8 9

> *Yes, I would very much like to marry you.*
> 1 2 3 4 5 6 7 8 9

> *Who knows, perhaps we could have saved our dream.*
> 1 2 3 4 5 6 7 8 9

> *Em nghi rang hinh nhu em trot yeu anh.*
> 1 2 3 4 5 6 7 8 9

THREE

THE THREE CHILDREN
OF THE SCHOOLTEACHER

Houston, Texas
the present

The day is long in March, and the hot and humid climate of Texas reinforces my self-indulgent illusion that sunshine will last forever. At six o'clock in the evening, the bright day has not died out, and the traffic of Westheimer Street is gradually turning into a beelike stream.

The patrons of La Griglia parade in, all beaming with their bright eyes, the women lifting the corners of their skirts, the men glancing at the gold watches beneath their gray coat sleeves. I am sitting at the bar, facing the front door, comfortable behind the dark sunglasses that hide my roving eyes so I can be free to become the people watcher of Houston. I first rest my eyes on the mannequin-like face of some Texas beauty, who reminds me of an unkempt peacock, with her turquoise frilly dress and beehive of purplish-red hair. I then move on to the beer belly of some Texas oilman, well covered under his navy blue coat jacket glamorized with a row of bright gold buttons that match his bright gold cufflinks. The Houston yuppies move leisurely to the front door from their shiny BMW convertibles and luxury Lexuses, replete with their alloy tire rims, leather seats, and customized license plates.

Inside the restaurant, the primitive colors of La Griglia's southwestern artwork take me to Mexico's green grass, brown earth, red sun, and the deep yellow grains of its corn tortillas. Gorgeous twenty-year-old waiters and waitresses sing the exotic menu of some twenty different kinds of salads, their rosy hands gliding baskets of hot bread wrapped in crisp white cloth across tables toward the tilting cups of glistening butter. Delicious oiled garlic and melted cheese fill the air, mixed with the aroma of fermented vinegar, tangy fresh tomato and tamarind sauces, the intoxicating scent of red and white wine, and the rich, floury smell of homemade pasta and tortilla.

I draw into my lungs the aromas of food and drinks, yet my palate remains immune to the seduction of the culinary art. People turn into robots through the lenses of my sunglasses until the familiar gait of an Asian male appears at the door in his khaki pants and denim shirt. I raise a finger and he sees me, the trade-marked boyish grin of my brother pulling his full lips upward and wrinkling the bridge of his elegant nose. That part of him has not changed and perhaps never will. Now perhaps he has gained a little weight around his waistline. Perhaps his thick, shining black hair has thinned a little. Perhaps his grin is only boyish in my mind. Pi is a man now, a head taller than the top of my teased hair, and he acts like a man. I slip down from the bar stool, and he places one arm around me.

His embrace is a grown-up's. There is nothing tradition-ally Vietnamese about it. In the old days, Vietnamese boys did not embrace their big sisters. Then, big sisters were treated like mothers, revered and bowed to. A big sister was expected to make sacrifices for her younger siblings and give them directions for the sake of the family, so she was given deference like a substitute mother. Now in stylish La Griglia, Pi could be mistaken for my boyfriend showing up for our early evening date. And he is embracing me.

"Hello, Mimi." He calls me by my American name. "Looking good, sis," he says. He is speaking English with a Texas accent, and we are meeting in La Griglia, where we act like yuppies, instead of in some Pho noodle shop in the Vietnamese neighborhood of midtown Houston, where our people suck in those long, flat, tasty noodles while they dip and stir their bamboo chopsticks in the meaty broth sprinkled with chopped chives and coriander.

Simone will be arriving late, Pi tells me as we sit at a table for four. He then launches into a full account of his Friday afternoon rat race—he has had to fight the four o'clock traffic to take my mother to his new home across town in an affluent suburb of Houston, the Woodlands. Regardless of when Simone arrives, he will have to leave before eight. Only I, unmarried and unattached, can stay past eight and sit idly at La Griglia to catch the attention of these young men, wearing white shirts and designer ties, arriving in the restaurant after they have valeted their BMW convertibles.

Once upon a time, we were three children inseparable in our daily routines, sharing a bowl of rice and splitting a piece of fruity American chewing gum into three parts. Simone used to put Pi up front and me on the back of her bike, and together we toured the streets of District Eight, Saigon, laughing at the dirt particles that flew against our young faces, in the heat rolling back from the dusty tires of those military trucks—the *camions* that graced Saigon's busy streets and spoke of a country at war fueled by foreign aid. But in those days I had no awareness of danger, whether from the *camions* that could crush our bike or the threat of war. Now we live in America, are afraid of high cholesterol and the health risks of overeating, and we see one another only at Christmas or for special meetings like this.

There will not be too many meetings like this, I hope, I tell Pi, and he shrugs. Someone calls, "Peter!" and Pi turns around to shake hands with a blond-headed young man in a starched white shirt.

"Meet my sister Mimi," Pi says to the starched shirt, and I take off my sunglasses at last.

"So this is the Harvard-trained lawyer," the starched shirt says in his distinctive Texas drawl, "the White House Fellow, the superwoman sister you always brag about."

According to Pi, the starch shirt works with Pi as a sale teammate at Hewlett-Packard.

I'm not really listening. "*Peter*?" I repeat the name his friend has called out to him, and my brother explains that he has officially changed his name from Pierre Phi Long to Peter. While the starched shirt is busy digging his fork into the grilled chicken breast topping his Caesar salad, I ask Pi why he prefers being called Peter. "Convenience," he says. "I am tired of being called *Peer* instead of *Pierre*. If I had ended up in France I would have been Pierre. But I am in Texas now. Pierre is too French, and it makes me unpopular among the guys at HP."

———

Peter Giang-Son. My brother's new name brings back my bittersweet memory of the day we were processed for naturalization. It was an important event. Even Simone had flown down to Houston from New York City for the special occasion, so we could all be naturalized together as a family.

Things went smoothly on that historic day until my father, in his stubborn way, decided to create a problem for all of us. My father's full name, the correct Vietnamese way, was *Tran Giang Son.* The family name came first; his compounded given name, *Giang Son,* came last. *Giang Son* means "river and mountain," a metaphor derived from the literary phrase *giang son gam voc.* "*Rivers and mountains, beautiful like silk and satin*" was the literary phrase, a metaphor for a beautiful country. So the literal translation of my father's full name was "Tran the Beautiful Country." If my father were to follow the American way, the family name would come last, and he would be *Giang Son Tran,* instead of *Tran Giang Son.*

No big deal, but ten minutes before our interview, my father announced, solemnly and adamantly, that he would not reverse his name to conform to the American way. The reversal destroyed the melody as well as the literary meaning, he said. It destroyed everything about him, he added. I couldn't understand why, but he kept repeating the word *destroy* in Vietnamese, and his eyes were red. He sat in a corner, reciting a Vietnamese poem over and over again, while his three children stared at one another, worried and confused, knowing that he had, again, slipped into his madness.

The madness had started on the day when my father foolishly stopped his car along Interstate 45, on the way from Houston to Galveston beach, in order to rescue a turtle crawling aimlessly across the freeway—the beginning of what we considered our father's harmless episodes of temporary insanity. Those days, my father had given up all hope of finding a teaching job. He had given up on writing or research. Instead, with cash from Simone and a loan from his Vietnamese friends, he had bought an old shrimp boat and rented it out to the Vietnamese shrimpers in the

Gulf of Mexico. Every week, he drove to Galveston to check on the boat and to collect his weekly rent.

That night, my father declared to us at dinner that he had adopted the poor little turtle as his fourth child to replace his firstborn Simone, who had married his American friend and boss at the news service in Saigon, the AP journalist Christopher Sanders. Mr. Sanders was more than twice Simone's age, and the marriage was entered into hurriedly a few days before the fall of Saigon to secure our departure for America. For years Mr. Sanders had never once contacted my father, and my parents never once talked about Simone's marriage.

Oblivious to our wide eyes and gaping, rice-filled mouths, my father declared he had even given the turtle a name. He called it Ali Baba, after a character from "Ali Baba and the Forty Thieves" in *The Arabian Nights*. We were all shocked. I was unsure if he was just joking or if he was truly bitter about Simone's marriage. Bitter to the point of replacing her with a turtle.

That summer, I had graduated from SISU and was living at home with my parents and Pi, prepared to enter Harvard Law School in the fall on a combination of scholarship and Simone's help in cash. My father had refused to talk to me about Harvard, never once congratulating me. He handled the news of my Harvard admission with the same silence with which he had treated the news of Simone's marriage. It was as though he were ashamed rather than proud, unable to bear the thought that I had come to Simone for financial help rather than asking him for a share of his modest income from the old shrimp boat.

But the shrimp boat, too, was partly the result of Simone's cash—something my father never wanted to admit.

I was puzzled, of course, but we exhibited little reaction or objection to my father's idiosyncrasy about the turtle. After the fall of Saigon, in our own quiet way, we had denied ourselves the luxury of outward reaction to shock. Besides, even in the old Saigon, my father had always had the reputation as a frustrated, impoverished, dissident intellectual. So, we quietly watched while our father put Ali Baba into a portable plastic sink and took it to the bedroom.

From then on, my father spent hours each day caring for his turtle. My mother, the classic subservient wife, went along and even helped him feed the little animal with bread crumbs, occasionally expressing her concern that the turtle might be ill. Worse, an ill turtle could even be toxic to the family.

We had taken the turtle for granted as my father's new toy, until one night, when my mother slipped out of their bedroom and told us in tears, "Your father has gone insane. He has been speaking to the turtle every night. Tonight," she said, "he called the animal Simone."

Pi and I tiptoed through the hallway and pressed our ears to the door to my father's bedroom. When we couldn't hear, we pushed the door open a little and saw my father kneeling on the floor next to the plastic sink where he kept his Ali Baba. He was indeed talking to the turtle, calling it Simone, his precious, beautiful, firstborn child. Pi could not understand the monologue, but I could. My father was reciting Vietnamese classical poetry, passionately and intensely, as though Ali Baba could understand every word. It had been years since I heard my father reciting those verses. It used to be a habit of his, in the old country.

In fact, I still have vivid memories of those nights in Hue, when Simone and I were not yet ten years old, bored and upset because our absentminded, clumsy father had decided to take over Grandma Que's role in our young lives by putting us to bed. Awkwardly, the young father first exhausted passages from

Alphonse Daudet's *Le Chevre de Monsieur Seguin*, the little goat of Mr. Seguin, running around somewhere in the countryside of France. He then progressed to a reading of Vietnamese poetry. I never forgot my father's favorite Vietnamese poem, which he read to us that night and many times thereafter:

> *Toi dung ben nay song,*
> *ben kia vung dich dong,*
> *lang toi do xam den mau tiet dong...*
> ...
> *I stood on this side of the river*
> *on the other side, the enemy's zone,*
> *in between lies my village,*
> *the haze of its horizon bearing the color of frozen blood...*

That night in Hue, Simone had pouted, asking my father to please go away. She wanted Grandma Que to sing the melodious folk tunes of Nam Binh. She wanted neither the little goat of Mr. Seguin the Frenchman nor the frozen-blood haze of my father's North Vietnamese village. My father, losing patience, spanked her, and she cried heartbrokenly.

It was the first, and the only time, he laid hands on her.

—

The year was 1979, in Houston, Texas, when my father recited again the same Vietnamese poem, this time to his Ali Baba in a portable plastic sink.

"What is he saying, sis? What does it mean?" Pi asked, rounding his innocent eyes. Pi had had no Vietnamese literature classes in the old country; he was too young when we left. Naturally I did not expect him to understand the words my father was reciting to his Ali Baba. Perhaps my father had realized this—the fact that in America, his youngest boy had become culturally alien to and isolated from him. Perhaps that was one more reason why he had adopted Ali Baba into his family, the poor abandoned, misplaced turtle from a Texas highway.

—

"Doi nguoc ho ten cha me dat, tap lam con tre noi ngu ngo." At the Immigration Office in downtown Houston, my father went on to sing another poem written by a friend of his—a Vietnamese writer living in exile. The writer could no longer write or publish; he could not speak English and had reversed his name to follow the American way. He subtly complained about all these things in a poem. In the early days of the Vietnamese resettlement experience, these literary products were printed in some crummy-looking newsletter distributed at Vietnamese grocery markets.

My father was murmuring his friend's poem to himself, the same way he had spoken to his turtle at home. I understood the meaning of those words. *I should not complain,* the poet admitted. *I am among the fortunate ones who should celebrate freedom. Just a little inconvenience here and there,* the poet went on. *For example, I reverse the name my parents have given me, and I become a child again, talking with my hands, babbling in a language I cannot speak.*

Stunned, I watched my father close his eyes as though he were meditating, traveling alone into his private world, saying his favorite exile verses over and over again like a chant, as though we no longer existed around him. In that moment, my father became a lonely immigrant who had slipped away from reality, shutting out his wife and children, accepting only Ali Baba the turtle as his trusted friend.

Before the immigration authority that day, my father officially remained Tran Giang Son, the new, middle-aged citizen of the United States of America. That was the problem. Without the name reversal, my father would be called Mr. Son, while Pi and I would be Pierre Tran and Mi Chau Tran. (The married Simone wanted to keep her full Vietnamese name as her middle name, so she would be Simone Mi Uyen Tran Sanders.) People in America would be asking why our father and his children did not have the same last name.

While the children kept discussing the issue, the immigration interviewer occasionally stuck her head out, calling the name of the next interviewee. We argued and argued, so urgently and earnestly in our staccato, clipped, tonal Vietnamese that the rest of the people who were also waiting for their interviews—Mexicans, Indians, Peruvians, Pakistanis, Iranians, whatever places they were from—were all staring at us. We must have looked like noisy clowns to them.

Amid all of this heated discussion, my mother had retreated to a corner, looking at a *Cosmopolitan* magazine, although her English was not good enough to understand it. When I looked at her to seek her opinion, she smiled feebly and said whatever name the immigrant officer would like to call her would be just fine with her. And then she told me, out of the blue, "The sky is blue, and I love America. It is my country."

For a moment, I was lost. Then, I caught on: she had practiced the sentence at home so that she could say it perfectly to the immigration officer. My father had worked with her diligently the night before our scheduled interview to suppress her Vietnamese accent, and to make sure she would not say the sentence the way she would if she were speaking French. To impress the immigration officer, my mother had to deliver the sentence in perfect American English, my father had stressed.

At the immigration office, my mother was practicing still, apparently in her head. In this emergency, my father had slipped into his poetry recitation, and my mother had taken refuge in the practice of her English. I had to become the take-charge daughter, a literary designer of a last name to solve the dilemma of the day.

I turned to Simone and Pi and announced I would be making the final decision about our last name. We would be taking my father's given name, Giang-Son, hyphenated, as our last name. That way, in the American way, we would all have the same last name, and as a family, we would be the Giang-Sons. I turned to Dr. Tran the Beautiful Country for his approval, but he was still closing his eyes.

The new family name made sense. First, I had hyphenated my given name for school, so hyphenating my father's given name into a new family name for all of us was naturally part of my innovative solution. Second, this hyphenation business went well with the territory. After all, in my mind, we were meant to be the new hyphenated Americans: *Vietnamese-Americans, Chinese-Americans, Japanese-Americans, Italian-Americans, Irish-Americans, etc.* The old country and the new country. We should all be "hyphenated" so that the old self and the new self could forever be connected into a single identity.

I reasoned to my siblings that, after all, Giang-Son did sound prettier than Tran. Giang-Son also sounded more Vietnamese, as the Chinese had Tran as a last name as well, so we would be maintaining our Vietnamese cultural identity better by being called Giang-Son, rather than Tran. Further, if the Americans misspelled Tran, we would all become Train, and that was no good. At least with Giang-Son, we would not run that risk. My logic must have been convincing, since everybody, including my mother, seemed happy with my literary design of a name. The three children would become Mimi Giang-Son, Pierre Giang-Son, and Simone Giang-Son (though of course Simone could choose to be Simone Tran Sanders, should she want to display her new "American wife" identity). Not bad!

That was how we were prepared and ready to throw away our old names, Tran Thanh Mi Uyen, Tran Thanh Phi Long, and Tran Thanh Mi Chau, those beautiful, lyrical Vietnamese names with special meanings that nobody here understood, names that consisted of foreign words too complicated and too long-winded to be remembered. Finally the matter of name was solved satisfactorily, and we all sat down, at peace, waiting to be called for the interviews.

—

Unfortunately, the problems of the day did not end there. Pi went in first for the interview. When he got out, he had officially become Pierre Giang-Son. My mother went next. When she exited the room, she told us what happened. There emerged the next complication.

During the interview, stressed out by my father's sudden episode of temporary insanity, my mother had broken out crying. The kindhearted immigration officer, a woman in her twenties, had gently asked my mother why. My mother's self-conscious broken English was inadequate for her to explain the complex turmoil of the soul, so all my mother could offer was a timid, shorthand explanation of the last-name business. She managed to explain that in the old country of Vietnam, a married woman could retain her maiden name. My mother had had the same name all her life, a vestige of her royal heritage. Yet that day she was all ready and prepared to change her full name from the long-winded Cong Tang Ton Nu Mi Suong to Suong Giang-Son, to conform herself to the American way and to be properly identified as Mr. Tran Giang-Son's lawfully wedded wife. Apparently, the immigration officer thought the name change had made my mother cry. So, she zealously pursued a mission to help my mother maintain her long-winded Vietnamese name. She told my mother that in America, no citizen could be forced to change or reverse her name against her wish, and women, in particular, could make their own decisions, especially on such a personal matter as her last name. My mother was indeed intimidated by the interviewer's long and forceful explanation of what America was about on the issue of names, but in the end, my mother got the message. The bottom line was, according to the immigration officer, my mother did not have to be called Mrs. Son instead of Mrs. Suong, simply to please her husband or to become American. She could be whatever she wanted to be.

The officer (not knowing she had unintentionally added to our family's identity crisis) also pointed out to my mother, conveniently and casually, the terrible disadvantage of adopting my father's last name, *Son*, even in the compound, hyphenated form. In English, *son* meant a male child. In the worst case, someone in America might even call my mother Mama San, instead of Mrs. Giang-Son. Mama San, that stereotypical and derogatory way of referring to an old Asian woman. My mother would not like that. On the other hand, my mother's own name, Suong, could be akin to *swan*. There was a huge difference between *son* and *swan*. Facing the unpleasant possibility of *Mama San* versus the beautiful image of a *swan*, in a split second and without further ado, my timid mother triumphantly said yes when the officer asked if she wanted to keep her old name.

So, thanks to the feminist officer, when my mother emerged from the interview room, this new citizen of *America the Beautiful,* timid and disoriented still, had remained proudly as Mrs. Cong Tang Ton Nu Mi Suong, the name she was born with—a testament to my mother's freedom of choice in her new country. The new citizen of America who emerged from behind the door of the interview room that day was Mrs. Cong Suong, wife of Mr. Tran Giang Son, and mother of Pierre Giang-Son. By then, the whole system of consistency I had devised for the last name business had collapsed, because our father was Mr. Son, my mother was Mrs. Suong, and their son Pi was Mr. Giang-Son. Where would that leave the two daughters? After all this work and discussion, we still ended up with different last names.

Back to square one. And the discussion started all over. All eyes in the room were on us again. We, the quarreling bunch, received all the hostile attention and curiosity of our fellow aliens.

It was then that Pi exploded. He said he had legally become Pierre Giang-Son and that was the end of it. All of this embarrassing discussion was the result of my father's nonsensical approach to the legalization of his own name on the piece of paper called the naturalization court order. After all, Pi did not care if he was called Mr. Son or Mr. Daughter.

Amid that heated and loud argument, the immigration supervisor—the big boss—stepped out, his six-foot-five body gigantic next to us.

"What's the problem here?" The giant cleared his throat, and we all quickly fell silent.

I caught my mother's frightened eyes. I could tell she was panicking—it was as though the glossy *Cosmopolitan* were withering in her hand, and her fragile frame withering with it.

Once again, in a burst of inspiration I arrived at a solution to the problem: the son in our family would be Giang-Son, and the daughters would be Giang-Suong, taking on my mother's beautiful first name, Suong, which could sound like Swan, *or* Sean. In Vietnamese, Suong meant "dew." Giang-Suong meant "river and dew." So, the men would be "river and mountain, the beautiful country," and the women would be "river and dew"—misty dew over a river, still a poetic image of a beautiful country. I was being my romantic and creative self, proud that I had managed to hold on to our literary heritage. Giang-Son for boys, and Giang-Suong for girls. Again, the rule made perfect sense.

I pushed Simone inside the room. The six-foot-five supervisor followed her and the door was shut. When Simone walked out, she told us that legally, she had become Simone Mi Uyen Tran Giang-Suong-Sanders, keeping all words and hyphenating them properly in the right places. She liked it, even though it was far too long. When Simone couldn't decide what to throw away from her wardrobe, she kept everything even if she never wore a piece again. The extraordinary length of her legal name simply meant that in her pretty head, she had managed to maintain all of her identities, or at least gather them all into the same drawer even if she didn't have enough space. In defense of herself, she told us that she could always shorten this very long new name of hers into Simone Sanders for practical daily use. The immigrant supervisor had asked her why the spelling of her Vietnamese last name was different from that of the men in the family, and she had simply smiled. "It is a complicated family, and a complicated place where we came from," she told him, urging him to move on with the paperwork and simply honor her wish.

I was the last one to walk through the door for my interview with the feminist immigration officer. I found out she was a graduate of Smith College, where all the feminist students in America congregated (or so she proudly claimed). She congratulated me on my new name and identity as existing on paper, Mi-Chau Giang-Suong, properly hyphenated per my request. In her enthusiasm, the officer even suggested, "If it were Suong-Giang, the two words transposed, that would make it sound like Sean Young, how beautiful! Welcome to America," she said.

As I later found out, this suggestion stuck with me in a surprising, unpredictable way.

After the arduous paper processing, we were sent home to await the court date, when we would be sworn in as new citizens, pledging our allegiance to America before a federal district judge.

On the way back home, we had no more discussion on the matter of name. My mother was happy that the immigrant officer had warmly praised her for making up her own mind and speaking beautiful English. "The sky is blue, and I love America"—my mother had delivered the sentence perfectly. My father seemed most pleased, and I understood why. Things had gone well. On the historic day, despite the ordeal regarding our name change, no real disaster had occurred, and he had gotten his way. He did not have to reverse his name like that poor poet. After all, Vietnamese or American, at least in name he was still Dr. Tran Giang Son, the schoolteacher in Vietnam, and not what he had become in America, the small-town entrepreneur whose shrimp boat broke down all the time because it was so old, and was used by no other shrimpers in the Gulf but the newly arrived, penniless Vietnamese who couldn't speak a word of English. Perhaps in his mind, his children would still bear the beautiful Vietnamese names he had carefully selected with the help of our sophisticated Grandma Que and a highly sophisticated Vietnamese dictionary. At home, we would always be Si, Mi, and Pi, the three children of the schoolteacher.

But it was important to us children how we were to be called. I felt terrible. I should have persuaded my father to reverse his name. That way, we could all remain the Tran family. Just a simple last name. Instead I had let my wild mind run, and my literary creativity had led to splitting the family in the domain of name. On the day we officially took our American identity, we had taken on different last names. Giang-Son. Giang-Suong. One of these days people would be asking us why the spelling of our last names was different, among brother and sisters, father and daughters, husband and wife. It would be a far too complicated, boring, and ridiculous story to tell. And nobody would understand, anyway. Perhaps we would just lie and blame it all on the towering immigrant supervisor in charge of processing our paperwork, or the overzealous feminist officer who encouraged my mother's freedom of choice. Perhaps we would just claim that the giant man had misspelled our name, so no more questions would be asked.

That day, I had no idea that later on, for phonetic convenience and in professional settings, I would adopt the kindhearted immigration officer's suggestion and allow myself to become Mimi Sean Young, a name that came to me so accidentally, bearing no trace of my Vietnamese identity or my nostalgia about the past. It started with Harvard Law School, where my Vietnamese legal name continued to become a problem as it appeared on the class roll. All this Vietnamese spelling was outright an obstacle to my gaining acceptance in a place that epitomized the American mainstream. Professors and classmates kept mispronouncing and misspelling Mi-Chau Giang-Suong. When the class roll was called, quite often I remained silent, not knowing I had been called on because the pronunciation of my Vietnamese name coming from the person at the podium sounded so far off-base I couldn't recognize it as my own name. There were days when the pronunciation sounded quite basic like *My Joe Juan Sung*; there were days it sounded more imaginative and fanciful like *Maya Joanna Gianni Song*; there were days when the humorous professor would just look up at the class, "Blah blah blah, you know who you are, Mister or Miss S-U-O-N-G, where are you?" He had spelled out loud the last name with a heightened pitch, creating an unintended change in the tonal accent and hence changing "dew," the Vietnamese meaning of *suong,* into "carnal pleasure," the meaning of *suo'ng*—the same word with a forward accent mark next to the *o*. Of course the genius Harvard professor had no idea he had just called me Ms. Carnal Pleasure in Vietnamese, in front of the whole class. Or, more often, professors paused with an obvious frown, showing their reluctant effort to figure out a way to say what they saw; meanwhile the whole class waited. I, too, waited nervously only to affirm my presence and to inform them, in my usual timid way, that they could just call me Mi, as in Mimi.

So, one day, I found myself writing down a different name. Mi-Chau became Mimi for daily use, and Giang-Suong was transposed into Suong Giang to parallel the closest pronunciation in English, Sean Young, just as the immigration officer had suggested. And then there came a time when enough coworkers and clients showed enough confusion and frustration in trying to remember the correct spelling or pronunciation of the hardworking lawyer's Vietnamese legal name, such that she should be just Ms. "My Young." So I ended up calling myself Mimi Sean Young all the time to avoid "My Young" all together. The next step was predictable: on office documents and correspondence, I began to appear as Mimi Sean Young. Finally, the inevitable had to occur: a court petition for another name change came so easily and painlessly as a natural event, a matter of fact. And, before I knew it,

I became Mimi Sean Young, legally and otherwise, and the issue of name was forever settled. The past was gone.

But my story of our naturalization day was never just about the ultimate Americanization of a name. Then, as we left the federal building in downtown Houston, all I felt was a vague sense of sadness, the kind that disturbingly lingered because I could not articulate its cause. The sadness grew as I looked back at the building where our papers would be processed. What I saw behind me was impersonal. All I could see was the gray facade of a concrete building. Just a building.

—

Just like me in the past, as of today, my brother—the boy I called Pi—has finally initiated a second name change for himself.

"OK, Pi, or Peter, as you now prefer, but to me, little Pi will always be Phi Long. Phi Long you are!" In this yuppie restaurant lounge in Houston, Texas, I call my brother by the first name he was given at birth, the masculine name meaning a galloping horse that turns into a flying dragon because of his unbeatable, magical speed.

"OK, I got it, sis." He blinks. "My sister, the writer, the romantic. You don't want me to forget my roots. OK, OK, OK, as you wish, I am Phi Long."

I am too romantic to hold a Harvard law degree, he says. Too romantic for the dreadful routines of corporate law, too romantic to play the stakes of Wall Street and get rich. Silently, I acknowledge the truth out of what he has said. In those places he mentioned, I have disguised my romantic self for a while, just enough so I would not be discarded and stepped on by the unromantic. In my mind, I add to his statement the fact that I am too romantic to get married and love an ordinary man. I want someone who calls me his first lady; on the day I die, I will still be waiting for him. It occurs to me that these statements—his spoken, mine silent—contain all the failures and dissatisfactions of my life. I have huddled within my romanticism as though it were the only abode left after an earthquake. And because I am romantic, I prefer calling him Phi Long now and then. My brother endures.

Someone is calling my name. "Mimi, over here!" I see Simone approaching in the New Yorker's signature little black dress that accentuates her slenderness. I have not seen her since last Christmas, and in the light of the early evening, despite the high-fashion-model look, her face appears drawn and her eyes perhaps slightly red. Her sleek, straight black hair has been layered and highlighted into a light-brown, wavy, Goldie Hawn shag. The furrows on both sides of her mouth are the only obvious sign of her forty-something vintage, yet the fine baby hair on the side of her cheeks still makes her skin appear translucently smooth. The tiny blood veins under her porcelain skin gives it the reddish pink shade of a young Chinese apple. My sister is the sweet child-woman, ageless always.

Finally we are together, the three children of Ong Giao, the Vietnamese schoolteacher who refused to reverse his name. (The starched shirt has said good-bye to Pi and has taken off with a brunette.)

The restaurant is getting crowded and I order foie gras mousse as an appetizer, in commemoration, I say, of Simone's and Pi's French elementary school—that time, so long ago, when Pi still wore his navy blue shorts and carried a *bidon* of water on a shoulder strap. "*École, école, école, je déteste l'école*—I hate school," he used to say. But I have no time to indulge myself in the nostalgia of childhood since Pi makes a hand gesture and anxiously dives into a discussion of family affairs.

"We can all spare childhood remembrance for now," he says. In his toastmaster public-speaking style, he expertly summarizes his case for our mother's living arrangements. I can see him making a presentation at work for Hewlett-Packard. He deserves every promotion Hewlett-Packard has given him. He acts like an American male, and there's little Vietnamese-ness, if any, left in him—that sullen, shy, uncommunicative, and scrupulous look from those dark eyes that are lowered and glancing sideways, and the perpetual smile that beams up a flat face—the signature of the Vietnamese spirit. "Praise a Vietnamese, he smiles. Beat him up, he smiles. Shoot him finally, he dies smiling," a Vietnamese author has written.

But Pi is not smiling scrupulously like a Vietnamese. Instead, he is professionally eloquent like a serious presenter, a straight–shooter, à la American style. He crisply justifies why our mother's better off living with him as the grandma-nanny for his baby girl. Our mother can't adapt to my single life or Simone's Manhattan existence. The problem, however, is Pi's dark-haired Irish-American wife, who may find the arrival of a Vietnamese live-in mother-in-law a culture shock. One does not expect the members of a host country to understand our Vietnamese way. Thus, our mother's living conditions in Pi's household can only be a tryout, to be revisited in the future.

And then Pi mentions the *Hy Vong Viet.* The *Viet Hope.*

Simone brushes her hair backward and pulls a scarf out of her tote bag. She wraps it around her head to cover up the dark brown shag. This I recognize as a characteristic nervous gesture of hers. Like our late Grandma Que, Simone has adopted the habit of doing things to her hair to hide her emotions, sometimes with the use of a scarf, other times with a hair clip. Since her husband died, she has reestablished her ties with the family, traveling to Texas once a year to see our parents. I have learned my big sister's nervous habit by observing her at these yearly Christmas get-togethers.

The mention of the *Viet Hope* must have hit a raw nerve. In Vietnam, my father wrote newspaper articles under the pen name "Hope," and the teenager Simone was known at the Saigonese National Press Club as Hope's beautiful daughter. For more than two decades of his life in America, my father never mentioned his former pen name, until a few months ago when he founded the magazine. He called it the *Hy Vong Viet,* roughly translated as *Viet Hope.*

"Dad has been asking me for five hundred dollars a month to support the *Viet Hope,*" Pi says, then takes a gulp of his iced water. "Five hundred dollars a month, you hear me? It's totally ridiculous. And guess what." Pi chews on his ice, and soon the glass is almost empty. "Dad does not want to ask the girls because he thinks the *Viet Hope* should be the responsibility of the boy in the family. *C'est moi,*" he says in French, pointing to the middle button of his denim shirt. "That's me."

The waiter is serving our foie gras mousse and a French baguette. I look past Pi's anxious face and see the profile of my father's face at sixty-five, his facial muscles sagging under the age spots that fill his cheeks. He has lost the elegant bone structure now distinctive in Pi's handsome Asian face. Only when the elegance was gone and the retirement papers properly signed did my father establish the *Viet Hope,* what Pi calls "Dad's one-man publishing house, one-man magazine dedicated to the 'revitalization of Vietnamese literature' and 'advocacy of liberal democracy in the Socialist Republic of Vietnam.'" Pi speaks comically of the *Viet Hope,* stressing phrases like "liberal democracy" as though they're punch lines. My brother is oblivious to the sadness that overtakes me. I have to turn away to hide the expression on my face. Pi's satire reminds me of that snowy day in Diamondale, back in 1976, when I skipped classes to mourn the unsolved death of a young man who had shared the same dream that drives my father's *Viet Hope*. My Crazy Man.

According to Pi, or Peter (per my brother's recent name change), my father has distributed two issues of the *Viet Hope* to Vietnamese grocery stores, unwelcomed by shoppers who prefer reading the community gossip. The magazine has consumed a good chunk of my father's modest retirement income from the school district, where he taught for years, taking care of underprivileged black, Hispanic, and Asian bilingual children from Houston's urban ghettos. The teaching job came after his shrimp boat went up in flames in the conflict between the Vietnamese Gulf Coast shrimpers and the hooded men of the Ku Klux Klan, which attracted national press in the eighties.

Finally, his retirement day arrived as a joyful escape from the routines of his life. My father could not wait to take off to California where his old buddies, the literati of the defunct South Vietnam, would jump in and help *Viet Hope* survive. These retired old men have all rid themselves of their jobs and are now dedicated full-time to the survival of the *Viet Hope*. Elsewhere, in La Griglia, for example, that spirit isn't to be found. My brother has no sympathy for it, and I have no energy to argue, explain, or plead my father's case.

It is ridiculous, Pi continues, that for decades we have become the supporters of unemployed relatives in Vietnam. We, the new Vietnamese Americans with one foot in the old Vietnamese culture, have been made into the unwilling rescuers of a failing Communist economy transitioning to the market model of the West. After years of sending home money to support poor relatives, gifts and contributions that cannot be deducted on our income tax returns, we are now being asked to support the revival of this *Viet Hope*, whatever that means to Dad. Pi's liberal wife, a former local administrator of the Houston chapter of the ACLU, has indicated she would not mind putting the money into a mutual fund for my father, instead of supporting this ethnic press of his. The magazine is a game or a tranquilizer for these old men, Pi says. Like playing bingo.

"I will take care of the five hundred dollars," Simone blurts out, and Pi's face turns red.

"It isn't so much the money," Pi insists, "it's the principle of thing, the ridiculous nature of the task." Soon they are both talking at the same time, and then I settle the matter by suggesting that we split the five hundred dollars three ways. Almost two hundred dollars per child to keep the old man happy. He may die tomorrow, I say, and there will not be a *Viet Hope* for us to argue about. When that sad day comes, the *Viet Hope*, whatever that is, will go with him to the grave.

At this point, Pi and Simone stop talking. The discussion is closed, and we each carry on our own thoughts. We choke on our foie gras mousse and French bread, and Simone complains that Houston restaurants do not have good French baguettes like Manhattan. So she decides to order a salad with the house specialty dressing: some sort of combination of garlic and mustard in cream.

When the salad arrives, we unconsciously split the dish three ways, the Vietnamese way.

———

"There is something else," Pi says, his angular face turning somber. "Hewlett-Packard may send me to Vietnam for three years to establish a new market. Top pay, of course, neat career move." Pi's tense, dark brows spell irritation and worry, contradicting his upbeat words.

"Then what's the problem?" I ask him. "You should be excited." I close my eyes and see Pi again as a child in his torn-open shirt and cotton shorts. "You will be seeing Saigon again. You'll go back to those places where we used to be. The house, the alleys in District Eight, the French school. Maybe you will return to Hue. Those *longan* trees and jack fruits. You'll eat them to your heart's desire. You'll suck the juice out of the peels and seeds," I say, lost in my dream of childhood.

"Except for that terrible *Viet Hope* of our beloved father," Pi says gravely. "It is an antigovernment publication, isn't it? It's like the Cubans' Bay of Pigs, isn't it? It may get me into trouble. Don't we all know the Communist government has the best under-cover system?" The deep vertical lines between his dark brows reflect both displeasure and paranoia. Pi's frown reminds me of my father's face years ago, the night we boarded the cargo plane at Tan Son Nhat airport. The brows came together the same way. Genetic.

"You read too many Tom Clancy novels," Simone sighs. "If it were me, I would be worried about something else."

"What?" Pi and I ask at once.

"The toilet. I would be worrying about the Vietnamese toilet. I wouldn't go unless Hewlett-Packard provides me with the best of housing, with an American commode that flushes properly."

All three of us stare down at what's left of the foie gras mousse. Childhood comes back to us all, not in the fragrant delight of tropical fruits, but in haunting memories of an impoverished country.

"I am sure corporate America can accommodate Pi's needs for a modern commode," I say, trying to join her joke in my usual anticorporate way. Pi is not smiling.

We should be laughing, and childhood memory can become funny. But somehow there's no joy among us. Without admitting it, we must all be thinking of the Tet Offensive. The Year of the Monkey. Nineteen sixty-eight. The three of us were old enough then to remember the experience. After all, we are the three children of Ong Giao, the schoolteacher. We are supposed to have inherited genetically the terrific memory, intellect, and sensitivity of the Vietnamese literati.

—

We were in the middle of New Year Celebration, and I was still on school break when the radio told us the Vietcong were moving into the heart of Saigon. They had staged an offensive line on the outskirts of the Capital City, and rockets would soon be flying over our head.

We were to report to the nearest army post, two blocks from our house, for a distribution of sandbags. My father made about fifty trips on his *motocyclette* to transport the sand. I watched my father, the schoolteacher, dig a square hole in the family room of our townhouse in District Eight, Saigon. We piled up sandbags, walling off the four corners of this hole. With a small shovel, Simone, Pi, and I helped him stuff and secure each bag. We were too little and weak to lift the bags, so my father moved them himself, one by one, upon his skinny back. He did not want my delicate mother to lift anything. We helped push the bags onto his back while he stood in the hole, and then he would bend low and lean sideways so the bag would fall to its proper place. His glasses kept falling off the bridge of his nose, and he would pick them up and dust the sand off them. Day after day we worked on building our harbor against the Vietcong's rockets.

At night we crammed into the square hole and listened nervously to the sound of rockets. First came the roar, then the *siu, siu, siu* as the rockets cut through the air, ending with a big noise, always sounding so far away. Sleeping together in the hole, we could not move without waking each other. "Like sardines in a can," Simone complained. To me, the discomfort of becoming sardines boxed between sandbags was more devastating than any threat from rockets.

During the day, we divided rice rations and helped our mother roast sesame seeds. She planned each meal such that we would have rice and sesame seeds every day. Before the New Year, she had filled up the rice container, which should last for a few months. My parents were tense, but apart from the nights in the hole, we three children enjoyed the break from school.

Our enjoyment did not last. The radio said the Vietcong had taken over Hue. Grandma Que was still there, where the fighting and rocketing were the most severe. Each night, I cried in my sleep, dreaming that Grandma Que had been shot—that she died alone in Hue, and I was not there to bury her.

But death had no real meaning to me until one night, when I heard a huge, ear-piercing noise, followed by cascading sounds of glass breakage. Pi woke up and started crying.

"Hush, hush, hush!" my father urgently silenced us. I was too shocked to cry. My mother began praying to our ancestors and all divinities. *"Lay troi lay Phat. Lay ong lay ba."*

I heard another noise. For a moment, I had thought my eardrums had shattered and I had gone deaf.

There was no more noise after that. Eventually, I fell asleep in the monotonous sound of my mother's prayer to Buddha: "*Nam mo a di da Phat...*" Her prayer became my peace.

In the morning, I crawled out of the square hole. Pi was still sleeping. My parents and Simone were gone. Where could they be?

I walked to the family room and found chaos. All the windows in our house had been broken; shattered glass was everywhere. I hopped over and tiptoed around the broken glass to the front yard.

All of the adults had gathered in front of our house looking onto the alley. I knew something terrible had happened.

The house in front of our house was gone. Debris had taken its place. People were pulling bodies out underneath bricks, burned wooden slabs, and sandbags. I caught glimpses of bloody arms and legs. Someone put bedsheets over them, and then the bodies were carried away.

The sandbags had not saved my neighbors.

I heard Simone weeping. My mother was still praying in small phrases. *"Nam mo a di da Phat."* The monotonous sound of her prayer blended with Simone's sobs. My mother placed a hand over my eyes as I strained my neck to look at the piles of debris that filled the alley. My mother told me to go inside and keep Pi from rushing out. Pi and I were to stay in the square hole with the sandbags.

I went inside and stared at the broken glass in the living room. I needed no more definition of death. It smelled like sandbags and blood, in the dampness of a square hole.

—

Life continued with our carefully planned rice rations and roasted sesame seeds. My mother handed us the last of the minced dried pork, and the three children shared their last meal with meat, knowing that the following day there would be nothing but plain rice and sesame. I longed for a piece of meat or fruit. There was no wet market, and we stayed locked in the house. My father glued his ears to the portable radio. The South Vietnamese army and its American allies had not lost control of the central radio station, and that was a good sign, my father declared.

The deaths of our neighbors proved that the sandbags were insufficient protection. So my father, the schoolteacher, devised another idea. Over the bathroom was a water tank holding the household's water supply. The bathroom was small and old, with no Western-style commode. Believing the water tank would buffer us against rockets, my father made us sleep in the tiny bathroom at night, when the rockets started roaring.

The bathroom floor was only large enough to hold two people, while there were five of us: parents and three children. So my father decided that each night, one parent and one child would sleep in the bathroom; the other parent and remaining two children would stay in the sandbagged hole. If the rocket hit and one half of the family was killed, at least one parent might stay alive to raise at least one surviving child.

"But," I argued with my father, "more than one rocket can hit our house in both places, and we can all die! It's better to die close together in one place than separately in two places!"

To this, my father remained silent.

"Do what your father says," my mother said in her tiny voice. "It's just a way to increase the chance for some of us to live. A chance to live is precious, and you must seize it, Mi Chau," she added quietly as though she herself were not convinced.

We, the children, hated the bathroom and preferred the square hole bordered with sandbags. Sleeping in the bathroom meant having our heads against the platform on which the old commode sat. It meant listening to water dropping onto the commode throughout the night. The old-style commode was built like a chair over a black hole. One pulled a string above one's head to flush. Water dripped down periodically in tiny drops, making dreadful noises all night. I dreamed of water dripping onto my hair, my face, one drop at a time, cold and ill-smelling, testing every nerve ending. Our feet were under the showerhead, and our toes almost touched the black hole where the water drained. My father had promised us he would renovate the old bathroom right after the Lunar New Year. No one had expected we would be sleeping in that dreary bathroom.

But we did, taking turns every night.

It was Pi's turn to sleep with our father in the bathroom one night when I was awakened by his screams. Between intelligible sounds, the three-year-old sobbed, babbling that he had awakened in the middle of the night to see a black snake crawling out of the black hole where the water drained. It was a tiny black hole the size of my ankle, providing barely enough room for the snake's pointed head to poke out, its pair of red eyes staring at Pi's toes. Terrified, Pi claimed that he had stood up and urinated right onto the snake's head. The stream of urine hit the snake's eyes, and the reptile withdrew into the black hole and disappeared.

Pi continued yelling his heart out throughout the night, and finally my father had to carry him into the sandbagged square. There, Pi kicked and wiggled and screamed his protests until he turned hoarse and his head dropped onto my mother's chest. Only when he collapsed and passed out from exhaustion did he stop screaming.

I had to join my father to take Pi's place in the bathroom. I sat up on the floor, quivering at the sound of my brother's shrieking.

My father had firmly made me stay. "Be a brave little girl," he said. "There is no snake. Repeat after me."

"There is no snake," I said timidly, my eyes fat with tears. "I don't want to sleep here, please."

"Do you want to die, like our neighbors?" my father asked.

"No."

"Good. Who's going to get that scholarship to Europe or America if you die under a rocket?" He told me again and again there was no snake. At worst, there might be an eel living in the sewage. Eels were harmless. People ate eels like fish.

I could not sleep all night. It was better to die under rockets, with bloody arms and legs buried under debris, and never to get that scholarship, than to face the terror of having that slimy black snake slither upon my toes and up my thighs onto my belly button. The disgust and fear made me nauseous.

I waited until my father fell asleep before I crawled out of the awful, humid bathroom and into the family room. I squeezed myself under the old upright piano my parents had purchased secondhand from a German priest. A sturdy piece of furniture, the piano should shield me against rockets. I smelled the pleasant smell of polished wood and slept peacefully even though the sound of rockets continued all night. In the early morning hours, I crawled back into the tiny bathroom. There I lay, next to my father, my legs curled up in my desperate effort to keep my sensitive toes away from the black hole where the black snake supposedly resided.

In the following days, I whispered my secret about my nightly escape to Pi, and we both did the trick each time it was our turn to sleep in the bathroom. Neither of us knew for sure whether our parents discovered we had slipped away at night to sleep under the piano. One day passed and a new day came. Rockets kept flying and we kept on living. At one point, I became convinced in my heart that I had become invincible, even though rockets had hit the neighborhoods of Saigon and had battered our neighbors after it had destroyed the forbidden Violet City in the heart of Hue. I firmly believed that I was destined to live so that one day I could return to Hue to rebuild everything. The notion became a conviction as compelling as what Grandma Que had instilled in me— that no matter where I went, I would always return safely to Hue.

I was right. Eventually, the South Vietnamese army and the American marines regained the ancient city of Hue. Shortly thereafter, the news came that Grandma Que was well and safe in her ancestral house. I thanked the Spirit of the River Huong for having protected Grandma Que, and I held on to my belief. The 1968 Tet Offensive made me believe that I would never die from the treachery of war.

—

Outside, the rays of the afternoon sun have wilted, and in the soft Latin jazz and dim light of La Griglia, the present has become surreal. Across the table from me, my brother's face resembles a marble bust. I can no longer see the few tiny wrinkles of age that distinguish the boy he was from the man he has become. His silence suggests he is perhaps still back with the slimy black snake of the 1968 Tet Offensive. Our eyes meet briefly in wordless acknowledgment that all three children of Ong Giao have carried Pi's little nightmare into America. The nightmare of childhood manifests itself in our daily lives in varied ways. We have all become sushi fans, yet we never touch eel—the disgust about a slimy black snake must have run so deep it takes away all appetite. Simone is perpetually irritated by the sound of water dripping onto a cold surface. For me, the nightmare resurfaced full-blown when I went apartment hunting for the first time in America. I did not like any bathroom where the tub sat right next to the commode. I could not enjoy a bath if the commode was within sight. Every time I submerged myself underwater and caught sight of the commode, I would snap up in panic, brought back to those hours, days, and months in Saigon when I was forced to lie in the tiny bathroom underneath a water tank, fearing rockets night by night and sharing Pi's terror about a slimy black snake.

We try to laugh lightheartedly, agreeing that if Pi goes to Vietnam, he should pack a portable toilet with him, together with an affidavit: *Dear Comrade, I know nothing about the* Viet Hope. *That magazine is the sole product and responsibility of my father. He is too old to lead a coup, a revolution, or to overthrow the current government. After all, the* Viet Hope *for democracy in Vietnam is just that…merely a hope.*

Our meal is almost over when finally Simone cuts to the gist of our meeting. She speaks in her soft, musical, and sometimes breathy voice, her best feminine feature that causes her friends to compare her to the soft-spoken American icon, Jacqueline Kennedy. I, on the other hand, have never been a fan of Simone's small, husky voice. The power of her lyrical soprano singing voice is more to my liking. I have always preferred female warriors and soaring birds to little whispering women or helpless butterflies.

Hurriedly Simone gives her report on the task assigned to her. She rushes through with such deliberate haste it is hard to follow her speech—an unusual departure from her demure, calming, and controlled demeanor. She's bought the land and chosen the spots at the recommendation of the Buddhist temple in southwest Houston. She's also consulted the Association of Vietnamese Senior Citizens, where old Vietnamese men and women gather and begin their monthly meetings with the salute to the defunct South Vietnamese flag. The rest of the world might have forgotten the flag, but not these old men and women. In the old, beat-up community center in midtown Houston, hidden modestly among rundown buildings and unkempt Vietnamese shops, every week the Vietnamese senior citizens stand up to sing the patriotic words of the defunct South Vietnamese national anthem, with the same ardor they exhibited in their long-gone youth. *"Nay cong dan oi, dung len dap loi song nui."* They are calling out to their fellow countrymen: *Let's answer the call of the* Viet Hope *echoing across rivers and mountains.* The phrase speaks of the beauty of my father's name, Giang-Son, rivers and mountains. Perhaps this is the embryo of the name of my father's magazine, in memory of his own youth. Youth may be gone, but not those words about *giang son gam voc*, those rivers and mountains of the homeland, beautiful like satin and silk—the metaphor that I had meant to become our last name.

The land Simone describes is a cemetery lot purchased predominantly by Vietnamese families, situated somewhere near the heart of Texas rather than among the rivers and mountains of Vietnam. My mother has urged us to prepare for her death. She's made it clear she doesn't want to be lonely in her "journey to the other side of the world," *ben kia the gioi.* This means she wants to be surrounded by Vietnamese-speaking neighbors—friendly Vietnamese ghosts to whom she can talk in Vietnamese about the old country and traditions, rather than baseball games or mutual funds. She also wants to be next to my father so she can continue cooking and caring for him.

Simone rushes through the financial calculations. We get a discount on the land, bringing our share per parent to a rounded figure—a total of twice that much for both Mom and Dad, then divided by three for each child. In addition, Simone says quickly, we should each contribute to a fund for their nursing home in the future.

An enormous lump rises into my throat, the garlic and mustard dressing going to my head. "I won't let my parents spend their old age lonely and isolated, in a nursing home," I say.

My siblings remain silent. For a long time. It is Simone who breaks the silence. "You're too Vietnamese," she says.

"She's just too romantic," Pi says, repeating his theory. "You can be die-hard cultural now, protecting the old way, but just imagine the day when they're too old to take care of themselves, their hygiene, their myriad old-age illnesses, and we're all tied up at our jobs, and with our spouses and children."

I have to interrupt him, unable to hide the anger in my voice. "Not too long ago, old folks in Vietnam lived and died among their grandchildren." I paint the romantic picture. "They died close to their kitchens, with their kitchen gods, in their altar houses, behind bamboo curtains, anywhere but a nursing home around nurses who don't speak the language. The old folks in Vietnam, too, had their hygiene, and myriad illnesses. What happened then? There wasn't any nursing home there and then."

"Go on, make your poem," my brother says, raising his voice, now traced with irony. "I don't know what happened then. There, life wasn't the same. We're in America now. Can you quit your job to stay home and take care of our senile parents, perhaps bedridden and out of touch with reality? Will you change their diapers and feed them spoons of rice congee? You're no nurse, and you have a job to go to…"

"But, Pi, I have already given up my job," I blurt out.

—

There's silence at the table. Finally Pi speaks.

"What? You must be kidding!" The alarm in Pi's voice is undeniable.

I shake my head, denying the reality of the uncertain future I have created for myself. I have quit my job as a lawyer to write full-time. I must look pained, since Pi has stopped talking, pulling his full lips into a nervous smile, his fingers tapping slightly on the table. He is stabbing the lettuce with the fork in his other hand. I know my brother too well to misinterpret his nervous gestures, because I knew the boy before he turned into the man. Pi thinks I have given up the argument. He is feeling guilty for cornering me. In a world that moves forward, guilt is the only link that forever ties us to the past.

And so in fashionable La Griglia, we discuss the deaths of our parents before they occur, and commit ourselves to the choice of the cemetery lot. Pi has no time for dessert, since he will be rushing across town to his suburban house where his beautiful children speak only English, and his beautiful Irish American wife is adjusting to the arrival of her Vietnamese mother-in-law. The new nanny, but only on a trial basis.

—

Simone and I see Pi off in the parking lot.

He is in his car, ready to drive away. He yells out at us, his two older sisters, "Mom wants to remind both of you that she's made a month's supply of frozen crabmeat egg rolls for each one of you."

The exhaustion of the evening has caught up with me, and I want desperately to go home to my mother's egg roll supply. My mind travels to that cemetery in southwest Houston, where some day she will lie among friendly Vietnamese-speaking ghosts. In that other world of theirs, perhaps the old men and women of Vietnam who lived and died in Houston will still be chatting about their unmarried children left on earth, those Vietnamese Americans who have no homemade egg rolls to eat because their mothers are gone.

There is no wind on a Texas night in March, yet I am chilled.

"Take care, sis," Pi turns back and yells to us again, before he drives away. A vague sense of sadness comes over me again as I realize that, these days, my brother is driving a fashionable sports utility vehicle, the luxury model. Apparently, the Vietnamese boy of my yesteryears has fully achieved the American dream.

I am left alone with my big sister.

"Let's go back inside and talk," she says.

I follow her back to our table. When she passes by me to sit down in the corner seat, I can smell her perfume. I may have imagined it, but I recognize the spicy fragrance of cinnamon. Back in Vietnam in the sixties, our maternal grandmother, Grandma Que, kept a cinnamon log in her ancestral house in the City of Hue. Cinnamon fragrance permeated Grandma Que's somber altar room. On the altar sat a solemn carved jade phoenix and two ivory plaques, vestiges of our ancestors. The jade phoenix symbolized our great-grandmother, a royal concubine of the last Vietnamese dynasty; the two ivory plaques, the *The-Bai*, were ID cards held by our great-grandfathers, commemorating their careers as mandarins and officers of the last Vietnamese imperial court. Grandma Que polished these artifacts every day. They smelled like cinnamon.

Simone leans over to blow out the candle in the middle of our table. Her face becomes dark like cinnamon, yet her eyes sparkle. "I respect you for quitting your job," Simone says, lowering her soft voice almost to a whisper. "It takes courage to change a course of life. But tell me why."

"Something happened to you during the fall of Saigon, during those critical hours," I say, evading her question. "That trauma has never left you, has it?" I am, of course, recalling my own trauma.

"It's my loveless marriage and the resulting bitterness that never goes away," she whispers. "I associated my late husband with the fall of Saigon in April nineteen seventy-five, and the injustice of it…"

"Something happened to me, too, in April nineteen seventy-five." I rush my words in one breath without looking at her. "Something terrible, and it's not just bitterness." I paused to take a deep breath. "I never told any of you. I wanted to tell someone once, in Diamondale, after you had left us for New York. I called him the Crazy Man. But he died. Untimely death. I mourned for a long time. I kept the secret for all these years until I met Brad. I told Brad, but he's gone now, and I quit my job. I want to reconstruct a diary of what happened."

I avoid her eyes. A long silence ensues. "Then tell me," she says at last, her beautiful eyes grabbing mine. "Tell me about the Crazy Man. Tell me about Brad. And tell me about this need to reconstruct a diary."

As I meet Simone's eyes, I might see a tear. I find in the darkness of her eyes underneath her moving lashes the shared knowledge of a time long gone called childhood and that passage from Vietnam to America.

We are sitting in such a dark space, yet I put on my sunglasses. And I begin to talk.

"It all began with the mirror, Simone," I say. "My mirror."

FOUR
THE MIRROR AND BRAD

Houston, Texas, 1999

I had the mirror on the third floor of my Victorian townhouse, against the wall opposite my makeup table. The entire third floor was given over to the master bedroom with its own bath, a bar, and a set of French windows opening to a balcony.

It was a massive, three-way mirror shaped like an armoire, the type of grandiose and archaic mirror used in dressing rooms of old-fashioned luxury department stores. It almost took up the entire wall. The mirror made the third floor into my private world. The more intense my law work became, the more time I spent on the third floor, at night, before the mirror. In fact, I bought the mirror on the same day I discovered a huge problem at Entran Corporation, my most important client. Entran, trading on the New York Stock Exchange, paid millions of attorneys' fees to my firm annually.

I found the mirror one Saturday morning at a boutique that was going out of business. That morning, the cumulative effect of things going wrong had become a turbulent sea swallowing into its waves the last victims of a shipwreck. I was that drowning victim looking for a floating board to hold on to. The workweek had been inundated with emergencies with Entran, a multinational energy corporation that built pipelines and energy plants all over the globe. A country manager stationed in India had contacted me with a request to perform a miracle on a plain-language provision of a 170-page contract for a power-generation complex already constructed there. He wanted to know if I could make the provision disappear, and he was persistent. In a moment of irritation, I blurted out to him that a good lawyer was not meant to be a god nor a mythical persona who could perform witchcraft to change events that had already happened.

Meanwhile, I had also found out that one of his senior project engineers had disbursed signature bonus money to a government official in the province where the power plant sat, in order to smooth out a disagreement with the Indian provincial government. "What's the big deal?" the country manager asked me over the phone. Giving money to a government official to improve government relations in foreign countries was the same as giving money to the Treasury, or the people, to benefit the poor province, he tried to reason with me. "There is a big legal difference under U.S. law," I said, cutting him off rather harshly. "Giving money to an official in a business deal is different from giving economic aid to the country. Here in America the law calls your gift to the Indian official a bribe." Upset, he told me he would have his boss talk to me, because easing their way through layers of governmental decision makers in India had been their course of practice, like "grease payment," as the slang went, and I was supposed to make it all legal.

Within the hour, I heard from Tracy Carr, the flamboyant female executive at Entran and president of its international division. The petite blonde, in her forties, had earned a reputation in the business community for being a tough cookie, having worked financial wonders and obtained all kinds of assets for the company in the developing economies of faraway places such as the remote provinces of China and India, where she allegedly traveled with a wardrobe and insisted on staying only at five-star hotels. The controversial and difficult India project had made headlines in the *Wall Street Journal*, and Tracy was credited for its success, having made news-making appearances in India in colorful saris that complemented her blonde hair, blue eyes, slender frame, and pale skin. Without Tracy, there would never have been the Entran power-generation complex in West India, the whole world had known. Tracy was also part of the Harvard alumni network, as was I. She was from the business school, and I was from the law school. Strangely, at times, the maître d' at the Petroleum Club in downtown Houston even got the two of us mixed up when we both showed up for the local Harvard Club's events, where typically Tracy proudly attracted all the attention, while I sat at a corner table hoping to avoid the hand-shaking routine. Despite her blondeness and my Asian ethnicity—and the obvious differences in our appearance, manners, style, and speech—the local Harvard Club and Petroleum Club people would still easily forget which woman was from the business school and which from the law school. With the Harvard label on us, we were either envied or hated, awed or ignored, yet in any event my Asian-ness would be overlooked for the Harvard label to take over, to make me into Tracy Carr, and it mattered not that we were so different, that she was all West and I was all East.

"What's the problem, Mimi?" she chuckled on the phone.

"No problem, Tracy," I said, knowing I sounded tired already. "No problem, but perhaps your guys over there in India have taken too much liberty, and they have walked a gray line with respect to the antibribery law of the United States; and perhaps you, Tracy, ought to do something about it." I stressed the last part of my sentence and she laughed.

"Don't you know by now, Mimi, that women like us have to walk gray lines all the time? Come on, Mimi, you'll work your magic wand. You're the lawyer." And then she hung up.

"I am the lawyer," I mumbled to myself. "I have a magic wand. Tracy Carr has walked her gray line, and I am expected to walk mine."

Out of nervousness, I stared at my own hands and my long, red fingernails. And then all of a sudden I panicked. There was no difference at all between Tracy Carr and me. We both had the same long red fingernails, meticulously manicured at the same beauty salon in the Village near Rice University. These red-nailed fingers were part of the magic wand we were supposed to wield in this world, a world that had sucked me into its vacuum—past the point of no return.

Then, to top it all, as I sat at my desk that day listening to the racing of my heart, I picked up the twenty-page legal memorandum prepared by a third-year associate at our firm, Kurt Fiesta, addressing another legal problem at a national bank, another big client. The memo was full of case law that contradicted the position the bank client had wanted to take, and I trashed it in a moment of despair. When the young man lurked in front of my door with anxiety on his face, hoping to receive my comments on his work, I was stricken with guilt, thinking of those younger days when I, too, had slaved in the library only for my work to end up in some big-shot partner's trash can.

And after all that madness, the air-conditioning in the car broke down. Friday night, I couldn't sleep. My limbs went numb as I lay in bed with no light on, my eyes focusing on a dot in the ceiling, and in that dot the years of my life appeared in the black print of international construction contracts. When the morning came I had this incredible urge to leave the house, but then

I realized I had had no time to take my car to the shop, and the idea of the heat boiling up from the leather seat made me nauseous. So I called Hertz to have a big Oldsmobile delivered and then drove on Memorial Drive all the way to the west part of town, with the air-conditioning in the rental car set at full force, the cooling breeze turning into a chill traveling up my naked arms to the base of my neck, making the sensation of being drowned more real.

I drove and drove until I realized if I kept going I would be in San Antonio, so I took a turn. Just any turn. I found myself in a shopping strip tucked underneath the beltway, and the next thing I saw was a big going-out-of-business sale sign. It was a women's clothing boutique named Vee, with the "V" in Christmas-green paint like an inverted evergreen tree. I parked in front of the set of glass doors, my eyes blurry from lack of sleep, the air-conditioning still going at full force. I had nowhere to go, so I wandered into the shop.

For a moment I thought I had gone insane.

I had been confronted by the image of a familiar woman in a tank top, her hair up in a little bun, her naked arms folded in front of her chest as though she had been in some very cold place and was trying to protect herself. I could see the black circles under her eyes, on a face so worn. I blinked. She didn't go away. I had turned and was about to run when I saw it. Everything made sense. I was not insane. There it was, the large mirror. It stood there greeting me, containing me, and I approached it. I saw the whole of me, front, back, side. I saw the smallness of the woman. The mirror became me. I had to take it home. To give the purchase an air of normalcy before the probing eye of the sales clerk, I threw in six T-shirts of the same size and style. I just pulled them off the rack, attempting to vary the color: white, gray, and black. I paid the shop owner an additional sixty dollars to have the mirror delivered the same day.

Life moved on from there. The car. The house. The health club. My busy and intense law firm with its own awful momentum. I was a salaried partner who earned a fixed income, as distinguished from equity partners who shared profit. It meant I had the title to impress clients and the legal community, but not the financial benefits of an owner, although I was entitled to attend all partnership and section meetings. At one of the power breakfasts, the senior partner told me the management committee had met, and they had turned down my request to go on a part-time schedule. The privilege was reserved for married lawyers with children. Me? Single and childless. Shouldn't even have applied. Life rolled on, but somehow everything was a little more tolerable, because I didn't care anymore about partnership protocols.

At least, I had the mirror.

Women like me, Harvard-trained lawyers and partners in big law firms, can afford personal therapists, but if we have any ambitions at all for judgeships or public office, we shouldn't indulge. Such women should be seen as having their heads impeccably well situated between their capable shoulders. For the rest of us, though, weekly therapy can be soul-rinsing, or at least ornamental and status confirming, like power breakfasts near the federal courthouse, gym work with a personal trainer at a private club, a Cartier watch for our wrists, or even a mink coat kept in our closets, though no longer worn in the era of animal activists' concerns.

But I was not like the rest of Harvard-trained female lawyers. The idea of sitting in a therapist's office, to me, was just as alien as running for public office in a country where any such position for the likes of me or the Crazy Man would be lifted as a symbol of multicultural diversity. In any event, if I had a therapist, he or she would be reduced to merely charging the hours I spent talking about Grandma Que and her *longan* tree, or about any other sacred objects on an incense-filled family altar that the therapist had never seen and perhaps could not even visualize. The therapist's hourly billing would be just like me keeping my timesheets for my law firm: a high number of billable hours paid by my corporate clients would represent my productivity, lawyering ability, and economic worth. My ticket to any public office in America would have to start there, with my billable hours for the big law firm.

Naturally, in her cultural and moral codes, Grandma Que would not have approved of any public office that depended upon productivity represented by a number associated with money. Nor would she be happy with the concept of therapy. In her world, psychic pain was locked in the heart and soul, within cerebral armoires of memory, and not to be spoken in words, especially to strangers or doctors. Occasionally emotional pain was even a badge of honor, not a disease to be cured by talking it away or taking a nerve pill. Women of queenly substance, in particular, should be guardians of secrets and sadness that test the strength of our soul in those matters of honor. The idea of pouring those secrets out to a therapist would be an act of betrayal. Even shame.

So, no therapy. No public office. I could become Mimi, but Freudian theories and America's "Democrat or Republican" campaign contributions had no appeal to me.

I turned to the newly purchased mirror instead.

In these days the mirror had become more than just a habit. In a perverse way, it was my best friend. In the mirror I could see myself. I could even see visions of all those dreams that I had gradually let go in the comfort of my life in America. I could see the old Mi Chau before Mimi took over.

I could even see past what I had become.

Before the mirror, I began to keep a sketchbook. In it, I sketched images of my past and even visions of a future that never materialized. These images would probably have made little sense to anyone but myself. At times, the sketching was so exhausting I had to leave the mirror. I had to maintain *some* sort of connection to the outside world. But I kept coming back, and the urge to sketch became a desire to put on paper something outside the law firm and myself, something about America. Not the side of America that had become my life, but a new America that I had not come to know—something vibrant, invigorating, and fresh that could be my mental reward.

So I developed a new habit. After spending Friday night with the mirror, on Saturday morning I would go to Hermann Park, sit with my sketchbook, and try to sketch what I saw around me— any sign of this newly discovered America that I hoped to see. Houston is often hot and humid, but in the early morning hours, there was enough of a cooling morning breeze to keep me going. I became fond of the park, and the sketching became a form of relaxation.

The sketchbook was how I met Brad.

—

I was daydreaming on a bench in Hermann Park when a tall blond man jogged up the path toward me. Instead of flowing past me like all of the other park runners, he stopped, smiled down at me, and said, "Hi." I jumped, startled as though an actor in a film I was watching out of the corner of my eye had suddenly stepped from the screen and spoken to me. My sketchbook tumbled from my lap, and the athletic jogger stooped to pick it up. I blurted out,

"That's mine," and the jogger said, "Yes, ma'am, I was going to give it back to you," in a Southern accent. Even after all my years in Houston, I found his Southern speech polite and soothing. All that business of calling a woman "ma'am."

But he did not just pick up my sketchbook. He stared at the cover for a second or two. I had written "Mimi" across it. "Is your name Mimi?" the jogger asked, and I nodded.

Strangely, he remained kneeling for a while. I did not know exactly how long, but enough time passed for me to realize that he was at my feet, away from the bench but sufficiently close to form an image of a tall man kneeling down respectfully before a petite woman. The stranger was looking up at me, holding my sketchbook with both hands as though it were a treasure accidentally found and he was afraid to break or damage it. His young face, with its cleft chin, registered an ardent and sincere curiosity. I saw the same inquisitiveness in the blue of his eyes, under a set of chestnut brown eyebrows. His sweaty face was very pink under the sun, making his soft eyes more distinctively blue. When I thanked him, the jogger said, "You're welcome, ma'am," in that same Southern accent of his. Still, he held on to my sketchbook, as though he really did not want to part with the object.

I had to lean down to take the sketchbook from him. He remained kneeling.

"Well, ma'am, I hadn't expected Mimi to be your name," he said, almost disappointedly, his chestnut brown brows drawn together into a faint frown. "Excuse me for being perhaps out of line, but I had expected, well, some sort of a long, winding, royal Asian name that I can't pronounce," he said.

He was just trying to make conversation, obviously, but why would he say "royal"? The word always reminded me of Grandma Que. Every woman who was Asian must have been "royal" to this jogger. After all, I was wearing tights, an old, loose T-shirt, and sandals, like any casually clad woman found in this city, or this park on a Saturday morning. There was nothing royal about a woman in tights and a T-shirt. All of a sudden, I became self-conscious.

"Oh well, you are American, after all," he said with a smile. "I can tell from the way you talk."

He finally got up and started jogging on. Perhaps he might have turned back to look at me once more, and then I was left alone. I had in my mind a vague image of a kneeling man, the short blond hair, a shade of baby blue for a pair of eyes, the profuse sweat, the respectful manners, and his Southern accent. So I opened the sketchbook and sketched what I thought was the combination of pale blue eyes and blond hair and drops of sweat all over a square face. Underneath my sketch—a mixture of chaotic lines and shapes—I wrote THE JOGGER OF HERMANN PARK and signed my name, Mimi.

About half an hour must have passed before I heard the Southern accent again. The man had returned, and he was standing before me, over six feet of him, his arms hanging awkwardly at the sides of his lean torso. He looked like a very big, elegant, but quite muscular doll, a marathon runner who had burned away all fat. His T-shirt was wet through with sweat.

I forgot how it went after that. My mind skipped the gap of memory and went straight to the point when he was sitting on the bench with me. I could smell his sweat, that unclean yet tolerable smell of a man who had just finished his exercise, something like red meat cooked in mixed spices and butter and strong alcohol and vinegar and Vaseline and old clothes and toothpaste and aftershave. So I kept a distance from him on the bench, yet I gave him my sketchbook and showed him the sketch I made of him.

"*ME*? *ME*?" he asked. I wasn't sure he was referring to himself, THE JOGGER OF HERMAN PARK, or to ME, MIMI, as my name appeared at the bottom right corner of the sketch. His eyebrows rose, and I told him to turn the pages, moving back in time.

"What's this supposed to be?" he asked, pointing to a different group of chaotic lines.

"A house and a tree," I answered. I was thinking of Grandma Que and her *longan* tree in the backyard of her old house in the ancient city of Hue, a long, long time ago. The jogger did not seem convinced. He turned the sketchbook sideways to look at the sketch one more time.

"Go to the next page," I said.

"Oh, now I can see that's a little girl," he exclaimed. "You, Mimi. So this is all about you and your childhood, isn't it?" This time he sounded convinced and completely self-confident.

What a good guess! I thought. What *else* could it be?

"Some place very far from here?" he probed. "Definitely not Atlanta, where I'm originally from."

So, he was from Atlanta. That explained the Southern accent.

I told him the place was Vietnam. "Oh," he said, and then remained quiet, perhaps as a gesture of remorse, or out of fear he might have invoked bad memories of the terrible war that had signified America's blunder and defeat.

We sat in silence until perhaps the morning breeze was felt no more. The heat of the sun was gradually taking over. I could still smell the sweat from the man. It was less unpleasant than before—just a reminder that the stranger had closed the gap on the bench and was now quite near. Perhaps too near, as though a slight tilting of my head could easily allow me to touch the hardness of his upper arms with my hair. All of a sudden, I felt a strange urge to put my head on the stranger's shoulders, and blushed at the impropriety.

"Why were you surprised that my name was Mimi?" I broke the silence.

He responded with a question. "Your Vietnamese name can't be Mimi, can it?" When I did not answer, he seemed a little embarrassed. "To me," he said, "Mimi is like…what's her name, Mimi Rogers, the actress."

I had heard of the brunette movie star, the older woman, ex-wife of the young Tom Cruise before he became America's block-buster leading man. At least she had dark hair and was more like me than…Marilyn Monroe. I shared this thought with him, and his eyes brightened.

"No, definitely not Marilyn Monroe…I mean not in physical appearance, but what about her spirit?" he asked.

"The broken spirit of a victimized woman who had the mis-fortune of having an outward sensuality that captivated too many, but it overshadowed her tender soul. Her tragedy." I became truly sad with my own rhetoric. The words I spoke were more like the monologue I would deliver to the mirror at home.

"Tragedy?" He repeated the word I'd chosen. "You identify with the tragedy of Marilyn Monroe?" The blue eyes registered a note of concern.

When I turned away, he apologized again. "I am so sorry if I asked the wrong question. You see, I'm a trial lawyer. I'm in the habit of asking questions."

Gracious, another lawyer! My heart sank at the thought I had let a lawyer get too close and see my sketchbook. Like any good lawyer, I had come to mistrust my own kind.

"I was an orphan raised by my aunt in Georgia," he went on. "She had dark eyes and dark hair…" he said slowly, his eyes lingering on my hair, "…like yours." He paused. "We were not exactly privileged, although she tried to hang on. So when I left Georgia for Texas, I went for life and livelihood. No dreaming. I became a lawyer."

Don't I know well the lesson of life and livelihood? The issue of survival? I carried on my internal monologue, still. Apparently he wanted to say that we must have shared a bit of sadness and struggle in our formative years, even if we were born oceans apart, perhaps even a decade apart.

His Atlanta. My thoughts went to the image of Vivian Leigh and her desire to hold on to her Tara. The past glory and mystique of America's South. There, people did not always talk, and everything, including illusions, was expressed with restrained and subdued gestures, perfect manners, and beautiful things. But there was poverty, war, hypocrisy, and destruction there, too, in the heart of America. After all, what did I really know about Georgia, except from novels, movies, and a few history books?

My thoughts went from Atlanta to Hue. My Grandma Que was also a dark-eyed, dark-haired woman like this man's aunt. So dainty and light that my Grandma Que walked around her old house in Hue without making any sound. She moved like a ghost among furniture and artifacts that spoke of a bygone past. Somewhere in Georgia, an impoverished Vivian Leigh had raised this baby boy with beautiful blue eyes. Somewhere in Southeast Asia, my Grandma Que had spoken to a baby girl about a monarchy that existed no more—the nine lords and thirteen kings who made up the Nguyen Dynasty before French colonization.

I kept these thoughts and comparisons to myself.

When he got no real reaction from me, the jogger silently turned the pages of my sketchbook. He had seen so many of my sketches. There was no sense in stopping him now. He frowned and frowned again as the chaos of my lines became more and more intense, complex, intricate, sharp, and bold. Like a bunch of entangled threads, ropes, all wrapping around repeated stabs at the page.

"What beautiful...violence!" he finally exclaimed, unable to hide the touch of sadness in his voice. I had to remind myself that this stranger knew nothing about me, or my mirror, and I had not even told him the Vietnamese name I was given at birth. Mi Chau meant a beautiful drop of pearl.

It was the same name as that of a Vietnamese princess who died because of love, in a folktale thousands of years old. Her husband betrayed her by stealing her country's defense secrets. He had taken orders from his father, a northerner, whose ambition was to take over the kingdom south of China. With the stolen defense secrets, the ambitious northerner finally succeeded. On the day when the capital city was taken, the defeated Vietnamese king had to run away on a horse, carrying his daughter behind him. When they got to the coastline, that was the end of their escape route. The turtle god appeared to inform the king that his real enemy was his own daughter. So the king killed the princess with his sword before he died. Her blood flowed down to the sea and was swallowed by oysters. Those blood drops turned into the most beautiful of pearls, found by villagers along the coast of ancient Vietnam. The legend went on to say that when the betraying husband found the princess's body, he held his wife in his arms and jumped into a deep well to kill himself. He had fulfilled his father's wish for the conquest of ancient Vietnam, but in discharging his duty to his ancestors, he had betrayed the woman who loved him and had brought about her death.

That was the meaning of my Vietnamese name Mi Chau. The most beautiful of pearls formed in the tragedy of love, patriotic duty, and ambition. This stranger knew nothing about this. To him, I was just Mimi, and this normalcy should be my safety net. Yet, it remained true that in the early morning hours of that Saturday in Hermann Park, I had let this stranger take possession of the images of my life that I had painfully recreated before the mirror. He had even wanted to discuss the matter of my Vietnamese name and posed the question of whether I, a petite Southeast Asian woman, could possibly identify with the tragedy of Marilyn Monroe, a five-foot-five blonde sex kitten and object of desire for millions of American men.

I sighed. They both died young, Monroe and the ancient Vietnamese princess Mi Chau.

By the time the heat of Texas had taken away all the coolness of the early morning breeze, we had exchanged telephone numbers. By then, he knew that I was Mimi "Sean Young," not the beautiful actress Sean Young of the Washington political thriller *No Way Out*, but the first and only Vietnamese female partner in the biggest law firm of the Oil Capital.

There was something in his Southern-accented voice and ardent manners that I instinctively trusted.

—

Later, not long after we became lovers, Brad told me the reason he'd come back to the bench where I was sitting. In his version of what happened that day in Hermann Park, he had seen me sitting alone in the park. The sight of a petite woman alone on the bench had moved him. So, he had changed his running route to pass by me and say hi. In his version of what happened, I had gone after my sketchbook and was almost squatting in front of him, at his feet, bending over and then looking up. He said I was crying. He saw tears in my eyes. He even asked, "Are you all right, ma'am? Why are you crying?"

My memory harbored no such moment.

He saw something else, he claimed. I had no recollection of that, either.

We were in a restaurant when he told me this. That evening I was all dressed up in a black sleeveless pullover dress, the hem of which fell almost to my ankles. By then we must have been sleeping together every night for about two weeks, and I was just getting used to waking up in the morning with Brad in my mirror, and the sex was intense and good. He had also developed the habit of squeezing my waist in public when we walked together, and so that night I had deliberately worn a silver belt, and when we walked into the restaurant, his hand was resting on the belt. For two weeks, never once had the memory of Grandma Que come back to fill my mind. Instead, my mind was filled with Brad.

In the restaurant, after our food had been delivered and the waiter had said *bon appetit* before he disappeared, leaving us at the table with our bouillabaisse and white wine, Brad started to tell me what he'd seen in Hermann Park on the day we met. As he was speaking, he looked to both sides to make sure no one at the restaurant was looking at us, then leaned over to press one thumb against the knit fabric of my dress, where my nipple was hidden. This reminded me how quickly I had become comfortable with Brad, to the point I had forgotten to wear a bra when I slipped on a dress to go out for dinner with him.

Brad removed his thumb after only an instant and said, "Please forgive me, Mimi, I couldn't help it." He kept apologizing for his sexual act even when his blue eyes were slightly red from the lust they bore. Yet I liked him for the genuine effort he made at being serious and polite even under the most ridiculous of circumstances. Brad said he had been watching my nipples harden under my dress because of the cold air-conditioning, and every time he saw them like that, he thought of the day we met.

This was when he swore to me that in Hermann Park he had seen at his feet a sketchbook and a crying woman, raising her face to him. He saw my nipple that day, he claimed. According to him, I was wearing a very thin, very loose oversized T-shirt, and it fell off my shoulder when I stooped down, and one of my breasts was showing. It was the size of a small, pointed pear, he said, and the chocolate nipple looked invitingly too large and plump. The whole scene—a woman squatting at his feet, reaching out for a sketchbook, showing him her nipple—moved him tremendously, Brad said. It wasn't sexual at all, he kept stressing. It was something emotionally very deep, in his gut, in his inner self, he kept telling me, and I wished I could believe him. When he'd jogged on that day, he said, he couldn't forget what he'd just seen because it had invoked something so very deep, so he made a full circle and returned to the bench, hoping I would still be sitting there. I was.

I, again, had no recollection of such an image or act. All I remembered was the tenderness of a kneeling man, and then later the quietness of the park as we sat together on the bench, when I let him roam through sketches that he could not fully understand. He saw no words. Only lines and shapes. But he did see everything. And made his conclusions.

—

In Brad's version of the beginning of our relationship, after I became *the-woman-who-showed-Brad-her-chocolate-nipple-in-*

Hermann-Park, I was *the-woman-who-ate-his-rose-because-she-wanted-to-go-to-bed-with-him.*

I loved the curve of Brad's mouth, those thin lips typifying my concept of the white man. When I kissed him slightly, I hardly felt the softness of lips. Instead, I felt the corners, then the contours of his lips, even the roughness of the unshaved skin around his mouth. I had to stay with a long kiss to feel his mouth, and whenever I kissed him like that, I always had the strange feeling that his mouth had become curvier under my lips. At times I had to stop and draw my head away so I could take a quick look at him to make sure his mouth had not changed shape. Yet there were times I wished his mouth would change entirely into a tulip, a rose, something very light, very surreal, so that his maleness and the reality of the flesh and taste of his mouth would not burden me so much, and then I could feel genuinely ethereal as though I were kissing a delicate flower.

I told him once of my desire to see his mouth change into a rose, and he was not pleased. He said a man did not want to be compared to roses. My idea, he said, was the feminine urge of a poet. And then he changed his mind and said it was more like the subliminal creativity of a woman operating in surrealism. He took the time to explain his theory of subliminal creativity. (It was rare that Brad did any kind of theorizing at all, but on that occasion he did.) He reminded me of the night after our meeting in Hermann Park, when I first asked him to come over for dinner.

Yes, for our first date, I asked him to come to my house, something I had never done before. I rationalized to myself that I would be in better control if we were in my environment, and I could be more at ease than in the formality of a restaurant, in public. That night, I had made a salad with raspberry vinaigrette dressing and had elaborately peeled a grapefruit and sprinkled pieces of its watery pink all over the salad. I had also elaborately broken up fresh pecans and sprinkled them, too, over my salad together with sunflower seeds. Later, reminiscing of our first home-cooked dinner together, Brad told me he he'd been afraid he would be hungry all night. All of my food was so light and intricately deco-rated that he did not dare to eat it, for fear he would be destroy-ing the aesthetic decoration. I told him I was merely adopting Grandma Que's style. The phrase just rolled out of me because I couldn't help ruefully mentioning her. Disappointingly, Brad asked nothing about that absentee grandmother of mine. Instead he was watching the vase of roses in the middle of the table. That night, being the Southern gentleman that he was, he had brought me a dozen red roses in a glass vase. The table looked fantastic and everything was perfect, and naturally it seemed exactly the kind of night for the first time of lovemaking.

According to Brad, I had leaned over and taken one of the roses out of the vase, walked over to the sink, and let water run over the rose. We were eating in the kitchen because I had no for-mal dining table. (The formal dining room had become a music room where my piano sat.) When I came back to the table, Brad claimed I had this strange look on my face. The rose I held in my hand appeared dewy because of the water residue, and when I sat down in front of my salad, I started peeling off the petals and sprinkling them over my plate. Certainly the rose had brightened the salad with its deep red petals. In front of him, I had slowly eaten the rose, and he had carefully watched how the deep red velvet petals disappeared in between my ivory rows of teeth. And he was saying to himself, "She is eating my rose!" He had made up his mind right then he would be making love to me that night, to the woman who ate rose petals. After dinner when he reached over and put one hand underneath my shirt, he had no shyness or fear or worry. He wasn't nervous. He thought it was meant to be because I was eating the rose he'd brought over.

Everything else about our first date seemed so perfect. The somber second movement of Beethoven's *Sonata Pathetique* sounded nostalgically sensual and did not make me cry as usual, and when the rondo of the third movement came, every note on the fast moving scale, every piano sound that reminded me of a beautiful rain seemed to synchronize with the pulse of my flesh, and Brad's arms and chest became that mossy wall from childhood—from that mystical city named Hue. On that sturdy wall I became a crawling vine, and flowers blossomed along my way. We smelled good, my bedroom smelled good, like the essence of lily or orchid (the result of my favorite Quelques Fleurs perfume from Neiman Marcus). I had served no coffee after dinner and had not even bothered asking Brad if he wanted any. Thank God he did not ask or insist on drinking coffee because I would have disliked his coffee breath. Instead I had served jasmine tea, plain, with no sugar or milk, the way jasmine tea was supposed to be drunk in the Far East. Naturally I had not asked Brad whether he wanted his tea the English way, although he had told me of his summer in England. He was doing a legal continuing education course in international law or commercial transactions with the European Union or something like that. By going along with my jasmine tea, not just one cup, but two or three, I couldn't remember exactly, Brad was already traveling with me to the Far East, such a nice debut to intimacy. The whole meal had no meat or heavy sauces, and Brad's kisses that night tasted like raspberry, grapefruit, pecans, sunflower seeds, and jasmine tea. When he eased himself into me, I smelled all these things.

I thought, too, of all of the green rice paddies of Vietnam, and the kite I never got to fly. I let myself fly with the kite when Brad's hands slipped under me. He raised me a little, and it seemed so easy, as though it were meant to be, and the nice moment came as naturally as his gentle yet persistent thrusts. Rare. Unfortunately too rare, and then it crossed my mind that perhaps he was the right one. Or perhaps it was the right combination of salad and Beethoven's *Sonata Pathetique* and Neiman Marcus's Quelques Fleurs. I teared up a little, he raised his head a little, and I could see he was looking into my eyes for a reaction; but the tears did not confuse him, because it was so conspicuous to him the nice moment was already mine to keep, and then he kissed my few tears away, and I thought it was so romantic of him to do that. That made him the right one already. At my age, the success or failure of any relationship with a man depended on how that first night went. And so Brad kept coming back, and before I knew it, I had my side of the bed and he had his, and I got into the habit of seeing him in my mirror, even if I never wanted him to be a part of it.

Whenever he recounted our first night together, Brad always told me that my wanting to see his mouth turn into a rose or tulip or any kind of smooth, velvety, deep-colored flower meant I wanted sex. That gave him the confidence to simplify my head, shut it off, and ease himself into me, again and again, days and weeks and months, without fearing the spiderweb within my head. And I let him be. I just let him be. The spiderweb that entangled my thoughts and separated them from his became the matter of my mirror acting as my confidante.

The mirror—this confidante of mine—was off-limits to him.

Here was the reason why.

I never told Brad the truth regarding our first date—what really happened to me during the dinner that I had cooked for him at my house. The whole time I was eating the rose, I was thinking of Grandma Que's diva lipstick. She wore it even when she was already sixty years old—a characteristic of the aristocratic women of Hue. That deep red of frozen blood. The color of a scab over a cut, a wound. French red wine. Wilting or dried red roses. The color contoured Grandma Que's thin lips when they pulled into a faint smile. She seldom smiled, and when she did, I often wondered whether she was truly happy, especially when her lips smiled and her eyes didn't. They gave off that tragic look of a beautiful woman knowing her beauty had become her curse.

In America, the sight of her face, eyes, and mouth always came back to me at the most unexpected moments. That night at dinner, I had felt angry for no reason at all. Perhaps I was angry at Brad for not asking me a follow-up question about Grandma Que, even though my mention of her had just been a slip of the tongue. In any event, there she was, appearing outside the window. She walked silently into the room, sharing in my anger at Brad. Her deep red lipstick smeared as she spoke the angry words in my mind, touching me with the very sadness and isolation of her face each time she appeared in America, in whatever crowd that made up my company at the time. That night Brad had been my one-man crowd. I had wanted so badly to make something beautiful, and the dinner for Brad was the chance to do it.

Only I knew Grandma Que was there, and the anger arose because the world was indifferent to her—the world as represented by Brad. I had not prepared dinner with the idea of going to bed with him. Nor did I think of being naked with him when I was chewing his rose. Sleeping with Brad was like a desirable accident that just happened, unintended. The last touch to something beautiful. But a nice, beautiful accident was still an accident, no more, no less.

Perhaps the accident happened because Grandma Que had come and had left, leaving me with the terrible loss of knowing she was gone, and there was not a single thing I could do about it. "It is your show, child! He is a nice boy," she said, her lipstick smearing again, and her eyes sprinkling a few tears. The frozen red wine of her lips traveled across the white screen of my mind, like the gradual spilling of ink onto a permeating surface, until the whole screen was transformed into the rich softness of deep red velvet. It felt like I had chewed a dozen roses, and all that fantastic redness filled up my gut and then quickly disappeared. When I looked down at my plate, all that remained before me was the fresh green of the salad, with no red rose petals, and my stomach felt light and empty. I turned that hunger onto Brad. The way he was looking at me across the remaining roses, eleven of them standing tall on thorny stems, made him into that last touch of beauty. Finally, I calmly told Brad I would light a scented candle. When the candle was lit, it shone onto a different world. The one I shared with Brad. Us alone. Without Grandma Que. I let the accident happen to me, in such a sweet, wonderful way.

To let this sweet accident happen to me, I had to construct a physical world outside of the mirror for Brad and me. It began with our first night after I had eaten his rose because of my memory of Grandma Que. She came to look at Brad, sharing in my anger, but then she left, leaving Brad to be my own show. Once I created that show, it had to be closed completely to Grandma Que, even if she had approved of it. She had to vanish with the rose I had eaten. The space that consisted of me and Brad could not have Grandma Que. Likewise, the world inside the mirror was opened to Grandma Que but not to Brad. To that world, Brad would always be the outsider. I had decided to make him so.

FIVE
HIS INTRUSION

Brad never asked me again about the shapes and darts of violence in my sketchbook. However, later, much later in our relationship, he wanted to make his way into the mirror. He wanted to share it.

I never intended for this to happen, the business of us sharing the mirror, although each time he stayed to spend the night, I let him share the third floor of my townhouse where the mirror sat. He had shared my sketchbook. And then my bed. My third floor. I had given him the physical world outside the mirror. Wasn't that enough?

So, waking up in the morning, I always turned toward the mirror, away from Brad. And that was how I talked, if I ever talked at all: into the mirror and away from him. I could see in the mirror the reflection of us, lovers, in the lazy hours of the morning. The lovers' scene was stagnant without the luxury and fluidity of words or interpretation.

My secretary said I was very lucky to have Brad, such a nice, good-looking young man. I thought of her statement every time I woke up and felt Brad's arm under my neck. I was the woman who was supposed to have everything, including this good-looking man. His presence alone confirmed my luck. No other words or interpretations were necessary.

—

In the morning, Brad's arm always extended beneath my mass of hair, and his skin looked too white next to the thousands of dark brown strands falling from my hairline. He often murmured something nice, something sweet, his sleepy voice sounding saccharin in those morning hours. At times, even though his eyes were shut, he would run his long fingers through the whole length of my hair, down to my rib cage. Other times he would stir and turn his face toward the ceiling, his eyes closed, his breath steady, but never did he move his one extended arm. It remained my pillow, the constant connection between us when our bodies separated. I could see in the mirror the contours of his biceps and triceps and the fuzziness of his heaving chest. It did not bother me if he was soundly sleeping when I was already awake.

Brad would never understand that my gazing into the mirror was not about me. I'd never been narcissistic enough to scrutinize myself for youth or beauty. My relationship with the mirror was about my past. The past that Brad could not share.

Even when Brad was not spending the night and I woke up alone, I always found myself on my side of the bed, the side that allowed me to face the mirror, and talked to the reclining woman in the glass. Her eyes told me she was already too tired to begin her day. For the entire year since my move to Houston for the job with the law firm, I had doubled the hours spent at the gym so I could lift those weights, swim those laps, and walk the treadmill religiously. I had hoped the rigorous gym routine would invigorate me and take away my morning fatigue. But the tiredness was like a morning sickness that struck and stayed. Eventually I accepted the malaise. As I learned to talk to the mirror, I felt that my eyes had become so wide-opened that I could see my words, my thoughts, the vibration of my brain cells, the throbbing pain inside my skull. My temples pulsed and my eyes stung as though I were seeing the world through a film of smoke. When I heard the birds twittering outside the set of French doors leading to the balcony, to fight the pulse inside my head and to get rid of that imaginary smoke in my eyes I would wrap a robe around me and walk toward the sun, out to the balcony where I could look down and see the top of my redbud tree and my magnolia bulbs in my front yard. At times, I saw the pink redbud flowers as clusters of dots, floating against purple and mauve magnolia blooms like viruses under a magnifying glass, engulfing and dissolving into one another. When I squinted my eyes, the dots turned into pink cotton candies—with minds of their own, congregating and then rushing toward a carnival candy stand, in front of a clown's mask, among colorful balloons and paper cups. I was a young girl dancing among cotton candies, balloons, and paper cups, smiling at a mask of clown, perhaps in an amusement park.

Those were the familiar images that once appeared to me from my confusing past. About the fall of Saigon.

But they made little sense. There were bazaars and festivals in Vietnam, but no carnivals or amusement parks. I often associated these concepts with the fun and ordinary good life of America, the type of things I often dreamed of, growing up in Vietnam.

When these confusing images appeared, I often had to shake my head to return to the reality of my front yard. Standing on the balcony, I usually found my peace in the pinkness of flowers below and the brightness of sunshine all around me. No more fog. No more pulse. Just the glorious, healthy sun and those gorgeous blooms among green leaves. They confirmed I was alive.

—

Quite often when the early morning sun crept into my third-floor bedroom and hit Brad's face brightly enough to wake him up, he would put his other arm over my shoulder and pull me in. His hand always felt rough on my skin, but some mornings his touch was very light, the way I imagined he would pat his child. That Asian child of his whom I had never met. I thought of her now and then, imagining what she looked like, and thoughts of her distracted my concentration on his touch.

We had been sleeping with each other almost nightly for months when Brad began talking of his child. We were meeting for lunch at a newly opened Irish pub near my house when he reluctantly told me he couldn't come over that weekend because he had to see his child. His three-year-old daughter was returning from Hong Kong, and it was his time to keep her.

By then I knew that Brad was thirty-three years old; I had seen his bachelor apartment and had made love to him on his leather couch, but never had I thought for a moment that the man might have a three-year-old child. I dropped the fork and pretended to wipe the corner of my mouth with the crisp linen napkin as he began talking about the girl's mother, a Chinese beauty originally from Shanghai, a second-generation immigrant and Hong Kong resident and British citizen and then Texas transplant, who had come to his law office to install his computer during his first year of practice. As a veteran lawyer, I knew exactly what a young lawyer's life was like during that testing period: then, the occupational stress had been overwhelming for me, the solitude and isolation as enormous as the Pacific Ocean. So he'd ended up taking this Hong Kong woman to dinner several times and eventually to his bed, and she became pregnant and they were married and the pregnancy became a trap; and they lived together and then they lived apart after the child was born, all of this happening so fast, before he knew what he was doing with his life. To save the marriage, they took a tour of Europe. That same summer, Brad enrolled in the international law course on the European Union in England, as he'd told me during our first date.

Mistake of youth, he said defensively, forcing himself to meet my eyes. Of course, I wasn't thinking of his European course. I was looking at the blond, blue-eyed man sitting before me and beginning to see the faces of so many of the other white men I'd dated throughout the years, men who knew nothing about me or my Far East yet shared a fetish for and stereotypical outlook of Asian women that led them from one to another, to the point that they felt they could never come back to their own kind. I felt heartsick to think that Brad had joined their number, that I had become just another in his long line of Asian lovers.

I did not want to know anything else. In the dark Irish pub I even put on my sunglasses and ordered a liqueur, but Brad must have seen the change of emotion in my eyes before I hid them behind the sunglasses, because he kept on talking about love— how strange a creature it could be, how fragile and unpredictable, and that if there had been any feeling of love between the Hong Kong computer woman and the young Anglo-American litigator, it had dissolved into nothing, yet the child and fatherhood had been a blessing he would never regret.

He kept volunteering all kinds of information, nervously and hastily, despite what had to be my obvious lack of interest. Through my sunglasses, I was looking toward the window overlooking Westheimer Street. He told me the Hong Kong woman looked like the movie actress Gong Li, and I said, "Thank you for telling me," thinking to myself that probably to his eyes all Asian women who went to bed with him looked like gorgeous Gong Li. There wasn't even one ounce of Gong Li on my face and body.

As if he had read my mind, he hurried to say that the Hong Kong woman was not at all like me. "Not even a scintilla," he said pleadingly. For example, the skin, hands, and feet, he said. She was a big, tall girl, about five-seven, with ivory skin and narrow hips. The big, dominant bone structure of her hand matched the computers she managed. I was an olive-skinned, petite, curvaceous Southeast Asian with tiny hands and feet, and long, slender fingers fitted for the touch of a piano's keyboard. And the soul. The soul. He kept repeating. She was commerce; I was art.

So, after a few months of sleeping with me, he knew my soul? And he knew art versus commerce? "Oh," I said, "so you have had the best of both worlds, traveling from the sunny beaches of Southeast Asia to the silky, jade-green East China Sea."

He stopped, confused. His long fingers trembled along the rim of the Irish coffee cup. I took off my sunglasses and looked into his pained blue eyes. I couldn't help smiling, knowing that the awkward man sitting before me was no sophisticated womanizer. A professional would not have thrown the corny metaphor about commerce and art at me, or dared to compare physical attributes. A professional would have handled the situation much more expertly, would have lied about the weekend plan and forever hidden the child from me. To reassure Brad, I touched his fingers clutching the coffee cup. His face relaxed, and the incessant talk about the other woman stopped.

But then he went on to say the strangest thing. He said I was such a small, compact, smooth-skinned woman that each time he held me in bed, he thought of his child and the way she was growing up, traversing the world between Texas and Hong Kong. He said even after sex when I cuddled against him, he would look down past my full head of hair and find the smoothness of my resting eyelids, and in those moments I looked so much like his child it was almost scary.

I put my sunglasses back on again and imagined how a child produced by a tall, blond American and an ivory-skinned, big-boned Hong Kong beauty of Shanghai origin could look like a dark-skinned, petite Vietnamese woman.

"It's my honest feeling," he said, frowning at my withdrawal, and I couldn't help smiling again at his ardor.

"Thinking of me as your child when you're fucking me?" I said, and he seemed stunned by my crudeness, and lost. So far everything had been romantic and sweet between us; I had never used a four-letter word with him.

"No," he said, too loudly. "I am not a pervert, please!" He looked genuinely stricken. "I mean after, *after*. The parental feeling toward you came after."

He took his wallet out and showed me a picture of a chubby Amerasian baby, almost bald-headed. He insisted the child resembled me, especially now that she had hair. Beyond the fact that the photo reminded me of the baby pictures I'd left on the other side of the Pacific Ocean decades ago, I decided the child did perhaps resemble me, due to our eyelids. I do not have the typical slanting, swollen Asian eyelids with their distinctive epicanthic fold, resembling a fine ink stroke. My eyes are more like the almond-shaped, deeply set windows of the soul of my ebony African American friends, more typical of South Asians or Pacific Islanders. Perhaps Brad was offering his perspective truthfully. I gave the picture back to him, commenting on how pretty the child was, then ended the lunch and headed back to my office.

The whole afternoon I was distracted and slightly depressed. I was not sure I wanted a lover who identified me with his Asian child. It was a cliché, but I wanted the man to make love to me, the woman, rather than a projection of his own inner world. Maybe I was expecting too much. A part of me liked Brad even more after the discovery at the Irish pub, because I intuitively believed in his honesty, or perhaps I just wanted to believe he was honest.

Around four o'clock that same day, the receptionist called to let me know a delivery had arrived for me: an arrangement of irises and orchids and a gift-wrapped box. The card said: *Thank you for letting me love you. B.*

I closed my office door, opened the gift box, and ran my fingers over the white silk camisole inside. Somehow the cool texture of the undergarment put me at peace. Brad and Mimi. Mimi and Brad. Sex and sex. *Thank you for letting me love you.* Should it be *Thank you for your body?* Or was it a roundabout way of saying *I love you?* Even if it were, I was old enough to know men rushed into the big word, love, in order to get to the big act, sex. In Brad's case, he had had all the sex there was for a few months. Apparently he wanted more.

For about a week I did not call him. I also had all calls screened at the office and avoided his phone calls. He left messages on my answering machine at home, and in his agitated, emotional voice, he asked that I grant him the courtesy of explaining why I might not want to see him again. Was it because of his Asian child, her Hong Kong mother, or was it because he had not told me about them right in the beginning? He raised question after question until the machine cut him off. I knew the decent thing would be to speak to him and answer his questions, but I couldn't, because I myself did not know why I wanted a break. I was afraid of complications, perhaps driven by an urge for self-protection that, at my stage of life, I could not ignore. Or maybe I was concerned I wasn't loved and only wanted as a sex object—a girlish notion and a cliché which, at my age, should be banned or discarded.

Finally a Friday night came, together with a roaring lightning storm and persistent rain. I fought the six o'clock evening traffic and went home exhausted. I watched old movies until I fell asleep on the couch. When I woke up at around eleven o'clock at night, the knowledge that another short-term relationship had begun and ended almost immobilized me, and I had to force myself to get up and climb the stairs to the third-floor bedroom. Once there, I could not go back to sleep. The rain was still pouring although the thunderstorm had subsided. I opened an umbrella, stepped to the balcony, and looked down to my front yard.

My heart throbbed at the scene.

Under the streetlight, I recognized Brad's jeep parked at the curb and could see his silhouette in the driver's seat, his sleeves rolled up and his hands resting on the wheel. He was an immobilized figure, just as I'd been after waking on the couch. God knew how long he had been sitting there, in front of my house, in the rain.

I went inside and frantically searched for my cellular phone. I stood on the third-floor balcony, looking down at his jeep, with an umbrella in one hand and my cell phone in the other hand. I dialed the number and saw the man in the jeep raise his phone to his ear. I heard Brad's voice on the line.

The sound of the rain could be heard in the background, filling up the unnatural gaps and pauses in our dialogues, which consisted of hellos and how-are-yous and I-am-glad-to-hear-your-voice and what-a-night-with-this-awful-rain.

I asked him to look up to the balcony, and he did.

"What are you doing in front of my house, Brad?"

He mumbled along and told me how he had been depressed because of my silence, that he had taken the wrong exit on the freeway and had driven to my house out of habit or subconscious desire. When he got here, he did not want to go back to his bachelor apartment on a rainy Friday night. He swore to me he had no intention of disturbing or stalking me, and understood that I did not want to see him.

As he was talking, he stepped out of his jeep, and the rain poured on him. He held the phone to his ear, and his head lifted to me on the balcony. He wore no tie and his shirt collar was open. I felt cold just thinking of the streams of rainwater crawling down his bare chest. He kept wiping the rain off his face with his other hand, and it struck me how beautiful he was, a tall, straight figure soaked in rain.

"Say you don't want to see me again, and I will drive away," he yelled into the phone over the sound of the rain.

I left the balcony to run downstairs and open the front door, and there he stood, shivering. He stepped inside, the rain dripping from him onto my hardwood floor. The cold, the rain, and his wetness passed on to me as I clung to him. We found ourselves in my living room and collapsed onto my accent Persian rug. We shivered together and our small kisses were cold and wet. I took off my terrycloth robe and wiped him with it. His hand, cold and wet, reached for me, and I saw that he was sobbing. His eyes had reddened, and I could not tell the tears on his face from the rain. "I am sorry, so sorry," he said, his lips trembling, and then all was silence.

—

Later that evening when Brad had dried himself and his wet clothes had piled up somewhere in my living room, we made love again, and I trembled in his arms because of the intensity of passion that seemed to match the persistent sound of the pouring rain outside. We lay side by side on the floor for a long time listening to the rain, and all this time he was holding my hand.

At last Brad rolled over and asked me again to accept his apology. What for? I opened one eye. He was, in his own words, "practically but not legally divorced." He couldn't tell me up front because the situation was complicated, revolving around an Amerasian child who, by the time she turned three, had many times traveled across the globe, in the web of a maternal extended family system that stretched from a mother in Houston to a grandmother in Hong Kong. He'd been afraid that if I had known he wasn't legally divorced, I might have turned away from him, and we would never have had a chance.

He was trying to explain why the divorce was not finalized when I began to think of the relationship between a child and her grandmother. I saw Grandma Que's face. She was standing outside the glass window, in a brown brocade *ao dai* tunic, the rain splashing around her. "Don't hold it against him," she told me. "He is a child himself." So I put a finger on Brad's lips and told him to stop talking. He held my finger in between his lips for a while, and then he raised himself and closed his lips on my breast. I heard the sobbing sound coming out of him again, and I held his blond head and the sobbing subsided.

I felt very, very sleepy and tried not to doze off. I heard Brad say, "Mimi, Mimi. Mimi. Do you like the white camisole I sent you?" I told him I had left it at the office. He was still talking, saying something like *let's drive to your office to get your camisole, let's get soaked in the rain, and let's make love again.* And then I might have heard him say, "Thank you for letting me love you." I dozed off, hearing myself uttering something stupid, something unintentional, something habitual, something totally unromantic. As my eyelids drooped heavily over my pupils, I either said it in my mind or out loud to my blond lover, "You're welcome."

—

We fell back into our routine then, until the morning before the mirror when Brad finally broke the norm. His pale blue eyes were opened wide to the glass, like mine. He began to ask questions, casually at first, then more persistently. I did not realize Brad could be so insistently probing. I had forgotten he was a good lawyer.

He was also looking into the mirror, into the glass that was my audience, my stage, my monologue. The scene of us together in the mirror had become the property of the blue of his eyes. If I turned around to look at him right at that moment, I would be looking at us on a blue backdrop. His eyes were a camera lens stealing my scene, and the mirror was no longer mine alone. I was spooned against him. I had expected to feel his hardness— perhaps he wanted to make love, and this line of questioning was just a prelude to morning sex. But his penis was warm and soft, and he was not rubbing against me. Instead, he was talking to me.

No, not exactly. He was talking past me, beyond me, to the woman in the mirror, lying nestled into him on her side, her hands pressed together like a leaf beneath her cheek. She was feline, a brown, sad, lazy cat. From the mirror, she was looking back at him, meeting his probing eyes, her naked thighs drawn up so that her knees almost touched the tips of her dark nipples. Brad, the man, my thirty-three-year-old Brad, was behind her, and she looked kind of lost against him. He moved a little, pulled the white sheet, and covered us up. Our bodies cut their contours against the thin, soft, white cotton, and the pinkness of him and the brownness of me shone through the fabric, which didn't cover anything at all when the sun hit the bed. All of a sudden I was overwhelmed with love. It was me in the mirror with a man, and he was close, too close, right behind me, next to my skin, sharing my scene and my mirror. I turned over to face him and impulsively kissed the corner of his curvy mouth.

Even driven by this tremendous feeling of love and spontaneity, I had to stop at the corner of his mouth and keep my lips sealed, fearing Brad would construe my kiss as a demand for sex. But he did not move, and for a moment I thought he was faintly resisting me and my lightest of kisses. Perhaps he was surprised. Perhaps, just like me, he was preoccupied with his own reflection in my mirror. I had rested my closed mouth there, right at the left corner of his mouth, expecting him to breathe more heavily so that I could feel his breath all over my face, down to my neck. I would try to breathe in unison with him.

Strangely, that morning Brad remained soft and warm, and the tip of his penis never rose between us, and I lost the corner of his mouth as he turned away. His mouth changed shape as he began talking; although his hand was cupping me, he did not roll over. Instead, he was asking me, again, about the Crazy Man. "You want to marry him?" he said. "You said so in your diary."

I felt a short, sharp pain under my ribcage. And then there was just a feeling of uncertainty and emptiness. He had read my diary. What was in it? I had only one diary, the one I had kept since the days at Diamondale. I did not recall filling all the pages, throughout the years.

He told me he had found the diary open to that one page, facing down, on the makeup table. He had not intended to look. But he did look, mistaking my diary for my sketchbook. Could this be possible? The books were roughly the same size. Naturally there could have been no malice. He had expected to find lines and shapes, yet found instead my words. To be exact, he found combinations of my nine words written for the Crazy Man, decades ago.

There wasn't much that made any sense in the diary. Only those words stood out as significant.

He did not apologize to me for having read my diary, just kept asking questions about the person I called the president of a new republic. Perhaps someone I'd met among the LLM foreign lawyers at Harvard? One of the "best and brightest" sent by some foreign country to absorb the Ivy League knowledge of America?

Brad didn't know how averse I was to this "networking" concept, this assumed web of connections with all other Harvard-trained lawyers around the world. Although I was privileged enough to have become the first Vietnamese refugee admitted to Harvard Law School, I had never learned to network very well. And seventeen years after graduation from Harvard Law School, at forty I was still working for hire, although I drove a nice BMW (with unreliable air-conditioning) and lived alone in a big three-story house, where the entire top floor was a huge bedroom with only three pieces of furniture: a bed, my makeup table, and the mirror. That was all.

Brad had gone to the University of Texas in Austin as a double major: English for his life and computer science for his livelihood. He had revealed these facts about himself quite early in the relationship. "That's a cliché," I told him then, too casually. "You could say the same thing about my choice to go to Harvard," I added. I was totally unprepared for his reaction. He jumped on me, heatedly pointing out how many times I myself had used clichés. I knew he would not have attacked me so vehemently unless the subject had something to do with Harvard Law School.

Brad disliked the Harvard Law label as much as he disliked lawyers—despite the fact that he was sleeping with a woman bearing the Harvard Law label and that he himself was a lawyer. The hatred of his own kind helped make him a terrific litigator. (We had this in common; we both disliked and disdained the majority of people in our own profession.) In trials and depositions, he did his job with the passionate hatred of his own kind and what he had become. He himself could not rationalize how he both loved and hated what he did for a living. I once mentioned to him that life was all about love-hate relationships and contradictions. For example, life and death: to be passionate about living was a way of loving death. Why else would people jump off airplanes and cliffs and climb rocks all the way to the snowy top of Everest to confirm their joy of living?

I immediately regretted uttering the word *death*. This was a raw nerve in Brad, I knew; he'd told me that he was allergic to talk of it. That had been why he'd become so concerned when I'd mentioned Marilyn Monroe during our meeting in Hermann Park, he said.

It was death that led him to law school, he had explained once. Only once. He was working at Texas Instruments as a programmer because there were no jobs for English majors. Then the news came: his former college roommate at University of Texas had committed suicide. The man had locked himself in his apartment and turned on the gas. An engineer, he must have known exactly how to do the gas thing. Texas allowed everyone to own a gun, but Brad's former roommate did not own one. He was anti-gun. When the news of the death came, Brad decided to quit his job to write a book about a man who couldn't understand why his college roommate wanted to die. Staying home to write full-time would be a dangerous act, Brad thought, referring to the life–livelihood cliché, so he applied to law school at University of Houston, intending to write during the day and attend law classes at night. That way, he would be assured of a job when the book was finished. The book was never finished, and Brad became a lawyer instead.

To Brad, Harvard Law School stood for a bunch of people who spent one hundred thousand dollars for three years to become lawyers and get jobs on Wall Street—the kind of thing neither Brad nor his college roommate would have done. Every year around the time bluebonnets were blossoming along Texas highways, he drove to Austin to visit the grave of the dead man. I asked him if he had a picture of his friend. "No, no picture," he said. "Pictures are like postcards. They capture a stagnant slice of life, not its essence. They can't replace life. All they do is capture memory, and memory hurts."

As I've said, he told me the story of his roommate just once, and then asked me not to mention death, ever. And now I had. I couldn't help it. Preoccupied with the romanticism of death, I'd let him down.

———

During that critical morning when Brad was determined to intrude into the world of my mirror, I was just thinking of his Asian child and reliving the whole episode of our mini-breakup, when Brad's fingers travelled down my spine and stopped at the dimple below my waist. I was turning away from my mirror but could imagine the scene—how his large, bony hand would look out of proportion on my slender back. He drew me into him and my head was lost in the immensity of his chest, and for a moment I imagined I had turned into his Asian child. All of a sudden I understood how parental feelings could exist between lovers, as he had tried to tell me they could, in that Irish pub. The sharing and giving of pleasure began with the unconditional bestowing of largesse and protection, to make sure the recipient was safe and whole. The recipient became small and lost and completely dependent. *In loco parentis* had to be the nature of all unconditional love. Pleasure began with the wholesomeness of unconditional giving. I became his dependent child.

But, the moment of spiritual *in loco parentis* quickly vanished, because he was also lifting me up so he could face me again, and our mouths met. This time he parted my lips with his tongue, and even though I was conscious of my early morning breath, I opened my mouth for him; and the father of the Asian child returned to being my thirty-three-year-old Brad. The tip of his tongue was as persistent as the tip of his penis, so close yet so aloof, like a bird I was trying in vain to catch, but I had to follow it; and the illusion of this spiritual parental relationship with Brad was gone. Forever gone.

For a time he was kissing me almost too violently, but then his hungry mouth slowed and finally released my lips and tongue. He repeated his question about the foreign students at Harvard Law School then—the part of me that defined to the world what I stood for: one of the first, the privileged few; the token, the high-achiever, the type-A personality, the model immigrant, the woman who had everything. The list of labels went on forever. Was the president of that new republic who appeared in my diary from Harvard Law?

"No, no, no," I said. I would not be writing about some Harvard man in my diary.

The blue of his eyes signaled his urgency to hear more. "No? Then who was he? Who else could have been a president of a new republic?"

I thought of Scheherazade of *The Arabian Nights* telling stories to her lover king to keep his interest. I might not have Scheherazade's skills to invent tales and mesmerize her king, but perhaps I should begin talking to keep Brad happy. I was not yet ready to answer his question, though. Instead, as I talked, I began to see in the mirror bits and pieces of my college and law school years.

SIX
THE BIRTH OF A NAME

Three years of undergrad went by fleetingly, and I achieved my goal. I graduated from SISU summa cum laude in only three years, at twenty years of age. On the day before commencement, I walked through Krost Hall to the forest between Krost and the University Theater for the last time. The beautiful sunshine of May brightened every corner of the forest, and leaves were not crying. There was no death. No requiem. This was supposed to be the beginning of my American dream.

Facing my future, I became aware of my dilemma. I needed a new name for my life in America. I was tired of being called My Chow or Chow Chow.

I thought of the Crazy Man. I had wanted him to know me as ME. ME. That day in the forest, I thought of how America should change my identity. I was not comfortable with any American or English name. I was comfortable as ME. ME. As the Crazy Man had known me.

Once in the ancient city of Hue, Grandma Que had taken me to a fortuneteller whose name, Mey Mai, meant "Old Wise Cloud." I had insisted on going because Simone had gone and had had her fortune told. When we later compared notes, Simone and I discovered Mey Mai had told us similar things—that Simone was bonded to a spirit who sang across the River Huong, and I was bonded to a spirit who lived in the green jade phoenix that brightened our ancestral altar. My sister and I concluded it was the same spirit—our great-grandmother the Mystique Concubine of the Violet City. We stood together, Simone Mi Uyen and her sister Mi Chau, small and insignificant before that mystical altar, two young girls holding hands, looking up at the radiant piece of jade, our souls full of awe, our eyes full of tears.

Mey Mai. Mey Mai. I repeated the name of the old, cheerful, melodramatic medium. Since childhood I had always liked the sound of the two *m*'s pronounced together by Simone in her sweet, breathy voice, the way her soft lips closed on each word, light like a cloud and slightly vibrating like the wind. The idea of a name came to me, flashing like a magical stream of light. I would change my name to MEME. It wasn't the exotic I was after. I just wanted to be ME. ME. Myself, the child of Hue whose fortune was foretold by an old wise cloud, Mey Mai.

I was sleepless that night, knowing the anxiety had nothing to do with the fanfare of the forthcoming commencement ceremony. I woke up several times, writing my new name down each time, staring at the piece of paper on which appeared my new name. I felt a stab in my rib cage, realizing that *meme*, in French, meant "the same." I threw the pen against the wall, hurried to the mirror in my dorm room, and looked at my face. No, no, no, I could not be *Meme*. It was all a mistake.

In the mirror I saw a skinny young woman with long, straight hair and a pointed chin. It was the same face that had been with me all these years, but I knew I did not want to be the same person. So I opened the desk drawer and took out the pair of scissors. I raised the scissors about five times, and then strands of hair were flying around me the same way leaves were flying around me that one day in the woods, the fall of 1976. I looked at myself again and found a new person. The uneven bob could be made fashionable, framing a face accented by thick, dark eyebrows, contrasting with a snub nose and thick mouth—the startling face of a curious cat, unobtrusive yet defensive, wide eyes carrying a bewildered look as though the cat had just seen her teased mouse turn into a scary witch.

I began writing my new name again, this time with a different spelling. I changed Meme to Mimi. Two notes on the piano keyboard. MI. MI. Repeated in the beginning melody of Beethoven's "Für Elise." *Mi–ri–mi–ri–mi–ri–mi*…Music was the only part of my past in Vietnam I consciously wanted to remember. When the back of my head hurt, I listened to classical music and the migraine went away.

That day, before the mirror and with my initiating haircut, I officially embraced my new identity. My obsession with mirrors must have started then.

———

I told Brad how I entered Harvard Law School as Mi-Chau Giang-Suong on paper and how I paid for my Harvard education with Simone's help and a scholarship. I told him how I became Mimi in the Harvard classroom after all the name confusion each time the class roll was called, ultimately leading to Mimi Sean Young as my permanent name.

I stressed the scholarship part so he would distinguish me from all those rich and supposedly smart kids who would pay one hundred thousand dollars for a JD degree from Harvard. He nodded, and his chin tapped lightly at the top of my head. I was delivering to both Brad and my mirror an honest monologue about Harvard Law School. He listened very patiently, although I knew he wasn't interested in all of the details about how awful that place could be.

Harvard Law School taught me how it felt to be ugly and tired.

The Gropias dormitory complex—a dreary, yellow-and-red block of old buildings bearing the look of a hospital built in the seventies, together with the arduous routines called the Socratic casebook study (meaning the reading of hundreds of pages of scholarly discussions of theories and abstract legal concepts), all had their way of making my skin grainy and my eyes muddy. The experience would create and deepen the circles under my twenty-year-old eyes (which, two decades later, turned into the slightly purplish sagging folds of skin that betrayed my youthful appearance and, under close scrutiny, would reveal my arrival at middle age). Those days at Harvard, blemishes appeared on my milky twenty-year-old skin. Tiny broken veins showed themselves underneath the small layer of derma-tissues once smooth, creamy, and translucent.

During law school, I disliked mirrors.

I told Brad how the buildings at Harvard Law School looked ominous to me at dusk in the fall, when I finished with my daily clinical trial workshop. How I had always walked back to the dorm room in the Gropias Complex slightly depressed. Brad nodded again so respectfully that I expected to hear the usual "yes, ma'am," but none of that polite Southern gentleman's talk came my way. He was quiet. He was waiting for that ultimate explanation about the Crazy Man.

But I kept going on and on about Harvard Law School, the grinding machine that crushed my ability to sense and feel.

———

Crushed. Crushed. Crushed. I turned to face the mirror again. My buttock was pressing against Brad's loins, but I could feel no sensation coming from the skin-against-skin contact. All I could focus on was the great institution's grinding machine that crushed me.

Crushed. Crushed. Crushed. I heard the word spoken and repeated to me by an auburn-haired woman wearing a black pleated skirt and matching suede boots in the Langdell Library my first month at Harvard Law School. She had the perfect bone structure and facial features of a movie star—that delicate jaw line, the dainty brows painted dark, and those thick mascara lashes over her deeply set, clear, green eyes. She wore a black wool turtleneck that shaped her pointed breasts and accented her fair skin. I had reserved a carrel in the stack room for my research, and she was sitting in my place.

"Excuse me," I said. "I've left my notes here." I pointed at the papers piled up inside the carrel. "Those are mine."

She looked up at me, down my body, and up again to the top of my head. She was assessing. Then she continued reading, ignoring me.

"Will you move, please?" I asked.

"You can't leave your stuff here and claim this space is yours."

"It's reserved under my name." I showed her the library card.

"I have half an hour to go." She continued working, ignoring me.

I sat on a bench nearby, waiting. Maybe the library staff had made a mistake.

Half an hour passed, and she was still working.

"Excuse me," I said again.

"I know," she said rudely, got up, and walked away. She turned to look back at me, her gaze coldly hostile.

I was just about to sit down in the carrel when I came across an object—a stylish gold watch. I picked it up and felt its cold touch on my palm. I stared at the Roman numbers on the square face contoured with diamonds. I read the inscription. *Cartier.*

"It's mine. You can't take it."

I looked up and found the black-clad, fair-skinned, auburn-haired beauty queen.

"I am not intending on taking it." I blurted out an awkward sentence as I often did when I became stressed out. I handed the watch over to her, and she took the time to put it on her wrist, too much time as though she wanted to draw my attention, again, to the beautiful watch. Through that deliberate watch-wearing process, she shifted her eyes toward me and continued her gaze, coldly.

"It's a very pretty watch," I said, trying to be friendly.

"Gift from my father. He went to Harvard. My grandfather went to Harvard. My family gave lots of money to this place." The hostility still laced her voice.

"I don't understand," I said, trying to remain calm, "why people have to be so rude and hostile."

"If you don't belong, don't come. If you do come here, don't expect kindness," she said, carefully enunciating her words. "If you expect kindness, then you don't belong, and you ought to leave. But if you're good enough, you stay. If you aren't, you'll be crushed. Crushed."

And then she walked away.

It was then that I decided that no matter what happened, unless I dropped dead, I would graduate with honors. The beauty queen was correct about the business of being crushed. Every week, I picked up piles of reading materials from the distribution center in Pound Hall—hundreds of pages of court cases, statutory material, and long, winding law review articles, the substance and application of which should all be cramped into handwritten words rushing out onto a blue exam book at the end of the semester, which determined my future. For three years I numbed my mind and filled it with judges' decisions, law review articles, Congressional records, and statutory interpretations. The determination to go through the grinding machine to make straight As crystallized into an iron will and remained the only thing that was not crushed, wiping out my daydream about *The Merchant of Venice* and replacing it with the perpetual weariness of eyes that moved across hundreds of pages deep into the night.

I was into the second semester and was about to leave the first meeting of Criminal Procedure when a chubby blonde girl, Tanya, who lived in my dorm, ran to me with a big smile. "Congratulations, Mimi!"

"For what?"

"Your name's on the list of law review. You made law review! It means you made straight As your first semester."

The grades had not been out, and I did not believe her. I had not felt good about any of my exams. In those marathon essay exams, I never had enough time to write down all I wanted to say.

"Go to the registrar's office and see for yourself. Yours is the only foreign-sounding name on the list. Do you know what it means to be on the Harvard Law Review? I'm beginning to be a fan of yours!" Tanya hugged me.

———

Crushed. Crushed. Crushed. I told myself not to be crushed when I stood in line to look at the list of Ames moot court participants. Tanya and I had teamed up. Two tall men were in line ahead of me. "Who are you going against?" the redhead asked the blond.

"No sweat. Won't have to prepare at all. Guess who I'm against? Mimi Sean Young," the blond man said. Sean Young was how all of them had learned to pronounce my Vietnamese last name.

"You mean that pretty little Vietnamese girl?" inquired the redhead.

"I thought she was Chinese," the blond responded.

"Oh whatever she is, she's just a lamb." The redhead shrugged. "She was in my Crim Law class. Never spoke a word. She's either very shy or a mute. You'll have nothing to worry about. You can sleep through the oral argument and still win against Mimi Sean Young."

Joyfully their palms touched, making a clapping sound.

I spent the rest of the day writing my argument for moot court, went back to the dorm, ate a cold can of soup, and practiced once with Tanya. I told Tanya not to worry. I would handle the argument. She just needed to back me up with case law and be prepared for the judges' questions. "OK," she said, relieved, "it's all yours." She just wanted to ride along, and she had become my fan.

I went to bed early. Why should I work and prepare all night while I knew that my opponents would be out drinking beer on Harvard Square because they thought Mimi Sean Young was a lamb and a mute? All the preparation would just make me stutter— that awful, uncontrollable habit that doomed my existence. The next day, I went to the moot court room, delivered my argument, and answered all the judges' questions while Tanya occasionally passed me her little reminder notes. Never once did I look at the redheaded and blond guys who were my adversaries. I concluded the show with a short rebuttal. I was so cold and angry inside all through the process that the rage overpowered any nervousness, and as a result, no lump rose in my vocal cord and I did not stutter.

I glanced at Tanya and then at my wristwatch, a birthday gift from Simone. I had finished. I was left with two minutes in the allotted time.

I told the judges I would like to use my two minutes to go off the language of appellate judicial precedents and into real life because the law, after all, was about life. The judges' stern eyes sparked with curiosity, and I took it as a sign of encouragement. I took a deep breath and spoke of the short little girl from Vietnam who went to Harvard and became a lawyer and represented a tall, Amazonian black girl from Mississippi who was told by a Southern college she couldn't play competitive college basketball together with tall white and black boys because the school, which received federal funding, had segregated athletes based on sex. I spoke of what it meant to both of them, counsel and client, Vietnamese and black, to read words of equal protection from the U.S. Constitution and words of antidiscrimination from the Civil Rights Act of 1964. Both girls had to decipher all that wisdom and intent that were reduced into words to make the vast land of America great. I called them *The Words*. *The Words* had meant nothing, nothing to the little Vietnamese girl, until she had turned Harvard lawyer and had to breathe life into *The Words* to vindicate the black girl's cause. Vietnam and Mississippi had seemed so far apart before then, until counsel and client both realized *The Words* had become the bond that united two very different females into one sameness. *The Words* continued to mean nothing unless they became real life to the people who were kept apart by rules that undermined *The Words*. Let *The Words* spread that sameness throughout the land and wipe out the barriers, white and black and Vietnamese, men and women, boys and girls, I said, and closed my moot court preparation notebook.

The judges announced the result. We won. The cause of my imaginary client from Mississippi was vindicated. I skipped the shaking hands with the make-believe opposing counsel, leaving Tanya to chitchat with the redheaded and blond guys, who all this time had sent nervous, embarrassed glances my way. I went back to my carrel in Langdell Library to study.

To this day, except for the color of hair, I do not remember my moot court opponents' faces, nor their names.

Much, much later on in my legal career, I discovered the true difference between moot court and real life. Only in a moot court could I argue a constitutional point with such intense passion. In real life, I worked like a dog for corporate law firms and made good money, but the Constitution receded to its book form. The question of what had happened to ideals became a luxury, which, like time, I could no longer afford.

—

Crushed. Crushed. Crushed. I stopped Brad from twisting a strand of my hair falling on my cheek, and my mind relived the isolation of a skinny girl from Vietnam finding herself at Harvard Law School in the early 1980s. The university theaters and writing labs of SISU were quickly replaced with panel discussions, moot courts, mock trials, student-held law and business conferences for alumni, and all the hotshot personae of American corporate life, guest lectures given by important policymakers of America, and on-campus interviews with mega firms from all over the country who gathered in the grand-styled, old hotels of Cambridge to handpick their rookies.

Despite the Ames moot court competition, I remained on Harvard Yard and at the Law School as the quiet Mimi. I no longer had my long hair to wrap around my neck in fall and winter. During the three years of law school at Harvard, I never grew my hair long again and had no time to experiment with makeup, although Simone occasionally sent me rouge and lipstick from New York City's Bloomingdale's, which Tanya happily purchased from me at half their market price. I became obsessed with the As on my law school transcript. The short hair and no makeup routine simplified my existence, which consisted of classrooms, the Langdell Library, the cafeteria in the Hark Common, and my dorm room in Story Hall of the Gropias Complex, large enough to hold a twin bed, a table and a chair, my three sweaters, two pair of jeans, my winter coat, two pairs of boots, and piles of case-books and class notes. Entertainment consisted of a walk across Harvard Yard to hear the bell tolling, to watch the earliest snow-fall of the winter in Cambridge, or to sit on the grass under the first stream of spring sunshine.

I no longer watched falling leaves of autumn. They held too many memories of the Crazy Man.

Occasionally my weekend was highlighted with a movie in Harvard Square and coffee breaks with Tanya, or a few interna-tional graduate students from Asia, those who were already law-yers in their home countries and who were pursuing the post-JD degree called LLM. I instantly bonded with them because no one in the class could pronounce our last names correctly—not that we ourselves could pronounce each other's last names correctly. (At this point in my recitation, Brad stirred slightly, and I could tell he wanted me to talk about the LLM students from abroad. Some man who later became the president of a republic. But all I talked about was the girls from Asia.) There were American-born Chinese, Japanese, and Koreans at school, but they did not become part of my small circle. I was always too conscious of the fact they looked much richer than I. The knowledge sank in when one of the Asian American girls in my class told me she had just purchased a Italian-made, chocolate brown, pebble-grain leather briefcase for one thousand dollars. It didn't match her gray interview suit, so she bought another one, a different color. Her briefcase alone cost half of my year's budget for pocket money sent by Simone. But even the LLM girls from Asia had their own routines, so throughout my JD years at Harvard, I had basically kept to myself, studied alone, and avoided the chance of running into another *Steve Something* or *Steve Whatever*, another black-clad auburn-haired beauty queen with her Cartier watch, the red-headed and the blond males and all of their friends in the moot court competition, those who told me they were utterly surprised if my moot court performance could be almost, just almost, as good as theirs. *Just almost.* I was afraid I would start to believe them, no matter how hard I had tried not to. And then there was the dreaded feeling when classmates started asking where I was from and how I got here. I was afraid of being identified with the Vietnam sore of America.

I heard Brad sigh. He took my hand and stroked my palm, but I could barely feel his fingertips. I saw in my mirror the messy kitchen of Story Hall where, at midnight, I fried my *tufu*, boiled my vegetables, and wrapped my lunches and dinners for the rest of the week. During law school, I no longer ate McDonald's Big Macs. But in the dorm, I could only cook when nobody else was in the kitchen. I did not want to be self-conscious about my ingredients like soy sauce, fish sauce, *tufu*, pungent herbs, or dried shredded pork that smelled funny to everyone but myself. It was the late seventies and early eighties, and there was no Vietnamese restaurant at Harvard Square. For my Oriental ingredients I rode the Tube to Boston's Chinatown. I stopped dreaming or shedding tears at night. Perhaps my subconscious mind finally cooperated with me and accepted the fact that as a Harvard law student, I needed a kind of comatose sleep at night to avoid daytime drowsiness.

Grandma Que came to me occasionally, wearing her deep red diva lipstick and brown brocade *ao dai*. One time I saw her behind a tree in Harvard Yard, looking at the blue sky of autumn. "*Be of first lady material, wherever you're going. And this place is supposed to help you get there*?" She sounded unconvinced, her eyes pondering the green grass of the Yard. "*But if you have chosen a road, as the Phoenix of Hue you must finish, and fly high.*"

That was how I conducted my existence in the early eighties as the oddity of Harvard Law School and Harvard Yard.

—

By the time I got used to being called "Mimi" at Harvard, I had acquired a few idiosyncrasies. Harvard Law School reminded me of how it felt like to sleep nightly with my casebooks for three years. After library hours, I continued my reading in bed. In the middle of the night, when I heard a noise, I knew the casebook had fallen onto the floor, and I instantly rolled out of bed, crawled onto the floor with my eyes closed, groped around, and fumbled in the dark for my casebook. The casebook became my security blanket at night through the long Massachusetts winters. By my third year, when I was finally called a 3L, eligible to be interviewed for permanent positions with Wall Street law firms, I had become addicted to my casebook as a bed partner. I worried whether I could leave Harvard and live my life normally as a lawyer without my casebook nightly in my bed.

When I was not studying, I wrote letters to myself and mailed them to my Story Hall address. In those letters, I recorded daily events, including my Sunday afternoon blues and how I felt alienated by the carefree JD students who drank beer and partied together in the Hark Student Center. By the time I finished law school, letters that I had sent to myself filled up shoeboxes under my bed at Story Hall. Just before commencement I went through the letters. I took out a match. One by one the letters went up in flame.

There was no Crazy Man, ever, on Harvard Yard.

SEVEN

A MATTER OF LIFE AND DEATH

My earlier years in America reappeared in my mirror as a marathon whose intensity was reflected in the frown on Brad's face in the mirror.

"Who is the president of a new republic?" he asked again, still pressing his original inquiry.

I realized how tired I had become.

"What is the dream you share with him? You mentioned the dream in your diary." Brad would not give up.

The dream. My dream. I was simply tired. Too tired.

So in my malaise in the early morning hours, I thought of a way to make Brad forget the words he saw in my diary. I turned away from my mirror, and for the first time in my relationship with Brad, I initiated lovemaking to stop the strings of words and to get away from his questioning. I simply did not want conversations about the Crazy Man, as it would lead to the things I left behind in Vietnam and the fall of Saigon. I moved against the cupping of Brad's hand, thrusting my pelvis into his palm, sliding myself underneath his muscular thighs, thinking of all kinds of things I could do to silence him, and to silence myself.

We had talked enough. He had asked enough. The mirror had had enough.

Brad was a tender and quiet lover. When I held on to his shoulders, I could feel every bit of his trembling, yet I had to listen very closely to hear the sounds he made. Watching him tremble and bite his lip was so poignant for me; it was as though he wanted to control the sounds and stop them from slipping away from him, like a yoga method of restraining himself and letting himself go at the same time. This inconsistency between self-restraint and release—an impossible effort for a human—made me want to cry. It had the same nostalgic effect as Grandma Que's forlorn eyes, or the slow, grave, sensual second movement of Beethoven's *Sonata Pathetique.*

I was still trying to slip under him when he turned over on his back, placed both hands behind his head, and stared at the ceiling. He was not cooperating, and the way he was lying on his back, facing the ceiling, made him so ready, so susceptible to conversation, which was exactly what I did *not* want. His lips started to move to form words.

So I rolled on top of him. I sat up and pressed myself on him, and that part of him rose. What I was doing must have consumed him, and he was no longer able to talk. He was looking at me half lustfully, half reproachfully underneath the thick blond lashes and the brows now drawn together into an expression of disapproval. He withdrew one hand from behind his neck to make a signal for me to stop. But I did not stop, and I felt him inside me, more and more distinctively. I felt him, yet I felt nothing of myself. I hypnotized myself with my own rhythm. I had never done this to him before, and he appeared defenseless underneath me. This way I no longer had his shoulders to hold on to. I could not disguise my ruthlessness. I did all the action in a frenzy and needed nothing, nothing to hold on to. I was master of my own fate.

Terror struck me.

The mirror showed a vulgar, ruthless, and selfish woman riding a man.

Oh gosh, I was simply raping him!

Yet I kept moving on so he would not have a moment to talk. The distance between us allowed me to see his face, so clearly, his eyes closely shut, his lips tightly drawn together. The grimacing spoke of pain rather than joy.

Brad had two deep furrows running from the sides of his nose to the corners of his mouth. These furrows leavened the boyishness of his face. When he was upset, the furrows deepened and his mouth curved down a little, just a little, enough for him to look unhappy, like a child disappointed by the lack of reward for his long day of schoolwork. I was looking down onto the furrows as they deepened and the corners of his mouth turned downward, and all of a sudden the terror struck me again that I was hurting him terribly, even though he rose inside me and his hips were moving against me.

I was looking down onto the face of an unhappy man, engulfed in some unknown sadness within himself, despite the hardening of his penis.

The terror that I was raping him returned and overwhelmed me, still. The terror continued as I realized that the pleasure I was giving his penis, keeping it rising and rigid, was everything he did not want and consciously rejected. His flesh was betraying him, and I was its accomplice at best, if not the culprit, the cause. After this, perhaps I would have damaged something so precious within him, or us, that there would be a certain emotional death. Some sort of irreversible, unmendable breakage that could make my soul bleed, internally and eternally, and cause the eventual death of the "us" I saw in the mirror.

Yet I kept on moving until his hardness became that piercing, heated stream that melted my reservoir of defense. Tears rolled down my face as his hands grabbed my hips and moved me fast, signaling the end of my ability to sustain the orchestrated gap between our psyches. He filled me completely, uttering the small, restrained sounds I had become accustomed to hearing. With his eyes still tightly shut, he did not see my tears. I collapsed onto him and he still pulsed inside me, my tears damping the curly, tiny, blond hair on his chest. His arms pressed onto my back and sealed me to him. He was trembling as usual. If I looked at his face at that moment, I knew I would see him bite his lip. I bit my own to restrain my sobs.

I lay still on top of him, my cheeks pressed to his chest, my arms circling his neck, his hands resting on my buttocks. We were sealed together, until through my tears I could see the violet horizon of Hue and Grandma Que's floating coffins on the green water of the River Huong.

Those floating coffins of the past!

My childhood in Hue had come back to me at this impossible moment, for the first time with Brad next to me, together with all the hurt in my soul.

Once, in the middle of the night, Grandma Que told Simone of a recurrent nightmare—my grandmother had dreamed of floating coffins on the River Huong. She was trying to catch them in vain. She also told Simone how afraid she was of dying alone, and then described the type of funeral she would like to have. She wanted to be buried in a lacquer coffin spiced with cinnamon fragrance. She wanted all her jewelry with her, arranged a certain way. The jewelry would safeguard her lonely journey into the other world.

I had woken up in the middle of the night. Overhearing that part of their conversation, I had run, crying, to Grandma Que and pleaded with her not to talk of coffins because I hated them. Grandma Que would never die; she was supposed to live forever. Both Grandma Que and Simone comforted me that night, and ever since then I thought of floating coffins as symbolic of the mystical yet tragic River Huong of my homeland, where violet met green and clouds met water, and all those elements merged and sparkled until the whole scene turned dark. I heard again those songs and sounds of childhood, that wailing sound of the pentatonic scale on a fourteen–silk stringed Vietnamese *koto*, the Dan Tranh—the desperately sad music of the East that belonged to my childhood. The sadness that had entered my psyche since the fall of Saigon.

—

When I opened my eyes, the music of childhood had faded away and I heard instead Brad's heartbeat. The pulsing of his penis had subsided, little by little, until the part of him that bound us together withered within me. His trembling had long stopped, and he lay still, so still, like never before.

I panicked. *Oh, Brad, have you died? Has your soul departed?*

I looked up at him and saw life in the curvy mouth that I had come to love. It turned into the shape of a talking rose. He was alive. The joy was so sudden that his talk became a gift. *Oh yes, Brad, please talk. Please let me know you are alive and you have not died.*

"Oh, Mimi, Mimi." He spoke my name and moaned. "I'm just a man, Mimi. Please don't do that to me again. I wanted you, and you gave me sex. Just sex. Please don't substitute yourself with sex."

Don't substitute yourself with sex. Oh, that was what I had done. I had substituted myself with sex. Instead of giving him myself, I could only give him sex.

I cried loudly. It was impossible to combine self-restraint with the release of the inner self.

I had never cried so openly before Brad. I did not just cry. Hysteria took over, and the tears were violent and without end. I gathered myself and separated myself from him, crawling toward the floor in the whirl of tears that distorted the face I saw in the mirror. Brad moved, too, crawling after me and catching my ankle, but I kicked and landed on the floor. I moved toward the part of the mirror that was not blocked by my makeup table so that I could see all of myself, and into the mirror I began to talk. Brad appeared behind me, and his arms extended forward until they became the shawl that wrapped around me and calmed me.

—

I'll start with that day in April 1975, Brad, when the assistant principal of Trung Vuong High School went to my class to get me. "There is an emergency call for you from a relative. You are to leave immediately," she said, and I gathered all my things and ran. The Trung Vuong girls of my class were all watching. The rumor about the U.S. airlift evacuation had been all over Saigon, and I heard one of girls say, "Good luck in America." I turned around and found the dimpled, ivory face of my best friend, Xuan. "You forgot your notebook, Mi Chau," she said, and handed me the hardbound purple notebook. That was my first collection of handwritten words and hand-drawn images. It had everything that Mi Chau the schoolgirl had cherished in her young and hopeful life: poetry, words from friends, famous quotes, cryptic statements made about all the grandiose dreams ahead of the would-be first lady of the republic, sketches of naïve art that had no hidden psychic pain, etc. I was going to take a scholarship abroad, France, America, Australia, England, Japan, any developed country that would welcome a straight-A student from Vietnam sent to represent her country. And then, I would go back home to marry the man who would head the republic, realizing my grandmother's dream of a revived Nguyen Dynasty. Together the man I loved and I would build and rebuild everything. No more Land Revolution. No more Mao or Stalin. No more war. No more bloodshed. Just beautiful concepts that came straight from the textbooks chosen and published by an idealized Ministry of Education completely free from corruption. Statehood and duty, that grand notion called *noblesse oblige:* a country is made up of territory, the people, and a government. A government must represent the people. The people must be independent and free to pursue happiness. All sound so easy and so simply stated they had to be absolutely right. A schoolgirl's mind was also very simple, just like that.

But, in April of 1975, all of a sudden things did not appear simple anymore. So I had circulated this notebook, called the *luu but* in Vietnamese, to all members of the class so the girls could each write a farewell sentence or two, since the school year was about to close and the college entrance examination was supposed to take place. There was more to these farewells than that, of course, with the Vietcong taking over a city per day. No one knew what would happen to all of us in a month or so.

The notebook had been circulated to all the girls and finally to Xuan, my best friend. Xuan's father was a South Vietnamese officer who was fighting the battles to keep the Vietcong from entering Saigon, so naturally Xuan could never hop on a plane to go with the Americans while her dad was still in battle. I could, though, and the girls must have known that was the reason for the phone call. Young schoolgirls like us did not get phone calls at the principal's office. So, Xuan was telling me, again, "Good luck in America," when she gave me the notebook. Her eyes were wet, but there was no time for us to say good-bye. I took the purple notebook from Xuan and ran toward the principal's office to take this fated phone call.

It was my sister Simone on the line. She told me to go meet her at the Continental Hotel downtown Saigon. There, she would give me a list. A very important list, she said, and guarding that list would be my mission. It would serve as our pass inside the airport, our ticket to America, and she had exchanged it with her life, she said.

"What do you mean you have exchanged it with your life?" I nervously asked her, but she didn't answer. Instead, she kept repeating the phrase "life and death." The list was a matter of life and death. She said I was to go meet her immediately at the downtown hotel to receive the list from her, and to take it to the airport to meet up with the rest of our family.

I can never, never forget how Simone looked that day in the lobby of the Continental Hotel in downtown Saigon. Growing up and living in the same household with her, I had taken her for granted. I never realized how beautiful my sister was until that day, when I had to face the seriousness of the situation and the possibility that perhaps, just perhaps, I would never see her again. She was devastatingly beautiful, wearing silk trousers and a black satin *ao dai* with an embroidered dancing dragon in gold threads, and a pair of spike-heeled pumps. This was the outfit of a Vietnamese queen. What was she doing in the Continental Hotel wearing that ceremonial outfit?

Whatever she was doing, she appeared in the hotel lobby, radiantly beautiful like a flower after a hard summer shower—somewhat shaken up, somewhat worked over in stormy weather, yet surviving and enduring still, brighter, wiser, riper, triumphant, but tragically full of the kind of sorrow that denoted a measure of self-pity. That day at the Continental Hotel, I knew intuitively that something had permanently changed in her—something at the core of her young adulthood. The sheer panic of a dying Saigon alone could not have occasioned such a tragic change in my beautiful sister. She exuded both a womanly, tragic air and a heroic effort at self-control that was almost too dramatic. It showed in the way she looked at me with her sorrowful eyes. The way her luscious hair was all messy and uncombed, so unlike her normal self, her eyelashes all damp as though she had been crying. Her fingers were trembling.

It was the same Simone, but to me she had aged internally.

In agitation, she gave me the list, telling me that it contained the names of our family to be airlifted from Saigon that very night.

"Tell me first how you got the list, sis," I said. "Tell me, or I won't leave."

I kept asking, and she kept shaking her head. I knew the source of this change in her was this life-and-death list. I refused to leave, and she finally had to explain.

What she told me made no sense.

She said she had gone to the Continental Hotel in the hope of finding a way out of the country for us, and there she met an old American man, a journalist twenty-five years her senior who was there covering the war, who had a big heart, and who turned out to be a benefactor. He helped her obtain the life-and-death list. Just like that. A good-hearted benefactor who appeared out of nowhere.

"Now I have to call and explain to Dad," she said.

I watched her make the phone call to my father from the Continental Hotel lobby. They talked for a short while, and tears rolled down her face as she whispered into the mouthpiece. She had told me to stay in one spot in the lobby, yet I aimlessly walked around and around, clutching the life-and-death list in my hand.

I scrutinized the list.

My father's name appeared as the payroll clerk of the American Defense Attaché's Office, the DAO, together with his wife and two children—Pi and myself.

Neither Simone nor Grandma Que was on the list. My brain registered the hard facts, and then I rushed back and yanked the phone from Simone. I demanded an explanation. The list had to have the whole family.

"I do not matter," Simone said. "I have my own way of getting out of Vietnam, and I'll meet up with you and the family in America." She looked away from me, her voice dropping down to a stop.

"What about Grandma?" I asked, fighting the urge to cry.

Simone said she would find a way to take care of Grandma Que. The list was a fake document, but even so, she could only secure four spaces, and a grandmother was not considered part of the immediate family under the American standard of evacuation. At the airport gate, the list was to be turned over to a DAO supervisor named George so we could be admitted inside. We would board a bus, she said. Eventually, we would board a plane. Freedom commenced with the typewritten list of names I held in my hand, and the bus ride that would take us inside the airport.

The phone was dangling on the cord hanging down from the hook when she pushed me away. "Go, go, go!" she told me. We would meet soon, outside Vietnam, she promised.

"But we can't just leave Grandma Que," I stammered, and Simone had to grab my shoulders. She said it was Grandma Que who had encouraged Simone to go looking for a way to exit the country. Grandma had removed the three sacred items from the family altar—the jade phoenix and the two ivory plaques. Grandma had tucked those precious items inside Simone's handbag, telling her to give them away to the first American who would value them enough to accept them in exchange for a flight out. Westerners liked antiques and history, Grandma reasoned.

We the granddaughters both knew that to Grandma, giving those heirlooms away were the equivalent of her own death. Yes, Grandma had told Simone, death was near. To us, the bourgeois and the intelligentsia, the Communists' hatred and condemnation of the South Vietnamese middle class would mean a death sentence. So, Grandma Que urged Simone, "Go, child," pulling the strap of her purse over her shoulder.

Move on, Simone told me. To carry out Grandma Que's wish, we the granddaughters would just have to move on.

And so with the list in my hand I was supposed to carry out my part of this life-and-death mission, and Simone and Grandma Que would meet us later outside Vietnam. I had Simone's promise. But even if Simone could not show up to meet us, she said, I was supposed to move on, take care of Mom and Dad and Pi in America, and in the worst case Simone would stay in Vietnam to take care of Grandma Que, and somehow in this mess the female Buddha Quan Yin would work her compassionate wonder and keep us all together, eventually, and Grandma Que would not spend her old age alone.

She told me what to do next and shoved me to the street, urging me to rush. Mom and Dad and Pi were supposed to be at the airport gate to meet me. All I had time to do was fight Saigon's traffic in all that heat to meet up with them, before the day was over.

———

"Simone kept part of her promise, Brad. She caught up with us, months later in America, without Grandma Que. In the refugee camp in Arkansas, we both turned silent, as though we both agreed to respect an implicit code. She never explained her escape in detail, and I had no energy to inquire. She had her secrets. I had mine.

"Oh, Brad, you want to know why I turned silent? You see, Brad, something happened to me during that hasty departure from Vietnam. I did my part of the mission she assigned to me, but not exactly. I deviated from the plan. I never told anyone what really happened to me outside the airport gate, that fateful day in April 1975.

"In America, we became a family again, except there was no more Grandma Que and her two granddaughters had changed. The new Simone eventually ran away to lead her own life in the Big Apple, and I, too, became the new Mi-Chau, the college graduate, who had had to hyphenate her Vietnamese first name and who had vowed to herself that she would forget the past. And then Mi-Chau turned into the Harvard law student who changed her name to Mimi."

—

I was blurting out words between sobs. I did not know I could produce so many tears. I leaned my head against Brad's arm and talked in a trance. In the mirror I saw a hysterical woman with a tear-streaked face seeking refuge in the perspiring pinkish body of an equally panic-stricken man.

I told Brad everything, everything I could remember. What happened to me in Saigon the day when the sun died and the night took over a city trembling in its historic fever, and I was still walking outside the gate to Tan San Nhat Airport, alone.

Crawling on the floor with Brad trying to catch me, I became a bruised and broken Scheherazade, pouring out my nightmare onto him. I wanted him to look into my nightmare with me— where I had seen a face that resembled the Crazy Man.

It started on that fated day, April 27, 1975.

EIGHT
APOCALYPSE

Saigon, April 27, 1975

Oh, Brad, oh, Brad. Hold me in my nightmare, my love, sweetheart, and share this pain with me. April 27, 1975. There will never again be such a day. The day is a virus invading veins, dormant at times, active at times. Occasionally, the day escapes me completely, and all I have is a blank screen, a terrifying black hole. Yet other times all events of that day rush back, uncontrolled, jumbled, entangled before they gradually settle into black-and-white film clips. Events move, I move, time moves, yet the day never ends. It repeats itself.

It was a hot, sunny day in April, as was every April day in Saigon. I said good-bye to Simone and left the Continental Hotel on my moped and rode through downtown Saigon, a young girl in a white uniform *ao dai* like any normal Saigon schoolgirl. Out of habit, I even put on my dark shades and white gloves, supposedly to protect my eyes and hands from the burning sun—the kind of things I did every day riding on Saigon's streets in the swarming traffic typical of Saigon thoroughfares. The flaps of my *ao dai* fluttered in the hot air as I sped and cut my way through downtown. I passed by the colorful fruit stands of the Ben Thanh market, where crunchy apples and luscious grapes were wrapped in white tissue paper and piled up into fresh, palatable mounts. I passed by the fashionable kiosks of Nguyen Hue Street, onto Justice Boulevard toward the concrete bridge that connected central Saigon to the airport. I passed through rows and rows of townhouses and shanties, closely packed—typical Saigon neighborhoods. The shanties had not turned into a raging inferno, nor disappeared in any holocaust. The familiar crowded urban sight had not been set in flame. No huge fireballs careened over treetops into the sky, nor did the horizon pulse with artillery flashes. Saigon traffic was noisy as usual, but no piercing or roaring rockets numbed my ears as they had on the nights of the Tet Offensive. No rattle of gunfire echoed through the center of town. On both sides of the more isolated thoroughfares crisscrossing with tree-bordered boulevards, the inhabitants of Saigon stumbled out of their flats as usual to gaze warily across the street or to peer timidly from their mopeds parked in their front yards. On the sidewalks, peddlers and their customers congregated around their food carts, carrying on their daily gossip and consuming their midafternoon snacks. Perhaps I had unconsciously slowed down to look and gauge the mood of the city. Perhaps there was a drumhead's tension in the air. Perhaps the traffic had snarled, and the onlookers all wore dazed expressions. Perhaps fear had spread from the lobby of the Continental Hotel all over town, but on the streets of Saigon that day I saw the same city, with no sign of imminent collapse.

A day like any day. Yet I was escaping, carrying with me Simone's life-and-death list. The list was supposed to be our savior, but it also announced the possible splitting of our family, the prospect of my separation from my big sister and Grandma Que.

Then how could the sight and sounds of Saigon be so hatefully normal, on April 27, 1975?

—

It was at the airport gate that I first detected the sign of collective panic, and the meaning of life and death.

"Move, move, move," the patrolling Vietnamese MPs shouted to the agitated crowd congregating outside the gate to Tan Son Nhat airport. I parked my moped and ran toward the crowd. No one there looked like travelers well prepared for an exodus. No suitcases, trunks, or boxes of belongings. I quickly located Mom and Dad and Pi in that anxious crowd. They clustered together, lost in the panic-stricken horde of people, yet I spotted them by the Pan Am bags they each carried on their shoulders. Those Pan Am bags. I had gone to the promotional event organized by the international airline in central Saigon, and had stood in line to claim those bags for my family. I never thought then that those white-and-blue fake leather giveaway bags would one day become our getaway luggage.

My family was waiting for me, as Simone had arranged over the telephone.

My father threw a Pan Am bag at me. My family had packed for me. I looked inside the bag and found a pair of trousers, sandals, a shirt, toothpaste, toothbrush, a pen, and my address book.

"Grandma Que is not here with us," I murmured, "so we are definitely leaving without her?"

The question was lost in the clipping sounds of Vietnamese mixed with the nasal slurring of American English spoken by the few Americans present. There were women who were weeping quietly, their sobs lost in the MPs' shouted orders and threats. Two American civilians were aligning the milling crowd into a single queue—a tall, bald-headed, middle-aged man and a shorter, younger man with a fat frame and a thick black beard. The pair were intensely talking and gesturing, making their way authoritatively among the MPs. I recalled Simone's instructions—I was to find a DAO supervisor named George. Like George Washington. I had learned from history books that he was the founding father of America.

"Stay here and wait for me," I told my father, pressing the life-and-death list into his palm. I tied the two flaps of my uniform *ao dai* together into a knot and crouched, then dashed, small and feline, right into the crowd and cut my way through the swelling mass of people toward the two Americans. I was ready to rip and claw my way through, if necessary, but then I found myself close to where the two Americans were standing, each holding a stack of papers in his hands. I stood panting, trying to listen to them. I had learned enough English in high school, yet I had to strain to understand their slurred American English.

"Look at this madness," said the bald man. "I'm dead, man. Dead on my feet. Tell me this is the last of them."

"There are more of them," the bearded man muttered wearily, "still waiting at the DAO movie theater, huts and gymnasium, and the DAO PX. There's a world of them."

—

Oh, Brad, Brad, please hold me. Love me, love me please, full and whole, and help me forget. But it is too late now, Brad, because it all happened and once it happened, it stayed on. Everything is coming back to me now so clear, so vivid. It's like an old movie, Brad. In that old movie, every frame of events was captured and stayed locked, forever and forever, in a place called memory. The heat. The sun. The crowd and those two American men who worked so hard like two machines to process us. I was awed. Just awed by them. Where are they now, Brad? The war was over and where did they go, these two American officials? Back to their home, America?

Where? Kansas, Illinois, Wisconsin, Pennsylvania, or California? Did they remember me at all, the young girl who pleaded for their help? Me, my weeping mother, my panic-stricken bespectacled father, and Pi, my little brother who got sick under Saigon's sun? We were outside the airport gate, in that desperate crowd.

There was "George," like in George Washington, the star of my world history book, but this George was short and stocky, and he said he was once Juan from Havana, who sympathized. He had a beard. And then there was that bald man, the older man who was there with George. Kirk, tall and lanky and pale. They were talking and talking, and I strained to listen. I used all of the English ability I had acquired as the straight-A schoolgirl who later found out, in America, she had the IQ of a genius. You see, even in Vietnam I spoke and understood English like a champ, having been chosen as the English rhetoric contestant for my high school to compete nationwide at the Vietnamese American Association on Mac Dinh Chi Street. We knew it then as the VAA, the promotional center of America's cultural presence in the heart of Saigon. Ironically, it was located on the same street that held the cemetery of South Vietnamese officers who died for their country in the war. At the VAA, President Richard Nixon had been replaced by President Gerald Ford as the honorary chair for the promotion of Vietnamese and American diplomatic friendship. I was told that if I won the rhetoric contest, I might receive a congratulatory note from President Nixon himself, forwarded by the VAA. America was our friend and ally, so the president of America definitely could care for the one and only girl who won the VAA English rhetoric contest! But there was never any English rhetoric contest organized by America for Saigon's youth, because the city fell and Russian tanks rolled in. I did not find myself at the podium for the long-desired contest. Instead, I found myself in front of the airport. So I used my English proficiency a different way, to listen to and memorize George's and Kirk's words.

That April afternoon I understood all those words spoken by the two Americans outside the airport gate, as they talked among themselves, thinking that the Vietnamese evacuees did not understand their private conversations. These words I overheard firmly registered in my confused mind during that one fated afternoon. For years and years I thought I had forgotten them all, but no, no they were still here, so fresh, so real as though spoken just yesterday. I remembered every word. Those words did not die with that day in April.

It's death, death, death, Brad. Now, Death with a capital D. Listen to me, listen to me, listen to the little girl! She had had to listen herself, trying to remember every word from George and Kirk because she wanted her family to be inside the airport, and those words might paint the way out. She had to be intelligent and resourceful. She needed to understand what was going on with the country. That meant paying close attention to words.

Words, words, words.

George and Kirk said they had stayed up around the clock, two conscientious American officials responsible for the evacuation. They worked the chutes in those fragile wood- and tin-framed buildings, the new DAO headquarters called Dodge City. Now that quaint name came back to me. The DAO was called Dodge City. Some of the Americans were still operating out of the Caravelle Hotel, laboring around the clock, secreting funneling Vietnamese into the processing center.

They mentioned their big boss.

The big boss had a name: Mr. Martin, the ambassador. The bald man, Kirk, asked if the big boss had ordered all processing of evacuees to be moved to the DAO annex. Among the brown-skinned Vietnamese, Kirk's freckled face was chalk-white, glazed with glistening sweat in the hot and humid air of April.

George said no, not the ambassador. Mr. Martin was sick like a dog and couldn't make up his mind on anything. It was the guys in the personnel division who prepared passenger manifests that moved the evacuation to the DAO. The air force and navy officers shared the onerous tasks of checking luggage for firearms and drugs. But on April 27, 1975, there was no more time for that. They said the evacuation was into "accelerated draw-down." They had to get on with the "nonessential" lists for the DAO. Were people like us on these nonessential lists? That day in April George and Kirk said it was just a short bus ride to the marshaling area near the DAO swimming pool. From there, Kirk and George would continue to haul the evacuees in vans or buses or even by a short walk to the flight line across the highway inside the air base.

They said they were not being yanked out prematurely, but they were as angry as the rest of the country and the South Vietnamese who panicked. They said that the average Vietnamese out there might not see what had been going on, but the city was a sizzling fuse. People were being put on vessels on the Saigon River to sail out at sea. Possibility of a river-borne evacuation to supplement the airlift. And all those black-market flights—slipping Vietnamese illegally onto the military airlift. The shrinkage of the foreign community in Saigon had aggravated tension, and Washington was not helping the guys on the ground like Kirk and George, let alone the desperate Vietnamese like us all over the city. Kind Mr. George, he said he wished he could find all those stunned Vietnamese a place in the chutes. But then Kirk told George not to be sentimental, even if George had gone through the Havana evacuation himself as a Cuban.

The sentimental George from Havana! He had the same first name as the forefather of my new country, and that day in April he made me a promise!

Oh, Brad, for the rest of my life how can I ever forget the name George?

—

That April afternoon, my ears had perked up at the sound of that name. The hope of survival came full and fine when I discovered I had found George. I had had to crawl by a few blocking bodies to face him. I stammered into his face. "Are you really George?"

"Yes." The younger American with the black beard focused on me. "I am George."

I turned and yelled across the crowd. "Dad! George is over here!"

My father heard me and was struggling against the crowd to get to me. Before my blurry eyes that day, the crowd moved like a wave, swept and swayed like wheat stalks in a strong wind. I kept my eyes focused on my father's bobbing bookworm glasses, which moved along in that human wave. He raised one hand over his head, cutting his way through the crowd, clutching the life-and-death list tightly with his fingers, guarding it above him like a sacred candle. Even with his tight grip, the piece of paper appeared vulnerable, moving above the wave of people as though dangling in the air.

"Over here, Dad!" I jumped out in front of the two Americans and waved my father over to them.

"Which one of you is George?" my father panted as he arrived before them, clutching the life-and-death list in his hand.

"I am George," the young bearded man repeated. "You and your family'd better hurry." He took the list from my father's hand and scanned it. He looked at my father skeptically. "What do you do, sir?"

"My father automatically blurted out the truth. "I teach at the university…"

Oh no, I lamented in my head. My father had screwed up our chance! I yelled defensively, "No, Mr. George! Don't take that to be true. I know it's not true. He is too tired; he doesn't know what he is saying. He is a DAO payroll clerk, and I am his daughter!"

My father's face reddened and then gradually turned pale and somber. Poor Dad, he remained silent, unable to react or correct his inadvertent mistake. The mistake of a schoolteacher's honesty, made under extreme stress. George put a finger on the tip of his big nose, pondering.

"What will happen to us, George?" my father finally said, trembling, enunciating his self-conscious English.

"Not everybody in this weeping crowd can leave," George said with a frown. "I can load only about a third of them. You, sir, apparently are a fraud—but you are an honest fraud, for a change, and your daughter is quick-witted, so I am going to put you and your family on the plane. What the heck, I'm Cuban; I used to be little Juan from Havana. You just arrived in time to catch the last bus for the day. To the DAO processing center inside the compound, and then to the airport runway. There's a pickup tonight. There may not be tomorrow, you understand."

The long bus rolled in, and George and Kirk shuttled among the crowd of anxious Vietnamese, ignoring their pleas, cries, and quarrels. The crowd had grown into a seething mob, pushing and shoving their way toward the bus door. The rest were shunted into long lines of passengers. Heavily armed Vietnamese police and MPs drew up a cordon around the bus to keep the crowd under control.

We stood well back in a long and lengthening line. Pi had squatted down on the ground, complaining constantly that he wanted some water to cool down in the heat, and my father had to yell at the child. I left Mom and Dad and Pi standing in line and wandered toward my moped. I opened my schoolgirl briefcase and tore a piece of paper out of my notebook. Leaning on the saddle, I wrote to Grandma Que. *Wait for me. I'll come back to be with you. Please don't give up on me.* I cried with each word. When I finished, I folded the paper and wrote our address in District Eight on the other side. I caught sight of myself in the rearview mirror of the moped. My face was swollen and my eyes red from emotional exhaustion and too much crying.

I returned to my family as they approached the bus door. They boarded ahead of me. As I mounted the step after them, something clicked in my head and I paused, craning my neck back to take one last look at the sky over Saigon. The afternoon was still hot and bright, and beads of sweat dropped down my hairline. I began to see the *longan* nuts in Grandma's Que mournful eyes in the white clouds that floated above. I looked at the letter I had written to Grandma Que, still clutched in my hand.

On the bottom step of the bus, I turned and gave my letter to George, who stood by the bus with his papers. "Will you mail this letter, please?" I pleaded, choking back tears. "It's my farewell to my grandmother."

"Yes," he said, taking the letter from me. His dark eyes were kind, and he patted lightly on the top of my hand. "Don't worry. Move on."

"It's very important to me, Mr. George. I promised her I will be back. You promise you will mail this right away, tonight?" I swallowed down the surge of tears.

"I promise," he said.

Somehow I was not assured by him; his voice was kind but mechanical. He was not looking at me but was wiping the sweat off his forehead and his dark beard, his eyes darting toward the end of the line of passengers. I was holding up the line. I heard Kirk shouting at the end of the line, "Move on! What's going on up there?"

Without him noticing, I slipped off the bottom step of the bus entrance and stepped down behind George. People were pressing against one another to squeeze themselves into the narrow door of the bus, and George was busy checking off his list, unaware of my movement and too busy to notice my action. The shell-shocked Vietnamese kept passing by him, one by one, to board. I sneaked behind his back. From there, looking up at the bus windows, I could see my parents looking for a seat. Quietly, I stayed behind George, unable to move. Something unexplainable was holding my feet in place, telling me to stand still. More and more people were boarding the bus. Kirk was approaching and the two Americans talked among themselves, blind to my presence.

"What was that all about, George?" Kirk said. "Who was holding up the line?"

"The schoolgirl worrying about her grandmother. She tried to take care of her distressed father earlier. And now it's her grandmother. Poor child wanting me to mail a letter to her grandmother who stayed behind. Yeah, right. Are you kidding? The Vietcong are marching in, and will there even be a post office?"

I jumped out from behind George. "You lied to me, Mr. George!" I screamed through the film of tears.

When I looked up, I saw my mother's panicked face pressed against a side window of the bus, looking sideways toward where I stood. She was waving her hand at me.

"Get on the bus, miss," Kirk barked.

"No! No!" I cried.

An MP sauntered over to me, his hand playing ominously over the gun on his hip. "Get on the bus," he said, "if you want to leave."

"No! Please!" I could hardly see through my tears. "Can you wait for me? I must go get my grandmother."

"So leave the line immediately, or I'll shoot," the MP said coldly. He touched the gun dangling on his hip, but I continued standing still.

My father's face appeared at the bus entrance. "What are you doing, Mi Chau? Get in!" he yelled at the top of his lungs over the curses of the horde of people in line behind me.

"No, no, no," I stuttered on. "I must go home first." A lump blocked my throat, and I could not articulate why I was not ready to board.

"Nonsense!" my father shouted hoarsely. "Get in!" The oncoming wave of passengers was pushing him aside, smashing him against the door, and the anxious evacuees behind me were protesting our blockade.

"No," I despaired, and the words finally escaped my mouth. "It's Grandma. I can't leave just yet."

My mother appeared behind my father. She was climbing over my father to reach me, pushing against the boarding line. She wanted out of the bus. My father attempted to hold her in place and pushed her back inside. My parents struggled at the bus entrance. I turned my head away and moved from the bus so I could no longer see them.

"Let me go! Let me go!" I heard my mother sobbing, her wailing in Vietnamese chasing me. "You take Pi to America alone. Our two daughters are in Saigon, together with my mother. I can't leave them. Let me go!"

My mother's heartbreaking voice trailed behind me. "My mother! It's my mother! My daughter is going back home for my mother. I am going home with my daughter and my mother!"

"No!" I turned back, parted the curious crowd, and reached out for my mother, who was leaning on the bus door at the top of the steps. "You stay!" I pushed her back inside. My father was holding on to her.

Slowly, I backed away from the bus. My feet felt incredibly heavy, and I was dragging them on. I shouted to my father during this excruciating process of dragging myself away from the bus, "I'm gone for an hour. I'll be back with Grandma. Both of us. I'll find the DAO headquarters. I'll find the airport runway. Trust me. I promise. Just wait for me inside the airport, wherever they put you!"

I was quivering, and my limbs had turned cold and weak. My father was about to jump out of the bus to go after me. I cried out, "No! Stay there, Dad!"

"All of you get back inside, or I'll shoot!" the MP shouted and stepped toward my father, one of his hands resting on his gun, his other hand pushing against my father's face.

I saw George step up and try to separate the MP from my father. "Let her go, for now," he said, then turned to my father. "Otherwise, all of you stay. I'll come back for her later. She'll be back." George turned toward me and shouted, "Be back here at five o'clock. I'll come back with the bus. Look for me, kid," the kind man said, then grabbed my father's arm and shoved him inside.

The bus was slowly moving and the door was about to close, except that George was hanging at the door. He turned toward me as the bus rolled on. "Five o'clock," he said. "Remember, look for me or the bus, or jump onto any army jeep if you can."

———

"Jump onto any army jeep if you can"—the words of the American named George registered firmly onto my mind.

I still saw my father's face underneath George's arm.

"Keep this!" My father threw a Pan Am bag at me, just before the door was completely closed.

The bus was moving faster. I saw Mom, Dad, and Pi rushing toward the back window. They were all reaching out for me, their mouths moving, but I could no longer hear them. I saw the wide-open eyes of my brother Pi and his tiny, extending hands next to my mother's red nose and tearful eyes. I caught a glimpse of the trembling downward curve of my father's mouth. His was the drawn face of farewell, without a trace of hope.

I ran toward my moped. I could still hear the bus engine behind me. I turned back once more to look.

Everything became a silent movie at that point. The last thing I saw at the back of the bus was my mother's slender frame moving frantically along the aisle, her fragile frame finally leaning against the back window of the bus. I saw her distorted face pressed against the glass window, as though the glass had become a sheer mask that compressed and deformed her facial features. Her lips moved against the glass. She was speaking into the glass, but I could no longer hear her.

The bus rolled away, and I was left outside Tan Son Nhat airport, together with the weeping crowd consisting of those who were denied access to the departure and those who had decided to stay.

Leaning against my moped, I unzipped and looked inside the Pan Am bag my father had managed to throw at me before the bus rolled on. My eyes became myopic at the pale green color that filled up the bag. All cash—brand-new Vietnamese *dong*, fresh-smelling and unwrinkled, tied neatly into bundles with rubber bands. For a moment, the smell of new money and fresh paper numbed my senses, and the sight of green blinded me. I had never seen that much cash in one place.

This must have been my family's life savings!

Sunlight was turning orange over the iron gate to Tan Son Nhat airport as I turned on my moped's engine and rode home. Down Justice Boulevard. On to the Turtle Square where a marble turtle stood in solitude in the center of a water fountain, marking the center of fashionable Saigon. On to Le Van Duyet street and District Eight.

Back to Grandma Que.

—

The small alley. Deep down into the back of the familiar alley in District Eight. My moped dashed through like an arrow. I rode like a warrior, with a purpose, oblivious to the bumps on the road that sent me up and down the saddle of my little moped.

I was approaching the alley's familiar dead-end. A small turn, and then I would be at the entrance of our townhouse—the familiar aluminum double doors between two concrete pillars leading to the enclosed, cement front patio. I had slowed to make the turn when I caught glimpse of Grandma Que standing at the entrance of our home. She stood alone, sad and lost, leaning onto the aluminum door around the corner from the alley. She had on a cone hat and a gray cotton blouse over black trousers—the traditional button-front blouse called *ao baba*, the South Vietnamese version of the Malays' *sarong cabaya* top.

Our eyes met for a fleeting second. She did not smile, and her brows raised into a question, very quickly, before she abruptly turned away, took off the cone hat, and disappeared behind the set of aluminum doors.

It was a split-second meeting of the eyes, and I saw so vividly her black *longan* eyes, the sadness within, and the farewell message.

Ngoai oi. Grandma!

I cried to her a sound of joy. But she was gone. The short path all of a sudden became a thousand miles.

I stopped the engine of my moped and pounded on the closed doors.

"*Ngoai oi!*" I yelled. "Grandma, open up!"

I must have yelled a thousand times.

No sound from inside. The doors did not move.

What felt like a decade passed, and within that decade I must have called out to Buddha, Jesus, Quan Yin, and all gods, saints, deities, and holy spirits. I knelt down before the entrance, pressed my cheeks against the aluminum doors, and cried.

Between tears I pounded on the closed doors until I could pound no more, my knuckles hurt so. I stopped pounding to sort through my confused mind. My grandmother had deliberately chosen not to open the door. She wanted to send me away. She did not want the good-bye heartbreak. She did not want to leave Saigon.

I knelt before the entrance to my home in District Eight, Saigon, where I had spent my childhood. The flaps of my white *ao dai* were stained with dirt. I placed my mouth against the cold, dusty surface of the aluminum doors and talked to her.

"Pack a Pan Am bag, Grandma," I said. "Oh no no, you don't even need to pack. Just leave. Leave with me. We'll get on a bus, and then a plane. Come on come on come on, we have to be back at the airport by five to meet an American named George. Go with me please," I sobbed.

The doors did not move.

I stared at the set of aluminum doors, and through them I imagined the sadness of her *longan* eyes looking out.

I knew, then, that the pain of separation in life was harsher than in death.

Someone was tapping my shoulders. I turned around and faced another pair of eyes. Slanting almond shape under dark eyebrows on a slender oval face, a little bluish in the chin. It was the fifteen-year-old son of our neighbor, my friend Nam. Nam was my only friend in the neighborhood. We had known each other for years.

"I talked to her earlier, Mi Chau." Nam was holding my shoulders. "She said a grandmother isn't supposed to go on the exit list that the Americans would approve. If she goes along, she can cause trouble for all of you and maybe the Americans won't let all of you leave because of her."

"Oh no, no, no, no," I wept.

"She wants you to go. She told me so," Nam said. "She said she would be fine. When the Vietcong come, they won't waste a bullet on an old woman, whom they once called mother of the revolution. She'll be fine in Vietnam and no good in America, she told me. Now go, Mi Chau, I'll stay here and keep her company."

I was still weeping.

"I'll take care of her," he said. I saw reassurance in his almond eyes.

My tears dwindled down, and then my sobs subsided into hiccoughs. "You promise? To take care of her on my behalf?" Finally I was able to speak intelligibly.

"I promise," he said, his almond eyes confirming his promise. "She'll be all right."

"No, she won't." I broke out in tears and my sobs returned. Somehow I just knew then, deep in my heart, that she would die one day, soon, wilting away, and I would be somewhere on the other side of the ocean.

"Black lacquer bed and lots of jewelry," I said in between waves of tears and hiccups. "Put her on a lacquer bed and have her wear a lot of jewelry. She wants all those things." I was dictating to Nam the funeral Grandma Que would want for herself.

"I promise." Once more the almond eyes gave assurance.

I turned on the engine of my moped and tied the two flaps of my *ao dai* into a knot.

"Please don't cry, Mi Chau," Nam said. "You are going to America, where there are golden leaves, pink flowers, and carnivals." Nam touched my hand.

"Carnivals?" Too much crying and confusion caused me to lose my capacity for speech; I was merely repeating after him. "Carnivals, carnivals, carnivals…"

Nam was my childhood friend. We hung out together in the small alleys of our neighborhood in Saigon's District Eight. We often talked about supermarkets, drive-in theaters, amusement parks, and carnivals in America—the things we read about from an English textbook called *English for Today.*

Upon the death of a city and the foreseen death of my beloved grandmother, there were supposed to be carnivals where I was heading. Clowns. Balloons. Somersaulting dancers. Cotton candies and multicolored paper cups. American Coca-Cola and chewing gum. All these among pink flowers and golden leaves typifying the change of seasons that was not found in tropical Southeast Asia.

I looked at the alley of District Eight one last time and envisioned Grandma Que as I last saw her. No more Madame Cinnamon. No more princess of the South Sea Pearl, the proud daughter of the royal Mystique Concubine of the Nguyen Dynasty. Just a pair of *longan* eyes fading into old age, a Vietnamese cone hat, salt-and-pepper hair in a bun, and black trousers and an old gray cotton *ao baba* blouse hanging over a fragile frame—a frail old Vietnamese woman standing in a Saigon alley, alone, one hot April day, with a sad countenance that spoke a hundred years of history and stories of separation and death.

Nam helped me get on the moped. "Wait a minute." He produced a roll of paper, fastened with a rubber band. "I made this for you," he said. "Take it to America."

Through the film of tears that blurred my eyes, I unrolled the paper and saw a watercolor painting of a forest with lots of red and golden leaves. My tears fell onto the paper and smeared the pointed tip of a golden leaf. Nam helped me roll his watercolor painting, and I threw the roll into the basket hung at the front of my moped, where the two Pan Am bags and my schoolgirl briefcase sat.

"Your sister Simone told me that in the West, leaves turn red and golden before they crumble. So I painted a red and gold forest for you," Nam said.

I wiped my tears and pressed my foot on the gas pedal.

"Don't look back," Nam yelled. "Go, go, go where you can do anything you want without fear. It will be beautiful where you go. Forests with red and golden leaves, gardens full of pink flowers, and colorful carnivals. Arrive safely in America. Who knows, one day, we'll be sending each other postcards. Plenty of postcards!"

—

Four forty. The afternoon of April 27, 1975. I was back at the gate in front of Tan Son Nhat airport twenty minutes before the hour. The crowd had dispersed. The line of patrolling MPs had thinned out. The sun was escaping behind those gray and orange tile roofs. Sunshine gradually turned mustard yellow, the color of dusk.

I walked around and around, conscious of the pain in my craned neck. The humidity of the air seemed to stick uncomfortably to my face. My shoulders felt heavy, and my skin felt sticky with sweat. My white schoolgirl *ao dai* was muddied and wrinkled. I saw no sign of George or the bus, and continued to walk my aimless steps. The remaining MPs, distracted and tired, let me roam because the gate was securely closed.

Five forty. Still no sign of George, or a bus. I touched the barricade and attempted to lift the bar to the gate. No use. It was tightly secured. A tall American MP shouted at me. "Stop! You want to get shot?"

"I must get inside!" I screamed back at him.

"Go home, miss. Tomorrow there'll be another crowd gathering and waiting. You can try tomorrow."

"My family is already inside the DAO compound. I must join them," I yelled again, my voice hoarse and flat.

The MP looked gravely at me. "All DAO pickups ended at four today."

"No," I voiced my despair. "I am promised another pickup at five by Mr. George, the DAO supervisor. He has my list. I'm on it. Please open the gate."

The MP touched his gun. "I know no Mr. George. I know no list. I will shoot you, and I won't open the gate. So go away."

Slowly, I backed away toward my moped. I rested my hands, and then my face, on its handlebars. I wept.

This was all hopeless.

I walked toward the row of houses just outside the airport gate, underneath rows of cooling tamarind trees. My disoriented mind wandered along in the shade of those trees. They were not tall and strong *longan* trees for healthy babies and happy adults, in a world where there could be no apocalypse like this day in April.

Small, dark alleys separated rows of square-box townhouses, typical of Saigon's neighborhoods. Small, scattered crowds of people were still congregating along the streets leading to the airport gate. Rows of parked mopeds bordered those streets, perhaps abandoned by those who had departed. My temples throbbed. My limbs felt heavy. I kept wandering around in hopes of seeing a familiar face, a familiar sight.

I spotted a jeep parking alongside an alley, underneath a tree shade. My heart leaped in joy, as I recalled George's words: "Hop in any army jeep, if you can." Relieved and rejuvenated, I ran toward the sight of hope.

A brown, pockmarked face looked out at me from the driver's side of the jeep, and all my hopes vanished. The man sitting in the driver's seat, breathing heavily, signaled for me to come close. He pinned the greedy gaze of his bloodshot eyes onto my torso. I took one step closer and smelled the heavy odor of Vietnamese hard alcohol, the *ruou de*. An odious sneer appeared on the stranger's face, showing his stained, brown teeth. His protruding lips, purplish and vile like pieces of rotten meat, vibrated slightly behind the rim of the white bottle he was holding in one hand. He was gulping down the colorless substance, smacking his lips with each swallow.

He pulled the bottle away and said, "Hello, beautiful. Call me Cho Den. The gang knows me by that name."

The foul-smelling creature of a man did indeed look like a pit bull, as he called himself. He slouched behind the wheel, empty white glass bottles and beer cans scattered around in the passenger seat on his right. He wiped his mouth with his sleeve, his bloodshot eyes affixed on me.

"Looking for me, *em be*?"

He had just called me his infant sister.

It was dark inside the jeep. I bent and craned my neck to look more closely in at the back seats. My eyes longed for any sign of George, only to be met with the disarray of more empty "Beer 33" bottles. The doglike man was extending his chapped fingers to touch my hair. "I am waiting for you, *em be*."

As he leaned forward, a beam of fading sunlight hit his body, and I saw that he was wearing the green South Vietnamese army uniform. Again my hope surged. He just said he had been waiting for me.

"Are you a South Vietnamese soldier, sent by Mr. George, the DAO supervisor, to meet me?"

"Right on, *em be*."

"You work with Mr. George and Mr. Kirk in the American evacuation?"

"Sure."

Somehow I was not convinced. My throbbing head attempted to reason. Before I could figure out a way to test him, the foul man cut off my chance to think. "Don't you trust me? I told you I work for Mr. George all right. The whole fucking country has been working for Mr. George. That's why I am here in this fucking place, because we all work for Mr. George, and I deserve better than the crock of shit coming from that suspicious look of yours."

I winced, repulsed by his obscenities, and dashed my eyes around the deserted alley. The last rays of the day's sun were stretching across the street, sluggish in the humidity of April. Particles of dust danced in the yellowish trace of sunlight. Night would be falling soon.

"Want to hop in? I can take you anywhere in this jeep." The foul man tapped on the passenger seat, clearing the empty glass bottles. He looked at me up and down.

I looked back at him and quietly reviewed my options. He was right. George did tell me to jump into any army jeep. This foul man's jeep was my last hope, and he was, after all, a man in uniform. Or I could go home to Grandma Que, who was determined to shut the door and would rather see me go to America. I would have partly failed the mission Simone had entrusted to me, and would never see Mom and Dad and Pi again. I did promise them we would meet in America, yet I deviated from Simone's instructions and had not tried my very best.

What a fool I had been.

I was just about to hop in the jeep with Pit Bull when my instinct stopped me, and I backed away from the jeep a few steps. Staring at the passenger door, I grew ambivalent. I was still trying to reason through my confused head when the ill-smelling soldier, behaving like a sniffing pit bull, moved his protruding purplish lips and stuck out his tongue to lick them, his bloodshot eyes darting up and down the frame of my *ao dai*. When I told him I needed to meet up with my parents inside the airport, he threw the glass bottle of *ruou de* angrily to the street, where it shattered with a crashing noise.

"So you're one of those privileged few, huh?" He stared at me with hatred.

I stopped talking, uncertain why he suddenly sounded so hostile.

"Getting a space out on a plane before the Vietcong get here, huh?" He was yelling at me.

I tried to talk, but he put a finger to his mouth, displaying his ragged nail, blackened around its corner. He was making a *hush* sound. "Hold your tongue and seal your lips, right now, or else I won't take you where you want to go. Rich parents, connected to the Americans, huh?"

He continued hissing between his syllables, his saliva foaming around his mouth. "Mr. George, high-ranked American, can help you flee, huh?" He jumped out of the jeep, walked around its front, and moved toward me. "So who's fighting this fucking war, if all of you just hop on a plane and flee?"

The sheer hostility of his words frightened me, and I did not know how to react. Yes, I would stay and fight if that meant the solution for the despair of this day in April, although I was just a high school girl who did not know how to shoot a gun. Pit Bull kept hissing at me like a venomous snake. His eyes were dilated, and the alcohol smell emanating from his mouth made me nauseous.

"I'll die in the jungle, in a jail, VC bullet shooting through my ass, and you and your precious family will be on the plane supplied by my American allies, heading to a resort, huh?"

He was in a rage, and he was vulgar. He was also drunk. But he wore a green soldier uniform and he was my only hope. I felt the need to justify myself. I told him my father was just a teacher, not a high-ranked official who abandoned his troops to leave the country. But my father was connected to the West. He was an educated man. We were considered middle-class Vietnamese and the Vietcong did not like us. It was common knowledge.

"Of course I believe you, *cung oi.*" He'd just called me little darling. His stinking, alcohol breath lingered on me, and I had to step away from him. "I'll help you find your family inside. That's what I've been doing all day. Getting paid to take people inside the gate in this jeep."

His talk reminded me immediately of my father's Pan Am bag stacked with freshly issued Vietnamese currencies, the *dong.* Thank God my father had tossed it to me! All of a sudden I felt confident. I had the means to ask for a favor from this man, whether or not he was sent by George, and regardless of how meanly he behaved. I could buy a ticket inside the airport.

"Mr. George is over there!" Pit Bull pointed to a dark little house around the corner. A few mopeds were parked inside its fence. The front yard had a huge tamarind tree. "We officers congregate with our American allies over there. Mr. George is just taking a nap waiting for you. He sent me out looking for you." Pit Bull was laughing as though he were mad.

My instinct took over again and I bit on one of my nails, my finger between my teeth. I should not believe him. I should test him.

"Will you describe Mr. George?" I asked.

"Sure, he is a *thang My trang*," he said, describing George as the "white American dude."

"Your George is neither young nor old, but tall and hairy like all *thang My trang*," he added.

"Not too tall," I corrected him.

"Come on, taller than Vietnamese dudes, the yellow shorties like your brother Pit Bull here," he said.

"Does he have a beard?" I probed.

"Sure he has a beard. Those American guys, they are all hairy."

I paused, trying to think of more things to ask. Pit Bull was getting more impatient and threatening. "I've had enough of you, little girl. I'm going to leave you here. You trust this American George to help you flee, but you won't trust your *dongbao*." He pointed to himself, as if I had forgotten he was my fellow countryman. "Come on. Do you want to meet up with your parents or not? Come with me to the house over there to see your Mr. George, before I change my mind."

I looked around for the last time. There was no other alternative. I had to get inside the gate tonight. I recalled George's words: "There is a pickup tonight, and there won't be tomorrow, you understand."

I gathered into my arms the two Pan Am bags—one full of the Vietnamese *dong* and one with my emergency belongings. I also had in my arms my schoolgirl briefcase and Nam's watercolor painting.

With my arms full, I went with him. The dark house was less than fifty yards away.

—

I followed Pit Bull to the townhouse and stopped momentarily at the chipped wooden door, slightly ajar. I could see a glimpse of the inside—dark and hideous, with dirty orange curtains and dark gray cement flooring. I heard voices of men inside—curse words in the crude southern accent of street Saigonese, in competition with the static coming from some broken radio.

Again my instincts took over. I turned around, intending to run back to the alley, but it was too late. Pit Bull had kicked the door wide open and was grabbing my arms. I started screaming, and he put a hand over my mouth. In less than a minute, he had me restrained, and I found myself dragged inside the house, the load of Pan Am bags and my schoolgirl briefcase pressed to my chest. My eyes could not focus in the dark, and I smelled mildew.

"Sh, sh, sh. Calm down. I'll take you inside the airport." Pit Bull nibbled on my left ear. The smell of hard alcohol and sour sweat emanating from him sickened me. He twisted my arms, and I had to bend and swing around to alleviate the pain. I dropped all my things, and they scattered all over the cement floor. Pit Bull had locked me in place with his arms, my back pressed tightly against his stomach, and I could not move.

Pushed, I lost my balance and fell onto the cement floor. I groped around, trying to gain my bearings. In the reddish light from an old lantern, I found two more Vietnamese men in the room, one stout and stocky, one toothpick-skinny, both shirtless, unkempt, and sweaty. I caught sight of their dusty army boots, knocked all over the floor, and damp socks hung on the iron headboard of a rusty hospital bed. The two men sat on the bed, among glass bottles of *ruou de* and Beer 33.

Before I could fully grasp the danger of this company, I heard the door shut. Instinctively I turned and attempted to head toward the door, but it was already tightly closed and Pit Bull was leaning against it.

"Where is Mr. George?" I tried to speak calmly.

"I am George." From the bed, the stocky man grinned broadly at me. I shivered at the sight of his gold teeth.

"What do you have there?" the skinny man howled at Pit Bull, pointing one finger at me.

"*Plush bo lac*," A lost pet, Pit Bull had just called me.

I thought of the *dong* inside my Pan Am bag. "I have money," I said. "I'll give you all of my money if you take me inside the airport." I picked up the Pan Am bag from the floor.

Pit Bull walked over to the old armoire in the farthest corner of the room, and motioned to me. "Take your money over here. I'll lock it up in this armoire, and then we'll go inside the airport. You'd better have a lot of money. If you try to cheat, I'll give you a good beating, *em be*."

Taking small steps, I moved toward him, bringing myself farther and farther from the shut door, deeper and deeper into the dark room. Pit Bull opened the armoire and grabbed a handful of some rectangular pieces wrapped in brown paper, imprinted with red ink. He held one to my face.

"See, these are gold taels. That's what it takes to get my assistance in this rescue mission." He stuck his tongue out at me and attempted to lick my cheek. I jerked back, wincing.

"I don't have gold taels," I said, trying to stand straight. "You can have what's in this." I handed my Pan Am bag over, and he clutched the zipper. He yanked it open, turning the bag upside down. Bundles of green *dong* fell onto the floor. A rubber band broke, and more green *dong* danced in the air. Pit Bull picked up one bundle, ripped it apart, and threw it at the two men sitting on the hospital bed. The money scattered onto the two men, all over the rusty hospital bed, and brightened the filthy floor.

Pit Bull's palm slapped across my face. I fell to the ground and saw stars, too stunned to feel the hurt.

"Fuck you. You think I'm stupid? I want American dollars. These are worthless." He turned to the other two men. "*Du me*," he spit out the worst Vietnamese curseword, motherfucker. "She cheated me. Missy here has connections to the DAO. Hear it, connections to the DAO." He stressed the last few words, pausing contemptuously on the word *DAO*.

"She wants me"—he beat on his chest—"me, the gang's Pit Bull, to take her inside the airport, to those fucking American allies, who'll give her plenty of dollars while I have none."

Pit Bull raised his hand again and was about to hit my face, but I crawled under his armpit and escaped the blow. I said in despair, appealing to his humanity, "You are a South Vietnamese soldier. You are supposed to help me."

"Are you nuts? Me, I'm no soldier, missy. I defected a long time ago to become the gang's Pit Bull. These uniforms can be bought at the flea market."

Too numb to react, I fully realized my peril. I was in the company of a bunch of angry, filthy, crazy men, the *con do cao boi du dang*, the outcasts of South Vietnamese society. There was no George waiting for me or picking me up, although he held my life-and-death list.

Before I could think through all possibilities, Pit Bull pushed me to the floor, pressing my face against the graffiti-filled wall in the back of the house. Strings of curse words were written with chalk and coal, or carved onto the wall with a knife. Pit Bull gathered my long hair around his fist and pulled me up. He locked his arms around me, pumping his stomach against my waist. I felt the sharp edges of his belt. "She smells good." He laughed into the back of my neck.

My face was pressed against the wall, my nose crushed against the hard, mildewed surface, against the hateful graffiti. The walls stank of human urine. I could not breathe, and the suffocation seemed to last a century, until he swung me around, pressing his stale-meat lips onto my face. He pressed his body hard against mine, and he groped for my breasts. I bit his purplish lips, and he removed his face from mine momentarily, but only to look up to the ceiling and howl like a rabid stray dog.

In that fleeting movement, I managed to turn my face to one side, away from Pit Bull, in order to get some air. The skinny man had moved away from the bed and was crawling on the floor gathering his boots. "What are you doing with the schoolgirl?" he yelled. "Don't tell me you want to fuck her. Don't. We are in deep shit already, idiot!"

"All right, *em be* can pay me some other way." Pit Bull grabbed my face and pulled it toward his own. I curled back to avoid the contact, kicking at his legs. He uttered a pained sound and yanked repeatedly on my hair.

I heard the skinny man yelling, "Come on, I won't be part of this. I want you to let the girl go!"

From the corner of one eye, I saw the skinny man standing up from the floor. He was holding onto a pair of army boots when the stocky man struck him on his head with a glass bottle. His emaciated body collapsed to the floor, together with smashed pieces of glass.

Pit Bull swung me around and pressed my face to the wall again. The vile smells of mildew and urine filled my nostrils. I saw stars among the dancing graffiti on the wall. I struggled to no avail. He was tearing off my *ao dai*. He licked the nape of my neck and yelled his hateful words into my ears, talking in a trance. "This infant sister is safely going to school and enjoying her privileged life, and now that the Vietcong are coming, she is to board a plane. She smells sweet like a jack fruit, and I'll say, since she has no money to pay for the rescue mission, why don't we just play a game before we kick her butt out to the plane with her goddamned fucking American allies?"

He locked my arms and wrists behind my back and smashed my head repeatedly against the wall. Moments passed and, lost in his monologue, he let go of my head, hands, and wrists, failing to notice that my right arm had been let loose, and I could now move one arm. I squatted down to the floor, and Pit Bull moved down with me, his lips grabbing mine.

Even in the state of despair and panic, I realized I needed a weapon. Any kind of weapon. In the struggle and in Pit Bull's crazed state, somehow I managed to move my head sideways, under his foul, grabbing lips, and I started surveying my surroundings in stolen glimpses. The empty space in front of me left me with no hope. The man's boots and beer bottles were all over the floor, yet out of my reach, although I could see them from the corner of my right eye. I caught sight of my schoolgirl briefcase, together with the rolled artwork Nam had given me. The two items were lying on the floor close to me. I stretched forward to reach the briefcase with my free arm, but it was out of reach. I grabbed the paper roll, Nam's artwork, instead.

"What are you trying to do, smart girl?" Like a barking dog, my captor yelled, exhaling a foul breath between each word. He delivered the last two words with slow deliberation, repeating them over and over again, mimicking a child's voice. "Smart. Girl. Smart. Girl. Smart. Girl." He uttered the words between his teeth with monstrous hoarseness, until the words blended into a hissing sound. *Zuzzzz.* He foamed. He was moving with me as I tried to reach for more objects on the floor; he yanked the artwork from my right hand and tore it up, tossing the pieces of paper into the air.

Nam's pointed red and golden leaves flew down onto my pained limbs. The sharp edges of the falling leaves hit my face, and I turned my chin up, recognizing the red and gold colors of the artist's forest filling the air and cascading down a dark, humid graffiti wall.

A thousand autumn leaves were flying in the air, witnessing my execution.

For a moment, I was blinded. Then, as I began to regain my vision, I was terrified to see Pit Bull take from the armoire a rifle. He pointed it at me.

I saw death.

These men would have no hesitation. They would kill me.

He pressed the rifle against my neck to pin me to the wall. I could not breathe. The icy coldness of the weapon against me, again, spelled death.

"You know what this is, baby doll, *cung oi*? Don't you want to know how your Daddy Pit Bull here got this beautiful M16?" Pit Bull hissed into my face nonstop, in a trance. "You hear, this beautiful thing was supplied by your Yankee friends. You know how much it cost me to get this thing? They use this to fire against the AK-47 made by the Russians. It's the Yankees and the Russians, and then the Russians and the Yankees and their M16 and AK-47, and they ain't give a fuck about your Daddy Pit Bull here, and your Daddy Pit Bull here ain't give a fuck about you, or them. Your Daddy Pit Bull here will just blow your head off in an instant with this thing, baby doll, *cung cua tao*."

Death was in the smell, feel, and sight of this M16 pressed against my throat. I would die in this filthy darkness, at the hands of these filthy men, these beasts fuming with hatred against anything that was human.

No one, nothing could save me now.

I closed my eyes and waited.

But there was no gunshot. I opened my eyes, still alive. Pit Bull dragged me to the bed, threw me on top, flipped me onto my back, and pressed one knee on my stomach. The stocky man held and crisscrossed my wrists over my head. Pit Bull placed the M16 along my side, close enough for me to feel the coldness of the metal. He climbed upon me and I cried out in pain. The two men turned into slow-moving specters. I attempted to raise my head, looking sideways from the corner of my eye, catching sight of the skinny man lying unconscious on the floor like a corpse amid broken glass. The stocky man raised his hand, waving it before my eyes. Through the cracks of the stocky man's fingers, I caught the menacing sight of Pit Bull. He was kneeling on the bed, in the space above my head, his tongue circling his purplish lips. He had a glass bottle in his hand, threw it onto the floor, and then moved his hands to his belt buckle. I heard the glass break and the movement of the brass buckle knocking against his knuckles. He moved down and yanked my legs wide open.

"My infant sister. *Em be.* You will be left to die. Die! Die for your Yankee friends. Die hoping they will come to airlift you from the Vietcong." He shoved me to the floor. "My infant sister, what a good day for you."

———

My nightmare began.

They did not need to fire the M16. Death was already here.

Those hateful hands blocked my nose and mouth. Fists and knees were on me and I was in pain, all over, bone and flesh.

I had been spun onto my stomach, and a beastly hand was taking hold of my head, raising it and banging it against the headboard. Unbearable weight was on me, and all I could hear was the rhythmic beating of my forehead against the wood surface. The rhythm became the pounding of nails on my own coffin where I lay underneath tons of stone, suffocated to death.

The pounding went on forever, and I gasped for air underneath my coffin lid.

The hands held my head and twisted my face to the side. My mind floated until the beastly hand let go of my face and a foul breath filled its place. It was Pit Bull's face upon my own, and his rough hand circled my neck, lifted my head, and banged it on the bed in rhythm with those stabs that cut my lower abdomen in two. Pit Bull's fingers blocked my vocal cords, and my cries for help could not escape my mouth, and my silent cries became words imprinted into my head. Grandma Que. The Spirit of the River Huong. That uncrowned queen of Annam. Future first lady of a new republic. I probed for any sign of a protector. Where was the spirit reigning over the River Huong, symbolized in a jade phoenix that graced Grandma Que's altar? Where was the almighty female Buddha Quan Yin, mankind's savior standing on her lotus blossom?

Save me. Save me. Save me. Save me. Save me. Save me…

No one heard.

—

In my nightmare, somehow my mind traveled to a vacuum in which I saw images of tales told to me in my peaceful childhood. Grandma Que once spoke of the white-turbaned knight and the black-clad knight of the East. They flew among mountaintops, carrying their magical swords, traversing the universe. They met up with the woman warrior.

There was no woman warrior next to me, and the knights had become gigantic, muscular reptiles wrapping around my limbs, their sinewy tails cutting their way through my lower abdomen and back. Pain entered in waves, and blood must have flowed. A hand slipped under me; I was being raised, and Pit Bull held a piece of broken beer bottle against the base of my neck. He told me to get on all fours or he was going to slit my throat. I got on all fours like a dog, and some sharp sword stabbed relentlessly at the lower part of me again and again, hateful stabs that traveled up and down to the end of my spinal cord and split me in half. I collapsed onto the bed, and the beasts pulled me up again and the stabbing continued. Pain tore through the center of me and ripped my flesh, and the beasts continued to laugh and their limbs wrapped around my limbs and their teeth bit down on to the back of my neck and shoulders. There was no white knight or black knight. Just beasts.

The excruciating pain lasted forever.

—

In the midst of that excruciating pain, I heard a loud noise. An earthquake, perhaps, or perhaps a building had fallen down, or the plane that carried my family to America had crashed. Like the breakage of me.

Right at the moment when I thought I had died, all of a sudden, the pain and the noise stopped.

Everything stopped.

The monstrous laughs stopped, the stabbing swords disappeared, and the weight was lifted off me.

A gap of silence ensued. The earthquake was over. At first, I thought I had died. But then I realized I was still breathing. The joy of knowing I was alive flooded through me, bringing with it the surge of renewed energy. I wanted to get up and run. I leaned my elbows against the floor and pushed myself up. Several times I collapsed. I tried again and again, and the pain alongside my legs and lower back still rolled through my body in waves as I tried to pull myself up. I continued trying. At some point, the joy of being alive overcame all pain.

I got myself halfway back up, pressing upon my elbows.

My eyes caught sight of a man's flight uniform, with its shoulder pads and flower-shaped gold pins. Reflexively, I jerked back in fear.

I saw, too, a revolver. Pointing at Pit Bull's face.

Pit Bull had no pants on, and the sight of his nakedness struck at my pupils, blinding them momentarily as I instinctively turned away in disgust. My skin felt cold, and I realized that I was naked and what was left of the torn *ao dai* uniform was still tangling around my pained body; instinctively I gathered the rags and covered myself. My eyes met the panicked face of the stocky man, lying on his back, panting, naked. A man's boot and pant leg were resting onto the stocky man's belly, pinning him down.

I saw another revolver. Pointing at the stocky man's face.

I backed myself against the wall. I breathed and felt a stabbing pain in my chest. Perhaps in the struggle I had torn a ligament. I leaned against the wall and looked up. I saw a face. A stranger's face. Someone I had never met before. Clenched square jaw. Brown skin. Fiery eyes. Crew-cut hair. Inflated neck. Tight lips.

I saw rage.

Somehow I absorbed this face into my mind permanently. And its rage.

The owner of that face and rage had on a flight suit, and he held two revolvers in his hands, one pointing at Pit Bull's temple, one pointing at the stocky man panting underneath the enraged man's boot. The stranger's boot was denting the stocky man's rippling naked stomach, pinning him tightly to the cemented floor.

"On your feet, girl." The stranger was talking to me.

I could not react.

"You just have to get yourself up," he yelled.

I sprang up and dragged myself along the wall, together with my torn clothes. I looked around and found my Pan Am bag. I grabbed it and pulled out the emergency pants and shirt. The pain temporarily retreated as my survival instincts kicked in. I ripped the rest of the torn *ao dai* off me, and I was getting dressed and all modesty escaped me, and then I stuffed my torn white *ao dai* and trousers inside the Pan Am bag. I hurried to finish dressing, and for a moment I thought life had resumed and my nightmare had just simply vanished. All I wanted was to run.

My shoes, I thought to myself. I still had one shoe on my foot and crawled frantically on the dirty floor to find the other one, which must have fallen off in my desperate struggle against Pit Bull. In all that destitution and despair, the burning will to run and live focused me on my shoes. I knew I could not run away very far without the other shoe. I found it.

The stranger started yelling at me again, telling me to go outside and wait by the tamarind tree. Automatically I followed his order. I ran away from my nightmare. Behind me, the stranger spoke to me still. He said there was something he had to do and I was not to step inside or look back.

I held the Pan Am bag close to my lap, dragged myself out of the house, and was faced with the night. The sky had turned dark, and I could see the emerging, milky moon among sparkling rhinestone stars. The humidity in the air hit my face, and I was aware, again, of my pain. My feet froze, and I could not step ahead into that dreadful night. So I sat down against the tamarind tree in the front yard, looking up at the branches spreading like a sheltering umbrella over my head. Beyond that omnipotent umbrella of protection, the sky over Saigon sneered down at me, flickering with an eerie silver glow, like a thunderstorm gathering wind.

"The night has its own face—the Face of Brutality," I heard Grandma Que's voice, telling me the story of the Mystique Concubine during my peaceful days of childhood spent in Hue. My great-grandmother believed there was a beast hidden in the threat of the night. Terrible things happened to people in the night's darkness. She personified this threat into a beast and called it the Face of Brutality.

In this night I had encountered the Face of Brutality.

It seemed like a century that I sat underneath the tamarind tree.

I could not figure out how much time had actually passed when I heard a gunshot. Automatically, I leaped to my feet and wanted to run. Yet I could not run, and then I heard more gunshots. A total of three, separated by only a short gap between. Matter of seconds. The last noise was followed by complete silence.

Someone was grabbing my shoulders and I jumped, dreading the possibility of another attack. Yet the person held me up and patted my back. I sobbed uncontrollably into the person's arms, and when I looked up, I saw the same square jaw, the sparkling eyes shining over the spark of flower-shaped gold pins on the shoulders of the flight uniform.

I was gradually coming back to my senses when I realized I was resting my elbows on his chest. I began to smell blood. My hands felt something slimy, wet, and soft on the lapel of his collar, and in the early moonlight I saw the red stains on his flight suit and the opaque, white substance my fingers had touched. The stranger took a handkerchief out of his flight suit pocket and wiped the white substance off my hand.

"I blew up Pit Bull's head," he said.

He held my elbow and moved me along to Pit Bull's military jeep parked outside the house. He placed me inside the jeep, in the passenger seat.

—

We sat in the jeep and night fell upon us as the round moon appeared demurely almost in her full shape. An unusual moon for April. The full moon usually appeared only in August.

I stuttered my way along to recount the horror to the stranger. That night in April I told him what had happened to me in the dark house outside Tan Son Nhat Airport, and he nodded, his dark brows coming together into a straight line over those fiery eyes.

When I finished, he touched my face and removed strands of dampened hair from my face.

"I don't know any Mr. George of the DAO, but I am a Republic of Vietnam Air Force officer, and I know all about the U.S. evacuation. It's been going on this entire month of April. I can take you inside the airport in this jeep to the DAO headquarters immediately, before it's too late," he said.

He turned around to the back seat of the jeep and reached for a flight bag. He opened the bag and took out a pill bottle and a Coke can and told me to swallow the pills down my throat with the Coke.

"You've been hurt terribly and need to see a doctor, but there's no time, so just take these pills. They're antibiotics." He threw the pill bottle into my lap.

I trusted him and swallowed the pills. In my nightmare he was the only human left on earth, and I had nowhere else to go, no one else to trust.

He pressed his boot on the gas pedal and the jeep rolled on.

—

I remembered nothing of the way from that dark house outside Tan Son Nhat Airport to the DAO headquarters on the other side of the airport gate that separated hell from hope. I had no recollection of how the army jeep driven by the man with dots of blood and human brains stuck to his flight suit lapel could have passed through the guarding MPs and the iron gate. It was as though the jeep were the only moving object on a dark road, and eventually the road was reduced to a bright dot in the middle of the night, dashing through without a course; and we simply followed the bright dot as through it were our destiny. I sat on the passenger side of the stranger's jeep, and when the jeep rolled on and I saw no more MPs and the dot began to move in front of me, I cried my heart out and washed my pain and shame away with my sobs and tears. In unintelligible sounds I called out to the Spirit of the River Huong who had failed to protect me from the brutal hands that grabbed my hair and banged my head and tore my clothes and blocked my throat. I mourned for myself, for every muscle pained, every vein broken, every tissue torn and bruised, all innocence of childhood ripped and destroyed in one dark, poisonous evening of April 1975. I mourned away the hurt and the rage within me. My body went into convulsions, and I wished I could cut off all the body parts that had been shamefully pained and bruised and slashed so that I could be free of all evidence of the nightmare that had happened to me.

The stranger sat behind the driving wheel and listened to my shrieking screams and at some point the jeep came to a sudden, violent stop, and I shut up, jerking myself backward, banging my head against the seat. To my left, I saw a gorgeous swimming pool, with its sparkling blue water under bright white bulb lights. A beautiful, tranquil sight of luxury. The DAO hotel.

We had stopped in front of a building with a beautiful swimming pool surrounded by an iron fence.

The stranger took me by my shoulders and shook. The stream of light above the pool poured across his face, and I saw his reddened eyes and tightened jaw, as he spoke between his teeth. "Stop this nonsense," he hissed, "and listen to me. Listen well. Something happened to you. Something terrible. Something hurtful. You got out from under those two beasts. You wrapped yourself and crawled back up on your feet. Quick and efficient. You ran to the door. You waited for me. You told me what happened. And now you must move on."

He let go of me, reached for his flight bag, and opened it.

"You see here." He showed me Pit Bull's leaflets of gold each wrapped in brown-grained paper, all stacked neatly inside the bag, those same gold taels I had seen in the armoire sitting against the back wall of that dark house. The stranger pulled my tangled long hair down and pressed my face close to the bag, letting me catch a glimpse of two black revolvers, tucked away among the gold taels at the bottom of the flight bag.

"You see this? I'm no angel. No one is at a time like this. I know Pit Bull and his gang. I organized them. I gave them this jeep, and they took passengers inside the airport all day. This has been going on as long as this evacuation has taken place. What else am I supposed to do when my commander has fled and my compatriots are flying their helicopters to Thailand and out to the Seventh Fleet? Tonight I was supposed to get my cut of the gold and give Pit Bull's gang the rest. You weren't supposed to be there, but you were, and so I changed my plan. I finished them up, and then I took all the gold. Past sunset tonight, I killed three men—two were your assailants and one was innocent, but I had to kill him, too, since he regained consciousness at the wrong time.

And then I took all the gold. It's cold-blooded murder, and you touched and felt human brain on my collar. You smelled blood on me. I could have killed you, too, but you deserve to live. Someone deserves to live."

I looked into his blazing eyes and saw the now-familiar rage.

"It is nothing." He clenched his teeth. "Get it into your head. On a day and a night like this, murders and rapes and robberies are nothing, absolutely nothing. Nothing matters. Nothing scars. Nothing hurts. That's how you survive. Repeat after me. You see nothing and feel nothing."

I repeated after him. I had seen nothing and had felt nothing.

"Repeat after me," he went on. "To survive, you forebear, forego, forgive, and forget."

I said the words. Forebear. Forgo. Forgive. And forget.

And then I froze into ice and listened on, his words painting for me the passage to survival.

"This is the swimming pool of the DAO's recreation center," he said, "the back door to where the Americans house Vietnamese evacuees before taking them to the runway. I'll throw you over the fence and you'll walk through the complex, and I am about to tell you exactly where to go, but you have to listen carefully and pull yourself together. Around the corner from the swimming pool, there's a shower facility, and you will stop by a restroom, where there're soap and towels, and you will clean and tidy yourself up."

He told me what to do, and I memorized every word.

"If you do what I've told you to do," he continued, "in less than half an hour you will find your family, and even if you don't find them, you will move on and get to where the Americans will be taking you and that's how you get out of this place and be united with your family elsewhere. Once you're inside the DAO compound, they no longer check you. You'll march on and won't turn back. You'll keep taking those pills I gave you, and along the way, you'll find some medical help. Then, you'll know what to do next and life will be fine.

"You are a very strong and smart girl, I can tell. Between now and then, you suck in your stomach no matter how much it hurts, and you will go on, as though nothing had happened. Nothing at all. And then you forget and don't look back. You are going to do this on your own, and nobody is going to stop you between here and the runway, and you'll be just fine wherever the Americans are taking you, to some better place I hope, 'cause too much is going on here and things are falling apart, and it's now just grab and run."

He took my Pan Am bag from me, reached inside, and pulled out my torn schoolgirl uniform—what was left of my white *ao dai* and matching trousers, shredded, dirty, stained with streaks of dirt and blood, all wrinkled up under his fingers.

He shifted and took off his bloodstained flight suit, displaying a white cotton T-shirt on a dark brown torso over some sort of lightweight Bermuda shorts, and I shrank from him, folding my arms over my knees. He smiled, showing an even row of white teeth. "You are afraid. Poor you, starting out your adult life this way."

He wadded his flight suit and my torn schoolgirl *ao dai* uniform together into one bundle and held the fabric ball in one hand. He sat in silence, resting his other hand on the wheel, staring ahead.

"Thank you," I said timidly.

Either the clear moonlight or the streak of bright light from the pole by the swimming pool struck its silver beam onto his cheekbones. I knew I would never forget that angle of his face, the way it appeared before me at that moment. In that streak of light, I began to scrutinize the man's face, every line, every contour, every pore that was visible to me, as though I were trying to paint or imprint that face onto my brain. Some time passed, and it seemed to me like a century.

———

"Who are you?" I had to ask. I had memorized his face, but he remained a stranger.

He did not answer me. Instead, he slowly undid the fabric ball and ran his fingers through his bloodstained flight suit: I saw a name tag sewn onto the front of the suit, but I could not read the name in the dark jeep.

"I have some civilian clothes in the back, and after tonight, this whole career is buried. This thing," he said vaguely, holding his flight suit against his chest. He held it there for a while. Under the beam of light, his face took on the greenish grayness of his flight suit.

"When you walk by that swimming pool," he said, "I will watch, and then soon I'll light a match. A few minutes of flame and your schoolgirl *ao dai* uniform and my air force flight suit will burn into ashes."

"What will happen to you?" I asked.

"I have the gold." He tapped his flight bag. "Maybe I'll grab a helicopter and fly off. Maybe we'll meet again. Maybe I'll just stay on to meet the Vietcong. Maybe I'll die with what's fated to die in this place. But I just know once you walk by that swimming pool, you will be all right."

He pulled the strap of my Pan Am bag over my shoulder. "Leave your torn *ao dai* with me to be burned, but keep this bag for your journey. You must forget, brave girl. There's no other choice but to forget." He was still clenching his jaw.

"Good-bye," he said the final words, "brave girl, good-bye."

He never told me his name.

———

On the night of April 27, 1975, I did march on as he told me to do. In climbing over the iron fence, I lost the shoes I had held on to, and thereafter went barefoot.

That fateful night, I walked by the DAO's gorgeous swimming pool and did not look back, knowing that behind me, the South Vietnamese Air Force officer who had killed three men for a bag of gold taels would be striking his match to his stained flight suit and my torn schoolgirl *ao dai* uniform. I followed his directions to the smallest detail, and sure enough, I was united with Mom and Dad and Pi inside the airport, in the DAO compound, where a horde of Vietnamese evacuees crowded the floor of the DAO headquarters. I found my parents and Pi squatting on the floor of the DAO annex among hundreds of stunned Vietnamese crawling among carry-on bags, bedsheets, and blankets. Their cries of joy gave me back my life. I explained away the cuts and bruises and smeared blood by telling my parents I had fallen off the moped. I told them, too, that Grandma Que did not want to leave with me, and chances were we would be starting a new life wherever the Americans would be taking us, without Grandma Que. All we could hope for was the possibility that Simone's plan went well such that she and Grandma Que would be meeting us outside Vietnam, in America.

I made it through the night of April 27, 1975, a consummate actress to myself and to my emotionally drained parents. I never saw the DAO supervisor named George again, and at about three o'clock the early morning of April 28, I held Pi's hands and limped my way, on bare feet, ahead of my panicked parents onto the airport runway. We boarded the cargo plane called C-130, together with other tearful, panic-stricken Vietnamese. My mother fainted and regained consciousness and fainted again, and at the time we clambered onto the icebox-cold plane, she collapsed and I helped my father hold her up.

In all my efforts to forget, I still have a vivid memory of the sparkling water of that gorgeous swimming pool inside the DAO compound—the signal of my survival. Nor could I forget the coldness of the metal floor of the cargo aircraft underneath my naked heels, or the stuffy air of that night in April. I also have a vivid memory of the roaring sound of the plane engine when it took off. How the passengers were incapable of talking. They merely wept.

I went on bare feet until I reached Clark Air Base in the Philippines, where a Red Cross worker handed me a pair of sandals as a welcome gift.

I limped my way on for the rest of the evacuation, from camp to camp—from the Philippines to Guam Island and eventually to Fort Chaffee, Arkansas, and my injuries healed along the way. I had kept the Air Force officer's antibiotics, and day after day I swallowed his pills until the vial was empty. I never saw a doctor. Youth, willpower, and my internal lust for life all kicked in and miraculously worked their magic to restore my health.

At Fort Chaffee in Arkansas we met up with Simone, without Grandma Que, and in the joy of reunion after the loss of a country, the two granddaughters of Grandma Que accepted the fact that life in America would be without our maternal grandmother. Our flight out was to be a one-way trip. I accepted, too, without knowing the details of my sister's escape, that something had happened to us both that day in April. It changed our lives, and because of it, we each closed up our heart.

To this day I have never seen the flight-suited stranger again, except that in the fall of 1976, in Diamondale, Illinois, on the SISU campus, I found the same fiery eyes, square jaw, and row of white teeth inside tightly pulled lips on the determined face of the Crazy Man. A sense of déjà vu.

Could they have been brothers, or related somehow? Or was the resemblance a product of my imagination resulting from the traumatic experience of my escape? I never had a chance to find out. The mystery remained what it was—a mystery, after the Crazy Man's untimely death.

My nightmare of that day in April has continued to haunt me at times all throughout my pursuit of the American dream, even in moments of peace, tranquility, or happiness. I went to college and excelled, achieving what the immigrant community viewed as American success—in a way it came too easily and brought no real joy. The child of Hue who taught herself how to read at the age of four—a genius mind spotted by the kind Professor Morgan of SISU journalism school—shrank into the predictable mediocrity of a successful, Harvard-trained lawyer. At every height of my professional success as a lawyer, and in moments of solitude when the nightmare of April 1975 returns to haunt me, I can't help but wonder, why me?

Why this price of freedom?

My success in America? A fallacy?

NINE
DEATH OF A DREAM

Brad's eyes, opened wide, registered panic and confusion as he tried to hold my shoulders when I sprang forward and waved my arms wildly in midair. I looked into the blue sky in his eyes and told Brad how for years I had not been able to forget those beasts and the gunshots outside Tan Son Nhat Airport. My mind drifted toward the oval shape of Grandma Que's somber face beneath a Vietnamese cone hat when she closed the door to the peace of home. Brad's blue sky deepened into my sapphire sea where in a dream my clothes floated and my beautiful sister Simone was gliding about, her hands extending toward me, uttering the words of the female Buddha Quan Yin, *"Nam mo dai tu dai bi cuu kho cuu nan Quan The Am Bo Tat."* Simone's melodic prayers were mixed with Brad's Southern voice, panic-stricken and full of anguish. "Oh God, oh, baby, how awful, calm down, baby, calm down." I bit down on Brad's forearm, and he grimaced, but made no sound. He was bearing my pain.

I broke away from him and moved again toward the mirror.

I moved on to SISU and its long winters. In the mirror I saw myself wandering around a small, dead Midwestern town, when all students had gone home for Christmas. There were no Christmas trees or Christmas presents inside the small dorm room at Smith Hall. I wanted no friend and needed no friend, and the deserted college town suited me just fine.

I told Brad what he had been wanting to know: all about the Crazy Man. How he had reminded me of the air force officer's face. How I had used the image of Sidney Poitier to justify the sense of familiarity.

Brad was a strong man, and he caught me when I collapsed. "It's OK, baby, I'm here. Go on and bite me, if that makes you feel better," he said poignantly.

I cooled down and kissed my teeth marks on his skin. "I'm so sorry, so sorry; I have hurt you," I murmured.

I sat in Brad's lap and talked to him about the small flame in my dorm room at Harvard the day I burned all those letters I had written and mailed to myself. It had been years ago, and I still remembered the flickering light. In that flame rolled the movie reel of my life as a lawyer on the East Coast.

—

The worst death of a dream is the kind that happens gradually over time. Neither law school nor the brand name "Harvard" made me into Portia. I did not save anyone I loved with my eloquence. Instead, I became an American lawyer. A fairly successful one. I started out full of idealism as a poor government prosecutor who made her reputation by winning a case against a seasoned litigator twice my age. My opponent, the youngest member of the Watergate investigative team in the seventies, made the same mistake as my moot court opponents at Harvard. All of them had underestimated the resilience of the shy and petite Mimi Sean Young, who managed to pull the rug under them. I won, and the case made headlines in the *Wall Street Journal* and the *Legal Times*. My reputation developed thereafter and brought hefty offers from Wall Street and D.C. firms. I climbed the corporate

ladder, yet descended into the mad existence of a big-firm lawyer defending corporations in commercial disputes that involved
millions of dollars, thousands of pieces of paper, and no heart.

Simone also graduated from Columbia Law School. She
went on to specialize in mergers and acquisitions at Wilkie Farr
Monahan, a blue-chip New York firm. We sisters easily became
the Vietnamese success symbols for the American dream. In
the rat race of our lives, the fact that we were Vietnam born was
overlooked. What counted were our billable hours and our ability to produce brilliant legal briefs and memoranda. While other
Vietnam-born lawyers made their fortunes representing non–
English speaking Vietnamese clients in personal injury, divorces,
and petty offense criminal defense, we sisters easily stepped away
from our own ethnic community, toward something more glorious among the cream of the mainstream's crop. As straight-A students in Vietnam and daughters of a college professor, we had no
problem with English, and we became lawyers in places where the
best lawyers were supposed to be: New York City and Washington,
D.C. The price we paid was just part of the immigrant's dream: we
readily enslaved ourselves to the big law firms of America, those
law partnerships that were called the "sweatshops" of the legal
profession, who rewarded us with six-figure salaries and bonuses
because we both billed over two thousand hours a year.

Then came the early nineties when Asia became the gold rush
for multinational corporations, I was again recruited by the big
law firms, and successfully transformed myself into an international transactions lawyer, following the footsteps of Simone and
her uptown Manhattan colleagues. I became the model immigrant, the legendary story of success among the Vietnamese community as the first Vietnamese woman who graduated summa
cum laude from Harvard Law School. I did more than that. I

wrote and published decent law review articles that solidified my reputation as a legal scholar. I volunteered for the ACLU and various public interest groups and worked incessantly on pro bono projects. All of those things helped me collect achievements like the White House Fellowship, the Young Lawyer of the Year award given by the Bar Association, and another graduate degree from Harvard.

Still, no political ambition in America. *America the Beautiful* could never be the republic that had wet rice paddies running all the way toward the horizon, with Grandma Que standing against the last sun ray of a dying day, on the bank of her historic River Huong, dreaming of the Nguyen Dynasty, its nine lords and thirteen kings. Likewise, I was determined never to walk into a shrink's office. How could one ever, ever explain to me the floating coffins from Grandma Que's nightmare?

In the rat race of the law profession, I had forgotten Steve Something's last name, Steve from the day of my drama practice, although in retrospect I realized he was prophetically right. My achievements were all decent, but I was never first lady at anything. Nor did I garner financial wealth, the result of not paying enough attention to invest well in Wall Street. The big firms' billable hours exhausted me, and I kept changing jobs—a pattern of life that repeated itself, foretold in that monologue I had composed and delivered to myself in the woods in the fall of 1976. *Separation is the spirit of the immigrant experience, so for the traveler living in exile, every departure is but a déjà vu beginning.*

As I worked incessantly at a series of law jobs, a part of me always viewed the square corners of my desk as a prison. I was too easily bored. Too easily bruised. When I found myself bruised, I wanted to fly away on a kite to some place where I could not be touched. So, at the peak of success in each job, I would have the urge to quit and move to a different city. Travelling across state lines made me feel like that kite stretching over one beautiful America, and nothing stopped me except the heaviness in my heart, which appeared and reappeared at times, pulling down the kite of my spirit. When real life caught up with me, I would ground my kite. The Harvard credentials and brand-name achievements would help me land on my feet in another prestigious law job, and I would soon pick myself up, break the prison of my law desk, and fly again, over the corn fields and orchards of the Midwest, over the tops of those old European buildings of East Coast cities and the flatness of Texas small towns and muddy waters of the Gulf Coast, through the fog and rain of the hilly Pacific Northwest, into the open blue sky over the sapphire blue Pacific Coast and the cool breeze of Southern California. When money ran low, I would go back to the prison of another law desk.

"I want to fly that kite with you, precious Mimi." Brad was speaking into the mass of my hair dampened with tears.

He did calm me down yet was unable to stop my strings of words. I went on and on, blurting out the disappointments of my life. A few years here. A few years there. An impressive resume stacked with brand names of a prestigious law school, corporate legal departments, and mega law firms in major cities of the U.S. Between jobs I kept seeing the flickering flame burning away the self-addressed letters in my Harvard dorm room. I kept seeing the young girl who had contorted herself every way on a small dormitory bed in order to write stories about Vietnamese immigrants on a notepad, the kind of thing I had not done since my graduation from Harvard.

Since I last saw the Crazy Man, I had had men who had loved me and had adored my body, but never had I found another man to whom I felt inspired to deliver combinations of my nine words. I imagined keeping the nine words in a magic bottle and closing the lid, together with my childhood in Vietnam. I imagined wearing this glass bottle around my neck all the time. Once, in the early part of my law career, when I was trying a case in court, my co-counsel mentioned that in the middle of oral argument, I often touched the base of my neck, where my magic bottle was supposed to be. An odd nervous habit, I told him.

Yes, in essence, to America, it was just a nervous habit.

I was still talking like a madwoman when Brad turned me away from the mirror to face him and kissed the base of my neck. "I want to look inside this magic bottle of yours. I don't know what to do. Tell me what to do, Mi Chau," he whispered. Even in my hysteria, I realized that he'd just called me by my Vietnamese name, and he pronounced it correctly. This made me cry even harder. I broke away from him again and reached for the woman in the mirror with one hand. I saw the tiny lines under her eyes and around the corners of her mouth.

Gone was the young freshman at SISU who'd performed Portia on stage. Gone was the 3L superperformer, iron-willed student at Harvard Law School.

Yet, never gone, the bruised teenager outside Tan Son Nhat Airport.

I said to Brad, "Do you know me now?"

"Yes I know you, and I am here for you, my Mi Chau, before the hyphenation," he said, and I responded with more tears. I touched the mirror again and wished I could embrace my own reflection, as I saw in the eyes of the woman the shape of her magic bottle, with nine words burdening her heart.

I turned to Brad. "My nine words," I said. "What you saw were my nine words."

"You can say your nine words to me, as you, now, Mimi." He pulled me to him.

"No," I said without thinking. "I am afraid there won't ever be another nine words that speak of a dream."

TEN
RETURNING TO DIAMONDALE

The crying must have caused me to pass out, or I must have fallen asleep.

Brad must have left and come back with a bowl of strawberries topped with whipped cream in his hands. When I opened my eyes, I found him holding the bowl. He fed me one strawberry at a time, and the whipped cream must have foamed around my mouth because he bent down and ran his tongue over my lips. He told me to stop crying because the swollen eyes would look bad for our dinner date that night—despite all that had happened, all my hysteria, he still intended to take me to dinner later. "My sweet Mi Chau. Sweet like these strawberries and the whipped cream I am feeding you," he said dreamily.

"Remember our meeting in Hermann Park?" I asked.

He nodded. "How could I forget? You were crying that day, too. Your eyes were like boats turning upside down on a deserted beach, and your lurking tears fell like rain calling those boats to the stormy sea."

No one had compared my eyes to boats turning upside down on a deserted beach waiting for the rain.

"When you cried, Mimi, it threatened me. I felt so helpless. I thought the boats would take off into a stormy ocean, unanchored, and I would not be able to hold on."

I told him no, I wasn't crying that day in Hermann Park. I was simply reflecting in the park, sketching images of Diamondale. A few days before I met Brad in Hermann Park, I had taken a business trip to Chicago. Instead of coming directly back to Houston, I changed my itinerary. I had the urge to return to Diamondale. It had been more than twenty years since I left. So I took a small plane from Chicago to the airport in Marion, the adjacent town, and as the taxicab rolled on into Diamondale, I recognized the Denny's where the Vietnamese Student Association of SISU had held its monthly meetings during those early years immediately after the Republic of Vietnam had become defunct. The cab rolled on, and when we reached the SISU campus, I discovered the coincidence. I had returned impromptu during spring break. There wasn't a soul around. The town of Diamondale was dead, as I had remembered it during my lonely Thanksgiving, Christmas, and spring breaks as a college girl. I saw myself, the skinny teenager, dragging her feet over the deserted streets of Diamondale, happily wearing her new contact lenses instead of old, ugly prescription glasses, thanks to the kindhearted Professor Morgan and the Hearst Scholarship.

The cab passed by the Communications and Fine Arts Building, and I could still see Dr. Morgan standing in front of the building, talking to the skinny teenager, in 1978.

"*Dr. Morgan, I am moving to Cambridge after graduation.*"

"*Cambridge, Massachusetts, or Cambridge, England?*"

"*It's Harvard Law School, I mean. My sister Simone is in New York City, and she has married a rich man. She is attending Columbia Law School. She is helping me out financially, and she has shopped around for financial assistance with the foundations. She helped me get a three-year scholarship! And guess what, I am the first Vietnamese admitted to Harvard Law School. We sisters are going to become hotshot lawyers, Dr. Morgan. It's our American dream.*"

"You never told me any of this."

"I was afraid you would not approve. You wanted me to become a journalist."

"Oh, My Chow. Harvard is a wonderful thing, and law school is awesome, but what about your writing? I've always thought you were meant to write creatively about the Vietnamese immigrants whom you called 'the new flowers of the United Garden of America.' See, that's part of your creativity. You saw the U.S.A. as a garden. You're a special girl, My Chow, because you have stories to tell in your heart. All of those excellent feature stories you wrote, the humanity you expressed, your prose, your metaphors. You are a natural storyteller, and such a sensitive person."

"I can always do that writing later. Now I am going to Harvard Law School. I have to be a successful immigrant, and that means Harvard Law School for now."

"Go then; you seem so excited. Best of luck to you. But remember to return to writing, when the time is right."

"When the time is right," I had promised the kind professor then. More than two decades had passed, and I had never written about the Vietnamese immigrants; and whenever Grandma Que came back to me, the sadness and desolation of her face stood out in an American crowd, mostly lawyers with whom I worked and against whom I argued. *Maybe it's enough if I just become a well-paid lawyer taking orders from corporate America. Where is the queenly spirit that once reigned in a radiant jade phoenix? Have I lost her, Grandma? She never protected me, so why should I believe in that kind of dream anymore?"* I shouted out my question to keep Grandma Que from disappearing again, but her melancholy face vanished, and I could not even hear the echo of my own unanswered question.

The cab circled the deserted SISU campus and the sleepy town of Diamondale. I never told the cabdriver to stop. I did not want to get out to walk, afraid the traces of memory would sadden me. When I got to my motel room, I asked the clerk at the front desk to find me a faculty directory of SISU. "It would take a while," he said. "We don't have it right here." I took a nap until the clerk delivered the directory to my room. I looked for Dr. Joseph Morgan in the journalism department, and there was no listing. He must have retired or moved away. I looked in the telephone book for the listing of one Joseph Morgan. Number eighteen Walnut Street. I tried calling the phone number listed, and there was no answer.

——

I walked on Walnut Street, in a rundown neighborhood with black men and women sitting on their crooked porches, some drinking beer, others reading newspapers. I walked and walked, and small black children were playing on the sidewalks, looking at me curiously and making way. I got to number eighteen, a yellow house, its color standing out in the faded neighborhood. But despite its distinctive yellow color, the house looked somber and uncared for, the wooden fence already damaged and broken in several places, the green paint of the shutters already chipped and dirty looking, the front door glazed with dust. The lawn had not been mowed, and weeds had grown high.

When I'd pushed on the fence gate and walked to the dusty, grimy porch, the black children followed. "Looking for Mr. Joseph?" A little girl looked at me intently.

"Yes," I said.

"He live alone. His wife die. He drink," the little girl said.

I rang the bell several times and no one came to the door.

"How old are you?" I asked the little girl.

"Eight." She wiped her nose with her hand. I took out a twenty-dollar bill and asked her to help me find Dr. Joseph Morgan. "He live here," she said, grabbing the bill, pointing to the front door.

"Could there be a mistake?" I asked the girl.

"No mistake. Only one white man in the neighborhood," she said.

All the other children had either left or stayed outside the fence, and only the eight-year-old girl had stayed on with me, carrying with her a baby girl. The baby girl could be one or two years old, with an inflated belly and a full mouth circled with dry milk. The curly hair was braided, and her eyes appeared too white on her dark, tiny face. Her chocolate skin was scaly.

The eight-year-old girl sat the baby girl down on the porch. "My sister," she said. The baby girl was standing next to me, pulling on the hem of my skirt and examining my panty hose.

"Mr. Joseph don't have no dog," the older sister said, dragging the baby girl away from me.

"No, don't drag your sister," I said, lifting the baby girl up. She nestled against me, playing with my pearls.

The eight-year-old walked around the side of the house toward the backyard and disappeared. I stood on the porch holding the baby girl, watching the sun go down. My thoughts went back to the afternoon when I last saw the Crazy Man in this town, in the fall of 1976. It was also sunset when I watched, for the first and last time, his warrior dance. I looked at the black baby girl's face and saw myself, one dirty child, with my sister Simone, running around the alleys of Saigon's District Eight after we had left Hue. Just like this. A little girl and her sister. Walnut Street in Diamondale became the little alleys of crowded, urban Saigon.

Simone was taking care of me, and together we strolled the alleys buying snacks from peddlers, most memorably the *canh bun*, a spinach and vermicelli hot-and-sour soup sold by an old woman who carried her coal stove and soup pot in a pair of baskets hanging on both sides of a wooden pole. Simone and I shared a bowl, sipping on the hot spicy soup. The woman dipped the empty bowl into a small aluminum sink containing the yellowish water that came out of the public faucet, where neighborhood women crowded and waited in line to take home their family's water supply in aluminum mini-barrels. The soup peddler splashed the oily water into the alley and placed the pole upon her right shoulder. The pole bent down at both ends where her baskets were slightly swinging, and off she went into the sunset.

This flash of Saigon memory vanished when I heard the eight-year-old girl yell, "Mr. Joseph! Some pretty lady looking for you." I was suddenly self-conscious of my sleek hair, black corporate suit, sheer panty hose, pointed heels, and pearl strand. I had not intended to return to this town this way and wondered what I might say to Dr. Morgan. That I had grown up, had grown older, had not contacted him in twenty years, and had not begun writing about the Vietnamese immigrants since I left his writing lab? The black girl had run back to the front porch, announcing to me that Mr. Joseph was sleeping in the backyard.

I walked back, my heels sinking into the grass and dirt. I recognized the old man sleeping on the lawn. It was Dr. Morgan, the sweet white father and defender of all communication and fine arts minority students at SISU, except he was now feeble, wearied, wrinkled, and old enough to die. He was wearing some loose denim shorts and no shirt. I could see the same mass of navel hair, except it was all white. His bird's-nest hair had thinned out quite a bit, and it was all white, too, instead of salt-and-pepper like old times. He looked peaceful in his sleep, yet diminutive, as though he had shrunk since I last saw him more than two decades ago. His wrinkles and the way he had brought his limbs together, close to his trunk, made me think of an uncomfortable death. I saw no trace of the zeal and abundance of the loud-mouthed, fat, middle-aged professor I once knew. Empty beer cans scattered all around him. Time and beer had had their effect on the man who helped me get through college.

I stood next to him and called his name. "*Dr. Morgan!*" He did not respond. I called his name again and he stirred, scratching his naked stomach. His eyes were still closed. The little black girl tried to shake his body and he pushed her away, turning slightly, his potbelly falling to one side. She almost crawled onto the side of his jiggling belly, and he opened his eyes eventually. His gray pupils fixed on me. His short, bushy, unshapely brows were as I remembered them, but all white. Folds of skin formed their creases around those fish eyes.

He looked at me as though I were a stranger, betraying no recognition of who I was or why I was standing here. My heart beat profusely and I began to speak, my voice trembling. "It's Mi Chau, My Chow," I said, recalling how he pronounced my name. He did not stir. "The Hearst Scholarship," I added, grabbing on to my own memory. He looked at me for a minute or so, closed his eyes, turned his white head to one side, and went back to sleep.

I took the eight-year-old girl's hand and held her baby sister, and together we walked to the street. I let them go, the eight-year-old clutching my twenty-dollar bill happily in her little hand. I watched them walk down Walnut Street, the same way I had nostalgically watched images of the two sisters, Mi Uyen and Mi Chau, return to time past.

Good-bye, I said to the images of the two Vietnamese girls.

Sunset was approaching. I turned around to look at the yellow house, capturing in my mind the image of the sleeping old man in his backyard, with his white hair, white brows, white navel hair, and protruding stomach, white like tuna fish and scaly and wrinkled like old age. I blinked my eyes. The coldness spread to my temples and numbed my face when I discovered I had not shed a single tear.

Good-bye, kindhearted Dr. Morgan, defender of all minority students.

Good-bye, Hearst Scholarship awarded for the birth of a writer. No writer has been born.

I have never written the life story of my Crazy Man.

Good-bye, birth of a dream that's no more.

—

The bowl of strawberries was empty and Brad was kissing my fingers. We were both sitting on the floor in front of the mirror, exhausted and sad. "Sorry, sorry," I kept saying. He wanted only nine words, so distinctively and cryptically, yet I had let out a sea of words and drowned him with it.

I took his hands and placed them on my breasts. "Love me," I said, "love me, please," and then I wrapped my legs around him. My hair brushed against his crotch, and his brows raised and the pair of blue eyes closed in on me, the blond head bending down on to my chest. I felt his lips on my nipple, yet again I felt nothing of myself except the wetness of saliva on skin, spreading the warmth to my heart. I held his head and stroked the short blond hair and told him I wanted all those letters burned in the Harvard dorm room back with me, so I could reconstruct my life into a real diary. I longed so badly to draft the nine words, any combination of nine words, even if I could never deliver them to anyone after the unresolved death of the Crazy Man. Just like the fall of Saigon, America had never explained his death—who killed him and why.

I realized the ridiculous fantasy the concept of my nine words represented. Even with the lucky number nine, nine words would never be enough for me to tell what I needed to tell. I needed to return to the contorted girl who wrote on a notepad. I needed a manuscript that kept growing, never ending, until I was exhausted and would fall over, unable to leave the game of words.

Brad let go of my nipple, sat up, and raised my chin. "You and I both want something else besides this comfortable yet dreadful life we lead, in which we let go of the dream and what we really want to be." He sighed into my hair and ran his tongue over my eyelids. "Our turmoil is our bond, the misfortune of the fortunate we both have become.

—

I opened my eyes and saw Brad sitting on the floor, leaning against the bed with one leg bent, one leg stretching ahead of him, beautiful and sad. I crawled over, curled up against him, glued to his lap, the same way his Asian child would have cuddled against him. The white bedsheet entangled us, his fingers were entangled in my uncombed hair, and our white and brown limbs were entangled.

In that entanglement I found rest.

We sat in this Siamese twin position until I felt dried and hot. Reality came back to me when the sun painted its arrows onto the champagne carpet. It was a Saturday morning, and we did not have to work, although I had documents piled up in the office and deadlines for the following Monday. Brad carried me to the bed and placed a pillow underneath my head. He bent over and stroked my face and told me how overwhelming all this had been for him, and perhaps I was so worn out he should make an appointment for me to see a doctor before he went jogging in Hermann Park.

I murmured something in response—I would never believe in a pill that changed my moods and a doctor who could fix everything, including wiping out yesterday and creating tomorrow. The dream I lost could not be rebuilt or replaced. Again, no public office in America. No shrink.

"Go away, Brad. Go jogging. No doctor, please," I told him.

And then I went back to sleep.

ELEVEN
RESOLUTION

For weeks after my nervous breakdown before the mirror, we did not make love, although Brad held me at night to sleep.

Before the night I told him my story, Brad had taken to leaving his clothes at my house and parking his jeep in my garage. Things changed, however. Many nights, Brad called to say he would not be coming over. I would drive to his bachelor apartment near Montrose Boulevard. We would pick up boxes of sushi from the signature Kroger and eat them before the TV, and then I would drive home to my mirror, sleeping alone, missing his arm extended under my neck. When we were together, he no longer placed his hand between my thighs. In my anguish over trying to figure out what was happening, I had almost forgotten the feel of him. When I sought a kiss, he would return it and then lower his face toward my thighs, apparently hoping to fulfill me that way. Our relationship went on like that for weeks, until I could stand it no more. At my house one night, I put my head on his extended arm as usual and asked him if something had gone wrong.

"It's funny, Mimi," he said. "The stereotype is that men do not want to talk, but in this case I was the one who asked all the questions, because I was growing so attached to you. And then when you told me all, it was so overwhelming I didn't know how to handle it."

"There is nothing to handle." I took him in my hand and guided him into me. He tensed and moved, with his head buried into the pillow, over my left shoulder, and I moved with him until he stirred and quaked, and it was all over.

"Isn't that what husband and wife do, Brad?" I asked. "A two-minute routine?"

He did not answer me. He must have gone to sleep. I stayed wide-awake, blaming myself for having released my marathon of words to him. I dozed off eventually and woke up in the middle of the night, my heart palpitating. There was no extended arm underneath the back of my neck, and my hand groped the empty space where he once lay. Panic struck me and then subsided when I rubbed my eyes and gained my focus. In the moonlight and the glow cast by the street lamps, I saw Brad sitting next to the bay window, smoking.

"Insomnia?" I asked.

"I have things on my mind," he said.

"When did you start smoking?"

A long silence ensued, and then he said, slowly, "Since the day you talked."

"Oh." I felt a sharp pain in my stomach.

He had extinguished the cigarette and was standing near the bay window looking at me in bed, a straight, tall figure amid beams of moonlight. I could only see a silhouette, just as I'd once seen him from my balcony, soaked in rain.

"I'm sorry, Mimi, but I am ordinary. I don't have your high IQ or scholastic achievement. Don't speak a foreign language. I am not royal. Have never thought of running for office, let alone the presidency. I have no capacity to reach out for any big dream. I burned my novel draft and became a lawyer. I was born into a normal society. No war. Just consumers. I don't worry much about ideals. I have never been to Vietnam or Hong Kong. Never thought I would have anything to do with either place. To tell the truth, I have never been comfortable around my Asian in-laws. Frankly, I don't want my child to grow up in that extended family network. I am afraid I won't understand her.

"I am *not* the man for you, Mimi," he said. Then, he lowered his voice. "I am not the man to whom you could deliver your nine words."

Irrationally, I thought that in all that moonlight beaming through the blinds of the bay window, I could see his pale blue irises in the dark like cats' eyes, the whites of his eyes reddened and wearied.

"Oh, Brad, come here," I said, extending my arms.

He walked toward me but stopped midway. "I talk and want to hear you talk; guys don't talk and don't want to hear women talk. I cry and I feel so much pain from life; guys don't cry and aren't supposed to feel pain. When I found you, I thought it would all be OK. I can be devoted to you, Mimi, yet I can't deal with your complexity. I was afraid of your silence, and when I finally did get you to talk, I was afraid of your words.

"The day you told your story, I understood your words, I got what happened to you; it's an awful thing. At the same time, I was lost. It isn't a stretch to say that, in many ways, I have no idea what you were talking about. I don't understand this business about how you guard your nine words."

No one understands how souls can be drawn together because they share the same hope and dream, unless the person is part of that hope and dream, I said to myself.

I sat up in the bed, and he took a few steps backward as though he were afraid I would move toward him. He stood in the middle of the bedroom, a loner delivering his monologue.

"I wish I could tell you I did not want sex from you. I am a man, and sex, especially with you, is a joy larger than life. But now that I know what happened to you and how you have carried this with you through the years, and that you don't want to give me your nine words, I am scared. When I reach for the inside of you, it doesn't feel the same any more, as though if I allow you to consume me, I will be sucked into something I can't understand.

"I guess I can just touch you and talk to you and pretend the turmoil doesn't exist. But it doesn't feel right. I wish I could make you believe in something corny. I don't understand it either, but despite all of this ignorance and desire and alienation and fear, I am still the guy who desperately wants to talk to you and to hear you talk, and I see myself in you, although I don't understand you. And it has nothing to do with sex, your pain, or my pain."

He moved toward me, knelt down by the bed, held his head with his two hands, and cried.

———

It was my birthday, and I had told Brad I would take a day off work to go to the spa for a facial and body massage to pamper myself. We made plans to meet at the French restaurant in the Riverway Hotel on Woodway, as Brad had an all-day deposition and would not be able to fight the rush-hour traffic to pick me up.

In a surge of workaholic energy, I changed my plan, postponed the spa appointment, and showed up at the office. The third-year associate, Kurt Fiesta, and I sat in a conference room with our laptops. We put together the legal memorandum for the board of directors of Entran. I addressed the various disputes with the Indian governments and the types of payments that the Entran engineer had transferred to the Indian official. I concluded that the payments were illegal under the Foreign Corrupt Practices Act and that the board had to remedy the consequences by taking certain actions. I decided to submit the memorandum to the Entran board weeks before the board meeting, long before the deadline for submitting agenda items.

For the advisory memo, Kurt had drafted the legal summary of the Foreign Corrupt Practices Act, and I had written my analysis and recommendations. We worked the whole morning to edit the final draft, and by noon, the sixty-page legal memorandum addressed to the Entran board was finished.

"I may be out of line here," the young associate said, "but may I ask you a question?"

I was editing the last page. "You've already asked a question," I teased. "Go right ahead."

"I know you were the first Vietnamese admitted to Harvard Law School and graduated summa cum laude from there. Why law? It would have been difficult enough to have simply survived that war and built a life in the U.S. But then, to push yourself to the top percentile of the law profession, so remarkably soon after getting here?"

The young man was probing, but I knew he had good intentions. I set down my pen. "It never really felt like a matter of choice," I told him. I closed the folder and handed it to him.

"The law was a choice, wasn't it?"

"Not exactly. Choices for immigrants are sometimes no choices. When Harvard chose me, the immigrant in me got stuck. If I hadn't been a first-generation immigrant, I might have rejected the traditional path of law school. I might have chosen to write, or to paint, for example, or even travel to Nepal and live in the Himalayan foothills as a hermit."

"Would you have?"

"Maybe. It's always easy to wish for an exotic alternative, the road not taken." I changed the subject. "Have the memorandum delivered this afternoon to the client. Call me on my cellular at four thirty to let me know it's done."

"Yes, ma'am." He paused pensively, and then, speaking slowly, "You might have known that I am the son of poor Hispanic parents who don't speak English. During college and during my three years at South Texas Law School, I worked in a Seven-Eleven store to help my parents." He trailed off, staring at his hands for a moment, then shrugged, looked up at me and chuckled. "I'm not sure why I'm telling you this, Mimi. I guess I'd just love to hear any advice you might have for me."

He had told me many times how glad he was to be working with me. I knew he saw me as a mentor, or at least wanted to—not just someone who'd critique his work and show him the ropes as a new lawyer, but someone who knew what it was like to try to build a career as the child of poor immigrant parents.

Kurt wanted more from me, but did I have it to give?

"I understand an immigrant's life, Kurt," I said to him with the same pensive tone. "I'll think about it, and you can be sure I'll do what I can for you. But not today."

He nodded, laughed nervously, and thanked me again.

I wondered what I should really be telling him, down the road.

About the death of a dream?

I sighed.

From the conference room, I hurried back to my office. When I looked at the calendar, I noticed a bar luncheon scheduled for the day to celebrate the new officers of the Lawyers for the Arts committee. I had not intended to go, but I was lured by the urge to leave the office and take refuge in a crowd. I buzzed my secretary, and she told me I could pay at the door or join the firm's lawyers at a prepaid table.

"I'll pay at the door. I don't want any more firm-talk today. I am taking the afternoon off."

"Happy birthday, Mimi," she said. "There's a bouquet of flowers from your significant other."

She brought the flowers in and placed the vase on my desk. I sniffed the twenty-four long-stemmed red roses and glanced at the note. *Will you eat my rose again? B.* I smiled. My thirty-three-year-old Brad might not be a professional ladies' man, but he could be clever with words. It had taken weeks for us to resume normalcy, yet we hadn't broken up. Meanwhile, my secretary continued telling me I was a lucky woman.

"How does it feel to be forty and look twenty-nine?" she called after me as I walked to the hallway.

"It sucks," I answered her, "because I am forty and don't look twenty-nine."

I could hear her laughing behind me.

———

The luncheon was an extravaganza hosted by Travis, Vince & Elms, the largest law firm in Houston. An ice sculpture, carved intricately into a flying bird, graced the buffet table. I glanced at the reddish-brown caviar that garnished plates of smoked salmon, cold cuts, and little golden quiches. I filled my plate with strawberries and cheese and picked up a glass of champagne from the white-shirted waiter, deliberately staying in a corner of the room to avoid the flow of colleagues.

"Hi, there!" A striking Amerasian woman in her forties was approaching me. "Long time no see."

Elizabeth Sung Foreman. I could never forget her name or her face. Her hair was highlighted burgundy red, with the big curls of a typical Texas beauty, and her Chinese eyes were adroitly made up, their Asian-ness contrasting interestingly with her high-bridged nose and dimpled chin—quite an unusual combination, and a tribute to the highly skilled knives of her plastic surgeon. The rumor mill at the Houstonian health club had it that she was addicted to going under the knife. Her huge breasts appeared constricted under the tailored black jacket that ended proportionately over an elegant short skirt. Sheer black hose and her matching Charles Jordan spiked heels were a fashionable touch and helped feminize her harsh manners.

Elizabeth Sung Foreman referred to me as her friend at cocktail parties, charity events, and happy-hour get-togethers of lawyers in fashionable tapas bars. A Texas-born second-generation Chinese American who spoke with a Texas drawl, Elizabeth was known as the tough, bitchy, hardheaded, and effective litigator, the only Asian female member of the Texas Trial Lawyers Association who could stand shoulder-to-shoulder with all the town's potbellied, celebrity male litigators. Once married to a wealthy oil and gas investor, she'd divorced him, retained her share of the fortune as well as his last name, and practiced law for fun with the top plaintiffs' firm in Houston, working exclusively on massive, multimillion-dollar plaintiffs' tort cases and class actions. Elizabeth had become the classic example of success as a brilliant lawyer, breaking the norm of the stereotypical submissive Asian female. She had established herself among Houston's socialites as an attractive, rich, coldhearted Asian-American woman who had also managed to gain acceptance as a Texas southern belle. She drove a convertible Mercedes with its top off on Houston's freeways, her scarf floating in the wind like the dancer Isadora Duncan, and supposedly performed acrobatics during sex. I was repelled by her as much as I respected her for what she represented—the persona I could never become, the type who could broker her Asian-ness and femininity whenever she needed to, and discarded her ethnic roots whenever this suited her.

Elizabeth Sung Foreman. A loud, cocky, obnoxious Amerasian Texas belle in a Barbie form, with the heart of Snow White's step-mother. In my few years of law practice in Houston, I had seen her being all of those things.

The Houston legal community had only two female Asian partners in prestigious law firms: Mimi Sean Young and Elizabeth Sung Foreman. Neither of us liked the other, yet both felt obligated to act as though we'd joined in a pact representing our kind—the Asian American pioneer female law firm partners, two exotic early birds in the profession, both serving on the board of the Asian American Bar and charged with the community responsibility of mentoring the new breed of Asian American female lawyers. We stood at two opposite ends of the spectrum. I was the reflective, intellectual Harvard-trained lawyer who slaved at a senior position, conforming to the image of a hard-working, conscientious Asian immigrant, while Elizabeth was the one-of-a-kind, hard-nosed litigator who'd fought her way to the top of the town's very small heap of multimillion-dollar lawyers.

"Looking slim, Mimi," she said.

"Same with you, Liz."

"I heard you are going to run for a judgeship." She winked.

"You know I don't have that kind of money, Liz," I said. "Nor would I want to become a judge even if I did have the money," I added truthfully.

"I would consider doing something like that only if it wouldn't interfere with my sex life," she said, vulgar as usual. "People watch you when you sit on the bench."

"Uh-huh," I said, looking off across the room to signal my lack of interest in the matter of her sex life. But then, my heart stung: I saw Brad at the other end of the room, talking and smiling in a group. What had happened to the all-day deposition? He was wearing the red tie I had given him. He did not see me.

"Alan Bradley Hurst," Elizabeth said, following my gaze. "Good-looking, nice guy. He prefers being called Brad. Not many people know that."

My heart stung again, and I couldn't help turning to look at her. "You know him?" I asked, trying to sound casual.

"We used to date. About three years ago," she said innocently.

I exhaled in relief, worried that Elizabeth would detect my nervous reaction. Three years ago I was still on the East Coast and had not yet met Brad. Only my loyal secretary knew about Brad and me, and she wasn't the type who gossiped. Brad and I implicitly avoided the public places known to be populated with lawyers, because we both disliked our own profession.

"Fabulous lay," Elizabeth continued.

I dropped a strawberry. She didn't seem to notice. I couldn't help looking over at her again, and since I was shorter than she, my eyes rested unintentionally on her large breasts. For the first time, I felt pierced by jealousy. I sorrowfully imagined Brad's handsome face against her breasts, his curvy mouth taking in her nipples, his hands molding the largesse I did not have. Where did this surge of jealousy come from?

"Sophisticated guy. Taking me to the opera and that kind of thing. I was sad for two days when I dropped him. I still miss the sex."

I let go of my fork this time. It dropped to the carpeted floor. I thought of how Brad and I spent the majority of our time at my house, in bed, before my mirror, rather than downtown commingling with Houston's connoisseurs of the arts. Maybe she was doing this deliberately, lying to hurt me. She had never liked me, and the friendship was phony. I regained my composure and finished my champagne. "You drop everybody, Liz," I said coldly. "You have the power to do it."

"Oh, no, no, with this one, it was different. I was genuinely fond of him. Still am. Sweet, tender lover. Quiet, but sensational. He utters tiny, sugary sounds. Untiring hip movements."

My heart stung again with every word she uttered. She tilted her head toward me and lowered her voice. "Occasionally he still comes back for old-time's sake, especially for that 'tie me up, talk dirty to me' ritual. In fact, just a couple of weeks ago…"

A dagger stabbed through my rib cage. Next to me she was still bragging, yet I could no longer absorb her words. She was oblivious to my pain. She could not be lying. She knew him. *Walk away, walk away, Mi Chau, before havoc is done.* I walked away from her and pretended to put down my empty glass for more strawberries. She followed me.

"I had to let him go because of his family situation. I didn't have time to deal with that. I didn't want to piss off Rebecca Kaw, of all people."

"Rebecca Kaw?"

"You mean you don't know? It's all over town, especially among the rich Asians. Oh, but you haven't been here for long. Only a couple of years, right? Let me fill you in. Alan Bradley Hurst is married to the only daughter of a Hong Kong multimillionaire."

"Oh, that. Yes, I might have heard. The computer lady."

"Yes. She's quite something."

"I heard she installed computers," I said, simply making conversation, not caring much about the gossip. If I had wanted to know, I could have asked Brad. But Elizabeth refused to let go of the topic.

"What are you talking about? You really don't know, do you? Rebecca Kaw installing computers? You've got to be kidding. She manufactured every computer in every law firm and business in town, in direct competition with the biggies like Dell, Apple, IBM, Texas Instruments. In fact, her company manufactured and masterminded the whole network system and software installed in Hurst's law firm."

I took in another strawberry and held it under my tongue. My heart was racing. *Walk away, Mi Chau, walk away. You don't want to know.*

"Rebecca came from Hong Kong, a thirty-something widow of an older man from MIT who started a very successful computer company which traded on the New York Stock Exchange. Its stock has gone *whoop*." She pointed her red-nailed finger to the ceiling. "The company is also a client of Brad's law firm. But Rebecca didn't just have a rich, dead husband. She also has her own money. Her family is filthy rich in Hong Kong and Singapore. She is the only daughter, only heir, and the dead husband's fortune only tops that. Her father builds golf courses in Houston and sells them to the Japanese. They were the first Asians in town who moved into River Oaks.

"Rebecca proposed to Brad and married him, and he stayed home in their River Oaks mansion to write some sort of a novel and she supported him and even got pregnant. But they didn't get along, and Brad went back to work and they were separated. The man would never get a divorce, Mimi. He might have come from some white trash Southern family somewhere from East Texas or Alabama or Mississippi, or maybe Atlanta, so he never had a taste of real, old Pacific Rim money. Rebecca gave him a golf course near Greatwood. He's still drawing income from it."

At the other end of the room, Brad was talking to a couple of young women in lawyers' suits. This wasn't the emotional, vulnerable, ardent Brad I knew, but a charming Brad who was relaxed, cheerful, suave, and open. Elizabeth's words continued to ring their wicked bell. *Walk away, Mi Chau, walk away. There is malice here.* My feet were buried in the ground, and I could not move.

"I don't mind filling you in. I'd better protect you. I can tell in your eyes the way you looked at him across the room that you like him already. Sexy Brad has a thing for rich, older, attractive Asian women. He went after me the first year he and Rebecca separated."

I swallowed the whole strawberry. She'd turned to look at me, and I met her eyes. I had no more champagne in the glass, but there must have been champagne on my cheeks.

"Thanks for your concern, Liz," I said, "but I don't fit the description. I am not rich."

"I may believe that, but sexy Brad may not know it, you see. In fact, I'm surprised he hasn't stopped by your office to introduce himself already. It's understandable why you two haven't run into each other. Different practices. You are…what? International commerce? And he's a local litigator. A very good one, I must say."

I thought of our chance meeting in Hermann Park. My sketchbook and the sweaty jogger. It had not been planned. I raised my eyes again to meet hers; they were difficult to read with all that careful makeup and the bright green contact lenses.

"He can fall for you, you know," she said, playing with the Chanel earring dangling from her earlobe. "No matter what, the dude is a romantic. And I can tell you are, too. Come on, go meet him with me. I'll introduce you two. At least seduce him for sex. I guarantee it's worth it."

"No, thank you."

"Come on. You can take the heat from Rebecca Kaw. I'm different. She's a friend and a supporter. She's too rich and too local to be my enemy. You, on the other hand, can always escape back East to your Ivy League crowd, or maybe find a teaching job with all those credentials of yours. Come on. You have my recommendation. You can have fun with the dude. Tie him up. Let him handcuff you. Try the Kama Sutra."

"Stop, Elizabeth," I finally snapped.

She stopped smiling. I looked away. At the other end of the room, Brad was shifting his weight, placing one hand in his trouser pocket. He still did not see me.

I turned to Elizabeth and softened my voice. "No thank you, Liz," I said, seeing the nauseating crudity and pettiness in her perfectly made-up face. "I already have a boyfriend," I added, pulling myself together.

She put away her plastic smile, stopped seizing my eyes with her green contact lenses. All at once, her gaze became tender, dreamy, and soothing, almost like that of my big sister Simone. "That's what I heard. You're seeing someone steady. Congratulations. He must be a lawyer, too. The way you work, you don't have time to meet anybody else. This is a small legal community."

She knows, Mi Chau, she knows. She is playing cat and mouse.

"I'm sure your boyfriend is good in bed...wait, wait, wait! Don't be prudish." Like that, the soft gaze had vanished and her wicked self was back. "I know you and I are the same type. The fearless and hungry. Competitive, overachieving women are highly sexual. Proud nymphos, we are. Don't deny it."

I put my plate down on the table a little too forcefully. It made a noise.

"If you didn't have a boyfriend"—she would not stop— "I would highly recommend Alan Bradley Hurst. He's a nice man, and he is discreet. Of course, you will have to live with the Rebecca Kaw situation, and that little girl of his, the baby heiress."

"Thanks for the society gossip, Liz. I have to leave." I listened to myself sounding aloof.

"*Au revoir,* Mimi," she said, imitating a French accent, the green contacts sending a different message: *Nice performance, Mimi. Don't expect me to quit that easily. I am still enjoying this.*

I started to walk away, but she kept talking. "So you didn't get to meet lawyer-gigolo Alan Bradley Hurst? Might as well. I think he's coming back to Rebecca. Just a couple of days ago, I saw them together for late-night champagne at the Houstonian Hotel."

I almost tripped on my heels.

"Watch it, Mimi," she called out behind me. "Well, if you two had met, I wouldn't be surprised if he would have fallen for you. In fact, if I were a guy, I would myself. You are one hell of a girl, Mimi."

—

You are one hell of a girl, Mimi. Rage overtook over me as I stepped into my car. My left leg scratched against something and a hole appeared in the sheer black hose. I cursed. I took the wrong turn twice on the way to the spa. Couldn't wipe out the words I had heard. *He's coming back to Rebecca. Just a couple of days ago*

I saw them together for late-night champagne at the Houstonian Hotel. I thought of those nights after our sushi meals, when I drove home to my mirror and slept alone. For weeks, his hands had no longer moved along my inner thighs in the familiar formula of our lovemaking. I had to take him in my hand and lead him on, and he buried his face into the pillow instead of seeking my lips. Painfully I reminded myself of how he had knelt down by my bed with his head in his two hands, pouring out those tears and emotional words. *He's a local litigator, a very good one I must say.* How could I have so quickly forgotten that my vulnerable, sensitive, awkward thirty-three-year-old Brad was one of the town's brightest young litigators, so quickly scoring victories in Texas courtrooms—in fact, who'd never lost a case? Litigators were good actors, and they knew how to invoke emotions and manipulate. I, of all people, ought to know better.

At the spa I took off my clothes and wrapped a Turkish towel around me and lay down on my stomach, my arms hanging down on the sides of the canapé. I told the masseuse to pound his hands on my wounded self and use all of his force. *Yes, ma'am. More force. Yes, ma'am. Do you have a lot of clients who are forty-year-old Asian women? A few, ma'am. Is our hairless skin smooth? Yes, ma'am. Do you like what you do? It's all right, ma'am. I don't like being a lawyer, but I do it for money. We all work for money, ma'am. Do you think Brad takes all Asian women in town to bed, and I am just one of those? Am I listed in his diary? A computer file somewhere?* The masseuse chuckled. *I don't know, ma'am.* I moved my head and turned to the other side. *Let's see: Rebecca Kaw. Elizabeth Sung Foreman. Mimi Sean Young. Who else? What do you think? I don't know, ma'am. I think I may have missed some local Asian celebrities. Tina Chen, the woman on the City Council. She's married and has a stick figure. Not his type. Besides, she is a public official. Bad risk. Donna Lee the Korean anchor—too young, too gamine. He likes older, voluptuous women. Patricia Chang, the assistant U.S. attorney. She wears a size twelve. He wouldn't go for that. What do you think? I have no idea, ma'am. You must know, you're a man. I'm married with three kids, ma'am. More force. I can't, ma'am, your bones are so small I can't take a chance. I say it's all right. Yes, ma'am. I have a boyfriend. He's lucky, ma'am. No, I'm lucky, my secretary keeps saying. You know why we are drawn together? We are both trapped. He's trapped in whatever he's trapped in. Rebecca Kaw. His job. His child. I'm trapped in my haunting past and my Harvard pedigree and investment in the law for almost two decades of my life. So he says he sees himself in me. We both hate our own kind. The more we hate, the more skilled we become at what we hate. Dreams die. The trap remains. My quilted Chanel purse. My Paragammo fine leather shoes. The silver-gray BMW 700 series with its unreliable air-conditioning. The three-story Victorian house in the museum district. Partnership meetings where we talk about people in numbers called billable hours. You know how much I billed? No, ma'am. Twenty-two hundred hours a year at over four hundred dollars per hour. I have made a bunch of us very rich. And they gave me a fancy title for it. I'm a law partner in a prestigious firm, I am head of a section, but behind doors I don't share in the profit, I make much less than the men, and the world is not supposed to know there is such a discrepancy in pay. By the way, what happened to the Human Rights Office at Harvard Law School? I don't know, ma'am. I haven't been to their potluck dinners for years. I've been busy doing client development at the Harvard Club. You know the Harvard Club? No, ma'am. Guess what, I am not a drinker but I had five glasses of champagne at lunch. I know, ma'am, you usually don't talk this way. You're usually very quiet. I don't think you are feeling well, ma'am. Your skin is very hot.*

I told the masseuse I would turn around on my back, and he turned away. I put the Turkish towel across my chest. He massaged my arms, and the pain ran from my fingers to the base of my neck. Brad's face hovered on the ceiling. He went from kissing the base of my neck—my magic bottle—to Elizabeth Sung Foreman's silicone breasts, to some tall, Hong Kong Gong Li look-alike parting her fishnet legs, another Brad resting between them. She brushed her black stream of Gong Li hair away from her face and laughed, and her teeth shone like a row of glistening white corn. I saw myself crawling on the floor holding my stomach, and then I fell down a cliff and the masseuse was catching me. *Be careful, ma'am.* The muscles on my face were twitching slightly, the result of the aging process, the stress of years of long workdays, and the sorrow inside my soul.

Who is the president of the new republic? Tell me, Mimi, who is he? My Crazy Man and the republic we would build together. We are both unusual people with unusual dreams, my Crazy Man and me, but what would we do in America? What would we be? He said he stopped writing the dissertation, but he still cared about the dream. My Crazy Man died before we could even kiss, and I had to deal with that loss on my own; I might have achieved my imagined American dream, but the real dream I shared with my Crazy Man was lost. The image of a sad and ignored Grandma Que kept appearing in America even though I knew she would be so out of place in America's crowds. Here in America, she was the unwanted ghost. What is the dream, Mimi? You wrote about the dream in your diary, Mimi. Tell me about your dream, my Asian child. You are like my Asian child. Oh, Brad. Oh, Brad. I touched the base of my neck and saw Brad, again, kissing my magic bottle. It spilled. *You can say your nine words to me, Mimi. After two decades of silence, I opened myself and gave the marathon of words to a man.*

I showed a man my dream and how it died, and then I found out he was a professional Asian woman fucker.

You're crying, ma'am. Do you want me to call someone? Get me my purse. Yes, ma'am. I took the cell phone out and realized there was no one in town I could call. Neither my friends nor my family knew anything about Brad. They had given up on me and my succession of no-name boyfriends. I put the phone down next to me and the Turkish towel dropped and my breasts were exposed. The respectful masseuse turned away quickly. *Thank God there are still respectful men like you, my masseuse.* I opened my compact and looked into its mirror at the twitching muscles in my face. *I want a facial. I'll make an appointment for you, ma'am. No, I want it now. Your strong hands, pound them on my face. I can't do that, ma'am. I can hurt you. No you can't, I'm already hurt. Can't you see my facial muscles are twitching? I can't see a thing, ma'am. I think you have a fever, ma'am, and you may be imagining things. Me, imagining things? Impossible. I can't be hallucinating. I am a top-notch lawyer, AV-rated, the top of my profession. But I just got defeated by a bitch named Elizabeth Sung Foreman who screwed my thirty-three-year-old Brad silly. It's nothing, nothing, believe me. This irrational behavior is what happens when Grandma Que's queenly grandchild is defeated. She thought I was strong but I wasn't. I am a fragile leaf falling from her* longan *tree, but she is no longer around to pick me up and replant my roots. Work your hands on my face, please. Sorry, ma'am. The cream can irritate your skin. I'll get fired. We'll get sued. It's against the spa's rules. Here is a hefty tip, fifty dollars, just for you. I'm a lawyer, I promise I won't sue you. Work my facial muscles, please. OK, ma'am, but I will be extra gentle. It's just a massage to keep you happy. You go to sleep, ma'am. I'll call the facial specialist and she'll take over. It's an emergency request by a longtime customer, I'll tell them.*

—

I slept away my sorrow and intense jealousy and broken heart. Reality came back when I heard the air-conditioning noise and felt the warm napkin they had placed on my face. The warmth gradually turned into cold air that soothed away the pain. I faced myself. *Oh goddamn you, Alan Bradley Hurst. I have fallen in love. I showed you my sketchbook. I told you my life story. I became your Scheherazade. I showed you the depth of my womb and I fell in love. What else can it be when I am this insanely jealous? Can't get out of my mind the thought of some other woman, Rebecca, Elizabeth, whoever they are, catching the tip of your tongue, the tip of your penis, the tips of your fingers, and the curve of your mouth. This pain is real. I must have fallen obsessively in love with a man to whom I should not be delivering my nine words.*

The cell phone rang and I grabbed it.

"Hello, Mimi, are you there?"

"Yes."

"This is Kurt Fiesta." I heard the voice of the third-year associate. I detected a note of alarm in his voice.

"What's wrong, Kurt?"

"I don't know. I had the memo delivered at one o'clock this afternoon, earlier than necessary. I was going to call you at four thirty as you instructed."

"Good, Kurt, good job."

"But, Mimi, by two o'clock, the client, Ms. Tracy Carr, called and said she was not happy and it was urgent that she talk to you. She wanted me to find you, and I said I would page. Your secretary said you were at the bar luncheon. I even went there. You had just left. I spoke to your friend, Ms. Foreman. She didn't know where you went. Assumed you went back to the office. Couldn't find you."

"OK, OK, Kurt, slow down. It's all right." I pressed on my elbows and sat up, wide-awake.

"Your secretary said you might be at the spa and didn't want to be disturbed. It's your birthday. Happy birthday, Mimi."

"Thanks, Kurt."

"Mimi, you will have to come in. I don't know what the client Ms. Carr has said or done, but at three I got a call from the executive assistant in the managing partner's office, and then the next thing I knew was that our very own Mr. Townsend was on the line talking to me directly. He has never done that the whole time I have been here working at the firm. He wanted me to find you. He set up a time for you to meet with him in the office. Four thirty this afternoon. The meeting is confidential. I asked Mr. Townsend what I could do to help you prepare, and he said, no, only Ms. Young could solve this."

"What time is it now, Kurt?"

"Three thirty."

"I have an hour. I'll be in. Don't worry, Kurt. I'll take care of it."

"Mimi, may I say something?"

"Yes, Kurt."

"I don't know what it is, but the memo is the best piece of work I've seen around this firm. It's legally correct. Morally, it's the right thing."

"I know, Kurt. Bye."

I sat in the ladies' room of the spa and took the emergency panty hose out of my purse. I pulled the silky sheer material to the tops of my thighs and carefully applied my makeup. The facial skin became translucently smooth and rosy after I applied foundation and powder and highlighted the cheekbones with nectar rouge. I smoothed the concealer cream over the dark circles underneath the eyes. I put conditioner on my lips and bordered them with a dark liner, dipped the brush into my neutral-colored lipstick, and filled in the shape. I put on the silk blouse and stepped on my high heels. The black suit came last. I placed the cell phone inside my purse and pulled the shoulder strap over my shoulder. I checked myself in the mirror. I was back to the poised, reflective, and perfect Mimi Sean Young.

I headed toward the marbled hallway and ran into the masseuse. His eyebrows raised slightly over his squinting eyes, which sparked with a myriad of dubious questions. "Ma'am?" he said. "I can't believe it. You look…so fine. I thought you were sick."

"I've recovered. It won't happen again. I was a little dizzy-headed from the champagne at lunch. Thanks for being extra-careful with my facial skin. I am going to a business meeting and it would have been disastrous had there been a bruise."

"You're very welcome, ma'am."

—

Burt Townsend was a stout Texan with a throaty voice and a thick, tanned face. He walked like a cowboy, his legs wide apart as though each were following a separate walking track; and his short arms curved into the shape of a fat *O* around his abundant frame. He smoked a pipe or at least always had it in his hand. His lips pulled perpetually into a half-moon shape, curving upward, giving the illusion of a smile, which remained on his face even when he talked. The authority he projected was in that perpetual smile, which could either be friendly to his clients or menacing and intimidating to his adversaries. The plaintiffs' bar had a nickname for him based on his perpetual moon-shaped smile—they called him, behind his back, the Joker, as in Batman comic books. On Fridays he wore a cowboy hat and boots to work. The law firm had grown more and more cosmopolitan and international, with my addition to the partnership as the expert on international transactions, yet Burt Townsend wanted to keep the distinctive Texas image. The Manhattan boys had to know they were dealing with Burt Townsend when they came to Houston, a statement for the great oil capital. A seasoned oil and gas and title lawyer, he talked with a smooth Texas drawl. One could see him in an oil field, smiling perpetually around oilmen or oil rig workers, as well as in a boardroom working out oil leases, but always in Texas. He would send the Ivy League–trained boys and gals of the Townsend firm to deal with the Yankees elsewhere.

Burt Townsend sat behind his mahogany desk, in front of his oil-on-canvas painting of an oil rig in motion, and signaled for me to sit.

"How's it goin', Mimi?" he said, his greeting loud and cheerful. "I heard it's your birthday. Happy birthday!" This was Burt Townsend's trademark. He was all into warmth and kindness.

"Thank you, Burt," I said. All the young associates called him Mr. Townsend. I had turned forty this day, with seventeen years of legal experience behind me, so for the first time in my years at the firm, I chose to address him by his first name, as did the senior partners in the firm.

He got up and walked around his desk toward the other chair facing me, in front of his desk. He drew on his pipe and swung it away adroitly. His movements were unexpectedly graceful and swift, considering his heavyset body. He sat down, stretched his short legs, and filled up the black leather chair. He leaned over and picked up my Entran memorandum sitting in the inbox to the left of his desk.

"Sorry for this unexpected meeting. I understand you were out celebrating your birthday. You know, as professionals, we put the needs and interests of our clients first."

Cut the bullshit on professional ethics. I've been through these meetings before. I've been a star performer for this firm, pulling in the billable hours to justify my existence. You've paid me not even one-third of the gross revenue I've generated. What have I done wrong? Client relations? I longed to spill the truth of my feelings, but I did not.

"It's all right," I assured him. "I pulled an all-nighter this week and wanted to recuperate. Actually, when you called I was at the gym working out with the full intention to return to work at four and work until nine tonight on the Dakota filing. It isn't due until next week, but I want to get it over with." I explained with a white lie, knowing the insane work pace was what he wanted to hear. In reality, I had planned to spend the evening with Brad at the Riverway. The Dakota filing was the following day's plan. *Play the game, girl.*

"Marvelous, marvelous." He put the pipe back in the corner of his mouth, his eyes lit up, the joker's perpetual smile appearing much more distinctively. Maybe this time he was actually smiling.

"I have fully expected this meeting, Burt," I said wryly. "I knew the client might have some reaction. It's a complex, delicate matter."

"Almighty fine," he said in his finest, most charming Texas accent. "Be that as it may, I wished you'd been here to take that call from Tracy Carr and *smoooth* things out," he drawled. "Anyway, here is the problem, and I'll leave it to you to solve satisfactorily." He pulled his fat frame up, filling the chair vertically, his manner congenial and fatherly. "You know we're all here bec'use of law. Law's law but it ain't law. It's bus'ness, you know what I mean. Bus'ness's law and law's bus'ness."

I don't know what you mean, sir, I said in my head. Yet I kept silent, and he turned the pages of my memorandum.

"Excellent work. You're an *alllmighty* fine lawyer. That's why we hired you away from the big boys on the East Coast and made you partner your second year here. *Uuunprecedented*, Mimi. We'd never done such a thing with anybody who came to us without an existing client portfolio like yourself. You have a*lllmighty* fine credentials.

"You amaze all of us," he continued, looking at me closely. "Summa cum laude undergrad. Summa cum laude Harvard JD, LLM. A fragmented work record, but, *alllmighty* fine! Our firm's growin' by leaps and bounds and we firmly believe in promotin' women and diversity and all."

He stopped to draw a smoke. "Sorry about the smoke, Mimi, my bad habit. I'll die one day smokin' my pipe."

I re-crossed my legs and turned away from the smoke.

"Anyway, it was I who recommended to the management committee that we open an international section for you to run to meet the needs of long-term clients doing bus'ness abroad like Entran. Our client's *reallly* big in Asia and Latin America both. Asia's your territory of cultural expertise, ain't it? You're very important to the success of this firm. Y'all have done a fine job."

"Thank you, Burt."

"The client appreciated your great work," he said, slowing down, the voice becoming dramatic. "But it ain't what they want." He inhaled on his pipe.

"What exactly do they want, Burt?"

"You see, Mimi, that's where you're off-base. You, as the lawyer, are supposed to know what they want. They want your help to solve a bus'ness problem." He drew another smoke.

"The country manager had already said he wanted me to make a contract provision disappear." I crossed my arms. "I can argue a point before an interpreting court all the way to the Supreme Court, but I can't make something in print disappear, especially when the contract was well negotiated and duly executed."

"Oh, that's preposterous!" He shifted his load in the leather chair already overloaded with his frame. "I hope the man's just jokin'. Now tell me"—he leaned toward me, warm and concerned like a father—"let's look at this together as a bus'ness problem. What happened?"

I knew what he would be getting at, ultimately.

"The senior project engineer made a huge payment to a foreign government official, which under U.S. law can be construed as illegal." I gave him the facts. "The Foreign Corrupt Practices Act, commonly acronymed as the FCPA..." I was speaking slowly and cautiously like a law professor, and he interrupted me.

"Hold! Hold it!" He raised one finger. "Stop right there. I'm not sophisticated enough to do international work, Mimi. And I don't care to. That's what y'all're here for, but of course I've heard of the FCPA. Serious stuff. I know about the Lockheed scandal in the seventies, all that bribery involving foreign government and all."

"Let me finish, Burt," I said. "The Department of Justice may go after the engineer for individual liability. We don't represent the engineer. We are here to save the corporation."

He leaned back and turned his head toward the ceiling. The smoke coming out of his pipe circled the air.

"Say, Mimi, if the client does what you recommend, discipline this idiot and all, it's all well and good, and maybe the Department of Justice would get this idiot and jail him, and God almighty, the fool deserves it, but what would happen to the contract they just won? Give up the contract? Void the bid? Bidding all over the second time? Come on, Mimi. What will happen to international relations if this thing gets blown up all over the media? You think bringing this mess to the attention of the board of directors and addressing it at the board's level, as you suggested, will solve this thing? Or will it just pass the bug onto the top and blow the mess out of proportion? That's why we need an almighty good brain like yours to solve this the way—"

"I did solve it, Burt."

"Hear me out, Mimi. It's a deal involving billions of dollars, years of courting the Indian government, thousands of hours of work of all kinds of personnel, the future employment of thousands of Americans and Asians in the next three years during construction and start-up, a heavy budget item on the client's balance sheet, stock price, shareholders' interests, all kinds of crap that they pay this firm millions of dollars a year, including your salary, to watch out for. Don't you think this ought to be resolved at the lower level, in a more pragmatic manner?"

I crossed my legs again. "Not taking action at the top, including us informing the board of directors, means risking shareholders' derivative suits and government prosecution of the corporation, and a violation of fiduciary duties…"

"Not if the whole thing goes away unofficially and quietly over there in west India. You can do better than just preaching about law, Mimi. Think creatively."

"I have."

"Come on. You underestimate your potential. A woman like you...Tell me, why did you go to Harvard?"

"Best law school in the nation, and they gave me a scholarship," I told him. *I was a first-generation immigrant. Straight-A student. Simone married old New York money and helped me with expenses. The scholarship came my way. I was raised by an old woman who believed in a queenly spirit. I was supposed to be the chosen descendant of a queen. I have a father who was a philosophy professor and a mother of fragile health who plants flowers. I wanted my version of the American dream, but I didn't know how else to go after my dream when the opportunity came my way to get a law degree from Harvard.* I carried on the monologue in my head, overwhelmed by the outward effort to control the need to cry.

"You also went back to Harvard for an LLM. You have a JD and an LLM from Harvard. Not many practitioners have such a glorious combination. Why did you do that, getting that LLM?"

"Intellectual stimulation."

"But you're not inspired to teach or become dean of a law school. You're here with us, instead."

"My father was college professor and life was hard for us. I didn't want to follow his footsteps. Well, come to think of it, I suppose Harvard also gave me contacts. Networking."

"There you go, Mimi. You've just hit the nail on the head. Now you're talkin'. How do you think the fabulous Tracy Carr got to where she is today over at Entran? She did wonders in India and Asia. She knows human relations. She smoothed things, wiped away events that weren't supposed to happen, and created events that should happen; and she climbed the corporate ladder quicker than a New York minute. Use her as a role model, Mimi."

For dramatic impact, he had paused to examine the pipe in his hand, keeping me waiting. "Mimi, I love this pipe. Don't you think it's *alllmighty* fine?"

I don't know a fucking thing about your almighty fine pipe, you asshole. Cut the bullshit, I cursed in my head. Only in my head.

"Your LLM class," he continued, "all of those top-notch over-achiever foreign lawyers and dignitaries. Some of them aimed to become the top in their respective nations. Surely you have a network of friends and classmates from Asia as well as in Washington, D.C."

He did not notice my sigh.

"I've seen you glow at this sort of thing in other situations. This week you've been tired. You haven't been thinkin' like a bus'ness problem solver. You resort back to the Harvard classroom. It may be legally and technically fine, but it's stale, academic thinkin'. It works only up to a point."

He left his chair and walked toward another oil-on-canvas painting of an old man, hung in the middle of the accented wall. The canvas showed the hard-edged face of a Texas oilfield worker in offshore platform gear. I looked around the room. There was no framed diploma or law book in his office.

"My daddy, Mimi." He pointed at the figure on the canvas. "He worked hard all his life. Maybe he would have loved for me to go to Harvard. I didn't. It hasn't hurt me a bit. Through the years I've learned one thing. We all need to cultivate people and utilize them later. And with that I founded this law firm."

"It's admirable, Burt," I said.

He stood still, looking at the painting of the oil rig worker. "No magic, Mimi. Just what's in your basket of tools. Think about how you can solve this beyond writing an almighty fine legal memo. Don't get me wrong. I am not suggesting any impropriety or illegality. Just a little finesse of people's contacts. I mean finesse. Of course, we're here in the bus'ness of law. We keep people legal and solve their legal problems."

"That's it, Burt. We solve legal problems only."

He abruptly turned around to face me. The perpetual smile had vanished. It was the first time I'd seen Burt Townsend's face without a smile. "The client didn't come to you because you could tell them about the FCPA. Many lawyers in this town can do the same thing, even if they may not do it as well as you. They came to you because this law firm has capitalized on your Harvard LLM network of international lawyers and government officials all over the world. Prove to us—" He paused. "Prove to us—" He stressed those words again.

I turn forty today, and I am tired of proving, I said in my head.

"Prove that you have all the good senses of a superb bus'nessperson."

He went back to his desk and smoked his pipe in silence. His meaty face was icy cold. His signature joker's smile had not returned. "I believe this whole mess may go away if you talk to the right person over there in India, who can make a clean sweep, as though nothing has happened…"

I stretched one hand over my knees. The red nails that represented the common physical trait among me, Tracy Carr, and Elizabeth Sung Foreman had become the diva lipstick of Grandma Que. I glanced toward the glass window and found her floating outside. The glass window became the mirror through which I could find her. In a split second, she passed through the glass and floated around Burt Townsend's office, curiously looking at the painting of the oil rig worker. Apparently, she had never seen a man like that before. She looked toward me and raised her painted brows. "*I don't know what all this is about, my child. But I know it is making you upset, and every time you are upset, you call upon me. I am here for you, but you are going to have to do this on your own. Don't let this man intimidate you, whoever he is. After all, you are of queenly substance. You set your own standards, and you will let this man know that. So I just stand here and watch."* She floated around the furniture for a while and leaned against the glass window at last.

I crossed my legs again and raised my eyes to meet Burt Townsend's. "You want me to be another Tracy Carr, whatever that means, to make events disappear or create them as called for. I wish I could." I paused. "You said I was to clean up the mess in India as though nothing had happened. But something did happen, Burt, and some people do believe that maybe even God almighty couldn't wipe out a fait accompli and turn back the clock. I had thought about this very carefully before I wrote the memo, Burt. I am here because I believe I am the legal expert."

I knew the famous Burt Townsend smile might never return to his face after my final words were spoken. But I went on. "The legal analysis is not that complex. The law is designed to deter bad acts. There was a bad act, Burt, and the whole question is who's the mastermind behind it. In fact, the country manager and Tracy herself seemed to imply that this particular bad act is just part of a corporate culture, a way of doing business over there in India. Naturally, one can't blame a culture for violation of U.S. antibribery law by U.S. persons."

Grandma Que shifted her weight slightly at the glass wall. *You sound good, Mi Chau. Is that how the famous school up there in the snow country of Boston has taught you to speak?* I looked at her and acknowledged she was somewhat proud of me. She couldn't help showing it. I went on.

"My legal memorandum is written to protect this law firm, as well as the corporation, within the spirit of the law, even if it means surrendering a bid contract that has already been tainted with international bribery. Now, if I hear you correctly, you are suggesting that I go along with executives like Tracy Carr in hiding the facts from the board of directors, while availing myself of the global Harvard network to somehow magically remove the taint, as though it never existed. You want me to work wonders and make the act of bribery disappear from the record over there in India. Certainly, the foolish engineer could not have reached into his own checking account to take out millions of dollars and transfer the fund to the South Indian chief."

Bad acts. Bad acts. Can they just be erased, because the good and almighty people involved cavalierly act as though the bad acts never existed? These words kept flashing in my head, and near the glass window Grandma Que nodded several times approvingly because she could see my thoughts. Of course she agreed with me. It was all about that first lady material—the *noblesse oblige* she had spotted in the little girl who crawled around under that beautiful *longan* tree of the past. Some place far, very far away.

My thoughts went back to the Crazy Man and the speech he gave on the steps of Krost Hall to passersby. A regime in a Southeast Asian country, symbolized by all the young men and women who believed in its cause, had been portrayed in the Western media collectively as corrupt and incompetent—the source of all kinds of bad acts, like bribery and the murder of innocent men and women, and thefts of public funds and foreign aid. When they lost a war, the world pointed its fingers and said, "It served you right," and the winner became the good guy, and all the bad acts and murders and thefts committed by the winners became nonexistent, and history was rewritten such that

the losers bore all the shame and became the culprit for a generation's guilt complex. Those losers happened to include the Crazy
Man and the few Confucian-minded teachers and intellectuals of
South Vietnam like my father, and all other unknown heroes and
heroines and the few good men and women of non-Communist
South Vietnam whose names and sacrifices never made it to the
media headlines or the final chapter of history. They never had
a chance. And all in that mess at the end of the Vietnam War,
there was a schoolgirl in that dark house outside Tan Son Nhat
Airport…such a small tragedy in the grand scope of things and
the immense treachery of war….

All of a sudden, I became very angry. I grabbed onto the arms
of the leather chair.

My past rolled through my head and I thought of how the one
SISU student had savored Portia's words on the meaning of justice and mercy. How the first-year law student—a 1L Harvard kid
from Vietnam had practiced the great art of lawyering by giving a
two-minute speech on the beautiful words of law that she believed
made America great. *The Words. The Words. The Words.* The flash
repeated itself in my head. My eyes felt watery, and I relived all those
moments before the plane took off from Tan San Nhat airport. I had
paid such a heavy price to be here, the brutal ripping of girlhood
from me and the subsequent breakage of my life. All I had to justify
the meaning of my existence here was a lesson of survival shown in
the beauty of *The Words. Those beautiful words. My Words.*

I remembered my idiosyncratic habit of touching the base of
my neck where I imagined I had the magic bottle that held *My
Words.* In Burt Townsend's office, I was touching the base of my
neck again. I did this whenever I felt I had to win the internal
battle that no one else knew about, except myself.

"We lawyers are all aware the FCPA requires knowing action and specific intent of a foreign bribery," I continued, completely oblivious to what was happening on Burt Townsend's well-fed face. "The project engineer who bribed is already on the hook. No one would protect him now, and he might not be rich enough to hire a lawyer who could turn black into white, the sort of lawyer with the type of contacts that the Harvard network could offer. The poor engineer is not an officer, so corporate insurance won't pick up his defense. He obviously would be pointing fingers at his bosses and the corporation, at individuals like the country manager and Tracy Carr, who were responsible for nurturing this wheel-and-deal corporate culture in business transactions abroad.

"Now the only question left is whether the corporation, and that means the board of directors, has shared in the not-too-clever project engineer's corrupt intent. How much does top management know? How much will the board know? Intent is a question of proof, direct and circumstantial. Firing the engineer, voiding the award of the contract, and informing the board are all part of management's effort to gather the surest proof to negate corrupt intent and insulate liability to that dumb and overzealous project engineer, and whoever else has authorized his decision to bribe. If that means the corporation may have to go back to America empty-handed, well…anything else short of that—any *finesse*, as you say…"

I stressed the word "finesse," adapting awkwardly his Texas drawl.

"Any efforts to hold on to the billion-dollar contract would cloak the corporation with the appearance of impropriety or possibly bad faith, leaving the corporation's intent an uncertainty—a matter of interpretation. A fact finder may very well interpret these facts to mean the corporation had the corrupt intent to benefit from the bribery. And the taint of a bad intent may attach to the corporation's lawyers as well, although the attorney–client privilege would provide protection of confidentiality and shield information from discovery in litigation. It means that you and I and this firm may also be implicated…"

I listened to the law professor in me talk. My voice rose to its own rhythm and intonation. At some point, the broken record player in my head took over. *The law. The law. The law. Words. Words. Words. Bad acts. Bad acts. Bad acts.* The repetition went on forever in my mind.

So this is my life. The law. The law. The law.

No genius. No queen of Asia. Just the law. Excellence in predictability and mediocrity. *The mediocrity of a well-trained intellectual lawyer working for hire.* Even at the height of rhetoric eloquence, I had seen myself. The sadness of seeing myself so clearly immobilized me. Yet, the broken record inside my head stubbornly continued. *The law. The law. The law.*

I was surprised Townsend had let me go on as long as I had. "It's my birthday, Burt, and I've worked hard all week," I said, finally lowering my voice. "I am tired and would like to call this off for the day. I am your employee, Burt, and a partner of this firm, although I don't earn equity. Tomorrow morning, I'll make phone calls to former classmates. I'll trace down someone in India or central Asia. I'll go through the Harvard international alumni network. I'll try to work something out within the parameters of the law. I can't promise anything, because I will not walk gray lines, Burt—not for you, not for this firm, not for Tracy Carr, or for any client. In sum, if Entran management wants bulletproof protection and clean hands, and that includes every member of the board of directors, the company had better do what I say in the memo, keep Justice prosecutors at bay, and leave the house-cleaning to that foreign government within its own borders. So far as the firm is concerned, it's time to bring into this delicate matter a white-collar criminal law expert, Burt."

The orchestrated menacing smile finally returned to Townsend's face, but his eyes remained grave and cold as dead fish. *The plaintiffs' lawyers are right. He does look like the hideous Joker in a Batman movie.* My mind flashed the image of the devil-ish Jack Nicholson in his clown suit, and I shivered.

"If that's your professional opinion, Mimi, this firm is behind you." The Joker had returned to being the fatherly, heavyset Burt Townsend. "This is a law partnership. We are all fiduciaries liable for each other's acts. But, first, please do your best to help the client solve a business problem, Mimi. Set your pride and rigid-ity aside. Don't sink the boat because a stupid lowlife deckhand made a stupid mistake. Don't make top management create a paper trail of knowledge with your memo, Mimi, and don't pass the bug on to this poor board of directors who, between you and me, don't know a thing! I think you should assume there hasn't been any proof that management or Tracy Carr was ever part of this mess, and so we—our firm as outside counsel—don't have to paper trail ourselves as knowing any linkage between this stu-pid engineer and top management. Why do we have to show that we know anything? Why does Entran's top management have to know because you told us and we told them? Why can't the 'knowledge' stop at the stupid engineer of ours?"

He stopped to relight his pipe.

"Take this memorandum back to your office, and think about what I say, Mimi. Maybe you never sent the memo, Mimi. Maybe this is just a draft and ought to be shredded. Maybe so far as the client is concerned, this payment business over there in India just didn't exist; at least, it didn't exist past this engineer!" He quickened the last few sentences, his voice dropping to a whisper.

"Think about problem solving, Mimi." His voice resumed its customary volume. "Think seriously of firm relations, client relations, international relations, and your future here in this partnership. What I am saying is, there is no need to crusade." He smiled his plastic smile, and his voice dropped again. "Hell, there are people who think the Foreign Corrupt Practices Act is bad law. Foreign bribery should be just a cost of doing business in those poor countries that don't share our American values. Maybe they should even be tax deductible. That's the argument. But, here in our home, we care about our American values."

Our American values. The twang in Burt Townsend's Texas drawl seemed to last forever. I looked for the silhouette of Grandma Que outside the glass window. I expected to find her hovering outside, dozens of floors above the hot and humid Texas ground. The Vietnam War had ended decades ago, and the little girl underneath Grandma Que's *longan* tree had lost her shade of cool when she became acquainted with the American values. What the heck were Burt Townsend's American values? Were they the same as *The Words?* Those words. The rhetoric I once spoke so passionately at Harvard Law School.

Or *The Nine Words* I had never delivered to My Crazy Man? Everything was just words. Words and words and words.

I stood up and Burt Townsend handed me my memorandum. My mind quietly registered the statements he had made. Again, words and words. *Maybe you never sent the memo, Mimi. Maybe this is just a draft and ought to be shredded. Maybe so far as the client is concerned, this payment business over there in India just didn't exist…Hell, there are people who think the Foreign Corrupt Practices Act is bad law. Foreign bribery should be just a cost of doing business in those poor countries that don't share our American values.*

He was still talking. He had not stopped.

"Mimi, don't make this into another Lockheed scandal if you can avoid it. If I can appeal to your social conscience, the Lockheed scandal hurt the American national interest as well as shareholders. But maybe for someone like you, the national interest of America is just secondary to your individual pride and sense of self-righteousness, and that means…"

I stopped him mid-sentence. "Burt, I hold a U.S. passport, and I was a White House Fellow once, and yes, I do care very much about the United States' national interest."

He ignored my comment, perhaps realizing his faux pas. He went on cleverly, sidetracking the implication of my statement. "The practice of law in a competitive world is never just about law, Mimi. Make those phone calls in the morning, tell us the results, and we'll have another meeting with the senior partner of your section and ultimately with Tracy Carr, perhaps, and together we'll decide.

"By the way, the management committee has sent you a bouquet of flowers for your birthday. It should be on your desk by now." He seemed to have finished.

I got up, walked toward the door, and turned around to look at him one last time. "Thanks, Burt, for a great birthday present. I'm sure the flowers are lovely. But most of all, thanks for sharing with me your thoughts about your father. And about the true meaning of a Harvard education. At least in your opinion, that is."

—

I stopped by my office and met my secretary's concerned eyes.

"How was the meeting? Is everything OK?"

"Everything is fine," I said.

"There are flowers for you from the management committee."

I handed her the memorandum and asked her to file it. I headed toward the elevator bank.

But then I stopped midway. I turned around.

The evidence!

Thoughts swirled through my head: *Young Mimi Sean Young was once a young government staff attorney who was trying to learn how to be a prosecutor of white-collar crimes. There's the lesson learned: One must hold on to the evidence to protect oneself. In protecting oneself, one can also protect the public interest.* After all, I was Mimi Sean Young, the woman who rewrote her name and who won the Harvard moot court, the symbol of successful diversity for the young and hopeful Kurt Fiesta.

"I changed my mind about that memo," I told my secretary. "I need it back."

She pulled the document from the tray and gave it back to me. "You're the boss!" She raised her eyebrows.

"Yes, I am the boss." I forced myself to smile. I looked at the piece of paper she had just handed over to make sure it was the right memorandum. It was.

"Go into the firm's network," I told her, "and find the electronic version of this memo. Get on your keyboard right at this moment, come on." I read the document number to her.

"There, it is on my screen!" She confirmed.

"Send it to this e-mail address, right away." I read to her my personal e-mail address. "And save a copy of the memo and all related e-mails regarding its research and distribution onto a disk for me, right now. I wanted the backup in case e-mails were lost or corrupted."

"Done, Mimi," my secretary assured me. I stood in front of her cubicle and patiently watched her perform the task. Finally, she handed me the disk, smiling. "Here it is, boss."

I thanked her and entered my office. Sitting down before my computer, I accessed the document on the network myself. My secretary had found the document. She had done everything I asked of her, before my very eyes. Nothing could go wrong. I just wanted to double-check, to be sure.

But something *was* wrong!

I executed the command to access the memo several times. Network rejected the command. It meant that the file was no longer there!

This had to mean that someone in the firm, privy to the document number and the network filing system, had got to the document right after my secretary. The person had deleted it, wiping away the evidence of my work and the advice that should go to the Entran board.

Could it have been my secretary, right after she accessed the document per my instructions?

Could it have been Kurt Fiesta, who worked on the document with me and hence knew the document number?

Or could it have been anyone acting at the instructions of Burt Townsend, who had had the document?

I took a deep breath to regain my composure.
My hands trembled. Hurriedly, I accessed my personal e-mail account. The nervousness made me enter the wrong password, and I had to redo the command.

I breathed out a sigh of relief.

The e-mail sent by my secretary appeared in my Yahoo! mailbox. I clicked. The attached document was there. Intact!

I inserted the disk and accessed it. All of the documents I wanted were there. Intact.

My secretary was, or could have been, a friend. She might have been the person who erased the document from the firm's network, at the instructions of someone from higher up, but she had also demonstrated her loyalty to me.

I forwarded my life-saving memorandum—a lawyer's ethical advice to be given to the Entran board—to one more e-mail address. It was the personal e-mail address of my former classmate and moot court partner at Harvard, the forever chubby Tanya. She was my confidante in the law, and the only real reward of my Harvard years. She would be glad to serve as my lawyer if I were ever in trouble.

I typed a cover note to Tanya: *Keep this for me, kiddo, just in case I need your help in the future. You are officially my lawyer. No questions asked, for now.*

In the subject line, I typed, *Communication in pursuit of representation and legal advice; confidential information absolutely protected by the attorney–client privilege.*

I had to make Tanya my lawyer. Giving the memo to anyone but my own lawyer would be a violation of the code of ethics. I was a lawyer myself, and the memo was my work product, communication, and advice to be given only to my client, Entran. I could not give the confidential document to any third party, except my own lawyer.

My "Sent" box showed that my e-mail to Tanya was sent. The evidence of my ethics was once more preserved. More importantly, I also had the hard copy.

I stepped out of my office and headed for the elevator.

"The flowers from the firm, Mimi," my secretary called after me. "Don't you want to take them home, or maybe you want to send Mr. Townsend a thank-you note?"

"No," I had to yell back at her down the hallway. "I am late for the celebration of my fortieth birthday."

In the elevator, I looked at my watch. In a couple of hours, Brad would be on his way from work to the Riverway Hotel.

In the parking lot, the tension finally caught up with me. I was exhausted. The urge to cry took away all efforts to retain my composure. I staggered along and fell into the driver's seat of my car. I had to sit still for a while, listening to my own heartbeats.

Finally, I drove home.

To my mirror.

———

In front of my mirror, I took off my work clothes and lay naked on my side of the bed. As usual, I faced my inanimate confidante. There was no Brad behind me, no arm extended under my head. *I am hurt, and the world seems to be falling apart, but I am missing you, Alan Bradley Hurst.*

Brad had a way of denying reality. Once the CD player was playing Beethoven's dark and grave *Sonata Impassionata,* and I was dancing my own version of Tai-Chi-cum-ballet on my king-sized bed, in front of the mirror, when he asked me, "When is your birthday?" He was sitting on the edge of the bed, with his computer address book in his hand. "I want to remember birthdays of the people I care for."

"December first, nineteen fifty-nine," I said.

"Nineteen sixty-nine," he said, and began punching onto the little computer keypad with one finger.

"No," I said, "nineteen fifty-nine."

"No," he said. "Nineteen sixty-nine. You misspoke. You could not have been born in nineteen fifty-nine. Don't joke with me. I will consider you a fraud. Lie down, Ms. Born-in-Nineteen-Sixty-Nine. Don't dance anymore. You're behaving like my daughter. You are small enough to get away with dancing on a bed, but you are causing me a headache."

I stopped dancing and fell on top of him. The belt buckle of his jeans rubbed against my belly. So in his eyes I was at least ten years younger than my real age. Or I was an Asian child dancing on the bed.

"It is you who defraud yourself, Mr. Thirty-Three-Years-Old," I said, laughing. "I am old, much older than you. I come from an ancient city ten thousand years older than America. Hue, my hometown, used to be the Kingdom of Champa, allegedly the original builder of the Angkor Wat, according to some who-knows-what theory. Around the fifteenth century, Champa disappeared on the world's map. You hear me? The Vietnamese robbed the Chams of their kingdom. Wasn't that awful? Just like that. Five centuries after the initial territorial conquest, the Cham culture almost went extinct. I have Cham blood in me, don't you know? I belong partly to an extinct species. That's why I have eyes that resemble an Amerasian's, like your child. I am not all pure Vietnamese. The Chams are genetically like the South Asians, the Indians, the Pakistani. They have bigger eyes and darker skin. So, you see, I am old, like Champa. Old like a vampire."

"Thanks for the history lesson. You have a tragic sense of yourself, yet entirely sensuous. A vampire? What a fine vampire you are. Some dark-skinned woman with delicate arms wrapping around my neck, gently sucking my blood. Let's see. You claim you are old, much older than I. Thousands of years, did you say? I want to examine the proof. Where are the wrinkles? I don't see any. I see a child's face. Like my child.

"Close your eyes for me," he said and smoothed my eyelids. He began tracing my body. Darkness fell upon my eyelids and I held my breath, my entire being focusing on the touch of his fingers, my heart pounding, every baby hair on my body raising and tingling underneath his touch. "Ms. Born-in-Nineteen-Sixty-Nine, I am looking for your wrinkles. I don't see any. Just a few lovely creases. A little hilly here. A little valley there. Lie still. All I see are delicious folds of skin. Smooth, dark olive skin. No freckles, even."

"You are so dumb, Mr. Thirty-Three-Years-Old." I opened my eyes. "I am too dark for my freckles and age spots to show. Look on my cheekbone. Both sides of my face. See them? Old lady's freckles."

"If I see them, I'll kiss them away. Lie still. You are through dancing."

He undid his belt buckle. I felt all of him. The shoulders that spelled anchor. The weight that bore passion. "Now, dance, dance, dance. Dance under me. Meet me. Meet me here, then dance for me," he said slowly, and I closed my eyes again. "You can dance your delicious dance now."

—

Nothing was delicious to me when I was lying in my bed, naked without him, sick of the practice of law, Burt Townsend's condescending words, and the trap of my professional life. At the Riverway, I would hope that Brad was sitting at a table, candlelit, perhaps, that same old dating ritual, not knowing what had happened in only one day. Why hadn't he called?

I reviewed our past episodes. I had seen such illusion. Such deception. Liz Foreman. Rebecca Kaw. Even over small things.

For example, he kept on wanting to believe I was Ms. Born-in-Nineteen-Sixty-Nine.

It made no sense. My purse always lay around; he could have checked my driver's license any time. My study showed degrees earned decades ago. I was a partner at an old-fashioned law firm and had three academic degrees. Couldn't have made it here at age thirty. He never asked. Never seemed concerned. He would celebrate my birthday, not caring to know my real age. I never intended to lie. I did not lie.

I got out of bed and stared at my naked self in the mirror. I tried to recall the chance meeting in Hermann Park. I examined my nipples, too large on small breasts, and too chocolate brown on mocha skin. Which one had he seen that day in Hermann Park, if I could believe him? I traced my body for the wrinkles he once traced. Creases. Folds of skin. All bearing traces of his fingertips. I put on an all-lace black bra and matching thong. I had turned forty. My body was still compact. Could his other Asian lovers look this good? I did not know what to do with my misery. I was an older woman in love with a younger man whom I could not trust. In the middle of my career crisis at work, I was still soaked and then dehydrated and weepy-soaked again with a burning desire for Alan Bradley Hurst. It terrified me.

I had a sheer, shimmering black dress that covered nothing. I had bought it at a specialty shop in New York City for the wild, wild night that existed only as a joke upon a husband-to-be. The dress needed a slip underneath. I rummaged around. Couldn't find the slip. I pulled the stretchy dress over my head and down to my ankles. It covered nothing, displaying my skin tone, the curve of my breasts, the muscles on my thighs, and the lace underwear set. Underneath the sheer, shimmering dress, the flowery black lace design patterns overlapped with the dark shade of my nipples and the space above my thighs.

I sat on the carpeted floor and painted my fingernails and toenails brown. I put on brown lipstick and bronze, shimmering eye shadow. I teased my hair and made it into a bird's nest in the style of Dr. Joseph Morgan, as though I had just made acrobatic love in bed. Like the legendary Elizabeth Sung Foreman.

I slipped on a pair of spiked heels.

I looked at myself in the mirror. I saw a high-class hooker. Not even high class: just a washed-out, badly made-up hooker.

I went through my closet on the second floor. I found a black, sheer silk scarf. I wrapped it around my neck. I found Brad's clothes. I put on his white shirt. I was so much shorter than he that the shirt became a shirt-dress, covering my reveal-all body. I rolled up the long sleeves.

And then I left the house. I headed for the Riverway Hotel.

———

I sat in my car in front of the hotel, and the valet attendant kept saying, "Excuse me, ma'am, aren't you coming in?"

"Give me a minute, will you please?" Stubbornly I sat in my car, blocking the driveway. The attendant paced back and forth in front of my car and then stood by the side of my window. I let him wait forever. He was hovering by the driver's side when I abruptly pressed my foot on the gas pedal and drove away. In the rearview mirror I could see the man's astonished face. To him, I was insane.

I drove around the corner of the hotel and parked below the window next to a row of red and white azaleas where I could look up and see the restaurant. I saw Brad. He was sitting alone, waiting. I got my cell phone out of my purse and dialed.

"Hello, sweetheart, happy birthday. Where are you now?"

"In the car. I am running late. Can you wait for me?"

"Of course. I have a surprise waiting for you."

"Me, too. I have a surprise for you. I will be very, very late. Something happened. I'll tell you later. By the way, how was the deposition?"

There was silence. *Lie, lie to me, Brad. Lie about small things so I can conclude you lie about the big things, too, and that will help me put closure to this.*

"Well…it went fine…I'll tell you later."

So he lied. I swallowed my pain.

"Mimi, is everything all right?"

"Everything is almighty fine."

"You sound upset."

"No, no."

"OK, I'll wait. I'll read a book. I have it with me. Anaïs Nin's *Elena*. One of your favorites, you said."

"You're right. It is my favorite. When a woman mixes sensuality with emotions, she creates too strong a bond, crystallized, blocking rationality or the intellect. She becomes a different kind of woman, different from the prostitutes of Paris, the type of woman who idealizes and poeticizes love, the kind of woman made up of legends. But in the essence of things, beneath her romanticism, she is nothing but a body like a prostitute, living and breathing for the needs of men." I couldn't recall Anaïs Nin's prose word by word, so it became my prose. "Brad, I believe that's the description of Elena."

At the other end of the line, he seemed to sigh. "Mimi, are you talking about us? Are you telling me something? You are too much. Too much for me. I don't understand, Mimi."

I took a deep breath and fought back tears. "Of course I am too much. That's because I'm not all-American, Brad. I have tried for more than two decades to become something I can never be. I don't expect you to understand. I am driving, and the phone can go out at any time. I want to read you something. Much more than nine words. Now, not later. I want you to listen to me carefully. Bear with me. I adore words. You know I am kind of crazy."

"Baby, something is wrong. I can tell. I'm listening."

"There was a Vietnamese writer, Brad, she said something similar to Anaïs Nin. She described the type of woman like Elena. She said, my feminine soul is forbidden territory, prone only to one kind of footstep—that of love. Like a gifted thief, love has the capacity of invading the forbidden territory, without a knock. It steals all that is valuable and gives it all to a stranger, someone I call a lover. Lovers construct a territory, a nation with its own rules incomprehensible to any third person. Such a nation exists on Earth but does not belong to Earth. Such a nation exists in the bodies of the lovers but does not belong to the bodies. Yet it relies on the bodies to express itself. As a result, there are women like me who cannot separate sex from love. And I can only wish the lover (whomever I choose), at times someone who, like a bystander, fails to understand, will cherish the code of love—the privately constructed nation and, in memory of what I give, will appreciate every inch of the body through which I wish to express."

I swallowed once more the surge of tears.

"Mimi, you must be talking about yourself. I am overwhelmed. I am going to book us a room in the hotel for a change of scenery. I miss feeling you, before all the turmoil began."

"Mahv-lous. Mahv-lous," I said, mimicking again the style of Burt Townsend.

"I'm waiting, Mimi, even if it means all night."

I turned off the phone and drove on Woodway to tree-filled Memorial Drive, and the night rose to greet me with its omnipotent presence. Grandma Que once told me of how the night could become a beast. She said her mother, the lonely and exquisitely beautiful Mystique Concubine of the Violet City, called the night the Face of Brutality. Grandma Que was brought up to believe that sweet, intimate night could turn into the Face of Brutality. She did not want her daughter and granddaughters to see the night in that same, haunting way.

Yet I was driving into the Face of Brutality.

I turned into a private street off Memorial Drive and parked my car. I locked the car door and sat underneath trees, watching that Face of Brutality emerge. Time passed. It was all dark, and I needed to sort out my head.

I drove back to Woodway, stopped in front of the Riverway, and left my car with the valet attendant.

"Good evening, ma'am," he said, taking my key chain. "You're back. I am glad. Your gentleman friend is waiting in the restaurant. He has been out here several times looking for you."

I walked into the restaurant wearing his white shirt. He was sitting alone at a booth, wearing glasses, bending over a paperback. Most diners had left. We were almost alone in the restaurant.

"Hi, Brad."

He stood up, taking both of my hands in his.

"Mimi, I was worried."

I sat down before him. Just as I had imagined, the table was dimly lit with a floating candle. Places like this were designed for lovers with money to spend. He had ordered a salad and it was half gone, and he had half a glass of red wine before him. The book by Anaïs Nin had fallen to the floor. Two gift boxes lay on the table, the small one on top of the larger.

"Mimi, you must be ill. Your skin is hot."

"My masseuse would agree with you."

"You are wearing my shirt. And this…Hollywood makeup. It isn't like you."

"It is me. You mean to say I am a mess." I stood up and posed, feeling like a topless dancer and a clown. "Would you like to see what is under the shirt?"

"Yes, very much, Mimi. But later. Sit down, there are still people around."

I took off the shirt.

Enter the clown! I said to myself.

He immediately popped up, put his arms around me, pulled me into an embrace, and sat me down in the booth right next to him.

Good. I am embarrassing him, but I am only hurting myself. I am the sad clown.

He hurriedly helped me put the shirt back on.

"You are practically naked, Mimi. Are you playing a game? Where have you gone, dressed like this?"

"To Memorial Park, alone, thinking about you and life."

"What's wrong, Mimi?"

"I want to know what's in the boxes."

"Your presents. Happy birthday, Mimi."

"Let me guess. Fishnet stockings and lace teddies from Victoria's Secret? I prefer La Perla, Paris. I am a material girl who can't let go of my corporate law practice and end up hating myself. What's in the small box?"

"I bought you a ring."

"You are not in a position to buy me a ring."

"It's a dinner ring, Mimi. Sapphire. Your favorite stone."

With money from his wealthy wife. The words appeared before me. My face felt feverish.

I undid his arms wrapped around my shoulders and stood up, walked around the table, and sat down across from him. I probed for the familiar blue eyes, always opened wide with vulnerability, and saw the same sensitive, thirty-three-year-old Brad.

"Brad, tell me about Rebecca Kaw."

His face immediately became somber. A long silence ensued.

"I thought you knew all along, Mimi," he finally said. "Thought we cleared that up the rainy night we almost broke up."

"That's right, I forgot. I understood her to be a computer programmer installing machines in your office."

"She was a computer programmer. That's what she studied, and that's how she met her first husband. I never said that was her job, but she did show up in my office installing my computer, and that was how we met."

"You are married to her forever, Brad."

"I never once said the word *ex-wife* to you."

"That's right. You said, the woman from Hong Kong. Your child's mother. I stand corrected."

"I am not enjoying this questioning and these sarcastic comments, Mimi. It's your birthday."

Angrily, I took off the silk scarf from my neck and tried to wrap it around my wrists. I failed. I put my wrists together and extended both hands to him.

"Brad, take the scarf and tie me up. Isn't that what you want to do?"

"Darling, I booked us a honeymoon suite upstairs, but…"

"I'm not opposed to this sort of thing." I talked breathlessly. "Once I was with a man who used handcuff on me and I let it be…"

"Stop, Mimi, stop."

I did not hear him. I continued nonstop. "I had too much pain within me carried from Vietnam, and I was so unhappy working within the grinding machine of my law firm that I had to torture myself, and then one day he had me cuffed to a four-poster bed. He was wearing a vampire cape and the light was dim, but I looked at his ridiculous self and there was nothing erotic about it, and worst of all he tripped over his cape and fell; he twisted his ankle and couldn't stand up, and I was cuffed to the four-poster bed, and right at that awkward, awful moment I had to laugh, saying to myself *what am I doing to myself, with this man wearing a theater cape crawling on the floor?* He was furious because I laughed…"

I had to stop to gasp for air.

"Mimi, please, I don't want to hear about your past."

"But you read my diary and asked me questions."

"I want to know a different past, not your being handcuffed by your ex-lover."

"Or, would you rather that I tie you up…"

"Oh, Mimi!"

"…so you won't have to go to Elizabeth Sung Foreman for that."

"Oh, no." He dropped his head onto the table for a moment and looked up at me, his face reddened. "You talked to Elizabeth."

"Today."

"You were at the lunch."

"Yes, while you were supposed to be at your deposition."

"I was, only in the morning. It adjourned early."

"Clever. You are a wonderful litigator with a bright future for manipulation, lies, deceit, and a talent for seducing successful aging Asian beauties."

He frowned, and the furrows around his mouth deepened. "I have never lied to you, Mimi. I may have been quiet about certain things because I thought you knew or didn't care."

"You are seeing Rebecca again. You two were seen at the Houstonian Hotel."

He looked away from me. "For weeks I was confused, Mimi."

"You lied to me."

"Mimi, since I've known you, I have not slept with anyone else."

"That can be contradicted by Elizabeth."

"Do not lower yourself to her. She is a monster."

"What's the difference between us? You fucked us both."

"Don't talk to me that way. The style does not become you."

"I don't know how to talk to you any other way when you cut me this deeply."

"You believe Elizabeth?"

"You tell me."

"I don't like being questioned or having to justify myself."

"Your tears, your words to me, were they real?"

"Yes," he said immediately, without pondering. "I'm not that good of an actor."

I wished I could believe him. The image of Brad and Elizabeth circling each other could make me bleed.

"Does she do gymnastics in bed like they say? I can't."

"Oh I can't believe this. You're jealous. It's on your face." I saw his eyes flash. "I don't like jealous, insecure women. Rebecca is over-possessive and…"

"Don't compare."

"Jealousy is better than the alternative, that you don't care."

"Yes, I am jealous. Shouldn't you feel triumphant?"

"We are hurting each other unnecessarily."

"I am jealous because—" My eyes were blurred with tears, and I saw his face, solemn and sad, moving out of focus in the film of tears before me. I spoke the final words. "All this pain, because," I choked, "I fell in love with you, Alan Bradley Hurst."

—

He searched for my hands, and I avoided them. My eyes felt watery, yet he did not offer a handkerchief nor tell me he wanted to kiss my tears away as he used to do. Instead, he sat still for a long time before he spoke.

"You said you fell in love with me. Does that mean right now you are not in love anymore?"

"I don't know if I should stay in love with you, Brad. Did you marry for money?"

He looked away.

"Don't tell me you married for the sake of your novel about your roommate's suicide, or that life–livelihood distinction."

"I am not telling you that."

"Did you go to bed with women, any women, specifically Asian women?"

He looked away again.

Anguished, I said, "We are so different, Brad. I can't marry for money, and I can't sleep with you the way I have and not love you."

He looked at me. "I am just a man," he said. "You are the idealist, and maybe that's why I'm so attracted to you. You are something I am not. On the East Coast, you worked incessantly, two thousand hours plus a year, and volunteered a thousand hours more to rescue boat people in Hong Kong from being repatriated to Vietnam, and senior citizens and the homeless and abandoned babies and battered women and whatever else turned you on. You did all these things to the detriment of yourself."

"So you checked me out."

"I know all about you, Mimi."

I know all about you. Someone said this to me, too, in SISU's Krost Hall two decades ago. Back then, I was a skinny, sexless, anemic teenager who had survived trauma, lived with nightmares in a small dorm room, and harbored secrets about apocalypse.

"What else do you know about me, Brad?"

"You idolize and convince yourself that you love a dead man who shared your culture and with whom I can't compete. And there are all the malicious things Elizabeth spread about you. That underneath the cool facade you were a basket case who couldn't handle corporate pressure. She hates you and wants you hurt, and she is succeeding."

Elizabeth Sung Foreman. The victor. I saw the redheaded, big-bosomed naked Amerasian woman rolling over Brad among bedsheets and pillows, and my head swung in a wicked circle of images. "When was the last time you sneaked from me to her?"

"I won't dignify that with an answer. You are behaving like a child on your fortieth birthday."

My fortieth birthday. He just said my fortieth birthday. Another lie. He knew my age all along. The circle of images in my head started to swing again. This time, images of Elizabeth were replaced with my own. *Lie still. No wrinkles. Just creases. Now dance. Dance under me.*

"I thought I was Ms.-Born-in-Nineteen-Sixty-Nine."

"Mimi, you are your marvelous self. Yearless and ageless. But you are also a woman. You are so wrapped up in your own sorrow you can't tell when a man loves you and is faithful to you."

"You've known all along I am forty years old."

"Not initially. But yes. It soon became obvious. I don't believe in making a woman self-conscious about her age. But it doesn't matter. You don't look forty, and I can love you as much as I love my child, in a different way."

"You lied to me. I fit the type. The older Asian woman. You've always known I am old enough to be your mother."

"Not exactly. Unless you could be pregnant at seven years of age."

His face was solemn and lucid, and even in my wretched state of mind, the unintended humor made me laugh. I couldn't help it. He laughed with me.

"Mimi, it's good to hear you laugh. We have cried together and laughed together. Just remember that. Happy birthday, Mimi Sean Young, and whatever else in that long, winding royal Vietnamese name of yours."

—

I wanted to leave, and he took me to the front of the hotel, where I nestled against him while waiting for the valet attendant to bring my car around. He was concerned about me being able to drive. He wanted to drive me home, and I said no, no, no.

He told me the honeymoon suite was still waiting for us, and that was a choice I could make. I looked at his ardent face and wanted badly to let him carry me up there, to let him kiss the burning creases of my flesh. I still desired him after all that hurt and pain. I longed to take the tip of his penis to the deepest part of me, as deep as any woman could give of herself, and then I would blossom underneath his persistent quest like Anaïs Nin's prostitute responding to a real man, not just an ideal of a man who lay underneath a tombstone in Southern Illinois, representing a republic that no long existed or was never built. While I kept longing for its revitalization, America and the real Brad stepped in and filled the void, like an adoptive parent, not understanding me, not feeling the pain of my loss, but real, so real and vivid, like Brad's thrust and the warmth of him, even like the traffic jam on Texas freeways or the morning breeze of one solitary America, stretching from coast to coast, the enormous *America the Beautiful* that had housed me for almost three decades of discovery.

Instead of going with him upstairs, I stood still in the cold, knowing I had not completely trusted him and knowing that, until I became whole, that lack of trust would always be my downfall, a sword that ripped the endurance of my skin and cut into my flesh; and the resulting pain would overcome all remembrance of the wonderful tingling under Brad's touch.

When the car came around, I held on to him and my eyes felt watery again.

"You shouldn't be too serious, Mimi. Don't cry too much. Those boats in the rain. I don't want to see them unanchored." There was a touch of sorrow in his voice, and he kissed me for a long time. The tip of his tongue felt so familiar, and it stayed in between my open lips and circled the width of my mouth. For a moment, I thought nothing had changed and life somehow was made perfect. But he let go of me and told me he would be sitting in the restaurant reading *Elena* to understand me better, and he would be waiting for me for the rest of the night should I change my mind.

"I think I'll be leaving you, Brad," I said.

"You may think you love me, but I don't think you do, Mimi," he said, stepping away from me and speaking in a voice so low his words became almost indecipherable. "Love can mean something uncomplicated. It means I am happy and you are happy when our legs intertwine. I fill you and you engulf me and there is nothing to deliberate or regret. You may never give me your complete nine words, but I have my own nine words to deliver. Here are my nine words, Mimi. I love you, I love you, I love you. Exactly nine words. I say them as a person without ideals. I say them without shame, fear, or complication. It has taken me too long to form my own nine words, and now I am just calmly brave and sure."

—

I drove away and parked again outside the window of the restaurant where I could see Brad pick up *Elena* off the floor, sit alone at the booth, and bend his head over the pages. I sat in my car for a long time, wishing he would run after me, as I needed the assurance beyond words to restore my faith. But he sat still and read on, as though there were no turmoil underneath the man who just said he was in love and watched his love walk away. He seemed absorbed in the book.

I saw him stop after a few moments to reach for his cell phone and begin to dial. I held my breath and reached for mine, ready to hear the voice I had come to long for. I would talk to him, seek assurance again, and then I would run upstairs and part my legs for the form of love that was instinctive and uncomplicated. But my phone did not ring, and inside the glass, I saw Brad speaking into his. I sat, stone-deaf, and the conversation he had, to which I was not privy, seemed endless. My heart sank in sorrow, and I knew I had no strength to continue doubting, questioning, and receiving explanations that either made absolute sense or sounded too clever and too perfect.

He was still talking inside, perhaps to his mother or child or colleague or another lover whom I might never know. My heart palpitated in pain and anxiety.

I thought of tomorrow. Mine only.

—

It was eleven o'clock at night, and I drove into the Face of Brutality again. I went to my law office.

Houston was cool at night in December. I had no coat and held on to Brad's shirt. My spiked heels made clicking noises on the cold and impersonal marble floor of the entrance to the building. I stopped momentarily to glance at the inscription of my name on the shiny glass stand that contained the building directory. I clicked my heels to the elevator bank.

It was midnight, and I was the only person walking down the hall. The plush carpet muffled the clicking rhythm of my heels. Empty secretarial cubicles took turns saluting me, their square shapes lining up with fax and copy machines and computer terminals. At random, I peeked inside the empty offices of colleagues and friends to take one last look, reminiscing over my professional life and law firm existence, thinking of the separation ahead.

I turned on the light in my office and looked at the city outside the window that separated me from the open air and all those sparkling lights. The floor-to-ceiling glass window of my high-rise law office became the mirror.

I saw in the glass the reflection of a woman in smeared, shimmering makeup, wearing a man's white shirt, standing on spiked heels, leaning over, looking back at me with rows of high-rises and bright urban lights behind her, against a blackened background. No moon, no stars, just city lights.

I also saw something else.

Directly behind the woman, looking in from the other side of the glass wall, I caught sight of a pair of beastly eyes. Red, squinting, moving at times, steady at times. Some animal, unidentified, was staring at me.

I remembered Grandma Que's stories of Hue. Once upon a time, in a different place, at a different time, my great-grandmother, Annam's royal Mystique Concubine, abandoned lover of an exiled king, saw a pair of eyes staring at her from the dark outside her half-moon window. The pair of eyes appeared most vivid during her last night in the royal palace of the Violet City, before her departure to the countryside in order to build a new life in the hamlet of Quynh-Anh. The beastly eyes followed the lonely woman. They haunted her a lifetime. So she referred to the threatening darkness of the night as the Face of Brutality. At one time the face resembled the French colonist who had exiled her husband, the king of Annam. In the end, the menacing face resembled the cruelty of fate. The lonely woman could change her place of abode, but she could never alter fate and be free of its burden.

This night, in America, outside the glass window of the high-rise office building in downtown Houston, I had seen my great-grandmother's haunting beast—the pair of eyes on the Face of Brutality.

I knew what this meant.

There had never been freedom from the past.

I had to go back to that past and make peace with myself.

The writing of a manuscript would be my emotional baptism. My rebirth.

I sat down at my desk and began typing a one-paragraph memo. The subject line said, "Resignation." I bold-faced and underscored the word. This time, I was not sure whether there would be another law desk prison awaiting me when the kite of my heart was pulled down.

I thought of the long years of my youth when I enslaved myself in supporting roles for hotshot partners of big law firms, how I had laboriously climbed the ladder to reach the top, where the only emotional reward seemed to be the perverted sense of self-importance: I no longer had to turn in legal memoranda that ended up in someone's trash can; instead, I was entitled to throw someone's work into my own trash can. Once and for all in my years of serving corporate America, I wanted to challenge the norm by way of a direct and concrete act.

So I stacked all documents relating to the Dakota filing into one folder and typed another memo, recommending that the assignment be given to Kurt Fiesta, the bright, young, conscientious third-year associate, product of a poor Hispanic family and an urban law school.

I held my spiked heels against my chest and walked barefoot down the hall, to the corner office of Burt Townsend. I slipped my resignation memo underneath his office door. And then I ran on bare feet toward the hallway.

Déjà vu. A journey on bare feet.

I made one last decision: holding onto the flaps of Brad's shirt, I thought for the last time of the honeymoon suite at Riverway.

I would not be going there.

I would be going home to my mirror.

I pressed my naked feet onto the carpet and deliberately shortened my steps. I was no longer running on bare feet down an airport runway, toward a roaring cargo plane in the middle of the night. Instead, there was an unspoken conversation between my bare feet and the carpeted floor of this impersonal law firm, already accustomed to the comings and goings of replaceable corporate lawyers and office workers.

My bare feet were telling the floor good-bye, farewell, so long, *adieu, adios, sayonara, ciao*...No, no, no, these feet would never turn back, even if the kite could no longer fly high.

THE END